The Sean O'Rourke Series
Book 5

Quiet Times?

by

Michael E. Cook

TELEMACHUS PRESS

Cover Designed by Telemachus Press, LLC

Cover Art: Samantha Paxton

Published by Telemachus Press, LLC
http://www.telemachuspress.com

Contact the author at cookorourkeseries@gmail.com

ISBN: 978-1-945330-65-0 (eBook)
ISBN: 978-1-945330-66-7 (Paperback)

Version 2017.07.07

Table of Contents

The Sean O'Rourke Series
Book 5

QUIET TIMES?

CHAPTER ONE

After Sean read the letters that Buck had in his valise, he asked everyone to come back to the table and join him. He filled everyone's glass again and told them to take a sip. Then he spoke. "I found two letters in Buck Slaughter's valise," Sean began. "One was from Bud and was addressed to Butch, and the other one was kind of like a "Last Will" and such from Buck. The one from Bud said that Butch would be the head of the family cause Goldie was dead and he was dying of the coughin' sickness. I reckon he meant pneumonia. Bud said that he was always proud of Butch and he expected him to get us killed. I have no idea why Buck had this letter and it didn't get to Butch."

"Well what did Buck have to say?" asked Maggie.

"He just said that if anyone was readin' this it's because he's dead and I better be. If I'm not dead, he's gonna come back and haunt all of 'em till they're dead," Sean said. "Then he said that Ruby probly took the rest a the clan back to the old homestead in Missouri."

"Well maybe this'll be the end of it," said Michael. "Was there anything else?"

"Ole Buck said that maybe he'd see me in hell," said Sean.

"Well maybe we're all going after what we've had to do," said Maggie. "I do recall something about "Thou Shall Not Kill." We've been doing a good bit of that lately."

"I been tellin' some a the ones we killed that I'm sendin'em ta hell, but I don't really believe in hell," said Sean. "I seen too much ta make me believe that there's somethin' that could be worse than what happened in the country the last several years." No one spoke for a few minutes. The undertaker came into the saloon and made his way to Sean's table.

"Excuse me Marshal," started the undertaker. "I discovered this on the body of that young girl when I was getting her ready." The undertaker handed Sean a derringer. "It was in her under-garments. I thought you might want it. I have no use for it."

"Thanks for bringin' it to me," said Sean. "Sorry to give you so much business all at once but it couldn't be helped."

"A man in my profession must take business when he can," said the undertaker. "Maybe one of these days you'll have all this outlawry under control and I'll be forced into waiting on folks to die of natural causes. Now good day to you all."

"You know Sean darlin', I think that man really likes his work," said Michael.

"Well if he doesn't, he sure came to the wrong place to set up shop," said Sean. "Let's have another drink. I feel like drinkin' today."

"We'll stay right here with you," said Michael.

"I'll have another one with you and then I'm goin' back out to the herd," said Jug. "Lolita, you can stay in town while I'm gone if you want. Ben and his boys'll bring in that other herd yet today and ours'll be in tomorrow. You can spend another night on that nice soft bed."

"I'd rather spend the night with my husband," said Lolita.

"Well Sean, looks like me'n Lolita'll be leavin' shortly and be back tomorrow," said Jug.

"You got a good woman there Jug," said Sean. "We'll see you again tomorrow." Lolita and Jug finished their drinks, then rounded up their gear and headed back to the herd. The rest of them stayed at the table and drank some more. After another hour, Jim decided it was time to see Sally. No one at the table talked much. They all finished their drinks and Sean went to the bar for another bottle. He came back to the table and filled everyone's glasses. He looked at Orry and spoke. "How bout you tellin' all a us bout yourself," said Sean. "Jesse told us you helped him some and you sure as hell helped us some here. We wanna know all about you. Start from the beginnin'."

"Well I was born up in Maine," started Orry. "It can get mighty cold up there sometimes. Made it through the grades all right. I just turned 18 not long ago. I thought about joinin' up durin' the war but my folks wouldn't sign for me. One day this train come inta town and it was full a wounded soldiers. I never seen so many men without arms and legs. After that I give up all thoughts a runnin' away and joinin' up. When the war ended I decided I was gonna go west. I didn't have much money. I kinda worked my way as I went. This is all the farther I got. I met Jesse at the little town just north a Cherokee land. I was in this saloon havin' a drink when he come in. I was with this fella named Nate Slaughter. He hired me ta help move some cows. I never knowed them cows was rustled. Anyway, Nate picked a fight with Jesse and Jesse broke his arm. I never seen nothin' like it. Nate went for his Colt. Instead a drawing his pistol, Jesse grabbed Nate's arm and broke it. Then he set it for'm. Would you a done that? If a fella wanted to kill me, I surely doubt I'd set his broken arm for'm. Anyway, I showed Jesse where them cows was. There was a fight. Nate and two others got kilt. They was all Slaughters."

"So that was maybe the first time you was ever in a gunfight," said Sean.

"Yes it was," said Orry. "I never shot nothin' 'cept deer and other critters. Jesse told me that them deer don't shoot back. I stayed with Jesse when he went down to "The Nations" cause I didn't think I'd live too long if I was out there by myself. Jesse's wife introduced me to this good lookin' young girl. She was Dawn's cousin. She's my wife now."

"That was mighty quick," said Michael. "Must a been one a them love at first sight things."

"It wasn't that quick," said Orry. "When Jesse went out with John Littletree, Charlie Redhorse and I went with 'em. We went all over the different tribe's land lookin' fer rustled cows and such. We didn't find nothin'. After Jesse sent ya that telegram, we was headed back when we come across them six killers. We had a scrape and I took an arrow in my left shoulder. Jesse got it out. We killed two a them Pawnee and them others high tailed it. We got down ta Jesse's place and I stayed at Laura's place for bout a month healin' up. Then I stayed with John Littletree. Me'n Laura got married bout three weeks before we come up here ta help out."

"You best git down there to your new wife," said Sean. "I don't reckon she liked it when you left."

"She didn't like it, but I told her Jesse was my friend and I needed to help my friend," said Orry.

"Well you sure as hell helped Jesse and us," said Sean. "Now you're our friend too. That wife a yours got herself a good man. What do you think Jesse?"

"He's got a ways ta go but he's gettin' there," said Jesse. "If he sticks around with the likes a us, we'll get all the rough edges off'm."

"So Jesse, when you figure on headin' back?" asked Sean.

"How bout I stick around till a few more herds come in?" asked Jesse. "Not all them Texas boys'r gonna behave as well as Ben Thompson's crew."

"One thing I do know," said Sean. "They'll behave in our place or they won't be in it."

~~~~

Ben Thompson and his crew brought in the Johanson herd that day. A telegram was sent to Don Johanson's wife telling her what had happened to her husband and that she would receive a bank draft for the herd. Ben and his men spent the night in town. All of them headed back to Texas the next morning. Later that morning, Jug brought his herd into town. He got a good price and gave his men a good bonus. He also informed them that if they wanted to remain part of his crew, they would behave themselves in town.

The first thing Jug did after he got paid for the herd was to go to Sean. He wanted to pay back Sean for the money he had given him to help start the ranch. Sean flat out refused to take the money. "Jug, I don't mean to insult you but I won't take your money," said Sean. "Things have changed some since you were here last. I got more money than I could spend in several life-times. I don't remember if I told you or not, but me and Maggie own "The Palace" in St. Louis now. Sam Draper had a lotta money in the bank when we took over. Sometime when we're settin' around havin' a drink, I'll tell you all bout gettin' that place."

"You know I'm gonna feel awful guilty about that money," said Jug. "It don't set right with me."

"Well Jug, take that money and git some more land and cows," said Sean. "Maybe you'll have the biggest and best ranch in Texas one day."

"I'd still feel guilty," said Jug.

"Well I'll tell you what Jug Carter," said Sean. "Whenever I'm havin' trouble with some bad outlaws or somethin' like that, you can come and give me a hand. You can consider that as payment."

"I'd do that anyway," said Jug. "You're my friend and friends always help friends."

"You're a good man Jug. I'm still not takin' the money," said Sean. "Now why don't you take that woman a yours and you two enjoy the hospitality of our tub. I'm sure she'd want to scrape off some trail dust. We can all have dinner together later."

"I believe we will," said Jug. "We'll see you later for dinner."

~~~~

After going to the bath house to clean up, about half of Jug's crew went to Maggie's Place and the others went to other saloons. The boys who came to "Maggie's Place" grumbled a little about check-ing their guns but they had themselves a very good time. Some of the boys were downstairs drinking with some of the girls and the others were upstairs with some of the girls.

Sean, Jug, and the rest of Sean's men and their women, were at their regular table having dinner, when one of Jug's men stumbled into the saloon and fell to the floor just as he cleared the door. He was beaten and bloody. Jug saw him and ran over to him. Tom was behind the bar and brought over some water and a towel. Jug noticed that the man's holster was empty. Jug sat beside him on the floor and lifted up his head. He gave him a drink of water and wetted down his face. "What happened boy?" said Jug. "Who done this?"

"Crooked card game," said the man. "I spotted'em cheatin' and called'em on it. Before I could do anything, two big fellas was whoopin' the tar outta me. Don't member how I got back here."

"Would you know them two fellas if you seen'm again?" asked Jug.

"Yes I would," said the man. "A woman was in on it too. She was behind me and lettin' them others know what kinda hand I had."

"Well boy, as soon as you can stand, me and some a the boys'll go over there and put a hurt on them fellas," said Jug.

"You know them card sharps'll be expectin' some cowboys ta go back there and do somethin'," said Sean. "They'll be waitin' for ya. I'll tag along ta make sure there's no gunplay. I want you and your boys ta leave their guns here."

"We won't need no guns fer what we're gonna do ta them fellas," said Jug.

"I'll go along too," said Jesse. Jug, the beaten man, and five of Jug's men headed to the other saloon. Sean and Jesse both had on their pistol belts. When they got to the saloon, Sean asked Jug and his boys to wait outside for a minute while him and Jesse went in first and had a word with the people inside. Jug agreed.

Sean and Jesse went just inside the door and stood. The place got very quiet. Finally the bartender spoke.

"What'r you doin' here Marshal?" asked the bartender. "You're not local law. There's nothin' goin' on in here that's any a yer business."

"Git that scattergun you got back there and hand it to me. Then keep your hands up on the bar where I can see'm and I mean right now," said Sean. The bartender did as instructed. "Now ever one a you that's carryin' a gun is gonna drop it on the floor now and kick it over ta me." There were twelve men in the place and not one man did as Sean instructed. "I can kill six a you before any a you can git clear a your holster," said Sean. "I got another pistol too. Jesse here's mighty good with his pistol too. Now I'm gonna count ta five. If I don't see no guns on the floor before then, I'm gonna start shootin'. Most a you know me and you know what I can and will do. Sean started the count. Before he got to four, the guns were on the floor and being kicked over to Sean. "Jesse, you take these guns and set'em just outside the door. These gentlemen, and I use that term lightly, can get them back when Jug and his boys'r done." Jesse got all of the guns outside and came back inside. "All right Jug, bring in that man a yers that took the whoopin' in here," said Sean. Jug came inside with the beaten man. The man could barely stand. "All right now boy, which a these fellas'r the card cheats?" asked Sean. The young man pointed them out.

"That woman with the blonde hair over at the bar is the one who was in on it," said the man. "Ever one a these fellas in here needs their asses whipped. Not one of'em lifted a finger ta help me while them two was workin' me over."

"All right young man, I want you to go back outside while we sort things out," said Sean. "Tell them other boys ta come on in." The man left and the others came inside.

Sean walked over to one of the card cheats. "You know mister, it's been my experience that card cheats always have a hide out gun," said Sean. "Hand it over."

"I already gave up my gun," said the cheat. Sean pulled a pistol and stuck it on the man's forehead. He waited a moment, then cocked the hammer. The cheat reached into his pants and pulled out a derringer. Sean took it. "Now the knife," said Sean. "You boys carry knives too." The cheat pulled back his jacket sleeve exposing a long dagger. Sean took it from him. Sean moved over to the other card cheat. He didn't have to say a word. The cheat pulled a derringer out of his right boot and a razor from his pants pocket.

"You know boys, I don't think you can be trusted," said Sean. "You two git your clothes off. I wanna see you two in your drawers pretty damn quick or I'll give that boy you whooped this pistol and let him shoot holes in ya." The two stripped as instructed. "All right Jug, they're all yours," said Sean.

As soon as the words were out of Sean's mouth, Jug and his men were tearing into the card cheats. Jug had gotten in one good punch on each of the cheats and then he started on other men in the saloon.

"So you just sat on yer ass and let them cheats beat the hell outta my boy," said Jug. "Well mister, you got a whoopin' comin' too." Jug tore into whoever was in front of him at the time. One time a couple of men grabbed Jug's arms while another one hit on him but Jug got loose and took the two men and cracked their heads together. The two men went down and didn't move. Jug and his men were outnumbered two to one but it didn't matter. Jug and his boys made sure all of them took a beating. The woman who was with the card cheats tried to run out a back door but Sean caught her and held her with her arm behind her back.

"I'm not into abusin' women," said Sean. "But if you don't stand still, I'll break that pretty little arm a yours right off." The woman didn't struggle anymore.

Jesse was enjoying watching the fight. It was almost over now. Josh and Wayne were holding up one of the cheats against the bar and taking turns hitting him in the gut. The bartender had stayed out of the fight but Jesse saw him duck down behind the bar and come out with a small club. He was about to strike Josh when Jesse spotted him and fired a shot into the ceiling. All of the fighting stopped and everyone looked around to see what the shooting was about. Jesse spoke. "That bartender got himself a club and was gonna brain that boy over there," said Jesse.

Jug ran over to the bar, jumped over it and tore into the bartender. Sean let him beat on him for a while and then went over to the bar. Jug and the bartender were on the floor and Jug was on top of the bartender beating on him. "Ya think maybe he's had enough?" Sean asked Jug.

Jug quit hitting on the bartender. "I reckon so," said Jug. "I'm gettin' tired anyway. C'mon boys. Let's let these fellas lay here and bleed for a spell." Jug and his boys left and headed over to "Maggie's Place." The cowboy who was beaten found his pistol among the ones that Jesse had set outside and put it back in his holster. Sean and Jesse waited a few minutes before they headed to the door. Sean still had ahold of the woman. The bartender pulled himself up behind the bar.

"That damn rancher's gonna pay fer these damages," yelled the bartender. "He's gonna pay I tell ya."

"Bill Thompson is a good friend a mine you piece a shit," said Sean. "He won't like it that you let cheatin' go on in his place. He won't like it that you let them cheats beat on that boy and didn't do nothin' ta stop it. He's in this town ta make money and he knows them cowboys won't go to a place where they'll get cheated. I'd say you'll be lookin' fer another job after I tell'em what really went on here. And I'll tell ya somethin' else mister. If you even look cross eyed at me on the street I'll blow your damn head off." Then Sean looked around at the other men in the saloon. A few of them were still unconscious but some of them were starting to get up now. "Any a you others got anything you want ta say ta me?" said Sean.

"This was none a yer business Marshal," one of the men yelled. "You had no call ta interfere."

"I didn't interefere," said Sean. "I just made sure it was a fair fight and nobody got shot. Now choke it down mister. You just got yer ass kicked and you deserved it. Git over it." Sean went out the door and started to "Maggie's Place." "Just what am I gonna do with you darlin'?" said Sean to the woman. "If you was a man I'd beat you till you couldn't stand. I know. I'll take you to Maggie and see what she says I should do."

"Please Marshal, turn me loose," said the woman. "I was just tryin' ta make some money. I never knew they'd beat on that boy like that."

"Sure, and I'm the Prince a Wales too," said Sean. "Now you walk along nice and behave and I'll let go a your arm. You take off runnin', I'll tell them cowboys know where ya went and let them have at ya." The woman nodded her head yes that she would behave and Sean let go of her arm. Jesse was several feet ahead of Sean. They had walked a little and Sean noticed that the woman was easing back. Sean stopped and turned to face her. "You're gonna run on me aren't you?" Sean said to the woman. As Sean was looking at the woman, he heard someone running on the sidewalk. He looked back to see. It was the bartender. He was running toward Sean. He had a double barreled shotgun in his hands. Sean pulled a pistol but the woman was right in the way so he couldn't fire. He grabbed the woman to push her out of the way. As he was pushing her, the bartender stopped running and fired the shotgun. Most of the buckshot hit the woman in the back but a couple of pieces hit Sean in his right thigh. The woman was knocked to the ground but Sean was still standing. Before the bartender could get the hammer cocked on the other barrel, Sean put a bullet in his chest. He hit the ground dead. Sean looked down at the woman. She wasn't dead yet but probably would be shortly. Jesse ran to get the Doc.

It didn't take long to get the Doc but by the time he arrived the woman was dead. Several people had gathered in the street to see what had happened. One of them was Bill Thompson. "What the hell is goin' on Sean?" asked Bill. "How come you killed my bartender?"

"Bill, soon as the Doc gits this buckshot outta my leg, I'll tell ya all about it," said Sean. "C'mon over to our place in a bit and you'll git the truth. I doubt you'll hear the truth if you go over ta your saloon. Them fellas over there are none too happy right now."

Maggie and everyone was in the street now checking on Sean. "Let's get you over to Doc's now and get that buckshot out of your leg," said Maggie. "Then you can tell us all about it." The undertaker heard the shooting too and came out to find that he had two more customers. He never said a word. He just walked back to his parlor and in a few minutes the dead bodies were removed from the street. He knew he would get paid.

~~~~

Doc had some whiskey so he let Sean have some good swallows before he probed for the buckshot. "Smells like you already had some whiskey," said Doc. "You probably won't feel a thing." Then Doc began.

"You're wrong Doc," said Sean. "I feel it plenty. Hurry up if you can. Gimme back that bottle." Doc let Sean have the bottle while he continued his work. It wasn't long till he was done.

"You'll be good as new in no time," said Doc. "Just keep them holes clean and you'll be fine. Neither one a them pieces hit bone."

"I thank you Doc," said Sean. "I'll do my best ta keep from bein' a customer in the future."

"As long as you're wearin' that badge, I'll probably see you on a regular basis," said Doc.

"I'm leavin' now," said Sean. "Talkin' ta you can be upsettin'."

~~~~

All of them went back to Maggie's Place and sat down at their table. "Jug told us all about the fight and such," said Maggie. "Now you can tell us about that woman and the bartender."

"Let's have some drinks and wait a bit," said Sean. "Bill Thompson'll be here shortly and he'll wanna know everything. If we wait on him, I won't hafta tell it twice."

"All right, I'll get us some more drinks," said Maggie. Maggie went to the bar and got everything. Lolita got some water and towels and then she and Maggie went around and cleaned the blood off of Jug and his men. "I sincerely hope the other fellas look worse," Maggie said to Josh.

"They do," said Wayne. "We made sure a that." Bill Thompson came into the saloon now and went to Sean's table.

"All right Marshal, tell me what happened," said Bill. "Every man I talked to at my place had a different story."

"Pull up a chair Bill," said Sean. Bill got a chair and sat down. "One a Jug's men got in a card game at your place," said Sean. "He found out it was crooked and a woman was in on it too. When he called'em on it, them two card cheats beat the hell out of'em. He was so beat up he barely got back here ta tell us. I had Jug and his boys leave their guns here and we went over there. I made everyone in there give up their gun. Then I let Jug and his boys have at'em. Jug and his boys was outnumbered two to one."

"So why in the hell did they beat up everybody and not just the card cheats?" asked Bill.

"I'll tell ya why mister," yelled Jug. "Cause them idiots sat around and done nothin' while them two worked over my boy. They deserved an ass whoopin' and they got it."

"So what happened with the woman and the bartender?" asked Bill.

"When the fight was over that bartender started yellin' at me and sayin' that the rancher was gonna pay for the damages," Sean began. "I told'm that he was a piece a shit and that he'd most likely be lookin' for a job after you found out that he was lettin' cheatin' go on in your place. And he also never done nothin' ta stop them cheats from beatin' up Jug's boy. I was takin' that woman who was workin' with the cheats over ta Maggie ta see what she thought I should do with her. That's when that bartender came runnin' at me with that shotgun. The woman was in the way and got shot. I killed the son of a bitch. Is that good enough for ya?"

"Well it looks like I need to get myself another bartender and some furniture," said Bill. "I'll do my best to make sure he's honest. Jug, I'm sorry this happened. You and your boys can have a drink on the house before you go if you'd like."

"Thanks Bill. I hope you do get yourself some good help," said Jug. "It was good luck this time. Sean was here ta make sure there was no gunplay and I was here with my crew. Any other Texas crew woulda rounded up all their boys and guns and the undertaker would be makin' some money."

"I'd say you were right," said Bill. "When things really get going around here, we'll definitely need to have some local law."

"Well for now we should enjoy the quiet times," said Sean.

"I guess we could call them quiet times," said Maggie. "There was only one beating and one fight today. I guess you could call it one fight even though there were eighteen or so men in it and only two people got shot and killed."

"Don't forget we had one more shot and wounded," said Sean.

CHAPTER TWO

Things were fairly quiet in town for the next two weeks. The herds came in and the cowboys did their drinking and whoring, but there was no real trouble. There were a few fist fights, but the men involved were too drunk to hurt each other. Some of the boys grumbled some when they had to give up their guns at Maggie's Place, but when they saw the girls, they didn't care. Michael ordered himself another piano because the Slaughters had shot his up pretty good. Several of the piano wires had been hit and it didn't look very good setting there full of bullet holes. The new piano would arrive in a month.

Jug, Lolita, and their crew had headed back to Texas. Jesse and Orry had left for "The Nations" to be with their wives. Jim spent his spare time with Sally and Jeb was a proud father of six. Another new storekeeper came into town and he had a female red bone hound. She and Jeb hit it right off. Barbara and Cookie were still acting like newlyweds and Michael and Betty slipped back to their house from time to time. Tom even snuck off once in a while. Maggie and Sean spent a lot of time in their room and in the tub. The herds were coming in and McCoy was counting his money.

The third week started out quietly. When the week was half over, some drunk cowboy fired his pistol into the air and then passed out in the street. That was the only gunshot that anyone had heard in town for two and a half weeks. Sean and Maggie hoped it would stay that way. At the end of the week a telegram arrived for Maggie and Sean. Susie and Dan were getting married in three weeks and would like it if they could attend. Maggie would be Maid of Honor and Sean would be the best man.

Maggie was thrilled about going. They could get there a few days before the wedding and have a good time shopping and such. They could even take a cruise on Horace's steamboat again. Sean knew they would have a good time, but he was worried that things could get rough in Abilene. He just knew that sooner or later a rowdy crew would come in and shoot up the town and just figure they were having fun and blowing off steam. It was their right. They had spent all that time on the trail. Sean figured they would be going to St. Louis, but he wouldn't commit himself until after another week of quietness. It remained quiet the whole week.

Halfway through the next week, Sean told Maggie that they would be going to St. Louis. She knew all along that they would go anyway. Before they left for St. Louis, both of them had long talks with all of their people. The main thing they talked about was their policy on weapons in the saloon. This would be strictly enforced with absolutely no exceptions. Michael and Betty would be in charge. Jeb would be staying with them. If the least little thing happened, they would only be a telegram and a train ride away.

They could now take the train all the way from Abilene to St. Louis, so it wouldn't take long to get back if something happened.

The wedding was a week away when they arrived. The first thing they did was head to the docks and check the schedule for Horace's boat. It was due to arrive in an hour. After it resupplied, it would be going out on a three day cruise. There were vacancies and Maggie and Sean signed up to go.

Horace saw Maggie and Sean on the dock as he landed the boat. He motioned for them to come aboard. They joined Horace in his cabin as the boat was being resupplied. Horace was glad to see his friends.

They had the same cabin they had their last trip. They had a wonderful time. They had dinner in their cabin two nights and dinner with Horace on the third night. Horace had also been invited to the wedding. He had become friends with Susie and Dan.

~~~~

Kathleen Jameson was sitting by herself at a table when Maggie and Sean arrived at "The Palace." It was still morning and the place was almost empty. Both Maggie and Sean had to do a double take when they first saw Kathleen. She looked enough like Maggie to be her sister. When Kathleen saw Maggie and Sean, she knew who they were right away. She got up from her chair and went to greet them. "I'm Kathleen Jameson and there is no doubt that you two are Maggie and Sean," she said. She and Maggie hugged each other and kissed on the cheeks. Then Kathleen hugged Sean and kissed his cheek. Sean was still mesmerized and didn't speak. Maggie looked at Sean.

"Well darlin', does she look like me or not?" asked Maggie.

"She definitely could pass for your sister," answered Sean. Susie and Dan had been in the office and came out to greet them. Hugs, kisses, and handshakes were given.

"I'm so glad that you could come," said Susie. "Dan and I really wanted you to be here."

"Well we're here," said Sean. "Have you got everything set on what you're doing?"

"We do," answered Susie. "After the ceremony there will be music and dancing and we'll have a great time."

"Are you going on a honeymoon?" asked Maggie.

"We are," answered Dan. "We'll be going to New York City and then stop at some of the big cities on the way back."

"Who'll be running the place while you're gone?" asked Sean.

"Kathleen will," answered Susie. "Dan and I have been working with her and we feel she can handle everything."

"Are you comfortable with that?" Maggie asked Kathleen.

"I am," she answered. "I'll have my own place someday and this will be a good experience. Don't anyone worry. I'll take care of things."

"So would anyone care for some breakfast?" asked Dan. "I can get the cook started if anyone wants to eat now."

"Sure, that would be fine," said Sean. "We'll get some breakfast and then Maggie and I will get ourselves a hotel room."

"You know there's rooms here don't you?" said Susie.

"Course we do," said Sean. "But we like that one room over at that one hotel."

"I understand," said Susie.

~~~~

Everyone had some breakfast and then Maggie and Sean checked into their hotel. They had their way with each other for a while and then took a nice long bath. Their room had a nice tub in it. It wasn't as fancy as the one back home, but it was nice. Afterwards, they spent the day shopping and just looking around town. They also stopped in to see Judge Sharpton. He was glad to see them and he was also glad that Sean hadn't been too busy with law enforcement. Quiet times were nice.

One evening, they went to a theater and watched a play. Sean thought it was silly, but Maggie liked it. They ate dinner at some nice restaurants and even visited some other saloons. Sean wanted to see what the competition was doing. After visiting the saloons, Sean decided that there wasn't really any competition.

~~~~

The day of the wedding, Susie was a nervous wreck. Maggie did her best to keep her calm. Dan was a little nervous too. Sean got some whiskey in him and loosened him up some. Maggie finally talked Susie into taking a drink and she calmed down too.

It seemed like there were over a hundred people at the wedding. They had closed "The Palace" a little early the night before so it could be decorated and the place looked really nice. There was a fancy carpet put down for Susie to walk on as she went down the aisle. No one gave her away. She wanted it that way. She was her own woman and she was giving herself to this man.

~~~~

Back in Abilene, a huge herd came to town. It was from a ranch known as the CC. This stood for Crying Comanche. The owner of the ranch, Clancy Evans, considered himself to be one mean son of a bitch and the best Indian Fighter in Texas. He was fast with a gun and hit what he shot at. He had a son, his only son, and the boy thought he was better than his old man. Everyone called him Kid because he was only 17, but his real name was Bart.

Clancy Evans was seventeen years old when he joined the Army in 1845. His parents and two older brothers had been massacred a few years earlier by a Comanche war party. He survived the massacre by fighting really hard. He personally shot three of the Comanche with his squirrel rifle and then clubbed another one to death with it. When the stock of the rifle broke, he took a bowie knife off of his father's dead body and cut two more Comanche. The Comanche respected his bravery so much that they let him live. Clancy hoped that when he joined the Army, he would be killing some more Comanche. The war with Mexico started and he ended up fighting Mexicans instead of Comanche. He mustered out after the war and joined the Texas Rangers. While he was with the Rangers, he earned a reputation for being very brave but also reckless. He carried two Colt Walker pistols and when he rode into an Indian camp, anything that moved got shot. It didn't matter if it was men, women, or children. Clancy didn't stay in the Rangers very long. He was not good at taking orders, especially when it came to Indians.

Clancy met his wife Emma, in a saloon while he was with the Rangers. She was a whore, but when she met Clancy, she fell head over heals for him. They were married in 1849. They started their ranch in Texas just east of Comanche Territory. Bart was born in 1850. Two other sons were born later, but they died shortly after birth. Life on the ranch was very hard. The Comanche were always raiding. Clancy was getting very good on figuring when the next raid would be. Whether it was luck or whatever, he always managed to kill some Comanche and not lose too much stock.

Clancy was a shrewd businessman too. He knew a war between the north and south would break out sooner or later, so he decided to increase his herd and ranch. A lot of Clancy's neighbors didn't want to sell to him, but one way or another, he got the land and cows he needed. He knew Texas would fight with the south, but Clancy figured he'd sell his beef to whoever could pay him.

Clancy believed the south had no chance to win the war once it started. All the big manufacturing plants were up north. All the south had was cotton, tobacco, and slaves. Clancy never knew anyone who owned slaves. He knew nothing about colored folks and he wouldn't join in a fight over something he knew nothing about.

During the war, most of the cattle he sold went to the Confederacy. Clancy received some payment in gold, but most of the time, it was Confederate paper currency. Sometimes, his cows were just taken. After the war ended, the Confederate currency was worthless. Times were tough in Texas after the war. Clancy had the biggest ranch in Texas, but no market for his cows. When the railroad went to Abilene, the slaughter houses in Chicago were begging for Texas beef. The Texas herds would go to Abilene for shipment to the northern markets.

As Bart was Clancy's only son, he was basically a spoiled brat. If he wanted a new horse, Clancy got it for him. If he wanted a new gun, he got it. Bart was fourteen when Emma died from influenza. Clancy was devastated. He mourned for almost a year before he got over Emma. Clancy took himself another wife not long after this. Her name was Shirley. She worked in a saloon , but wasn't a whore. She was fifteen years younger than Clancy and everybody thought she married him for his money. Clancy didn't care what anyone else thought. He thought he was a young buck again.

Shirley and Bart didn't get along at all. Bart thought she was just after his Pa's money and he always let her know it. Clancy put more than one knot on Bart's head for being rude to his step-mother. Bart didn't like it that he had taken a back seat to Shirley. Before she came around, Bart was the center of attention. Now he thought he was treated like one of the hired hands. Little by little, Bart began hating his father.

Shirley was a very attractive girl and was only seven years older than Bart. Bart had a lot of fantasies about being with Shirley. He remembered something that he had heard from a bible thumper a few years back . It was from the Old Testament. When King David's son decided that he was going to oust his father, the first thing he did was have sex with all of David's wives and concubines. Bart envisioned himself having his way with Shirley and then killing his old man.

Clancy didn't go on the drive to Abilene. The Comanche were doing some raiding and he wanted to stay home and protect his young wife. Maybe he'd kill some Comanche too. He had eight hands with him at the ranch. His foreman on the drive was Sugar O'Reilly. They called him Sugar because he liked his sweets. He was also a tough Irishman and liked a good fight now and again. Clancy also knew that Sugar would keep the Kid in line. There were twelve other hands on the drive.

Michael had a bad feeling as this herd came into town. It kept coming and coming. It was huge. The pens wouldn't hold all of it.

It would take a while to get the whole herd loaded and headed out. This extra time it took to get the whole herd taken care of was making the Kid and the other hands restless. Sugar wouldn't let anyone go into town until the whole herd was penned up. It was all he could do to control his men.

When the last cows were finally penned up and loaded, Sugar got the men paid and turned them loose. They all took off for town and were shouting and firing their pistols into the air. Some of the boys took some shots at some signs and some watering troughs. Sugar was going to have a tough time babysitting tonight.

Some of the boys went to a bath house and cleaned up, but others went straight for the saloons and whorehouses. Michael watched them as they entered the other saloons. They were pretty rowdy now. What would they be like after they got liquored up? Several shots were fired in the other saloons, but no one yelled for the doc. Apparently no one had been shot yet. It was almost midnight before some of the hands of the CC made their way to Maggie's Place.

Michael was playing his new piano when the Kid and six of them walked in. Not one of them paid any attention to the sign about giving up their weapons. They sat down at two different tables and started yelling for some whiskey. Tom and Betty were behind the bar. Jim was nowhere to be seen. Jeb had been over by Michael and when the boys walked in and ignored the sign, he started a low growl. Tom and Betty reached down and grabbed the shotguns that were always behind the bar. Michael left his shotgun at the piano, got up and walked over to Kid's table. He had his pistol in his belt. Jeb went to the other table.

"Get this mangey dog away from me," shouted one of the cowboys. Jeb's growl was getting louder.

"Not now Jeb," said Michael. "Don't kill the young boys till I tell you."

Kid stood up and looked Michael in the eye. "Get the hell away from us old man and get that damn dog away before I blow his head off," said Kid.

Michael remained polite. "Now tell me boys, which one of you thinks he's in charge of this group?" asked Michael.

"I am, you old old son of a bitch," said Kid.

"Well now young man, you and your friends will remove your weapons or I'll let Jeb over there rip your throats out," said Michael. "Or, me and Jeb might just back up and let them two with the shotguns over at the bar blow you all to hell." The boys looked over at the bar to see two double barreled shotguns pointing at them.

"Them fools won't shoot," said Kid. As he said those words, he was reaching for his pistol. Michael saw this and struck Kid with a right to the jaw before the pistol was pulled. Kid was knocked back so hard that he landed on the next table. He was out cold. It looked like his jaw could be broken. The other cowboys dropped their gunbelts on the floor. Jeb was still growling.

"Knives too," said Michael. Three of the boys had knives and dropped them on the floor. Jeb quit growling. "Now you boys are welcome in here if you behave yourselves. Or you can leave and take your friend with you. We got a good doctor in this town. He might need him." The cowboys all looked at each other and decided to leave. They had just started picking up Kid when Sugar walked in.

"I can just about guess what happened," said Sugar. "That jaw a his might be broke. Get him outta here and find a doctor."

"What about our guns?" asked one of the cowboys.

"I'll make sure you get'em back," said Sugar. "Now git." The boys carried Kid outside and went looking for the doctor. "Now who in here done that to that boy?" asked Sugar.

"That would be me," said Michael. "Now you can check your gun at the bar."

"I never wear a gun in a bar," said Sugar. "People get shot that way." The two men sized each other up.

"You got a wooden leg or I'd hafta whoop you some," said Sugar. "That boy's papa would expect me to do that."

"Well don't let this wooden leg stop you sir," said Michael. "So let's two Micks have a go round."

"Have it your way stumpy," said Sugar.

"Stumpy huh, prepare to kiss the floor," said Michael.

The two men squared off. Michael was fairly good on his feet for having a wooden leg. It surprised Sugar. He was even more surprised when Michael caught him with a good left and knocked him sideways. "Not bad stumpy," said Sugar. "Care to try that again?" This time Michael caught him with a right to the jaw and Sugar went down. "That's about enough a that," said Sugar. "It's your turn to go down." They sized each other up. Sugar caught Michael with a good right to the gut but Michael didn't even flinch. Then he hit Michael with a left to the jaw and Michael just shook his head a little. "Damn stumpy, what are you made of, iron?" said Sugar. Michael smiled and never said a word. Sugar caught Michael with several rights and another left. Michael almost went down once but caught himself. Then he caught Sugar with a good right to the chin. Sugar fell straight back and landed on a table. He got back up and shook it off. He went for Michael again. They stood there sizing each other up.

"Couldn't we settle this in a more gentlemanly manner?" asked Michael,

"And what would that be?" asked Sugar.

"Irish whiskey," answered Michael. "We can see who can drink the most."

"Nobody can beat me when it comes to Irish whiskey," said Sugar. "And how do I know you have Irish whiskey?"

"Because my friend, I'm part owner in this place and we always keep Irish whiskey on hand," said Michael.

"I haven't had any Irish whiskey for years," said Sugar. "I forget what it tastes like."

Tom got out a bottle and two glasses. He sat them on the table closest to the two men. "Join me, my Mick friend," said Michael.

"I believe I will," said Sugar. The two men sat down. Michael filled the glasses.

"How about a toast," said Michael. "Here's to not getting killed."

"That's a good toast," said Sugar after he had taken a drink of his whiskey.

"My friend and I started that toast in the late war," said Michael. "Were you in the late war?"

"Yes I was," answered Sugar. "I was with "The Irish Brigade.""

"Well let's drink to the Irish Brigade," said Michael. The men took another drink.

Several more toasts were made and soon the bottle was empty. Tom brought over another one.

It was apparent that neither of the men were drunk when the second bottle was empty. Michael asked Tom to bring over another bottle. "I think I better stop now and see what other trouble my boys are finding," said Sugar. "How bout we call it a draw for now?"

"Fine by me ," said Michael. "It's been a pleasure meeting you. Good luck with your boys." The men shook hands. Tom gathered up the cowboy's weapons and gave them to Sugar. Sugar waved goodbye as he went out the door.

Sugar found most of his crew in another saloon, but Kid and two others weren't with them. They said they had no idea where they were. After Kid left the doc's office, he and two others disappeared. The other men just figured they had gone to a whorehouse. Sugar passed the weapons out to some of the boys who had left them at Maggie's Place. He sat with his boys but didn't drink. About an hour later, Kid and the other two boys came into the saloon where Sugar and the boys were. Kid was sober. "I'm gonna kill that son of a bitch," said Kid. "Nobody does that to me and gets away with it."

"Sit down Kid and have a drink," said Sugar. "You're lucky that man didn't kill you."

"I'm gonna kill'em," said Kid. Kid was having a hard time speaking. His jaw hurt bad. Doc said his jaw wasn't broken, but might be cracked some.

"You kill that man and they'll hang you boy," said Sugar. "I found out somethin' while I was drinkin' with him. He's a Federal Deputy Marshal. His boss is that O'Rourke fella that everybody talks about. There's nobody faster than him with a pistol and they say he can kill you at a thousand yards with his Sharps. He's good with his fists too. You don't mess with these Federal boys."

"Just wait till Pa hears that you were drinkin' with the man who done this ta me," said Kid. "He'll shoot you himself. Hell, I might just shoot you."

"I wouldn't try it Kid," said Sugar. "You pull a gun on me and I'll take it away from you and shove it up your ass. Then I'll slam you around some till all six shots go off. Now you just shut up." Kid didn't say another word. He sat there and started drinking.

Sugar thought it would be best if he stayed up all night and kept an eye on the boys, but around 3am, he fell asleep in his chair at the saloon. Kid motioned for the other boys to step outside with him. They all went outside. Sugar was still asleep. "I'm gonna go kill that bastard," said Kid. "Who's with me?"

"I'll have no part a murder," said one of the boys. His name was Del. "I had me enough liquor and women. I'm goin' to my hotel room." Most of the others followed Del.

"Suit yourself," said Kid. Then he ran over and grabbed a pistol from one of the other boys. "You boys go on now. I got business to take care of." Kid had a pistol in each hand now as he and the two others walked towards Maggie's Place. It was fairly dark outside, but the lights inside the saloons lit the street up some. They were about two hundred feet from Maggie's Place when Betty and Michael came out the door. Jeb was with them. They started for home.

The boys saw them and ducked into the shadows. After Michael and Betty had come about a hundred feet, Jeb started growling. Michael knew something was not right. "Who's out there?" yelled Michael. "You better come out before I turn Jeb loose on you." It was silent for a moment and then a shot rang out. Betty was hit and went down. Jeb took off at a run towards the shooter. Another shot rang out. Jeb was hit and went down.

Michael checked on Betty's wound. He pulled a pistol and knelt down next to Betty and tried to spot the shooter. Another shot rang out and Michael was knocked the rest of the way down. The bullet had hit his wooden leg. Michael fired a shot at where he had seen the muzzle flash. As soon as he fired, he was struck by another bullet and went down. Kid walked toward Michael.

"I'll finish these two off now," said Kid.

"I'll have no part of murderin' a woman," one of the others said. He and the other boy turned to walk away. Kid shot them in the back as they were walking away.

"Damn cowards," said Kid. Sugar finally woke up from all the shooting and went outside to see what was happening. He walked down the street to see Kid standing over Michael and Betty. He was about to shoot them again.

"You'll hang for this Kid," said Sugar. "I'll see to it personally."

"The hell you will," said Kid. He raised a pistol and shot Sugar in the forehead. Just as he fired, he heard someone running toward him. It was Tom. He had been almost home when he heard the shooting. He didn't keep a gun at home so he ran to the saloon and got one of the shotguns from behind the bar. He saw Kid kill Sugar and saw Michael, Betty, and the other two cowboys on the ground. He knew that Kid had just shot all of them. He wanted to fire the shotgun but was not close enough and he feared that he might hit Michael or Betty. When Kid saw Tom with the shotgun, he took off running. When Tom got to Michael and Betty, he fired both barrels at Kid. Tom saw him stumble, but he kept going. Then Tom knelt down and looked at Betty and Michael. Both of them had blood all over their chests. He started screaming for Doc Rawlins, but Doc had heard all the shooting and came running. Jim showed up. Some other cowboys who had been in a whorehouse came over to see if they could help. Betty and Michael were carried to Doc's office. Doc could only work on one of them at a time, so he started on Betty. He had Jim hold a bandage on Michael's chest to help slow or stop the bleeding. Cora helped him as he worked on Betty.

The bullet had not gone through and had to be dug out. Betty was unconscious so she didn't care. It took a while, but Doc got the bullet and stopped the bleeding. Cora bandaged up Betty while Doc started on Michael. The bullet in Michael was dangerously close to his heart. Doc worked slow and meticulously but he got it out and didn't rupture the heart or any of the big arteries and veins. Doc and Cora bandaged up Michael and sat down for a minute to relax. Doc was about to have himself a drink when Jim said. "You got another customer Doc. Jeb's been hit."

"I'm not a dog doctor," said Doc. "I don't know what I can do." Some men had carried Jeb onto the porch in front of Doc's office. Doc got a lantern and took a look at Jeb. "Looks like he got shot in the head but he's still alive." Then Doc felt Jeb's head. "The bullet just creased his skull. He'll be all right. He'll just have a headache for a few days." Doc cleaned up Jeb's head as best he could and then put some salve on the wound. Jeb came to just as Doc finished. He didn't look happy. He looked like he wanted to hurt someone. Doc let him into the room where Betty and Michael were. Jeb laid down on the floor at the foot of Michael's bed.

The next morning, Tom sent a telegram to St. Louis for Sean. It went as follows:

Federal Marshal O'Rourke

Three men murdered by Texas boy<<stop>>Betty and Michael badly wounded by same<<stop>>Jeb wounded<<stop>>believe I wounded boy as he ran<<stop>>hurry back

Tom

Everyone had a great time at the wedding. The drinking and dancing went on till the wee hours of the morning. Sean and Maggie were having a late breakfast the next morning when the telegram came. When Sean read it, Maggie could see fire in his eyes. She took the telegram from him and read it. She started crying. Sean let her cry for a little while before he spoke. "We'll be leavin'," said Sean. "Once I make sure Michael and Betty are all right, I'll be goin' to Texas. Jeb better be all right too. I'll show that son of a bitch that there's a lot of different ways to die and some of them can be pretty slow."

"You hurt him and you hurt him bad," said Maggie.

"I will darlin'. I will," said Sean.

After breakfast, Sean went straight to Judge Sharpton's office and told him about the killings and the woundings of Betty and Michael. "I'll be going to Texas after him," said Sean.

"You go ahead and hang'em when you chatch'em," said the Judge. "Hang'em before he kills someone else." Sean left the Judge and he and Maggie were on the next train.

~~~~

The next morning in Abilene, the cowboy named Del went looking for his foreman. He had slept through the shootings during the night and had no idea what had happened. He found most of the other cowhands. Four people were unaccounted for. Sugar, Kid, and two cowboys couldn't be found. Del went into Maggie's Place to see if anyone had seen these men. He went to Tom at the bar.

"My name's Del," he began. "I'm looking for our foreman and some others. We brought a herd in yesterday. Have you seen any new faces in here?"

"Young man, there was some shootings in town last night," started Tom. "Three men were murdered and a man and woman were badly wounded. Some young fella did it. I saw him shoot the big fella. He ran off when he saw me coming with a shotgun. I fired and he was hit. He stumbled some but didn't go down. He got away."

"What did that young fella look like?" asked Del. Tom gave a description of the shooter as best he could. "That was Kid," said Del. "Where's them bodies? Maybe it's our boys who got shot."

"They're over at the undertaker's," said Tom. "Best git over there before he gets'em boxed up." Del went over to the undertakers. The three men were laid out. The undertaker and his help were about to box them up.

"I need to take a look at these bodies," said Del. "I think they're part of our crew."

"Help yourself," said the undertaker. "If you do recognize them, I'll be able to put names on the markers," Del took a look at the bodies.

"This one is Sugar O'Reilly," said Del. "And this one is Joe Riley and that other one is Walt Darcey."

"You can take their weapons if you want," said the undertaker. "I have no use for them." Del took the pistols and gunbelts off of Joe and Walt. Sugar wasn't wearing his gunbelt. Del checked the pistols to see if they had been fired recently. They had not. Kid had murdered his own people. Del went back to Maggie's Place. He went to Tom.

"Them were our men over at the undertaker," said Del. "That big fella was our foreman Sugar O'Reilly. The other two're Joe Riley and Walt Darcey. I checked their pistols. They haven't been fired. Kid done all the shootin'. You got any law in this town?"

"We don't have any local law, but the fella that got badly wounded is a Deputy Federal Marshal and he works for Federal Marshal Sean O'Rourke. I reckon you've heard a him."

"I have. I think everybody has," said Del. "Where is O'Rourke right now?"

"He'll be on his way back here," said Tom. "He was in St. Louis for a wedding."

"Well me and the other boys'll be leavin'," said Del. "Make sure you tell O'Rourke that none of us had anything to do with these killins' and such. It was all Kid's doin'. His old man's got about the biggest spread in Texas. It's the CC. The old man's name is Clancy Evans. He's not that old, mebbe forty. He think's he a gunmen. I seen him shoot. He is fast and he loves ta kill Injuns. Kid's real name is Bart. Everybody calls him Kid cause he's only seventeen. Me'n the boys'll be leavin' after we get somethin' ta eat. We'll be lookin' fer work somewheres else besides the CC. We don't wanna be anywhere near there when O'Rourke shows up. We know all about him and what he can do."

"Well why don't you and the other boys have breakfast right here on the house," said Tom. "We got us the best cooks in town.

And I thank you for all that information. The Marshal will be needin' it." Del rounded up the crew and they had their breakfast. Del thought of something else he should tell Tom.

"One more thing before we go," said Del. "Kid'll go to the ranch and tell his old man some big story about someone else killin' our men and how he just got away with his life. The old man'll believe'm. Now we'll be leavin'." Tom thanked Del again for the information.

~~~~

Jim went over to the Doc's to check on Betty and Michael. Cora answered the door when he knocked and took him to Betty and Michael. Doc was there with them. "How are they doing?" asked Jim.

"Betty'll be fine," said Doc. "If Michael makes it through the day, I believe he'll make it. Nothing we can do but wait. Now why don't you take Jeb here with you when you leave. He don't need to be in here." Jim stayed for a bit. Betty and Michael were asleep so he didn't stay long. He tried to get Jeb to go with him when he left, but Jeb wouldn't leave Michael and Betty. "I guess he'll be here till Sean get's back," said Doc.

~~~~

When Maggie and Sean got back to Abilene, Tom told him everything that had happened and gave him the information he had gotten from Del. Jeb was so glad to see Maggie and Sean that he started howling and woke up Michael and Betty. Michael was now out of danger. He and Betty would be at Doc's for a few more days. Doc didn't want them moved just yet. After Maggie and Betty did some crying, Michael told them about the events in the saloon and the shootings that night. The talking wore Michael out and he fell asleep after he told Sean everything. Maggie stayed and talked with Betty for a while. Sean went to the telegraph office. He sent a telegram to Jug Carter. It went as follows:

Jug

Will be coming to Texas<<stop>>three men murdered and Betty and Michael badly wounded by Bart Evans<<stop>>Bart also known as Kid<<stop>>Evans ranch is CC<<stop>>will need your help

Sean

Sean knew that it might take several days for the telegram to get to Jug. He would wait patiently. He would also make sure Michael was healing while he waited to hear from Jug.

~~~~

It took four days for Jug to get Sean's telegram. Josh had gone into Ft. Worth for some business and brought it back with him. Jug sat down with Lolita and told her he would be helping Sean. She was very upset about Betty and Michael getting shot. She was also concerned for Jug's safety. "That man that owns the CC is nothing more than a bully and a gunmen," said Lolita. "They say he got his ranch and cattle by killing and running off honest folks. He murders Indians too."

"I've heard that too," said Jug. "Sean is our friend and I'll be helpin' him. Josh and Wayne can take care a things while I'm gone. I'll be sendin' a telegram back to Sean tellin' him to come on down. I'll have Wayne go to Ft. Worth and get it sent. We got a while before Sean'll be here. I'll make sure everything is all right here before we go after Kid."

"Well in the meantime, we can get started on some of those children we want," said Lolita. She took Jug by the hand and led him to their room. They spent most of the day in their room. The next morning, Jug sent Wayne to Ft. Worth to send the telegram to Sean.

~~~~

Back in Abilene, Sean waited to hear back from Jug. Michael was doing well now and he and Betty were back home. Doc checked on them regularly. Sean also decided that when he headed to Texas, he would swing down through "The Nations" and pick up Jesse Strong. He, Jesse, and Jug should be able to handle anything that would come up.

It had been fairly quiet in Abilene. The cattle drives had come in and the cowboys did their drinking and such. Word had gotten out about the shootings and for the most part, the cowboys behaved themselves. They knew O'Rourke was back in town and he would be on the prod. No one even looked cross-eyed at Maggie's Place.

CHAPTER THREE

When Kid took off from Abilene, he headed east. He found a small town in Missouri that had a doctor and had four pieces of buckshot taken out of his legs. There were three pieces in his right leg and one in his left leg. The doc scolded him for not taking care of it right after it happened, but there was no infection. The holes had started to scab over so the doc had to open them up again to remove the buckshot. Kid didn't want to be put to sleep, so doc had him drink as much whiskey as he could stand. Kid still did a lot of screaming. Kid passed out when doc was removing the last piece.

When Kid woke up a couple of hours later, a tall, slender, middle aged man was standing beside him. He had on a tied down colt and was wearing a star. Kid looked up at him. "Who the hell'r you?" asked Kid.

"I'm Sheriff a this county," he answered. "Name's Don Bowden. Just who are you and how did you get yourself shot and what happened to your jaw?"

"I'm Hank Owens," Kid said. "I was walkin' my horse when I got shot. Never seen nobody. Maybe it was somebody out huntin' and I caught some stray buckshot. I fell and hit my jaw on a rock. Lucky my horse wasn't hit. I headed this way lookin' for a doc."

"Where you headed boy?" asked Don.

"I was goin' down Texas and get me a job on one a them ranches," answered Kid.

"Well soon as you feel up to it, you git yourself headed that way," said Don. "Don't quite swallow that story a yours, but I don't know nothin' otherwise. I got no posters that fit your description."

"I'll be leavin'. This don't seem like a very sociable place," said Kid. The Sheriff left.

Kid thanked the doc for telling the Sheriff he was there and then headed for the nearest saloon. He had a couple of shots of whiskey and something to eat. He got on his horse and headed out of town. As he neared the edge of town, the Sheriff was riding back into town. When they got almost to each other, the Sheriff stopped. Kid stopped too.

"Don't be comin' back this way Hank, or whatever your real name is boy," said the Sheriff.

"Don't you worry yourself sick about me Sheriff," said Kid. "I won't be around here ever again." Kid gave his horse a kick and started on his way. The Sheriff did the same. After he was about twenty yards past the Sheriff, Kid turned to see if the Sheriff was watching him. He wasn't. Kid pulled his pistol and shot the Sheriff. The bullet struck him in the middle of the back and he fell dead out of the saddle. Kid galloped away.

A few days later, Sean received a telegram from Judge Sharpton. It went as follows:

Federal Marshal O'Rourke

County Sheriff murdered in Missouri just across
state line from Kansas<<stop>>suspect had buckshot removed from legs<<stop>>Sheriff ran sus-
pect out of town<<stop>>could be your man

Federal Judge Sharpton

"That's gotta be our boy," said Sean after he read the telegram. "He swung over that way to find a doctor. Sheriff musta
made him mad. Yep, that's our boy. He got a taste for killin' and
he likes it. He'll be headin' down to Texas. I bet he'll kill again before he gets down there to the ranch. Sean was right. Kid got himself to Texas, but just across the Red River, his horse came up
lame. He came across a lone cowboy one day and shot him and
took his horse. Before he got to the ranch, he came across a traveling preacher. He killed the preacher out of just plain meanness.
The preacher didn't have a thing the Kid wanted. The preacher
had two biscuits in a pouch and his bible and that was all he had
except a very old horse. Kid shot the horse, too.

~~~~

By the time Kid got to the CC, his legs were healed up pretty good.
Clancy was sitting in a rocking chair on the front porch of the
house smoking his pipe. "It's about time you got back boy," said
Clancy. "What took so long and where's everbody else? Where's
Sugar?"

"Sugar's dead Pa," said Kid. "Some gunman killed him and Joe and Walt. Them other boys run off. I tried to help Sugar, but someone opened up on me with a shotgun. I fell and hit my jaw on a rock too." Kid pulled up his pants legs and showed Clancy the buckshot wounds."

"Why would anyone kill Sugar and them boys?" asked Clancy.

"I really don't know Pa," answered Kid. "The shootin' had already started when I got there. I heard someone yell out "O'Rourke." I got out a there before they killed me too."

"I heard a that name O'Rourke," said Clancy. "He's a Federal Marshal, but he's nothin' more'n a gunman. Is there anything you're not tellin' me boy?"

"I hit one of'em before I was hit with that scattergun," said Kid. "I seen'm go down. Don't know who he was, but he was doin' some a the shootin'."

"Where's the money for the herd?" asked Clancy.

"It's in a bank in Abilene," said Kid. "Sugar paid everyone off and then put the rest in the bank. He was gonna get it out or get a bank draft when we left."

"Why didn't you get the money or a draft before you high-tailed it?" asked Clancy.

"I told you Pa. They was tryin' ta kill me," said Kid. "I got outta there before they did."

"I suppose I can send a telegram to that bank and have them send me a draft," said Clancy. "Are you sure you're tellin' me everything boy?"

"That's everything Pa," said Kid. "Like I said, the shootin' had already started when I got there. Don't know what it was about or nothin'."

~~~~

A few days later, Sean received the telegram from Jug. Sean would be leaving the next day. He would head down to "The Nations" and get Jesse Strong. Then the two of them would head to Jug's ranch. Michael and Betty were healing well. Betty was able to get up and move around some. Michael would get out of bed and move to a chair. He would do his necessaries and then lie back down for a while. He wanted a drink badly, but Doc Rawlins wanted him to wait a few more days. While Betty and Michael were house bound, they had some serious talks. Betty wasn't sure she wanted to stay in Abilene. Maybe a nice quiet town would be better. Abilene was becoming a very violent place. How many times had Michael been shot already? Michael was deciding that he had been shot enough times too. Maybe they would find a nice quiet town.

Sean had a nice long talk with Michael the evening before he left. "I'll get the son of a bitch for you Michael," said Sean. "I'll get him for you and Betty. Nobody shoots my friends and lives to tell about it. He will die slowly. I promise you."

"I had an idea on how I'd like him to die," said Michael. "I want him to watch his own blood leaving his body. I'd like him to bleed to death while Jeb watches."

"I think Jeb'd like that too," said Sean. "I reckon I could take Jeb with me this time. So I've been hearing rumors that maybe you and Betty are thinkin' about movin' to someplace that's nice and quiet. Michael, I fully understand. You and Betty deserve a good life together. You need to live in a place where you don't have to worry about gettin' shot all the time. How many times you been shot already? Hell maybe all of us should leave this place. Abilene's just gettin' started as a cow town. It'll be a lot worse next year and the year after that. I don't want to be shootin' drunk cowboys all the time."

"I do love owning a saloon," said Michael. "I feel at home when I'm in a saloon."

"That's because saloons are supposed to be a place where a man can go to enjoy himself," said Sean. "Nothin' wrong with havin' some good whiskey or beer and relaxin'. Maybe there is a nice quiet place out there. I bet Maggie's startin' to feel that way too. Well Michael, I need to get some sleep so I can get an early start in the mornin'. You and Betty take care while I'm gone."

"Make sure you come back," said Michael.

"Oh I'll be back," said Sean. "You can count on that."

~~~~

That night, Maggie and Sean had a nice long talk as they laid in bed holding each other. What Maggie said didn't surprise Sean at all. She was thinking that maybe they should leave Abilene for a quieter place. There were other towns out there. They could even try St. Louis for a while. "That's been on my mind some too," said Sean. "I'll think real hard on it when I get back. But I gotta get that Kid first. I'll be takin' Jeb with me this time too. Is that all right with you?"

"It'll be all right," said Maggie. "Things do seem quieter now. Jim's here and Tom and Cookie. It'll be all right. If things were to get too much out of hand, I'll just board up the place. Nobody who works for us will get shot while you're gone. I promise."

"You're a good woman Maggie. I love you," said Sean.

"I love you too darlin'," said Maggie.

Sean was on his way at daylight. He left well provisioned. He rode Billy and took a spare horse and a pack horse. He wore two pistols and had his Winchester and Sharps in scabbards on each side of his saddle. His ten gauge was on the pack horse. He had plenty of ammunition on him and there was a lot more on the pack horse.

~~~~

A few days after Sean had left for "The Nations," Clancy Evans decided it was time to wire the bank in Abilene and get his money. The nearest town was Smithton and it was a hard days ride away. Smithton was a small town, but it had everything a person needed. There was a General Store which was also the Post Office and Bank. There was a saloon and it had a few working girls. There was also a livery stable that was attached to the saloon. There wasn't a hotel in town, but the saloon had extra rooms when the girls weren't using them. The town had a part time Marshal and he was also the Justice of the Peace. Sometimes on Saturday night, he would arrest a drunk when they got out of hand. There was no jail, so he usually handcuffed the drunks to a hitching post or in a stall at the livery. One thing they did have in town was a telegraph office. They put one in Smithton because the Army would pass through from time to time while they were chasing Comanche or Kiowa.

Clancy rode into town and went straight to the telegraph office. He sent a telegram to the bank in Abilene and asked that his money be sent to him. He would accept a bank draft. Clancy went to the saloon while he waited on a reply from the bank in Abilene. He went to the bar and ordered a whiskey. Right after the bartender poured it, the part time Marshal approached him. "Mr. Evans, I got somethin' here you should see," said the Marshal. "Maybe we should sit at a table and have a little more privacy."

"Just what the hell is your name anyway?" asked Clancy. "And what would you have that I would need to see?"

"First off, my name is Roy Dobbs," said the Marshal. "And I'm sure you'll want to see what I have. No one else in town has seen it. I wanted you to see it first. It came in a couple days ago." The two men went to a table.

"All right Roy, show me what it is you think I need to see," said Clancy. Roy reached into a pocket and pulled out a piece of folded up paper. He took care when he unfolded it. He didn't want to tear it. When he had it unfolded, he handed it to Clancy. Clancy stared at it for several minutes.

"This is a wanted poster for my boy," said Clancy. "What the hell is this all about?"

"Well, Mr. Evans, I got a telegram the other day about this poster," started Roy. "Your boy murdered three men and badly wounded another man and a woman. A witness said he saw your boy shoot your foreman. Apparently he had shot the man and woman first and then shot two cowboys in the back. Their names were Joe Riley and Walt Darcey. When your foreman ran out in the street to see what was going on, he killed him. The man and woman weren't dead yet and he was about to shoot them again when a man with a shotgun chased him off. Your boy was hit with the shotgun as he was runnin' away. Not long after this, a County Sheriff in Missouri was murdered. Some doc in a small town took some buckshot out of a young man's legs. The doc told the Sheriff and the Sheriff run the fella out of town. Later, they found the Sheriff dead, shot in the back. They think Bart kilt that Sheriff too. Oh, and some cowboy named Del identified the bodies. He also said that your foreman wasn't wearin' a gun and them two cowboys never fired their guns. One more thing, that man that was badly wounded, he was Sean O'Rourke's deputy and that woman was his wife."

Clancy wasn't sure what to think about all of this. Was his boy capable of all that killing? "Are you sure about all this?" Clancy asked Roy.

"Mr. Evans, a witness saw Bart kill your foreman," said Roy. "Someone did hit your boy with some buckshot before he could shoot that man and woman again. That's what I know to be true. The rest could be true, but I can't say for sure. I do know one thing Mr. Evans. If they catch your boy, he'll hang. O'Rourke'll make sure of that. I've heard that O'Rourke hanged some men even after they were already dead." Clancy sat there in a daze for a while. He drank his whiskey and ordered another one. After he finished it, he thanked Roy for the information. He went to the telegraph office and got word from the bank in Abilene. Then he finished his business in town and headed home.

Clancy started the ride home at a slow pace. The more he thought about what his son had done, the faster he moved the horse. He had almost run his horse to death when he realized what he was doing and gave the horse a rest. Should he kill this horse just because his son was a murderer? When he got home, he was going to give Bart the beating of his life, and then he was going to turn him over to the law.

It was late when Clancy arrived at the ranch. When he was about a mile from the ranch, he took off his gunbelt and placed it over the saddlehorn. He didn't want to lose his head and shoot his son. He wanted his son to hang. When Clancy was in sight of the ranch house, he could see Bart sitting on the front porch smoking. He rode straight to the porch and stopped just shy of it. Before Bart had said anything, Clancy slid down from the saddle and ran over and grabbed Bart. "You're nothing but a damn liar boy," yelled Clancy. "You murdered Sugar and them boys and mebbe that Sheriff. I'm gonna beat the hell out of you and then I'm giving you to the law." Bart had on his gunbelt. Clancy saw that he had on his gunbelt. Clancy punched Bart in the gut and when he bent over, Clancy grabbed his pistol and threw it. Then he proceeded to beat on Bart. Bart tried to fight back but it was like tangling with a grizzly bear. All he could do was take the beating. Clancy got careless. He wasn't paying any attention to where Bart's pistol was. Bart was pretty beat up, but not as bad off as he acted. He knew right where his pistol was. The next time Clancy struck him, he staggered over and fell right on top of it. He was laying face down and was pretending to be out cold. When Clancy grabbed him to turn him over and beat on him some more, he was staring at a Colt revolver. Not one word was spoken. Bart pointed the Colt at Clancy's chest and fired. Clancy was knocked backwards. His shirt was on fire.

Shirley had been just inside and was watching the beating. She came running out now and went to her husband. She took her hands and beat out the fire on Clancy's shirt. Before she could say or do anything else, Bart took the Colt and cracked her on the head. She fell limply to the ground.

The next thing Shirley knew, she was naked and tied to her bed. Bart was on her and was pumping away. When she screamed, Bart slapped her across the face. When he was finished, he went into another room and came back with a bottle of whiskey. He took a few swallows and then forced himself on her again. When she screamed again, he hit her with his fist and she was knocked out.

An hour later when the ranch hands came back from their days work, they found Clancy laying by the front porch in a pool of blood. He was just barely alive. One of the men thought he heard a scream and he went inside. He found Shirley tied to her bed. She had been beaten and raped. He gently covered her and untied her. The man with the fastest horse was sent after the nearest doctor. It took Shirley awhile to regain her composure, but when she did, she told the men what had happened. She told them that she had heard Clancy say that Bart had murdered Sugar and some other boys and maybe a Sheriff in Missouri. Clancy had said that he was going to beat him and then give him over to the law. "When Clancy got here," started Shirley. "He wasn't wearing his pistol. He grabbed Bart's pistol and threw it. While he was beating on Bart, Bart was able to get his pistol and shoot Clancy. I put out the fire on Clancy's shirt and then the next thing I know, I'm tied to my bed and Bart is raping me." Shirley was crying now and showed no signs of stopping. The men tried to comfort her as best they could. They brought Clancy inside and cleaned him up as best they could and waited for the doctor.

Doc Clemmons didn't make it till the next morning. He rode half the night to get there. Doc Clemmons was a good doctor. He served with the Army of Northern Virginia and this was nothing compared to what he had done years earlier. The bullet was close to Clancy's heart and should have killed him, but for some reason, it didn't. It took Doc a while, but the bullet was removed. There was nothing he could do for Shirley except give her something to calm her down. Shirley wouldn't take the medicine and wanted whiskey instead, Doc obliged her. Doc did all he could and said he'd be back in a day or so to check on Clancy.

One of the hands had always heard that Clancy had a safe in the house where he kept some cash on hand. A couple of the men went looking for it. They found it. It was in a room Clancy called his office. It was a small safe and was under a desk. The door of the safe was wide open and the safe was empty. Only Clancy knew how much money Bart had gotten. Shirley never knew how much money was in the safe at any one time. Clancy had never given her the combination. There was no need. Whenever she needed or wanted something, Clancy got it for her. Clancy was good to her and she loved him for it. She knew that everyone thought she was just after his money, but she didn't care what other people thought. Clancy might have been a son of a bitch at one time, but he was her son of a bitch and she loved him.

~~~~

Sean had no trouble at all on his way to "The Nations." He passed a few settlers and a group of buffalo hunters who were heading west. The settlers were tired of drought, Indians, and outlaws and were heading back east to Ohio. One of the buffalo hunters had heard of Sean and how he had lived with the Cheyenne. He asked Sean where the big herds would be this time of year. Sean just said one word, "west," and then moved on. He heard some of the hunters grumble a little as he left them, but he really didn't want to get into a fight right now. There were four of them. Sean could probably take three of them, but the fourth one could be a problem. That is unless Jeb helped out.

John Littletree was at the edge of the village when Sean arrived. He recognized Sean right away and went to his friend. "Good to see you again my friend," said John as they shook hands. "I don't imagine you're here for a social visit."

"It's good to see you too my friend," said Sean. "And no, this isn't a social visit. I'm after a killer and I came for Jesse. Is he in the village?"

"Him. Orry, and some of the other men are out hunting for some fresh meat," said John. "They should be back this evening. You can go to Jesse's cabin and wait for him. I'm sure Dawn would be happy to see you. I'll take care of your horses."

"Thank you," said Sean. He handed John the reins to his horses and walked to Jesse's cabin. He lightly knocked on the door. Dawn answered it. Jeb went inside just like he belonged there. Neither of them said a word for a moment. Dawn hugged Sean and stepped back. Sean could see that she was with child. She was maybe six months along. She spoke.

"Yes Sean, I am with child," said Dawn. "The baby should come late fall or early winter."

"I'm happy for you," said Sean. Then he hesitated for a moment. "You know I'm here to get Jesse don't you."

"I knew that as soon as I opened the door," said Dawn. "Are you afraid that I might not want Jesse going with you since I am with child?"

"That crossed my mind some," said Sean. "I'm after a killer. He's gotta be stopped."

"Sean, if it wasn't for you and Maggie, Jesse and I would probably be dead," said Dawn. "Of course I'll worry about Jesse going with you, but I know that you won't let anything happen to either of you. So where are you headed?"

"I'm picking up Jug at his ranch and then we're headed to a ranch called the CC," said Sean. "It's sposed to be about the biggest ranch in Texas. The man that owns it has a son. It was his son that did all the killin'."

"How many did he kill?" asked Dawn.

"Three for sure and maybe more," started Sean. "He also shot Betty and Michael."

"Oh my God, are they all right?" asked Dawn.

"They are now, but Michael was bad off for a while," said Sean. "That fella might be the one who murdered a Sheriff over in Missouri too. I intend to kill'em." Just as Sean finished speaking, Laura Brownshirt knocked on the door. Dawn let her in. Sean took a good look at her. "I see you and Orry been busy," said Sean. "Your baby'll be here a couple months'r so after Dawn's."

"Yes it will Sean and it's good to see you again," said Laura. "Who you after now?"

"Goin' to Texas after a killer," said Sean. "I came here to get Jesse."

"You won't be needing Orry, will you?" asked Laura.

"No, me, Jesse, and Jug'll be enough," said Sean.

"I know he'll be wanting to go with you and Jesse," said Laura. "Seems like wherever Jesse goes, Orry's gotta go too."

"They're good friends," said Sean. "Friends like to help their friends out. But I won't need Orry. He'll need to be here to look after you two while we're gone." The three of them had some coffee and talked. They hadn't finished one cup when the men got back. They had done well and came back early. There were four of them who had gone hunting and they came back with three deer and two bears. Jesse saw the extra horses and the pack when they entered the village and he knew that Sean was there. He went to his cabin. He went to Dawn first and gave her a hug and a kiss. Next he gave Laura a kiss on the cheek. Then he went to Sean and gave him a hug and a handshake.

"Good to see you my friend," said Jesse. "Who we after this time?"

Sean was surprised that Jesse went straight to the point. "Goin' to Texas after a killer," said Sean. "We'll pick up Jug at his place and then head to a ranch called the CC. It was the owner's son who done the killin'. He shot Michael and Betty too."

"We best get'm killed," said Jesse. Orry came into the cabin now. He went to Laura and gave her a hug and kiss. Then he went to Sean and shook his hand.

"Who we after now?" asked Orry.

"We, that is, me, Jesse, and Jug'r goin't to Texas after a killer," said Sean. "You are stayin' here and takin' care of the women and the place."

"So yer sayin' that you don't need me?" said Orry.

"That's what I'm sayin'," said Sean. "Someone needs to be here and you're that someone."

"I guess Laura wouldn't want me traypsin' off again anyway," said Orry. "So Jesse, you gonna help skin and cut up these critters we shot or are you gonna socialize?"

"I'll be there in a minute," said Jesse. "I just needed to greet my friend."

"I'll help you boys," said Sean. "I got a good skinnin' knife in my pack. We'll be done in no time."

Sean was good with a skinning knife, but Jesse was really good. He just made the whole process look effortless. They got the meat divided up in no time. By the time they got back to Jesse's cabin, the women were just about done fixing dinner. After a fine meal, they all sat around and talked. Sean had a bottle with him so he and Jesse sipped some whiskey while they talked.

They headed south the next morning at daylight. Jesse was well provisioned too. He took a spare horse and a pack horse. He wore two Colt revolvers and had his Spencer in a scabbard on his saddle. He had plenty of ammunition for both. Jeb seemed anxious to be going. Maybe he knew who they were after.

CHAPTER FOUR

The ride through Creek territory was uneventful, but when they got to Chickasaw land, some young hot head thought they should pay a toll for going across Chickasaw land. Sean assured him that no toll would be paid and if he didn't want to get hurt, he should get away from them. The young brave did get away from them, but later on, he tried to steal some of their horses.

It was getting late and they were almost to the Red River so they made camp for the night. Sean knew that something was going on. Billy seemed a little restless as they rode and Jeb would stop from time to time and look behind them. Sometimes he would disappear and come back in a few minutes. They made a big fire that night so if they were being followed, the person or persons following would have no trouble finding them. The horses were hobbled and tied tightly when Sean and Jesse turned in for the night. After about an hour of darkness, Jeb had a very low growl going. "I hear him too," Sean said to Jeb. "How bout we wait till he starts to untie one of the horses and you go bite him on the ass." Jeb stopped his growl and eased over near the horses. Jesse was awake too. He and Sean laid there pretending to be asleep. It wasn't long and they heard a blood curdling scream and then Jeb barking fiercely. In the firelight, they could see the young brave running away with Jeb after him. Sean was sure he saw blood on the brave's backside. Sean called to Jeb and he came back. He saw some blood around Jeb's mouth. "You did bite him on the ass didn't you boy," said Sean. "Damn if you're not the best damn dog ever." Sean got on the ground and was rolling around wrestling with Jeb. Jesse sat there and laughed at them.

"If that young boy got himself a woman, what do you reckon he gonna tell her bout what happened to his ass?" said Jesse. Sean just laughed.

~~~~

They crossed the Red River the next morning and were in Texas. It would take another good four or five days to get to Jug's ranch. The ground they traveled on was taking a pretty good beating. Several herds had come that way and the land was almost barren. By the fall, the trail would need to get wider if the cows were going to get any grass to graze on when herds bedded down for the night. They passed two herds the first day they were in Texas. Sean liked to watch the cowboys work. There was always some longhorn who didn't want to cooperate and was always making for some brush. The cowboys didn't get much easy time in the saddle.

On the third day as they approached another herd, they could see that the point man was wearing a sling on his left arm. When they got closer, they could see blood on his shirt. As they approached the man, he pulled out his pistol. "Keep your distance mister," said the man. "I'll shoot you if I have to." The point man couldn't have been more than eighteen years old.

"Easy now fella," said Sean. "I'm Federal Marshal O'Rourke and this man is my deputy. Looks like you had some trouble." Sean showed the man his badge.

"Yes Marshal, we did," said the man. "Name's Lonnigan, Thomas Lonnigan, and this is my Pa's herd. We got hit yesterday by rustlers. They cut out about five hundred head and skedaddled. One of us got kilt and three others got wounded. Don't think we hit any of them. My Pa's riding on the cook wagon. He got hit in the leg. His name is Thomas too."

"Well we'll have a talk with your Pa when he gets up here Thomas," said Sean.

"That's some dog you got there Marshal. Would you sell him?" asked Thomas.

"Not for any amount of money," said Sean. "He's a good cow dog too. If you're wantin' a good cow dog, when you get to Abilene, go to the livery and find a boy there named Billy. His dogs is good cow dogs and they might have some pups."

"Thanks Marshal," said Thomas as he rode away.

It took a good while for the cook wagon to get to Sean and Jesse. The herd was stretched out a good ways and they were in the middle. Thomas saw Sean's badge as the cook wagon approached Sean and Jesse. "You're just the man I'm lookin' for," said Thomas. "Damn rustlers hit us. Took mebbe five hundred head. One got kilt and three of us wounded. Don't think we hit any of them."

"How many of them were there?" asked Sean

"There was at least eight that I saw," said Thomas. "Seemed like this real young fella was shoutin' out the orders. Never seen none of'em before. What brings you out here Marshal? Are you chasin' rustlers?"

"No, I'm after a killer by the name of Bart Evans," said Sean. "They call him Kid cause he's only seventeen. His Pa owns the CC ranch."

"I seen a poster on him last town we passed," said Thomas. "Surprised me. I don't know that boy's Pa personally, but why would a boy with a Pa who owns the biggest ranch in Texas be killin' folks?"

"Hard to tell," said Sean. "Maybe he likes it. So which way did them rustlers head after they took your cows?"

"They headed east," answered Thomas. "We heard that there was a lot of border gangs on the Kansas Missouri border."

"We cleaned some of'em out a while back," said Sean. "Looks like more have taken their place. Might get worse now that all these Texas herds'll be goin' to Abilene. Well, you boys take care now. Don't let no strangers get too close. We gotta be movin'. If we run into them rustlers, we'll kill'em for you. What's your brand?"

"It's the T/M," answered Thomas.

"Next town we get to that has a telegraph, I'll send a telegram to Abilene and let'em know that if any cows with the T/M brand show up before or after Lonnigan's herd does, they're stolen cows," said Sean.

"Thanks Marshal. Good luck catchin' that killer," said Thomas.

~~~~

When they came to a town with a telegraph, Sean sent the telegram to Abilene. He told the operator to make sure that all of the cattle buyers knew about the stolen cows. Two days later, they arrived at Jug's ranch. Sean was impressed. Jug had fixed up his place real nice. Jug was out with some of them men when Sean arrived. Lolita went to Sean and Jesse and hugs and kisses were exchanged. One of the hands was there and took care of their horses. They all sat down on the front porch and Lolita brought them some fresh coffee. "So you're going after Bart Evans," said Lolita. "That ranch is southwest of here three days ride or more. They say that boy's Pa is a tough son of a bitch and he likes to kill Indians."

"Well Jesse and me are tough sons a bitches too," said Sean. "But we won't kill no Indians unless they're tryin' to kill us."

"They say he's good with a gun too," said Lolita.

"Are your tryin' to scare me?" asked Sean.

"No, I'm just worried about Jug," said Lolita. "I'll always worry about him."

"Well Maggie always worries bout me," said Sean. "That's just the way it is."

"Yep, and Dawn always worries bout me too," said Jesse.

"How about ole Jeb there. Does anybody worry about him?" asked Lolita.

"We worry some," said Sean. "Ole Jeb got shot when Michael and Betty got shot. A bullet creased his skull. I actually believe that Jeb knows we're after the fella that shot him and Michael and Betty. I won't tell you what Michael said about how he wanted that fella to die. It's not pretty."

"If he did all that killing he deserves to die," said Lolita. "I was raised Catholic, but I never had much luck with that turning the other cheek stuff or forgiving folks who did some bad things. So Jug should be back before too long. I must get started on dinner. Feel free to look around if you want. I can get you something stronger to drink if you like."

"We'll just look around for a spell," said Sean. "We'll probably have a few drinks a little later." Lolita excused herself and went to the kitchen. Sean and Jesse wondered around the place checking things out. The bunkhouse was almost identical to the one where they had the shootout with George Anderson and his men. When they went inside, Sean relived the shootout in his mind. "Let's get on out of here," said Sean. "You seen one bunkhouse, you seen'em all." Jesse had never heard about the bunkhouse shoot out, but he knew something was on Sean's mind and it wasn't something that was pleasant.

Jug had almost all new fences around the barn. A lot of the work around the place had been recent. Jug had himself a real good crew. The cook was in the cook shack starting on dinner for the men that evening. Sean and Jesse exchanged a few words with him. Just as they left the cook shack, Jug came riding in. He rode right to Sean. He slid out of the saddle and gave Sean a hug and shook his hand. Then he did the same with Jesse. "It's good to see you boys," said Jug. "I heard something when I was out with the boys. Don't know if it's true or not."

"Well, tell us," said Sean.

"There was a cowboy out lookin' for work. We run into him out on the north range," said Jug. "He had been over at the CC lookin' for work before he came here. Some of the hands there told him what had happened. He said that Kid shot his old man and darn near killed'm. Then Kid raped his stepmother and robbed the place. No one knows where Kid is now."

"Well we better go there and find out if this is true or not," said Sean. "Mebbe if Kid did shoot his old man, the old man might have an idea where Kid would go."

"You got a plan on how we're gonna get this done?" asked Jug.

"No, we'll see what Kid's Pa and Ma say after we get there," answered Sean. "Hopefully, they'll know somethin', or maybe one a the hands might."

~~~~

Lolita made a fine meal for the men. Sean remembered that she was a good cook, but whatever she made today, she outdid herself. They all sat around the table after the meal and sipped some whiskey. Jug told them all about how it was in Texas. He told them that some of the other ranchers were a little upset with him because he let Bear Claw's people have a steer from time to time when they needed it. He couldn't get it through their heads that it was easier to give the Kiowa a steer from time to time than it was for them to be stealing them from the ranches. This way nobody got hurt. There were plenty of longhorns anyway. Most of the other ranchers just plain hated Indians. They were raised that way and nothing was going to change it. Jug was called an "Injun Lover" more than once. Most of the time it didn't bother him. Other times, someone's jaw got broken and it wasn't Jug's.

The next morning after a big breakfast, the three men headed southwest. Sean could tell by the way that Lolita was hanging onto Jug that she didn't want him to go. Jug also had a talk with Wayne and Josh. He considered both of them to be foremen and they would be in charge during his absence.

~~~~

They rode fairly hard for the first two days. There were plenty of unshod pony tracks on the second day. Sean was very cautious and expected trouble, but there was none. He knew they were Comanche ponies. The Kiowa weren't this far south. They stood watches at night and the horses were hobbled and tightly tied. Jeb never let out one growl these two days and nights.

The third day, they had ridden for over a half day and stopped to rest the horses. The area they were in was almost totally open plain. As Sean looked to the southwest, there was a big rise about a mile off. There couldn't have been more than five trees between them and the rise. "If I was gonna take a shot at someone, I'd do it from that rise over there," said Sean. "There's no cover between here and there. Some Comanche could be on the other side waitin' for us too. There's pony tracks everywhere."

"So what're we gonna do?" asked Jug.

"I think we'll just set up camp early today," said Sean. "If there are some Comanche behind that rise, maybe they'll get impatient and come out after us. If they do, then they'll have no cover and we'll pick 'em off when they get in range. If nothin' happens, then after dark, I'll slip over there and see if we got company or not.

The men set up camp and acted like they were relaxing and taking it easy. A few hours went by and nothing happened. It was starting to get dark so they got a fire going and cooked their supper. Sean wanted a big fire. Anybody watching would be paying attention to the fire and not him. Jesse was doing the cooking tonight. The men would have ham and beans and biscuits. Two hours after dark, Sean and Jeb moved out. Sean took his Winchester, one pistol, and a knife with him. There wasn't much of a moon but Sean still moved slow and easy.

It took Sean over a half hour to get to the east side of the rise. He and Jeb slowly worked their way around the rise. As he neared the back of the rise, he heard voices. Jeb started a growl but Sean told him to stay quiet. Jeb did as he was told. The voices sounded like they were coming from the top of the rise. Sean and Jeb slowly moved up the rise. The top of the rise was another two hundred yards. They had just started their move, when Jeb started a good growl. Sean knew that something or someone was near. Then Sean heard two dogs barking. The barking was getting closer. One dog was well ahead of the other. Then he heard someone yelling at the dogs. "Jimmy, Sonny, get the hell back here now," the man yelled. The two dogs didn't obey and were coming right for Sean and Jeb. Jeb took off at a dead run right at the lead dog. Sean couldn't tell what kind of dog it was in the darkness, but it was a big dog. It was almost as big as Jeb.

When the two dogs met, there wasn't much of a fight. Jeb got ahold of the other dog's throat and it was over. The dog died quickly. Jeb was just turning to face the other dog. The other dog took a close look at Jeb and turned to run. It had only gone a few yards when Jeb caught up to it. The other dog let out a yelp as Jeb lit into him. Sean felt sorry for the dog. It seemed that Jeb was taking his time and just playing with it. One more yelp and the dog ran back up the rise. Jeb walked over to Sean. There was something bloody hanging out of Jeb's mouth. Jeb dropped it on the ground in front of Sean. Sean picked it up and held it toward the sky so he could tell what it was. It was one of the dog's ears.

When the dog got back up the rise, Sean could hear voices again. "Damn Sonny, what the hell did you get into it with?" said the man. "We didn't see no wolf sign out here."

"Well somethin' sure as hell bit his ear off," said another man. "Where's Jimmy? Jimmy, Jimmy, come on back Jimmy." I spect I better see if I can find Jimmy. One a you see if you can get Sonny's bleedin' stopped." When Sean heard the man say he would be looking for Jimmy, he and Jeb moved about fifty yards from the dog's dead body.

They could see the man looking around for the dog. Then they saw him fall down. "What in the hell?" the man yelled. He had tripped over the dog. Sean swore he heard the man crying. "Boys, there's gotta be a wolf around here," the man yelled. "Jimmy's throat's been ripped out. Nothing could do that ceptin' a wolf. Better check them horses and make sure they're tied tight. We'll be startin' two hour watches. Ronnie, you're first. Howard, you're next. Then you Luke. I'll go last."

"Why don't we have a fire," yelled Luke. "If there's a wolf out there, a fire'd help keep'm away."

"Yeh, and a fire will give our position away too you fool," said the man. "If O'Rourke's comin' like Kid said he would, we don't want him knowing where we are. That could be his fire we're seein' way off. But I wouldn't think O'Rourke'd have a fire like that out in the open for all to see."

"There's nobody within' a mile of us Al," said Luke. "Ceptin' maybe some Comanche and they won't tangle with us. If they seen us already, they know we got these long guns."

"They say O'Rourke uses a Sharps," said Al. "They say he can kill a man at a thousand yards. None of us are that good."

"I bet I can hit a man that far away if I got time to aim good," said Luke.

"You're dreamin' fool," said Al. "Now shut up. We're not havin' no fire."

"Mebbe I oughta just shoot yer ass and take yer money," said Luke.

"Feel free to try it any time you son of a bitch," said Al. "If you was somehow lucky enough ta kill me, you'd never get the rest a that money from Kid. I'm the only one here that knows what O'Rourke looks like. I seen'm once in Kansas City. Now go ahead and try it if you got the nerve." Luke just shook his head and walked away. "I didn't think so," said Al.

Sean heard all he needed. He and Jeb started working their way back to the others. They moved slowly and it took close to an hour to get back. Jug and Jesse were waiting anxiously when Sean got back. "Well, what's over there?" asked Jesse.

"There's four of'em on the other side of the top of the rise," answered Sean. "From what I heard, Kid hired'em to kill me. Kid figured we'd be going this way to get to his Pa's ranch. They had a couple a dogs with 'em. Jeb killed one and ripped up the other one. They think a wolf done it."

"So how we gonna get'em?" asked Jesse.

"I heard one of'em say that they all had long guns," started Sean. "And they think the fire they been seein' was probly some Comanche and he said the Comanche wouldn't tangle with 'em cause they had long guns. So they don't know we're here. I was thinkin' I'd get a little sleep then slip back up there and steal their horses."

"How bout that other dog?" asked Jug. "He'll hear or smell you before you get close enough."

"Jeb'll go with me," said Sean. "When that dog saw Jeb and what he done to the other dog, he turned and ran. Jeb caught'm and chewed him up some. I'd say that dog'll be too scared to do anything but whimper. Dogs are like wolves. When the leader of the pack tells his boys ta shut up, he means it. If they don't do as he says, then he runs'em off or kills'em. If they submit, there's no problems. That dog knows who's boss."

~~~~

When Kid rode off from the ranch, he had $30,000 in his pockets. He rode hard when he first took off, but the farther he got, the more confident he became. No one would be after him for a good while. Kid decided to head for San Antonio. He'd never been there and had heard it had just about anything a man could want. It took a few days to get to San Antonio. He stopped at a few small towns along the way. Every saloon he went into, he asked people if they knew anything about Federal Marshal O'Rourke. Nobody knew him personally but almost everyone knew his reputation. O'Rourke wasn't a man to be messed with.

Kid decided that when he got to San Antonio, he would try and find some men who would kill O'Rourke for him. Finding someone shouldn't be a problem. He had plenty of money and money buys about everything. When he rode into San Antonio, he went straight to the biggest saloon he could find. He tied his horse to the hitching post out front and went inside. As soon as he cleared the door, a whiskey bottle went flying past his head just missing it. It crashed into the wall and shattered. There was a big fight going on. From what he could see, it looked like four men who were dressed like buffalo hunters were into it with six others. The six men looked to be cowmen. They all were wearing pistols, but no one was pulling theirs. The bartender was ignoring the fight. He did reach up and take down a big mirror that was behind the bar. Some working girls were standing on some stairs cheering the boys on. A medium sized man wearing a badge walked in right behind Kid. He yelled for the fight to stop. The fighters ignored him. Then he pulled a pistol and fired a shot into the floor. The fighters still ignored him. He was about to fire another shot into the floor when someone slipped up behind him and hit him with a chair. He fell to the floor out cold. The fight continued. Kid took a seat out of the way and watched. After a good while, the four buffalo hunters were getting the best of the cowmen. The fight was almost over when one of the cowmen pulled a pistol and took a shot at one of the buffalo hunters. The shot missed but it ripped the man's jacket at his right shoulder. All of the fighters stopped and looked at the shooter. The shooter had his hammer cocked and was about to fire again, when another shot came from somewhere else. The shooter was struck in the chest and hit the floor dead. Kid stood there with his pistol in his hand. "I couldn't let him kill that fella like that," said Kid. "Somebody had to do somethin'."

"Damn right somebody's gotta do somethin'," said one of the cowmen. The cowman went for his pistol. Before he cleared the holster, Kid's pistol fired again. The man hit the floor dead. The other cowmen stood there in amazement.

"Just who in the hell're you?" one of the other cowmen asked.

"None a yer damn business," said Kid. "Now does anyone else feel like dying?"

"Put that shooter back in yer holster and we'll see if you can kill a man when the odds're even," said the cowman. Kid holstered his pistol. The two men looked into each other eyes. The cowman had his pistol out first and fired, but he missed. Kid didn't miss. His bullet caught the man dead center in the chest. He hit the floor dead. Just as the man hit the floor, the man wearing the badge came to.

"All right now, somebody's goin' to jail," he said. "I wanna know who hit me with that chair and I wanna know now. No one answered. "Who done all this killin' in here?" asked the lawman.

"I done it," answered Kid. "That one cowman pulled a gun and was gonna kill one a them other boys. I shot'em ta keep'm from killin'm. Then another cowman tried to shoot me and I killed'em. This other one thought he was faster than me. He was, but he missed and I didn't."

"That's right lawman," said one of the buffalo hunters. "That fella woulda kilt one of us fer sure. This fella didn't do nothin' wrong. These killins' were all self defense'r somethin' like that."

The lawman looked at the remaining cowmen now. "Is this all true?" he asked the cowmen.

"It is lawman," one of the cowman said. "We were havin' a good fight when one a our boys pulled a gun. Weren't no need fer that. No sir, weren't no need."

"Well just who in the hell are you mister," said the lawman. "Or should I say boy. You look mighty young ta me."

"I'm called Joe Tucker," said Kid. "And my age is none a yer business."

"Supposin' I make it my business," said the lawman.

"How bout I let my pistol do my talkin'," said Kid.

"Are you threatenin' me boy?" asked the lawman.

"You can take it any way you want lawman," said Kid. "I done kilt three men today. One more won't matter."

"I think I'll put you in the lock up for a while," said the lawman. "We'll see if the Judge thinks these killins' were justified'r not. Let's go boy. Gimme that pistol."

"Yer not gettin' my pistol unless I'm dead," said Kid.

"Suit yerself boy," said the lawman. The lawman went for his pistol. He cleared the holster before Kid, but Kid fired first. The lawman was thrown backwards as the bullet tore into his chest. His pistol fired into the air as he fell. He hit the floor dead.

"You best git yourself outta town right now," said the bartender. "That fella you just kilt is kin to the Judge. They'll hang ya sure."

"I'll have me a drink first," said Kid. "Set'em up for my friends here." Kid and the four buffalo hunters went to the bar.

"So you say that lawman is kin to the Judge here," Kid said to the bartender.

"Yep, the Judge is his Uncle," said the bartender. "He got the deputy job cause the Judge is friends with the Town Marshal."

"Where's the Marshal now?" asked Kid.

"He had to go to Austin to testify in some trial," said the bartender. "He should be back any day. I wouldn't be here when he gets back. He'll take in a man anyway he can. He's a big pistol whipper and he don't care which way a man is facin' when it comes time fer a shootin'."

"That's good to know," said Kid. "We'll be leavin' now." Kid looked at the four buffalo hunters. "I said we'll be leavin' now." Then Kid handed the bartender $200. "This is for the damages," Kid said. "Go git yer horses boys. I said we're leavin'." The buffalo hunters hesitated for a moment and then did as Kid said. Once they all had their horses, they rode out of town heading northeast. The buffalo hunters had a couple of dogs that went with them too. The dogs had been at the livery. They gave some young boys two bits to watch them while they got a drink.

None of them talked until they stopped right before dark. One of the buffalo hunters spoke first as they set up camp. "Name's Al. Them others is Luke, Howard, and Ronnie," said Al to Kid. "Seems ta me, you want somethin' from us."

"That's right Al," said Kid. "I figure you boys owe me. Some a you would be dead if it weren't fer me."

"That's right Joe, or whatever yer name might be," said Al. "What is it you want?"

"I want you ta kill a man for me," said Kid. "He'll be comin' after me afore too long."

"Sounds like a lawman ta me," said Al. "Who is it?"

"O'Rourke," answered Kid.

"I heard a him and I seen'm once," said Al. "He's not a man to mess with. You best git someone else."

"I'll give you $200 each now, and $300 each more when it's done," said Kid.

"Hell, I'd kill the Pope fer that," said Luke.

"The Pope won't be shootin' back," said Al. "We'll kill'em for ya. How do we know you'll give us the rest when it's done?"

"You don't," said Kid. "How do I know you won't just take the front money and run?"

"You don't," said Al. "I give you my word. We'll get'm kilt for ya."

"All right, now when you get it done, word'll spread fast," said Kid. "It'll be in all the papers and such. When I see it in a paper somewhere that O' Rourke's killed, I'll head for Ft. Worth and stay there till you all show. I'll wait two weeks. That should be enough. My real name is Bart Evans. They call me Kid. My name's on some wanted posters."

"How much you worth?" asked Luke.

"$500 last I saw," said Kid. "Are you thinkin' bout tryin' fer that money?"

"No, just curious," said Luke. "Killin' O'Rourke pays better in the long run."

"Well let's get some food and some sleep," said Kid. "I'll be takin' you to a place that would be perfect fer you to kill O'Rourke. You boys are good shots with them long guns aren't you?"

"We are," said Al. "We was goin' ta western Kansas after buffalo, but this'll pay a lot more and is easier work."

"Next time we pass a town, you boys need to provision up," said Kid. "Might have a wait on O'Rourke, but he'll come."

"Why you so sure he'll come?" asked Howard.

"Cause I shot his deputy and the deputy's wife in Abilene," said Kid. "He'll go to my Pa's ranch lookin' for me. I shot my Pa too."

"Damn Kid, you sure been doin' a lotta shootin' lately," said Ronnie.

"Some people need shootin'," said Kid. The four men weren't quite sure what to think of Kid. They quit thinking when he handed them each $200 the next morning. When Kid handed Luke his $200, he knew Luke was wondering how much money he had on him. "Luke, I know what yer thinkin'," said Kid. "Best git those thoughts outta yer head. If you don't, there won't be no thoughts in yer head, just lead."

When they came to a small town the next day, the men got their provisions. When they started getting close to the CC, Kid stayed just off CC land. It took a couple of days to skirt the ranch. They finally came to the place that Kid thought would be perfect for killing O'Rourke. He took them to the top of a rise. It was almost totally open plain. You could count the trees in all directions on two hands. From the top of the rise, a man could see almost a mile, farther if he had a good spyglass. There was a water hole about two miles from the rise. Kid showed them where it was. "Now all you gotta do is wait," said Kid. "He'll be comin' from the northeast and headin' right for you if he does what I think he will. Whatever he does, you should be able to spot him from here. Now don't get ansy while yer waitin'. It might be two, mebbe three weeks before he gets here, but you got purty good pay fer settin' on yer ass waitin'. I'll be leavin' now." Kid took off headed east. When he was about five hundred yards out, Al could tell that Luke was having some thoughts again.

"Don't be havin' them thoughts," said Al to Luke. "We done give our word to that man. Our word is our word."

"You give yer word, not me," said Luke. Luke went to his saddle and pulled his Sharps from it's scabbard. He shouldered it and took aim at Kid. As he was about to cock the hammer, he felt some cold steel at his throat.

"You lower that buffalo gun or this blade'll find your neck bones real quick like," said Al.

Luke lowered the rifle. "I wasn't gonna shoot," said Luke. "I was just practicin' my aimin'."

"Sure you was and I was just gonna make sure my knife was sharp," said Al.

~~~~

Sean got his three hours of sleep and he and Jeb headed back to the rise to steal the four men's horses. Sean took his time and was as quiet as a cat. When they got close to the four men, Sean could see that one man was on watch and the other three were asleep. The horses were hobbled and were tied to some small bushes. The dog Sonny was about twenty yards from the man on watch. A bandana had been tied around his head to help stop the bleeding where his ear had been ripped off. Sonny had seen Sean and Jeb but remained quiet. The man on watch had no idea anyone was near him when Sean cracked his head with the butt of his Winchester. Sean slowly untied the horses and led them back down the rise. After they had gone about fifty yards, Sonny joined them. He went to Jeb and took a submissive posture. Jeb stood over him as he lay there. After maybe a minute, Jeb let Sonny up and it was like they were good friends now.

They had moved three hundred yards from the rise when one of the horses let out a whinny. Sean tried to quiet the horse. He got that horse quieted, but then another one decided to make some noise. Sean mounted one of the horses and took off at a gallop. He let go of the rope that was tied to the other horses. He knew Jeb would make sure the other horses went where he did. Right after he had mounted the horse, he heard someone on the rise let out a yell. "What the hell's goin' on here? Where's the damn horses? Howard, where the hell are your Howard? Get up boys. The horses is gone. Probly them damn Comanche." Then one of the men found Howard.

"Weren't no damn Comanche," said Luke. "If it was Injuns, Howard'd be dead. He's just knocked out. Where's that dog? Where's Sonny?"

"Well we can't do nothin' till daylight," said Al. "We'll just wait till daylight and then see what we can see. We got bout three more hours till daylight. I'll stay on watch. You two get some more sleep."

~~~~

Jesse and Jug were wide awake when Sean got back with the horses. The horses were tied and the men sat around the fire. "I see Jeb's got a new friend," said Jug. "Looks like he's seen better days."

"He'll be all right," said Sean. "Jeb took his ear off. They're friends now. Sonny knows who's boss."

"So you're Sonny," said Jesse. "Maybe you'll come home with me." Sonny went to Jesse and sat down beside him. Jesse petted him and rubbed his belly. Sonny was Jesse's dog now. "So what're we gonna do bout them fellas on that rise?" asked Jesse. "Did you kill one of'em when you took the horses?"

"I just knocked one out. I spose I should have killed'm. Probly will before this is over with. I figure we'll wait till daylight and see what they're up to," said Sean. "Let's get some more sleep."

~~~~

When Al and the men on the rise woke up at daylight, Al decided it was all right to have a fire and cook up some breakfast. "Whoever's out there knows we're up here anyway," said Al. "I need me some hot coffee." They got a fire going but when they filled the coffee pot with water, they discovered that was all the water they had. "We'll get us some more water after breakfast," said Al. "Two of us can go after water and two of us'll stay here with the supplies. Luke, you and Ronnie'll go after the water."

"How come I gotta go after water?" asked Luke. "I went last time. Besides, there's somebody out there."

"Well you been sayin' how you're such a good shot with that buffalo gun," said Al. "There's hardly any cover down there. If anybody comes at you, you should be able to see'em a good ways off and kill'em before they get close."

"I think I'll just shoot you one a these days," said Luke. "I'm just bout tired a you hackin' on me."

"Just shut up you big baby. You're goin' after water and that's that," said Al. Luke didn't say another word. After breakfast, he and Ronnie grabbed all the canteens and water bags and headed for the water hole.

Sean and the boys didn't have a fire the next morning when they got up. They had some biscuits from a previous day and chewed on some jerky. Sean got out his spyglass and watched the rise. It wasn't long and he saw two men walking to the west. They were loaded down with canteens and water bags. "Two a them fellas are headed for a water hole," said Sean. "Must be some water to the west a bit. I'm gonna git on Billy and swing way out. Maybe I can find that water hole and get to it before them two does. If I don't beat them there, they'll be loaded down on their way back up the rise." Sean saddled up Billy and took off at a gallop. Jeb and Sonny went with him. There was a little more cover as he swung out to the west. It wasn't long and he spotted where he thought the water hole should be. There was a grove of trees in the open. The water hole should be right there. He could ride up to the water hole on the opposite side of the two men and not be seen. As he neared the water hole, he could see the two men approaching the other side. They were still close to a thousand yards away.

There was some brush around the trees and Sean was able to tie Billy where he couldn't be seen by the two men. Sean sat and waited. Jeb and Sonny sat with him. When the two men got closer, Sean spoke to Sonny. "All right boy, it's time to earn your keep," said Sean. "Now you go on over to them two fellas over there. Act like you missed'em and such." Sean had no idea if Sonny understood what he had said or not, but Sonny got up and went over to the two men just like Sean had told him. Luke and Ronnie were glad to see Sonny too.

"Where the hell you been boy?" said Luke. "Did you just run off or what? Well, no matter." The water hole was just a small pond and was only about fifteen yards across. Sean was in the brush opposite Luke and Ronnie. The two of them went to the edge of the water and started filling their canteens and water bags. Sean let them fill a few of them before he spoke.

"You boys stand up and drop them gunbelts right now," said Sean. Sean had his Winchester trained on the two men. Ronnie stood up first and when he did, he went for his pistol. The Winchester fired and Ronnie was stuck dead center in the chest. He was thrown flat on his back. Luke stood now and dropped his gunbelt as instructed.

"Just who in the hell're you mister?" asked Luke.

"Name's O'Rourke," answered Sean. "Jeb, git over there and don't let'm move. If he does, he's all yours." Jeb went over next to Luke while Sean kept his Winchester trained on him.

"What the hell kind a dog is that?" asked Luke. "I bet he's the critter what ripped out Jimmy's throat."

"That's him," said Sean. "And he really enjoys doing the same to men he don't like. Now you stay put while I git over there." Luke didn't move one bit while Sean moved around the water hole. Sean stood in front of Luke. "Now are you gonna tell me all about Kid hirin' you boys ta kill me?" asked Sean.

"Why should I tell you anything?" asked Luke. "You're gonna kill me no matter what. I hear you like killin' folks."

"You can think what you want fella," said Sean. "I have killed a lotta folks. Can't say as I always liked it, but I'll tell you this. When I kill Kid, I'll like it."

"Why don't you give me a chance lawman?" said Luke. "Let me put my gunbelt back on. Let me die tryin'."

"You got some cajones mister," said Sean. "If these trees were bigger, I'd hang you right here. What the hell. Go ahead and put on your gunblet." Sean backed away from Luke. Luke stood there and didn't move. Jeb got out of the way. Luke reached down for his gunbelt. As he was putting it around his waist, he was hoping Sean was off guard. He pulled the pistol from the holster with his right hand as he was fastening the buckle with his left hand. Sean wasn't fooled. His bullet struck Luke in the forehead. The back of his head was blown off as he fell backwards.

Sean pulled the two dead bodies away from the water hole. He didn't want their bodies rotting and contaminating the water hole for others. He went through their pockets to see if there was anything important in them. Each man had $200 on him. Sean just shook his head. He grabbed their guns and then mounted Billy. He headed back to Jug and Jesse. Jeb and Sonny followed.

"We heard shootin'," said Jug as Sean returned.

"They tried to shoot it out," said Sean. "They're dead."

"How we gonna get them other two?" asked Jesse. "They still got the high ground."

"They're out of water," said Sean. "Cover's a little better to west. We'll move to the west a bit. We'll turn a couple a their horses loose. I'll have Sonny run them horses to where them two on the rise can see'em. They'll try and catch them horses and get to that water hole. When they do, we'll catch them."

Al and Howard had heard the shooting in the distance and were figuring the worst. "That weren't no buffalo gun," said Al. "That first one was a Winchester or a Henry. That other'n was a six gun. Luke'n Ronnie's dead. I just bet O'Rourke's out there."

"Well what can we do?" asked Howard. "He'll kill us sure."

"He will," said Al. "I reckon we made a bad choice when we said we'd kill O'Rourke. I spose we better stay put till dark. Then we'll head to that water hole. We don't git some water, we'll be dead in a few days anyway."

Sean and the boys swung out and moved to the west. They went to the water hole and let all of the horses have a good drink. Then they tied off most of the horses in the brush around the pond. Sean told Jeb to stay with the horses. He, Jesse, and Jug moved a little closer to the rise. Two horses and Sonny went with them. There were a few trees about a mile from the rise. They were small trees but there was a little brush around them. There were a few more trees about a thousand yards from the rise and there was brush around them too. Sean and the boys took cover in the brush while Sonny moved the horses to within five hundred yards of the top of the rise. Then Sonny came back and sat beside Jesse. There they would wait for the men to try and catch the horses.

Al and Ronnie were worried about O'Rourke. They were so busy talking about O'Rourke that they weren't watching around them at all. Finally, Al took a look around to see if anything or anyone was coming after them. He almost cried when he spotted the two horses grazing about five hundred yards away. "Ronnie,

Ronnie, take a look down there," said Al excitedly. "Them's two a our horses. They musta got loose from whoever took'em."

"That could be," said Ronnie. "Or mebbe they turned them horses loose to flush us down off this hill. They could be hidin' in the brush."

"I don't see nobody in no brush," said Al. "I'm goin' after them horses. Stay here if you want."

"Oh hell, I'll go too," said Ronnie. "We're gonna get shot sooner'r later. Might as well be sooner." The two men headed for the horses.

Sean had his Sharps with him and he took aim on one of the men as they came down the rise. He let them get within fifty yards of the horses before he spoke. He made sure he had a clear shot and the horses were not in the line of fire. "You boys stop right where you are and drop them pistols and long guns," yelled Sean. The boys stopped but didn't drop their weapons. Sean waited a moment and then squeezed the trigger. The Sharps barked. Ronnie was thrown backwards and hit the ground dead. Sean quickly reloaded. Al didn't drop his weapons. He laid down flat on the ground and started firing at the brush where he had seen the smoke from Sean's Sharps. Jug and Jesse fired a couple of shots toward Al to let him know that Sean was not alone.

One of the horses had fled when the first shot was fired, but the other one ran straight toward Al for some reason. It didn't budge as the other shots were fired. The horse moved now and was between Al and Sean. Al got up his nerve and stood up. He grabbed the horse's mane and mounted the horse. Before he was fully on top of the horse, Sean's Sharps barked again. The horse was struck in the neck. It reared up and fell to its left. Al had fallen off to the left when the horse reared. When the horse came down, it landed on top of Al. Al's chest was crushed. Sean and the others went over to him. Blood was coming out of Al's nose and mouth. He was still alive, but just barely. "You done killed me O'Rourke," said Al.

"Well isn't that what Kid hired you ta do ta me?" asked Sean.

"I reckon so," said Al.

"How much was I worth?" asked Sean.

"$2000," answered Al. "He give us $200 a piece to start and then we was gonna get $300 a piece when you was dead."

"Are you gonna tell me where Kid went before you die?" asked Sean.

"All I can tell you is he headed east," said Al. "After we got you kilt and it was in all the papers, he was gonna meet us in Ft. Worth and pay us off. Now how bout you puttin' a bullet in my brain. I don't wanna still be alive when the coyotes or buzzards start eatin'." Sean obliged him.

"We gonna bury these fellas?" asked Jesse.

"Nope, they don't deserve buryin'," said Sean. "Go through their pockets. Should be $200 on both of'em." Jug and Jesse checked the men's pockets. Ronnie had $200 and Al had $180. Al must have been the one who bought the provisions. "You boys can keep that money," said Sean. "Here's $400 more. I don't need it." Sean handed the money to Jesse and Jug. "I guess we best take their guns with us. Don't want some Comanche gettin'em."

CHAPTER FIVE

When they arrived at the CC ranch, the place looked deserted until they got about a hundred yards from the house. As they got closer, armed men started appearing. Sean counted six men armed with rifles. They were in different positions. One man was in the hay loft. Another man was on the roof of the house. The other four were behind other buildings. All of them had their rifles trained on Sean and his men. When they were about fifty yards from the house, Clancy came out and sat down in a rocking chair. "State your business," said Clancy. "If I don't like what I hear, my men will cut loose on you."

"Name's O'Rourke, Federal Marshal O'Rourke and these men are my deputies," said Sean. "We're here after your son."

"Stand down boys," said Clancy. "The law's here. Come on over to the house and we'll talk. Fred, Sam, take care a these boy's horses." Sean and the boys dismounted and let Clancy's men take their horses. They walked over to the porch. Clancy shook each of their hands. He hesitated some when he shook Jesse's hand. "Are you a lawman big fella?" Clancy asked Jesse.

"I am," answered Jesse.

"That's somethin'. I never even heared of no colored lawman afore," said Clancy.

"You got somethin' against colored folks?" asked Jesse.

"No I don't," answered Clancy. "I never had no slaves and I never fought in that damn war so some rich son of a bitch could keep his. I never knowed any colored folks. I seen'em, but I never knowed'em."

"Well now you know me," said Jesse.

"I reckon I do," said Clancy. "You boys take a seat. I'll have the wife bring out somethin' cool to drink, or would you like somethin' stronger?"

"We might have somethin' stronger later," said Sean. "Right now, we need to talk about your son."

"Shirley, bring us out somethin' cool to drink would you please?" asked Clancy in a loud voice so Shirley could hear. "I guess I'll sorta start from the beginnin'," started Clancy. "Bart was my first born son. Me and Emma had two boys later that died. We was a pretty close family. I guess I spoiled my boy. Taught him everthin' I know. He's pretty fair with a six gun. Anyway, my Emma died when Bart was 14. We started driftin' apart then. I mourned that woman for bout a year and ignored my boy. When I snapped out of it, I took another wife. She's a young thing. Everybody, my son included, thought she was just after my money. I never cared what folks thought. Her and my boy was always at each other. I put more'n one knot on his head for disrespectin' my wife." Just then, Shirley came out with some drinks for the men. They could see that she was a young and very attractive woman. They could also see that she still had some bruises on her face that were not quite gone. Shirley went back inside. "You see them bruises on her," said Clancy. "Bart done that while he was rapin' her. I stayed here when the cattle drive left. The Comanche was raidin' some so I stayed here. When my boy got back, he give me some big story bout some big shootout and how some other men kilt my foreman and my men. He said he heard your name mentioned, O'Rourke. He said he hit one of the men who was doin' some shootin' and he got hit in the legs with some buckshot. Said he fell and hit his jaw when the buckshot hit'm."

"That's some story," said Sean. "Course you know it's not true don't you?"

"I do," said Clancy. "I went inta town ta see bout gettin' my money from the herd in that bank in Abilene. The local law showed me a wanted poster with Bart's name on it. Also said he got a telegram sayin' that a witness saw Bart shoot my foreman and was bout ta shoot that man and woman again when a fella with a shotgun chased him off. That's when he got hit in the legs with the buckshot. They also think my boy kilt a Sheriff over in Missouri."

"Well, Kid killed three men in Abilene for sure and shot my deputy and his wife as they were going home for the night," said Sean. "My deputy smacked your boy in our saloon when he wouldn't give up his pistol. We don't allow no firearms'r knives in our saloon. Don't know fer sure bout that Sheriff in Missouri, but I'd bet that he done it."

"I'd bet that too," said Clancy. "Anyway, when I knowed my boy was a murderer, I made up my mind I was gonna beat the hell out of'm and then give'm to the law for hangin'. When I got back from town that day, I proceeded to beat the hell out of'm. I had my pistol on my saddlehorn. I took Bart's pistol from'm and threw it. I guess I got careless when I was beatin' on'm. He got his pistol back and shot me. I guess he was sure I was dead. When

Shirley ran out of the house to look after me, he cracked her over the head with his pistol. Next thing she knows, she's tied to her bed and he's rapin' her. When he got his fill, he stole $30,000 out of my safe and took off. The hands found me'n her when they came back after their day's work. Doc said that bullet shoulda kilt me cause it was so close to my heart, but it didn't. Took some time, but I'm healin' all right now. It'll take Shirley a while ta git over what happened ta her. I never thought I'd say anything like this, but I want my boy dead. If you don't git'm, I will when I'm healed good."

"We'll get'm for you and he's gonna die slow," said Sean. "So have you got any idea where he would go?"

"I wish I could help you but I really got no idea," said Clancy. "I doubt Bart'd go to any of the places where folks know the both of us. I was gonna put up some more bounty money. There's $500 on him now. I was gonna make it $2000."

"So is there any law around here who could help you out?" asked Sean.

"This is a big county," said Clancy. "The Sheriff is over a hundred and fifty miles away. I hear he's got his hands full with bandits and Comanches. The Rangers is after Injuns and bandits. Don't know what the army's up to. Them fools couldn't catch a Comanche if he walked up to them and gave himself up. Probly got some West Point desk sitter who don't know a damn thing bout Injuns."

"I hear you're an Indian fighter," said Sean.

"I killed me some Comanche over the years," said Clancy. "They massacred my family back in the forties. They let me live cause I fought so hard. That was their mistake. I git even whenever I git the chance. So'r you a Indian fighter?"

"I lived with the Cheyenne for several years after my family was massacred by white outlaws," answered Sean. "We had scrapes with the Pawnee and Comanche from time to time. I won't kill no Indians now unless they're tryin' ta kill me."

"They say you're the best there is with a pistol or a long gun," said Clancy. "You must favor a Sharps."

"I do," said Sean. "My Pa bought two of'em before we left ta go ta Oregon. I used my first Sharps almost clear through the war. It got blowed up around Atlanta. I got me one now that uses metallic cartridges. Best rifle around that I know of."

"I like a Sharps too, but you can't beat a Henry or a Winchester when you need some quick firepower," said Clancy. "Why don't you and your boys join us fer supper. My Shirley is a fine cook. Mebbe tomorrow you can talk with some a the men. One of'em might have an idea where Bart mighta went. So what kind a dog is that big fella. I never seen no dog what looks like that. Big too."

"Don't know what breed Jeb here might be," said Sean. "All I know is he's a good cow and stock dog and he loves me, my wife and my friends. Anybody gives us trouble, they got Jeb to tangle with. He's killed a few men. Bit the hand clear off one fella. Got him and some other dogs from some outlaws a while back. Them outlaws is dead now."

"Was any a them other dogs females?" asked Clancy. "I could sure use some good cow dogs around here."

"I give them other dogs to a boy in Abilene," started Sean. "He works at the livery. There's been some pups. If you ever get to Abilene, ask for Billy at the livery."

"So what happened to that other dog's ear?" asked Clancy.

"Ole Jeb bit it off," answered Sean. "Sonny here and another dog was with some buffalo hunters that your boy hired ta kill me. That other dog and them buffalo hunters is dead. Them fellas said Bart was gonna give'em $2000 for killin' me."

"Well, Bart had $30,000 on'm," said Clancy. "He could hire it done I spect. Before I forget, I got a picture a my boy. You can have it since you never seen'm before." Clancy went inside and returned with the picture. "This picture is bout two years old, but he still looks like that," said Clancy. "He's got a few whiskers but not enough ta grow a beard'r mustache yet."

"Thanks, that picture'll be a big help," said Sean. "Them wanted posters don't have a likeness on'em, just a description."

They talked about another hour and Shirley called them all to dinner. Clancy was right. Shirley was a good cook. They all ate their fill and then had a glass of whiskey. It was about an hour till dark and Sean wanted to talk with some of the hands. Not one of them had any idea where Bart would go. One of them said he had heard that Bart always wanted to go to San Antonio. Maybe he went there. Clancy said he had a spare bedroom in the house and one of them could sleep there if they wanted. There was also plenty of room in the bunkhouse. Clancy still didn't have a full crew yet. Bart had killed his foreman and two others and some of the others had run off when they found out O'Rourke would be after Bart. He needed men. There were a lot of men looking for work, but very few of them were good cowmen.

It was dark now and all of them decided it was time to turn in. Sean decided he and his men would sleep in the bunkhouse. Some of the hands gave Jesse some pretty dirty looks when he laid his bedroll down on one of the bunks. "Yer not figurin' on sleepin' in here with the white folks are ya boy?" said one of the hands. Jesse just ignored him. "I said yer not figurin' on sleepin' in here with the white folks are ya boy?" the man repeated.

"If you don't want me to break you in half, BOY, you best shut your face right now," said Jesse.

"Who you callin' boy you damn nigger?" said the man. Sean and Jug didn't say a word. They knew what was going to happen. Any second now Jesse was going to get up and hurt that fella real bad. A few more words came out of the man's mouth. "Get your black ass—" He couldn't finish. Jesse had ahold of him and was beating him senseless.

"Don't kill'm Jesse," said Sean. "Just teach him some manners."

"I don't know bout no manners, but this white boy gonna learn somethin' bout respect," said Jesse. Two more of the other hands sat up on their bunks. They were thinking about helping their friend. Jeb went over and sat down in front of one of them and Sonny sat down beside the other one. They both had good growls going. The man by Sonny was slowly reaching for a pistol that was in his gunbelt. The gunbelt was hanging on the head of the bed frame. Before his hand got to the pistol, Sonny jumped up and sat on the man's bunk just daring him to move. The man moved no more.

"Remember now Jesse, don't kill'em," said Jug.

"Just bout done here," said Jesse. The man was out cold and hitting him anymore wouldn't help anything. Jesse picked the man up and laid him on his bunk. "Anybody else got somethin' ta say?" said Jesse. No one opened their mouth. Jesse went to his bunk and laid down.

"Any a you boys get any ideas durin' the night you best keep'em to yourself," said Sean. "Me'n the boys is light sleepers and these dogs wouldn't mind makin' you bleed some. Now I'll say goodnight."

Nothing happened during the night. One of the hands woke up and was getting up to visit the outhouse. When Jeb came over beside him and gave him a low growl, the man decided he could hold it till morning.

The next morning, Clancy invited Sean and his men to breakfast. Shirley made them a big breakfast, flapjacks, sausage, and eggs. As they were eating, Clancy asked them if they slept all right.

"We slept real good," answered Sean. "One a yer boys slept really well."

"How do you know that?" asked Clancy.

"Cause he said some wrong words to Jesse here and Jesse taught him a little respect," said Sean. "Don't think he'll need any medical attention, but he might not be much good on a horse for a few days."

"I'm sorry bout that," said Clancy. "I guess I never asked the men what they thought bout Jesse here stayin' in the bunkhouse. Some folks is funny bout such things. I can understand them not wantin' some Injun in there, but I don't understand nothin' bout why folks don't like coloreds."

"It's the way they was raised," said Sean. "They're scared of people who'r different."

"I spect that's true," said Clancy. "I guess there's lotsa folks who'r scared a them Chinese people too. I seen some of'em once. They were sittin' round eatin'. They were using some sticks instead of forks and such."

"Them're called chopsticks," said Sean. "That's what they use over in China and other Asian countries. Doubt if I could figure out how ta use'em. Well Clancy, I want to thank you for your hospitality. I have a favor to ask of you."

"Sure, whatever you want," said Clancy.

"I'd like for you to hold off addin' to that bounty for a while," said Sean. "They'll be enough bounty hunters after Bart as it is with $500 on his head, but if it goes up to $2000, they be comin' from all over to try and collect. I don't need no bounty hunters messin' things up for us and gettin' in the way."

"All right, I'll do that," said Clancy. "I'll wait another month. If I haven't heard nothin' by them, I'll increase the bounty."

"That's fair enough," said Sean. "Now me'n the boys'll saddle up and head out. I believe we'll head to San Antonio. If nobody's seen hide nor hair a Bart down there, we'll head back to the east. If you hear anything, send a telegram to some a the bigger towns. I'll check with telegraph offices whenever we get to a town and see if there's anything for us."

~~~~

They went through some small towns on the way to San Antonio. In each of them where there was a saloon, Sean talked to the bartenders and asked if they had seen Kid. When Sean produced Kid's picture, the bartenders remembered seeing him. One of the bartenders remembered Kid asking him and others in the saloon if they knew anything about O'Rourke. They all remembered that when Kid left town, he was headed southwest toward San Antonio.

When Sean and the men rode into San Antonio, it was early afternoon. They stopped in the middle of town and looked around. "I'll meet you boys at that saloon over there," said Sean.

"I'll be talking with the Town Marshal if he's in town. Jeb, you and Sonny go with Jug and Jesse." Sean took off looking for the Marshal and Jug and Jesse rode over to the saloon. They tied their horses out front and went inside. The place had three men and a bartender inside. Two well dressed men were sitting at table not far from the front door and one man, probably a cowhand, was standing at the bar. There was a half empty beer glass in front of him. Jug and Jesse sat down at a table not far from the bar. Jeb and Sonny sat down next to them. They waited a few minutes to see if the bartender would ask what they wanted. The bartender ignored them. "We'll have some whiskey over here bartender," said Jug. Still the bartender ignored them. "I'll get it myself if it's a problem for you," said Jug.

"Do yer drinkin' somewheres else," yelled the bartender. "This is my place and I don't allow no niggers, greasers, or chinks in here."

"We're Federal Deputies," said Jug.

"I don't give a good Goddamn who or what you are," said the bartender. "I don't serve no niggers in here and since yer his friend, I won't serve you neither. Now git the hell outta here." The man who was drinking beer at the bar must have figured there was going to be a fight. He left without finishing his beer. Jug stood up and turned to face the bartender.

"Bring us some whiskey over here while you're still able you son of a bitch," said Jug. The bartender never said another word. He reached down behind the bar and produced a sawed off double barreled shotgun. He pointed it at Jug and Jesse. Before he could get the hammers cocked, Jeb lept up and was standing on the bar right next to the bartenders face. Jeb was just daring the bartender to make the wrong move. "You best put that shotgun away," said Jug. "Ole Jeb'll kill you before you can get them hammers cocked." The bartender didn't speak.

"I'll kill you before that dog kills me," said the bartender.

"Go ahead and try it," said Jug. "It's your funeral." The bartender hesitated for a moment and then slowly moved his right thumb to cock the hammers. As soon as Jeb saw the thumb move a little, he had ahold of the bartender's throat. He had a low growl going but he didn't bite down. The bartender's face turned a strange color. "I told you, you fool," said Jug. "Now real easy like, and I mean real easy, you lay down that shotgun." The bartender did as instructed. Jeb kept his mouth on the man's throat. "Now, real nice soundin' like, you say, sorry Jeb. I won't shoot no one now," said Jug. "Go on, say it now. If you don't say you're sorry, Jeb'll take it bad. He might kill ya anyway."

The bartender was shaking badly now. "I'm sorry Jeb. I'm really sorry. Please don't kill me," said the bartender.

"He said he's sorry Jeb. Go ahead and let go of'm," said Jug. Jeb let go of the bartender and went back over to Jug. "We'll have that whiskey now," said Jug. The bartender needed a moment to regain his composure. In a few minutes, he took a bottle and a couple of glasses over to their table. The two well dressed men in the saloon had watched the whole time and never said a word. When it was over, they went back to their own conversation.

The man who had left the saloon didn't leave just because there might be trouble. He knew where the Town Marshal was and went for him. All he told the Marshal was that there could be some trouble over at the saloon and he should get over there. The Marshal and a deputy headed for the saloon. The Marshal was wearing a tied down Colt and carried a Winchester. His deputy had a Colt and was carrying a Sharps Carbine. As soon as they went inside the saloon, the bartender started yelling. "Them two sons a bitches there're givin' me trouble," said the bartender. "I told'em ta git outta here, but they wouldn't. That one dog there was gonna kill me."

"That's right," said one of the well dressed men. "Go ahead and arrest them two."

"All right Judge, yer a witness," said the Marshal. "You boys drop them gunbelts."

"We're not droppin' nothin'," said Jug. "We're Federal Deputies. Now back off if you know what's good for you." The Marshal cocked the hammer on his Winchester. His deputy, cocked the hammer on his carbine." Jug could tell that Jeb was itching to get at the Marshal.

"Stay still Jeb. Don't do nothin' till I tell ya," said Jug.

"I'll kill that dog if he even starts my way," said the Marshal.

Sean had looked all over town and couldn't find the Town Marshal. He was about to give up and head to the saloon where Jug and Jesse had gone, when he heard someone on the street say something about trouble over at the saloon. Sean headed back to the saloon. He eased his way to the door. Inside he could see two men with their guns pointed at Jug and Jesse. He eased his way inside. The Marshal was about ten feet from him now. The bartender saw Sean now and let out a yell. "Behind you Marshal, look out." Before the Marshal could turn to look, Sean had a pistol out and cracked him over the head. Before the Marshal hit the floor, Sean moved quickly and cracked the deputy over the head.

"You're obstructing justice," said the Judge. "You just assaulted a Marshal and his deputy. I'll see you in jail for that."

"You shut your mouth Judge or you'll get yourself assaulted next," said Sean. "Jeb you go over and keep an eye on the Judge. If he moves, you know what to do. Judge, if you're packin' any weapons at all, I'd advise you to leave them alone. Now boys, what went on here?"

"That bartender give us a hard time," answered Jug. "Didn't wanna serve Jesse and me. Ole Jeb straightened'm out. Then that Marshal and his deputy showed up. We was havin' a few words when you showed up."

"Well take them guns away from them boys," said Sean. "We'll wake'em up and have us a talk with 'em." Jug and Jesse took the weapons from the unconscious lawmen. "Bartender, git me a bucket a water," said Sean. The bartender didn't move. "You git that water and I mean now or me and the boys'll be havin' some target practice in here. That big mirror sure looks nice. The bartender didn't move. Sean pulled a pistol and took aim at the mirror.

"All right, all right, I'll get the damn water," said the bartender. The bartender was gone for a moment and then brought a bucket of water over to Sean. Sean dumped half of the bucket on the Marshal and the other half on his deputy. They came to spitting water out of their mouths.

"What the hell and who the hell're you?" said the Marshal as he took a look at Sean.

"Name's O'Rourke, Federal Marshal Sean O'Rourke," answered Sean. "And I hear you're the local law here."

"That's right, I'm the Town Marshal. Name's Riley, Tad Riley," he answered. "And this fella here is my deputy."

"Well Riley, why did I come in here and find you pointin' guns at my men?" asked Sean.

"Some fella told me that there was trouble at the saloon so I got my deputy and came over," Riley answered.

"Was it necessary ta be pointin' guns at my men?" asked Sean.

"I reckon not," said Riley. "I just don't take no chances no more. We've had a lotta trouble here. Anymore, I always have my guns ready. We had a deputy and three cowmen killed in here not long ago."

Sean pulled out the picture of Kid. "Was it this fella?" asked Sean as he showed the picture. The bartender took a look at the picture.

"That was him," said the bartender. "He kilt them fellas and left here with four buffalo hunters. He even paid for the damages from the bar fight they had."

"Well them buffalo hunters is dead," said Sean. "Kid hired them to kill me." Just then, Jeb had a good growl going. Sean looked over at the Judge.

"I was just reaching inside my jacket for cigar," said the Judge. "Call off your dog."

"Don't think I will," said Sean. "Jeb don't like you and neither do I. You just sit there and behave. How the hell did an asshole like you git ta be Judge anyway?"

"I'll have you know that I was a Judge out here for many years before you Yankees started that damn war," said the Judge. "Durin' the war, I was an aide to John Bell Hood."

"Well whoopdedo," said Sean. "I never knew the Yankees started the war. Thanks for the history lesson. Now you listen ta me Judge. I don't give a shit about your glorious service with the Confederate Army. The war's over and your side lost. Jesse don't much care if you like'm or not, but you will respect him. You said you were gonna see me in jail. Judge, if I even hear a rumor that you've put out a warrant for me or my men, I'll come back here and send you straight ta hell. If you don't know bout me and what I'm capable of, you just ask around. There's no need for you ta even reply. You git up off yer ass and git outta here. Let'm go Jeb. You might get poisoned if you bit him anyway." Jeb went back over beside Sean and the Judge and the other man left.

"Now Riley, will there be any more trouble before we leave this town?" asked Sean.

"Not if I can help it," said Riley. "And I apologize for bein' so skiddish about yer men. There's just too much goin' on around here. Mebbe I oughta give up this job. It's drivin' me nuts."

"Not everyone can be a lawman," said Sean. "Sometimes I think bout givin' it up too, but there's just too many bad people out there. Someone's gotta do the job. Besides, I'm good at it."

"Well I hope yer good enough to catch Kid," said Riley. "He seems ta like killin' folks. Some men're like that."

"We'll catch'm and when we do, He's gonna die slow," said Sean. "He's killed seven men that we know for sure and probably another one. Plus he tried ta kill my deputy and his wife and his own Pa. Yes sir, he's gonna die slow."

"You got any idea where he could be?" asked Riley.

"We know he headed northeast when he left here," answered Sean. "We killed them buffalo hunters not far from his Pa's ranch. Plus on the way here, we come across a trail herd that'd been hit by rustlers. They said some young fella was shoutin' out the orders. There's a chance it coulda been him. We'll find'm. It might take a while, but we'll find'm. This fella does like ta kill and the more he does it, the more he'll want ta do it. We'll find'm."

CHAPTER SIX

When Kid left the buffalo hunters, he didn't have much faith that they would get the job done, but he was hoping. He also knew that with a bounty on his head, other men would be after him too. If he was worth $500 to a bounty hunter, why couldn't he hire several bounty hunters to work for him. Hell, he had plenty of money. Bounty hunters were not known to be pillars of the community. They would probably do about anything for money.

It took Kid a while, but he made his way to Dallas. As far as he knew, his Pa hadn't been to Dallas for a lot of years and he himself had never been there. No one would recognize him. Kid called himself Harley Tipton when he rode into Dallas. He went into a few bars and had some drinks with a few men. He told them he was looking to hire some bounty hunters for his Pa's ranch. They were having trouble with critters killing their calves and they didn't have the time or manpower to hunt the critters down, whatever they were. Kid had always heard that some bounty hunters hunted critters as well as men. Kid wasn't having any luck in the saloons. He spent the night at a hotel and after some breakfast, he went to the Marshal's office. The Marshal was at his desk looking at some wanted posters. "State yer business Mr." said the marshal without even looking up. "I got work to do."

"Name's Harley Tipton," said Kid. "My Pa's got a small ranch and we got problems with critters killin' our calves. We don't have the manpower or time to hunt'em down. I'm lookin' ta hire some bounty hunters." The Marshal looked up now.

"Probly just some damn coyotes," said the Marshal. "They'll kill calves when they get the chance. You oughta be able ta kill a few coyotes."

"We're just gettin' started Marshal," said Kid. "Hell, we don't even got a shack ta sleep in yet."

"Well there's a couple a fellas just north a here that go after bounty money when it gets up around $200 or more," said the Marshal. "They're man hunters. I doubt you could pay'em enough ta kill some coyotes or whatever's killin' yer stock. I'd stay away from'em if I was you young fella. They're mean. And I mean real mean. They're brothers. They call one Stew and the other one Chili. Chili's the bigger one. Their last name is Potts." The Marshal hesitated for a moment and then took a good look at Kid. "What did you say your name was?" asked the Marshal.

"It's Harley Tipton," answered Kid.

"I got a poster here for a fella named Bart Evans," said the Marshal. "They call'm Kid. This description here fits you pretty good. You best look over your shoulder once in a while. Someone might mistake you for that fella." The Marshal looked away from Kid for a moment and was looking through his posters. Kid had on his gunbelt, but he also had a long bladed hunting knife on the left side of his gunbelt. As the Marshal was looking down at his posters, Kid slowly pulled the knife with his left hand. When the

Marshal looked up at Kid again, Kid reached across his desk and stuck the knife deep into his throat. It didn't take the Marshal very long to bleed to death. Kid wiped the blood from his knife on the Marshal's shirt and walked out of the office like nothing had happened. He noticed a little blood on his lower left arm so he wiped his arm on the back of his pants. He mounted his horse and headed north to find the Potts brothers.

A half hour later, one of the deputies came back to the office and found the Marshal dead. The town went crazy. No one knew what had happened or why anyone would do this. No one had seen anything. Some of the people wanted to get a posse together and go looking, but who would they look for? No one had a clue.

~~~~

It took Kid half a day to find the Potts' place. It wasn't much of anything. There was a small shack with a well out front. There was a lean to type shelter where it looked like they kept horses and a small corral behind the house. One of the Potts men was drawing some water from the well and the other one was chopping some wood for kindling. The one chopping wood saw Kid first. He let out a yell to the other one and ran into the shack. He came back outside with a Spencer rifle in his hands. He chambered a round. When Kid got about a hundred feet from them, the one with the Spencer spoke. "Who in the hell're you and what do you want?"

"I came out here to discuss some business with you boys," answered Kid. "I hear you boys're bounty hunters."

"What we do is our business, not yours," the man said. "Now tell us who the hell you are before I put a hole in ya."

"Name's Bart Evans," answered Kid. "They call me Kid."

"I seen a poster on you boy," said the one by the well. "We was thinkin' bout goin' after you when we ran outta money."

"Well I'm right here," said Kid. "You don't need ta go after me."

"Shoot'm now Stew," said the one by the well. "He's worth $500."

"You must be Chili," said Kid.

"How'd you know my name?" asked Chili.

"I talked to the Marshal about you in Dallas," said Kid.

"Go ahead and shoot'm Stew," said Chili. "We never made money this easy afore."

"Now just wait a minute," said Stew. "This fella knew we was bounty men when he came out here. Let's hear what business he has to discuss with us."

"You're a smart man Stew," said Kid. "Now tell me how you boys take care a business."

"When we get low on money, we just go after another man," said Chili. "When we get'm, we live off that money till it's gone. We get us some women and whiskey and supplies. When the money gets low, we go after anothern. That's what we do. We don't go after a man unless the bounty is for dead'r alive. Most of'm don't come in peaceable like."

"So are you boys good trackers?" asked Kid.

"Yep we are," answered Stew. "Our Pa was raised by Apaches. He taught us everthin'. Our momma was white and Messican. Our Pa just loved our momma's chili. He said it made him horny. That's how Chili got his name."

"That's interesting. So you boys don't mind killin' folks if you have to?" asked Kid.

"No, we don't mind," said Chili. "As long as we get paid, we don't much care who we kill."

"That's good. So would you boys mind making more money than you ever seen before?" asked Kid.

"What you got in mind?" asked Stew.

"Well first off, I'll give you boys $250 a piece," started Kid. "That's what you woulda got for bringin' me in. Then I think we should do some cattle rustlin' and mebbe rob some banks over in Missouri."

"They hang cattle rustlers," said Stew.

"They gotta catch you first," said Kid. "Got any friends that might want some easy money?"

"We know some boys," said Stew. "They be some cousins a ours. They rode with some a them border gangs along the Kansas Missouri line a while back. They know their way around. I spect their names'r on some posters. We'd go after'em ceptin' their kin. We won't kill no kin."

"So how soon can we find your cousins?" asked Kid.

"We can find'em in a few days hard ride," said Stew.

"So when do we leave?" asked Kid.

"As soon as we see the color a yer money," said Chili. Kid reached into a pocket and pulled out five one hundred dollar bills and handed them to Chili.

"You boys can worry bout splittin' it up," said Kid. "All I got on me is big bills."

"What makes you think we won't kill you and take the rest a yer money and then turn yer body in too?" said Stew.

"Cause I'm faster with a gun than you and you know that there's more money out there than what I got on me," said Kid.

"How do you know you're faster than us?" asked Chili.

"You boys can try me any time you like," said Kid. "But I'd rather work with you than kill you. There's a lotta cows out there just waitin' for us and cattle prices are really high since they got that railhead in Abilene. That means there'll be money in them banks too. There's not much law around either."

"What about that O'Rourke fella," said Stew. "I hear he's the best with a long gun, pistol, and his fists. I hear he lived with the Cheyenne and he can track too. He's kilt a lotta men."

"They got caught," said Kid. "We won't. You boys say your Pa lived with the Apache and taught you all he knew. Don't you think Apaches is better'n Cheyenne? You boys start thinkin' like Apaches and we'll be all right."

~~~~

They rode hard for four days. On the fifth day they came to a series of hills. The ground was brushy and desolate. It looked like nothing could live on it but rattlesnakes and prairie dogs. There was a small trail that led into the hills and they followed it for a couple of miles. They stopped for a while to rest the horses. As soon as they dismounted, they heard the unmistakable sound of a lever action rifle chambering a round. Then they heard it again. "You boys step away from them horses and keep your hands where we can see'em," said someone. "One wrong move and you'll meet yer maker."

"Cousin Lukey, is that you?" yelled out Stew.

"Yeh it's me," Lukey answered. "Who the hell's that with you?"

"It's Kid Evans," answered Stew.

"How come he's still breathin'?" asked Lukey. "I seen a poster on him for $500."

"He is worth $500," said Chili. "But now he's payin' us ta work for him. Can we come on in to your camp now?"

"Sure, come on in," said Lukey. "Just follow the trail. It's not far." The boys mounted their horses and followed the trail for another half mile. When they got to the end of the trail, they didn't see anything right away. Then they looked harder. Over in some trees and brush was a small shack. Next to the shack was a small corral and a shelter for horses. A small stream was behind the shack. When they rode over to the shack, they could see several horses in the corral. Some of horses were branded and some them weren't. None of the horses that were branded had the same brand. These boys had been stealing horses.

Lukey and the other man, rode in behind Kid and the Potts brothers. They all dismounted beside the shack. "So what do you think of our place?" asked Lukey. "Hard to spot isn't it?"

"Gotta look hard ta see it," said Chili. "Where's the rest a the boys?"

"Oh, they're out workin'," said Lukey. "Me and Slim stayed here to watch the place. They'll be back this evenin' or in the mornin'."

"So are you makin' any money stealin' horses?" asked Kid.

"We do all right," answered Lukey. "Slim here is real good with a runnin' iron. He can change any brand and make it look good."

"So you reckon you and the boys would mind rustilin' some cows and robbin' some banks?" asked Kid. "Cattle prices are high in Abilene."

"If we take stolen cows to Abilene, we'll end up hung," said Slim.

"We won't take no cows to Abilene," said Kid. "After we rustle some, we'll change the brands if they're branded. Then we'll sell'em to another drive or ranch. We won't make the high price they'll be payin' in Abilene, but we won't hafta take all that time drivin'em to Abilene."

So yer sayin' we rustle some cows and then sell'em to maybe the next drive that comes along?" asked Lukey.

"That's pretty much what I'm sayin'," said Kid.

"What makes you think a drive would buy more cows from us?" asked Slim.

"Cause they would make money off'em," said Kid. "If we sold 500 head for $10 dollars a head and they get $40 a head in Abilene, they'd be makin' $30 a head. That's $15,000 profit for them and $5000 for us."

"What makes you think the boss of a trail drive has that kind a money on'm?" asked Slim.

"Most likely, he won't, but I'll bet he could write a bank draft," said Kid. "Most banks'll cash any bank draft if it looks honest. Then maybe we could visit that bank later and make a nice withdrawal."

"If we steal cows, I think we should take'em all the way to Abilene and get top price," said Lukey.

"That's cause yer stupid Lukey," said Kid.

"Don't be callin' me stupid boy," said Lukey. "I'll rip you ta pieces."

"Maybe you will and maybe you won't," said Kid. "Have you ever worked longhorns day in and day out? It's a lotta work. Some of'em would soon as gore ya or stomp ya as look at ya. If we do things my way, the money's a lot quicker and easier. Let someone else do most a the work."

"So what would you tell some ramrod about why you want to sell yer cows?" asked Slim.

"I'll just make up some story and look honest tellin' it," answered Kid. "Hell, I could tell'm that we got hit by rustlers and this was all we had left. I'd say we was tired a the trail and bandits and such and we was goin' back home. He'll, I'd believe that story if someone told it ta me. Even if we didn't get the brands changed and word got out that some cows was stolen and had a certain brand, the fellas that bought them cows would get blamed."

"Well let's give it a try," said Slim. "I'll go fix up the brands on them horses and we'll be ready ta go." Slim got busy with his branding and Lukey started making supper for the boys. Lukey was their designated cook. He did a better job with beans than the rest of them.

It was a little before dark and they were about to have supper when three riders arrived. They were some of dirtiest, nastiest looking men Kid had ever see. Not too many men bathed on a regular basis, but these three looked like they hadn't ever used a bar of soap in their lives. "Kid, these three is Sol, Barney, and Clyde," said Lukey. "They be our cousins. Boys, this new fella here is Bart Evans. Everbody calls'm Kid."

"I can see why," said Sol. "He looks like he's still draggin' on the teat. Why's he here?"

"Sol, don't let my years fool ya," said Kid. "I could kill ya before you batted an eye. And if I was draggin' on a teat, it'd be cause some sweet young thing wanted me too."

"So yer a killer, huh boy," said Sol.

"He is," said Stew. "He's got $500 on his head."

"Then why is he breathin'?" asked Sol. "You boys shoulda kilt'm and collected already."

"We're workin' fer him now," said Chili. "He's got things all figured out."

"So what're we after, horses, cows, banks?" asked Sol.

"We'll start with cows and then mebbe some banks," said Kid. "I got me another idea while you was talking. I think we should rob some banks in Missouri. Everybody'll think the James Younger gang done it. Hell, they're gettin' blamed for everything that happens in Missouri anyway."

"That sounds good but if them fellas find out someone else is messin' in their territory, then we'll have them and the law after us," said Barney.

"So what, yer already wanted men aren't you?" said Kid. "We don't hafta rob banks just in Missouri. They got banks in Texas and Kansas and other states. Should be a lotta money in Kansas with all these cattle drives goin' on. Mebbe in Kansas, we won't hafta rob banks. We'll just find who the cattle buyers are. Them fellas always have lotsa money on'em. So, are you boys in?"

"I reckon so," said Sol. "Might as well make some money since everbody else has got so much of it. Should be 'nough to go around fer us."

"Well we can get started soon as you boys think yer ready," said Kid.

~~~~

Kid and his gang took off two days later. They headed over to the cattle trails and waited. When the Lonnigan herd was half way past them, they struck. They cut out around 500 head and headed east. One Lonnigan man was killed and three were wounded. None of Kid's men got a scratch. They kept their small herd bunched up about 2 miles east of the main cattle trail and waited. They let one herd pass the next day, but when the second one came by, Kid went to some of the drovers and asked to see the ramrod. The drover took him to his boss. Kid acted like he was a scared boy when he spoke to the ramrod. "We was hit by rustlers," started Kid. "They took most a the herd. There's bout 500 head left. We got'em bunched up a little to the east. We want ta sell'em and go home. We had enough a outlaws, Injuns, and no water, or dust storms. We'll take whatever price you can afford."

"Slow down son. What's yer name?" asked the ramrod.

"It's Tom Lords," said Kid. "My Pa was with us, but we buried'm a ways back."

"How many cows you say you got?" asked the ramrod.

"Should be bout 500," answered Kid.

"I can give you a bank draft if that's all right," said the ramrod. "I don't got no cash to amount ta much."

"A bank draft'd be fine," said Kid.

"I'll give ya $15 a head," said the foreman. "That is if your boys'll bring'em over ta our herd. Does that sound all right."

"That'll be fine," said Kid. "We're gettin' outta the cow business. Too damn dangerous." Kid went back to his herd and he and the others drove the herd over to the main herd. The ramrod wrote out a bank draft to Kid and Kid wrote out a bill of sales. They shook hands and Kid and the gang moved on.

After Kid and the gang got out of hearing distance, one of the ramrod's men went to him. "Boss, I bet ya them cows is rustled," he said. "I just can't believe someone'd come this far and then sell out just like that. Not when the price in Abilene is so high."

"I figure them is rustled cows," said the ramrod. "But them buyers don't care bout brands. They just want their beef. A steak tastes the same if it's from a legal cow or a stolen cow. Besides, we got a bill a sale."

~~~~

Kid and the gang rode to the closest town that had a bank. He cashed the bank draft and then all of them went to a saloon. Kid gave all of them their cut. None of these boys had ever seen $900 before. Most of them slammed down some whiskey and had some whores. The whores that Sol, Barney, and Clyde had, made the boys take a bath before they would bed them. The boys grumbled some, but they took a bath. Sol was not happy about taking a bath. He took one, but when he was done, he gave the whore a black eye. Stew and Chili were a little more civilized about it. They went to a bath house of their own accord and cleaned up before they found some whores. Kid let them drink and whore for a couple of days. Then he told them it was time to move on. Before they left, he told Sol, Barney, and Clyde that they should get themselves some new clothes. Even though they had taken a bath, they hadn't bothered to clean their clothes and their clothes still were pretty rank. Kid didn't mess around with any whores while the other boys were busy. He found some sweet young girl and sweet talked himself right into her drawers. Of course he told her he loved her and she believed him. That is till she found out he had left town.

~~~~

They headed east and out of Texas. When they got to Arkansas, they sold their horses and took a train up to Missouri. Kid decided that the train stops were in the bigger towns. The bigger towns would have banks in them. They stayed on the train for almost a day. They were about in the middle of Missouri on the western half when they got off the train. They got themselves some more horses and supplies and then made their plan.

Robbing the first bank was easier than Kid thought it would be. When the bank opened the next morning, four of them went inside and four stayed outside and kept watch. Once inside, the four men covered their faces and informed the bank employees that this was a hold up and no one would get hurt if they handed over the money. The bank employees handed over the money and the men left. Once outside, they all rode out of town to the west. After a few minutes, one of the bank employees went to the Town Marshal and told them there'd been a robbery and the gang headed west. They had gotten away with $5000. The Marshal tried to round up a posse but no one would go with him. Everyone figured it was the James Younger gang and they weren't messing with them.

When the gang realized they weren't being followed, they slowed down. When they made camp for the night, Kid divided up the money. These boys couldn't wait to rob another bank.

Kid waited a week before his gang struck again. This time it wasn't that easy. A bank teller didn't want to give up the money and he didn't believe he would be shot. He was wrong. Kid shot him right between the eyes. When the bank manager started yelling at Kid, he shot him too. They made off with $10,000 that day but they got shot at as they rode out of town. This time a posse was after them. Kid had an ambush all set up for the posse, but right before they opened up on them, the posse turned around. It seems that they had gone into another county and were out of the local law's jurisdiction. Kid decided they should hole up somewhere for a while. They went into "The Nations."

CHAPTER SEVEN

Back in Abilene, Maggie was feeling lonesome. It had been a long time since Sean had been gone this long. And there was another reason she was missing Sean. Maggie was fairly certain that she was with child. She had missed her time right before Sean had left. It had been over a month now and she missed her time again. She was having some morning sickness too. Betty and Michael had healed well and were spending more and more time in the saloon. Betty saw Maggie acting sick one day and she knew right then that Maggie was pregnant. The cowboys who came in with the herds had been behaving for the most part, but the place was just too busy for Maggie to handle. There were nights when none of the saloons in town closed. Cookie and Barbara were working themselves to death in the kitchen. Tom was at the bar sixteen hours a day. Jim was on the floor from noon till they closed, if they closed. Michael and Betty did what they could, but they were not one hundred percent yet. Maggie needed more help. Even the working girls were getting worn out.

One morning, Maggie sent a telegram to St. Louis. It went as follows:

Susie and Dan Taylor
Palace Saloon

Susie and Dan<<stop>>need help at sa-
loon<<stop>>Sean after outlaw<<stop>>very busy
with cattle drives<<stop>>can you spare any-
one<<stop>>will pay well

Maggie

Maggie received a telegram the same afternoon. It went as
follow

Maggie O'Rourke
Abilene

Kathleen Sara Doug will be there in a few
days<<stop>>Hope that is enough

Susie and Dan Taylor

Maggie was relieved when she read the telegram. She did not
know Sara or Doug, but she knew they were good people if Susie
and Dan were sending them.

When they arrived in town, Maggie and Betty met all of them
at the train station. Betty did a double take when she saw
Kathleen. "Are you two related?" Betty asked Kathleen.

"No we're not, but we could probably pass for sisters," said Kathleen. Kathleen introduced Sara and Doug and then Maggie took them over to a hotel to get them a room.

"Your room will be paid for while you're here," said Maggie. "Get yourself settled and then come on over to the saloon. I'll see all of you in an hour or so." Kathleen and the others went to their rooms and got settled. Kathleen was the first of them to head to "Maggie's Place." As she left the hotel and was walking down the sidewalk, a couple of cowboys saw her coming toward them. As she got closer, one of them spoke.

"What do I hafta do ta get ta know you better darlin'?" the cowboy asked.

"I'll be over at "Maggie's Place," said Kathleen. "Just be a gentleman and ask for Kathleen."

"I sure will Miss Kathleen," said the cowboy. Kathleen smiled at the two men and then continued her walk to "Maggie's Place." "I'm gonna go git me a bath right now," said the cowboy. "That woman's got quality and she won't want no fella that smells like cows and horse piss," the cowboy said.

"I believe I'll git me a bath too," said the other cowboy.

Sara was a looker too and when she started down the sidewalk for "Maggie's Place," she had several cowboys wanting to escort her. "You boys can call on me at "Maggie's Place," Sara told them. She blew them a kiss and then continued on to the saloon.

Doug was a tall handsome man and when he started down the sidewalk to the saloon, several ladies in some of the stores gave him a welcoming smile. Doug sure hoped those women weren't married. He always had luck with the ladies and he always stood by his rule. Never, ever, mess with a married woman. This had kept him out of trouble over the years.

When they were all there, Maggie sat down with them and introduced everyone. She told each of them what was expected of them. The most important thing she told them was to remember that this wasn't the big city. This was a cow town and very few of their customers had good manners, but they were not to let anyone give them a hard time. If someone didn't check their weapons when they came in, they would be asked to leave. If they didn't want to leave, they would be forced out by whatever means. No one had any questions. Betty showed the girls what rooms they would be using and Doug got with Tom and he showed him where everything was.

Word must have gotten around about Kathleen and Sara because the place filled up very quickly that evening. A few of the cowboys grumbled about giving up their guns, but they got over it when they saw Maggie's girls. All of them were gorgeous, not just Kathleen and Sara. But Kathleen did stand out with that red hair of hers. Several times that evening she was asked if that was her painting on the wall. She would always say, "Maybe you'll find out later."

The second night, they found out that Doug was pretty good with his fists. Some cowboys were fighting over who would be with Kathleen next. They weren't drunk either. Doug broke up the fight, but he had to give both of them a couple of rights and lefts to their jaws. When he had finished breaking up the fight, he sat the two men down at a table and had a small talk with them. "Look boys, we have all these beautiful women here," he started. "Neither of you is leaving here without being with them. Just relax and enjoy your drinks while you're waiting your turn. Don't waste your energy fighting each other. You'll want all your strength for the women. Now I'll give you a drink on the house.

You two shake hands and be friends." The two cowboys shook hands. Doug brought them their drink. As they were sipping on them, Kathleen and Sara both went to their table. They both extended their hands toward the cowboys. One of them took Kathleen's hand and the other one took Sara's. They went upstairs. A half hour later, they traded off.

Maggie was happy about the way Doug handled the cowboys. A situation like that could have gotten way out of hand and a lot of damage could have been done. Maggie thanked Doug and when the two cowboys finally came back downstairs, she thanked them for controlling themselves. One of the cowboys took a hard look at Maggie and then a hard look at the painting on the wall. "That's you isn't it. You're Maggie aren't you," he said.

"Yes that's me and I am Maggie," said Maggie.

"Maggie, you are a goddess," said the cowboy. "That painting is good but it doesn't do you justice. May I kiss your hand?"

"You may," said Maggie. "But I must tell you, I am an owner of this place. I am not a working girl."

"I hope that I didn't imply that Miss Maggie," said the cowboy. "Your beauty has me in a trance."

"Where'd you learn to talk like that young man. Cowboys don't talk like that," said Maggie.

"My father spent some time as an actor back east," said the cowboy. "He was always making us kids recite Shakespeare. He even sent me to an acting school for a while. I hated it. The other kids were too uppity. I'm more at ease around these cowboys Miss Maggie. No uppittyness in them at all. What ya see is what ya get."

"Well young man, what's your name?" asked Maggie.

"It's Simon, Simon Miller," answered the cowboy.

"Well I'm Maggie O'Rourke and I'm pleased to meet you," said Maggie.

"You said O'Rourke, didn't you?" asked Simon.

"I did," answered Maggie. "You've probably heard of my husband haven't you."

"I sure have," said Simon. "Everybody's heard a him. Wouldn't want ta be on the wrong side of the law and have him after me. Is he here tonight?"

"No, he's out after an outlaw," said Maggie. "You ever heard of Bart Evans? They call him Kid,"

"I don't know'm personally but I saw him and his Pa once down in Texas," said Simon. "I seen Kid's name on some wanted posters. I guess he turned bad. That's a shame. His Pa's got the biggest spread in Texas and that boy wouldn't want fer nothin'. Don't make sense him killin' folks like that. Hope yer husband gets'm killed. I knew the CC foreman Sugar O'Reilly. He was a good man. I worked fer him when he was with another ranch before he went to the CC."

"Well Simon, it was nice meeting you," said Maggie. "Maybe if you get tired of pushing cows around, I could let you work for me."

"That's somethin' ta think about Maggie," said Simon. "I sincerely thank you for your kindness. Now I must be on my way."

"Remember what I said Simon," said Maggie. "Now you take care of yourself." Simon nodded his head and then he and the other cowboy left.

"What was that all about?" the other cowboy asked Simon when they got outside the saloon.

"That was just some polite conversation with a beautiful woman," said Simon.

"You got it bad fer her," said the cowboy.

"I don't think so," said Simon. "Did you hear who her husband is?"

"I did," answered the cowboy. "But she sure is somethin' ta look at isn't she?"

"She surely is," said Simon. "Maybe I will quit pushin' cows around and see if she would give me a job."

"You'd be some bartender," said the cowboy. "You'd be too busy lookin' at the women ta do yer job."

"I believe I could look and still do the job," said Simon.

"You better learn how to fight better if yer gonna work in a saloon" said the cowboy. "That fella in there kicked both our asses."

"Well if I do git me a job there, I'll ask that fella ta show me some things," said Simon. "Why am I talkin' ta you about this? I'm goin' over there in the mornin' and see if she was serious about giving me a job." The cowboy just shook his head and the two of them went to their hotel rooms.

The next morning, Simon was at Maggie's Place when they opened for the day. He walked in and found Maggie standing behind the bar. He went to her. She saw him as he approached. "Mrs. O'Rourke, if you were serious about giving me a job I would like the opportunity to become one of your employees," said Simon.

"I was serious," said Maggie. "If you work out, I can promise you work while the cattle drives are coming to town."

"That's fair enough," said Simon. "I do have a small favor to ask of you though."

"What would that be?" asked Maggie.

"I'd like for your man to teach me some better fighting skills," said Simon. "I think I'll need them in here sometime."

"That's not a problem. I'll have Doug show you some things," said Maggie. "Pay's $60 a month and you can start right now."

"That's twice what I make pushin' cows," said Simon.

"Don't worry. You'll earn every penny of it," said Maggie. "Some days you'll put in sixteen to twenty hours. Now can you handle that?"

"I'll give it my best," said Simon.

"Have you got a place to stay?" asked Maggie.

"I do not," answered Simon.

"I have a room out back you can use but you have to share with Jim," said Maggie.

"I won't mind if Jim don't mind," said Simon. Jim walked into the saloon now.

"Jim, come over here," said Maggie. "Jim Stewart, this is Simon Miller. He'll be working with us. I told him that you two would be sharing the room out back." The two men shook hands.

"That's all right by me," said Jim. "I spend a lot of time with Sally so I'm not in the room a whole lot. Go get your gear. I'll show you your new home."

"All I got is a bedroll, horse and saddle, and a pistol," said Simon. "Let's go see the room now." Jim took Simon to the room. "This'll be just fine. This is more'n I've had for a good while."

"Well if you got any money left, you should get yourself some new clothes," said Jim. "Looks like your duds is bout worn out anyway."

"I was thinkin' I'd get me some," said Simon. "Maggie probly don't want me lookin' like a drover anyhow."

"The other women'll like you better too," said Jim.

"So what is it you do here?" asked Simon.

"I basically just watch out for trouble and head it off before it gets goin'," said Jim.

"Where was you yesterday when me and that other cowboy was fightin'?" asked Simon.

"I was here," answered Jim. "I was on my way over when Doug beat me there and took care of it. He's pretty good with his fists, isn't he?"

"He is," said Simon. "My jaw's proof of that. I'm hopin' he can show me some things."

"I'm sure he will," said Jim. "Now if I was you, I'd ask Maggie if it'd be all right to go buy some new clothes."

~~~~

Maggie agreed that Simon needed some new clothes and she let him take off to get some. He came back an hour later looking like a totally different person. He had bought his clothes and then gone to a bath and barber shop. He bathed, got a shave and a haircut, and then put on his new clothes. When he walked back into the saloon, he caught Sara's eye. She was impressed. Maggie was impressed too. After complimenting him, she put him to work. It wasn't long and Maggie knew that she had made a good decision when she hired Simon. He was a good worker.

Simon caught on really quick and after a week, he was doing about everything around the place. Doug had showed him a few things and he felt somewhat confident that he could break up a fight or take care of himself if the need arose. Sara did take a liking to Simon. Maggie figured it was because of the way he talked to women. He was always the perfect gentleman. One night, a couple of drunk cowboys were giving Sara a rough time. They had already drunk up all their money and were trying to talk Sara into giving them some free ones. Sara was as polite as she could be, but the cowboys started getting rough with her. One of them shoved her and knocked her to the floor. The other one was about to kick her. Before he brought his leg back to kick her, Simon was on him. Simon grabbed the cowboy from behind and turned him around. As the cowboy came face to face with Simon, Simon gave the cowboy a right to the chin and the cowboy was out before he hit the floor. Then Simon turned on the other cowboy. He grabbed him by the front of his shirt and forced him out the front door of the saloon. Once outside, he hit the cowboy with a left to his jaw and down he went. Then Simon went back inside. He grabbed the unconscious cowboy and dragged him outside into the street. Then Simon went behind the bar and got a bucket of water. He went back outside and threw some water into the faces of the cowboys. As they came to, Simon was standing over them. "You boys are welcome in here anytime, but while you're in here, you will treat the ladies with respect," said Simon.

"Just who in the hell do you think you are?" asked one of the cowboys.

"I'm the man who's gonna stomp your ass if you mistreat any of the ladies again," yelled Simon. "Now you boys move on or I'll give you some more."

"We want our guns back," said one of the cowboys.

"I'll get them for you," said Simon. "What kind do you have?"

"We both got Army Colts," said one of the cowboys. "You'll see some letters scratched on the handles. Mine is a B for Ben and his is H for Homer."

"I'll get'em and be right back," said Simon. Sara had been standing by the door and watching everything that went on outside. She gave Simon a look of approval when he came back inside to get the boy's guns. Simon found the pistols with no problem. These pistols were cap and ball too. Simon pulled a pocket knife out of his pocket and opened the blade. Then he removed the caps from each of the nipples on both pistols. He went back outside and handed the cowboys their gunbelts. No words were spoken. The cowboys strapped on their gunbelts. Simon turned to go back inside. When he had gone a couple of steps, he heard the unmistakable sound of hammers being cocked and then the hammers striking. He turned to face the cowboys. "So you sonsa bitches woulda shot me in the back," Simon yelled at them. Then Simon held out his hand and showed the cowboys the caps from their pistols. He stood there and threw the caps at the cowboys. "You boys sure are some brave men," yelled Simon. "First you rough up women and then you try ta shoot me in the back. Do you know what the penalty is for attempted murder in this state. If O'Rourke was here he'd hang you. You boys get the hell outta town before I have you locked up." The two cowboys didn't say a word. They looked at each other and then turned and walked away. Simon watched them for a moment and then went back inside. Sara was there by the door.

"I'll see you when I get done for the night," said Sara. Simon smiled at her and went back to work.

Maggie had watched most of the happenings and went to Simon when he came back inside. "That was good work Simon," said Maggie. "But you keep a good watch. Them two cowboys might hold a grudge for a while."

"I'll be careful Maggie," said Simon. Doug came over to Simon now.

"That was good work Simon," said Doug. "I probably wouldn't have woke them up though. They might have woke up in the street and not remembered how they got there. Anyway, Sara's taken a fancy to you. Treat her right."

"I will," said Simon. "I will."

~~~~

Simon spent what was left of the night in Sara's hotel room. Simon wasn't a fool. He knew what Sara did for a living and he knew that there would never be anything serious between them. But he felt special when he was with her. He knew that she liked him and that was good enough for him for now.

~~~~

Maggie's morning sickness seemed to be getting worse. It just didn't happen in the morning either. There were times when she was in her room and everyone else could hear her heaving. There were some days that Maggie didn't want to come downstairs at all.

The long days were also taking a toll on Michael and Betty. They had healed from their wounds but they just didn't have the stamina that they had before. There were days that Michael didn't play his piano at all. Betty worked behind the bar and took care of tables, but she was not able to work the whole time the place was open. Even with the extra help from St. Louis, everyone was dog tired most of the time.

Maggie made a decision. "Maggie's Place" would close at 2am. Last call would come at 1:45am. All patrons would leave at 2am of their own accord or be thrown out. All of the employees agreed that this would be all right. Usually there weren't that many customers in the wee hours of the morning anyway.

Maggie had a big sign made and they put it right next to the sign that said for the customers to check their weapons. The first night the sign was up, they had to help a few customers out the door, but there was no serious trouble. On the third night, there was a big poker game going on. High rollers were playing and not cowboys. Every so often as closing time got closer, one of the employees went to the table and reminded the players of closing time. Of course one of the players was consistently winning hands. Some of the other players were whining to continue so they would have a chance to win their money back. The last hand was dealt at 1:55am. The man who had been winning was the dealer. He won the hand and informed the other players that the game was over for the night. He would be glad to continue tomorrow night. "Never seen anyone win that many hands before," said one of the gamblers. "I think maybe we should take a look up your sleeves and check your pockets."

"Very well," said the winner. He stood up and took off his jacket. He turned the sleeves inside out. He pulled up the sleeves to his shirt. He turned his pants pockets inside out. The he pulled off his boots and turned them upside down. No extra cards were found or seen. "I suggest you boys learn to play the game better," said the winner. "Poker is a game of skill, not luck." The winner put his jacket back on. "Now if you'll excuse me, I believe this establishment is closing for the evening. I will entertain the thought of another game tomorrow night if you wish." The winner nodded his head to Maggie as he left. The other gamblers grumbled a little but they finally they got up and left. None of these gamblers had checked any weapons when they entered the saloon that evening.

The next evening, the same gamblers were at it again. Michael got to watching them. The man who had won the night before was very good and he was not a cheat. As Michael was watching, he was sure that he noticed a bulge on the waist of two of the other gamblers. Michael watched them for a good while and then had Doug watch them. Doug also noticed the bulges. The same man was winning again and the other gamblers were starting to complain some. "I can see no reason this game should continue," said the winner. "You people are obviously convinced that I am a cheat. I suggest you find someone else to play with. If you'll excuse me, I'll be leaving." As the winner stood and was about to leave, the two gamblers with bulges at their waist's, reached for something at their waist. Just as they were about to produce pistols, two hammers were heard cocking. Michael had cocked his pistol and had it pointed at one of the gambler's head and Doug had a pistol cocked and pointed at the other one's head.

"You two will take those pistols by the butt and lay them on the floor," said Michael. "Do it now." The two men seemed to be doing as instructed. As they were laying the pistols down, one of the gamblers changed his mind and started raising his pistol to fire. The other gambler saw what the other one was doing and started raising his pistol too. Michael and Doug both fired their pistols. The gamblers were struck in the head. One of the gamblers had managed to get his pistol cocked. When he fell to the floor, the pistol fell from his hand. When it hit the floor, it fired. Michael was struck in the leg. Michael looked down at the small hole in his pants leg. The bullet had struck his wooden leg. Betty ran over to make sure Michael was all right. "Don't worry Betty darlin'," said Michael. "This wooden leg came in handy again." Betty didn't say anything. She just cried a bit.

The undertaker had been in the saloon having a drink when the shootings happened. He finished his drink, rounded up his help, and took the bodies to the parlor.

The winning gambler went to Maggie. "I'm sorry to have caused so much trouble," said the gambler. "Is there anything I could do for you that would ease the pain I have caused in here?"

"Nothing that happened here was your fault sir," said Maggie. "Poker is a game of skill and if someone's not good enough, they shouldn't play the game. What is your name?"

"I'm Anthony Balducci, and I thank you for your kindness," said Anthony. "And you must be Maggie."

"Yes, I'm Maggie, and Anthony, you are welcome here any time," said Maggie. Anthony took Maggie's hand and kissed it. Then he nodded his head and left.

Doug and Simon helped the undertaker's men get the bodies out of the saloon. They cleaned the floor as best they could and business went on as usual. When the saloon closed at 2am, Simon had a talk with Doug. "Have you ever done that before?" asked Simon.

"That's the first man I've killed since the war," answered Doug. "Never thought I'd kill another man after that."

"Does it make you feel bad?" asked Simon.

"Yes it does," answered Doug. "I don't enjoy taking a life, but I wasn't gonna let them fellas kill that other man. Maybe you'll get lucky and you'll never have to shoot anyone."

"I hope so," said Simon. "I hope so."

CHAPTER EIGHT

The Comanche were known to be one of the fiercest tribes on the plains and had been known to hold a grudge for whatever reason for years. When Sean was with the Cheyenne and the Comanche war party was on their way to attack their village, Sean and Braddock had killed many of the Comanche at long range with their Sharp's rifles. The remaining Comanche fled but they swore they would get "the one who kills with the long gun and the big pistol." A few years later, the village of Comanche from which the war party had come, was practically wiped out by smallpox. A young brave survived. He became a leader of his clan and led them in many raids against settlers and ranchers. Two of his brothers had been killed when their war party went after the Cheyenne village. He swore that he would personally get "the one who kills with the long gun and the big pistol." He would shoot his belly full of arrows and scalp him while he was still alive. Then he would cut out his heart and feed it to the coyotes. His name was Mad Buffalo.

Mad Buffalo was a tough customer. He had been shot at so many times by soldiers, Rangers, and others, and had never been scratched. He believed that bullets couldn't hurt him. He was a proud man and never used white man's weapons. He had his bow and arrows, lance, a tomahawk, and a hunting knife. He didn't mind if his people used guns as long as they used them to kill their enemies. Whenever his clan went on a buffalo hunt, they used bows and arrows and lances. Ammunition was reserved for soldiers, Rangers, and settlers.

The Comanche got most of their guns when they killed settlers and soldiers, but some of them came from trading with Comancheros. The Comancheros were always trading for horses. Mad Buffalo was a smart man and if the guns were defective or old, he wouldn't let his people trade for them. More than one Comanchero was killed trying to trade defective or old guns.

Mad Buffalo knew that "the one who kills with the long gun and the big pistol" had become a lawman and was called O'Rourke. He had heard that he spent most of his time in Kansas, but at times he had gone to Texas after outlaws. Perhaps one day he would see O'Rourke in Texas. One day when some Comancheros were at his village trading, the leader of the group told Mad Buffalo that he probably wouldn't be back for a good while. He had heard that O'Rourke was in Texas and was after an outlaw. He didn't want to be anywhere near O'Rourke. The Comanchero wasn't sure where O'Rourke was now, but he had heard that the man he was after was the son of the owner of the CC ranch. Mad Buffalo knew the CC ranch. His men had raided there many times over the years.

Mad Buffalo had several braves who could speak American and a few who could speak Spanish. He himself spoke American. He sent scouts out to see if they could learn anything. There were five sets of scouts and two braves in each set. One of the two in each group could speak either American or Spanish. The first set of scouts were sent to watch the CC ranch. If they could, they were to grab someone off the ranch and force them to talk if they knew anything. Two sets of scouts went south toward San Antonio and the other two sets went northeast. They would all stay out for a month if necessary. None of the scouts knew what O'Rourke looked like, but they knew what a lawman's badge looked like.

~~~~

Sean wasn't quite sure where to go next. He decided they would spend the night in San Antonio and he would send out some telegrams and see if anyone had seen or heard about Kid. The boys were sitting in a café having breakfast the next morning when a man walked in and noticed the badges on them. Then he thought he recognized Sean. He had seen him once in Kansas City. He walked over to Sean's table. "I'm sorry to interrupt your meal, but are you Marshal O'Rourke?" asked the man.

"I am and these are my deputies," said Sean. "Who are you and what can I do for you?"

"Name's Oren Bradley. I seen you once in Kansas City," said Oren. "I just got here not long ago from Dallas. Strangest thing happened there."

"Well what was it?" asked Sean.

"The Town Marshal had his throat slit right at his desk in his office," said Oren. "Weren't no witnesses'r nothin'. A deputy found him mebbe a half hour after it happened. They wanted to form a posse, but no one knew where to go or who to go after."

"What was the Marshal doin' at his desk at the time?" asked Sean.

"They said he musta been lookin' at wanted posters cause he had a pile of'em on his desk," said Oren. "The one on top was for some fella named Bart Evans. It was covered with the Marshal's blood."

"How long was you in Dallas?" asked Sean.

"I was there for two weeks," said Oren. "I'm a whiskey drummer. I had been travelin' a lot and was stayin' there ta rest a bit."

"So you probly spend a good bit of your time in saloons." said Sean.

"Of course I do," said Oren. "That's where I make my livin', plus I indulge my self too."

"Do you remember seein' anyone there in those two weeks that you hadn't seen before," asked Sean.

"I'm not sure. I see a lotta different faces," said Oren. "No wait a minute. There was this one fella. He was real young. I heard him askin' folks if they knew where he could hire some bounty hunters. Said his Pa was startin' a ranch and they was havin' trouble with critters killin' their calves. I remember now. I think someone told him he should go talk to the Marshal."

Sean reached into a pocket and pulled out the picture of Kid. "Is this the fella you saw?" asked Sean.

"This fella looks a little younger, but it sure looks like him," said Oren.

"That's Bart Evans, also known as Kid," said Sean. "He's killed a buncha men and wounded others. He's worth $500 dead'r alive."

"He wasn't much more'n a boy," said Oren.

"Don't let his looks fool ya," said Sean. "He likes killin'."

"Would I be eligible for any reward?" asked Oren.

"If you catch'r kill'm you are," said Sean.

"But I told you where he was," said Oren.

"So you think he's just sittin' in Dallas waitin' fer us to grab'm," said Sean. "Look, thanks for the information. I wouldn't tell a soul you told us you saw him in Dallas. If he'd find out, He'd kill you. Now me and my boys gotta make some plans. Now please excuse us." Oren turned around and left.

Sean waited till Oren cleared the door of the café before he spoke. "I'd say our boy killed that Marshal," said Sean. "He musta recognized Kid from his poster and Kid killed'm. Just why would Kid want bounty hunters?"

"Bounty hunters is man killers," said Jesse. "I'd say he startin' himself a gang and he wants men who don't mind killin'."

"That makes sense," said Sean. "With all that money he stole from his Pa, he could hire a lotta men. I think we'll head over to Dallas and see if we can find anything else out. I'll get us some tickets on the stage. Should get us there quicker. They finished their meal and Sean went to the stage dept. There was a big sign that said "No Stages Till Further Notice, COMANCHE." Sean talked with the clerk at the depot.

"We're not makin' any runs anywhere till the Army gets here and gives us escort," said the clerk. "Them Comanches is at it again."

"How soon before the Army gets here?" asked Sean.

"You ever been in the Army?" the clerk asked Sean.

"I have," answered Sean.

"Then you know the answer. The Army'll be here when they git here," said the clerk. "Probly got some shavetail in charge who don't know where he shit last."

"I know what you're sayin'," said Sean. "But give'm a little slack. Them Comanche are a tough bunch."

"Yeh, and the Army can't be everywhere at once and there's not enough of'em anyway," said the clerk. "Say, aren't you that O'Rourke fella? Who you after down here?"

"After Kid Evans," said Sean. "He was here not long ago."

"I'll be damned," said the clerk. "I heared bout that deputy gettin' shot. Was that Kid?"

"Yes it was," answered Sean. "He likes killin'."

"Don't understand why anyone'd like killin'," said the clerk. "I see more'n enough of it durin' the war. Don't wanna see no more of it."

"Good luck with that," said Sean as he was leaving. He met the others at the hotel where they had spent the night. "Well boys, stages aren't runnin'," said Sean. "I guess they're worried bout Comanche and won't go out without an Army escort. We'll get some more supplies and then head out."

An hour later, the men were saddled up and headed toward Dallas. They saw no other people their first day back in the saddle. The next day, they came across a trail drive. It was a huge herd and stretched out for miles. They stayed to the west of the herd to keep from choking on the dust the herd made as they moved along. The third day, Sean spotted some unshod pony tracks. He knew they were Comanche. There were only two sets of tracks. Sean followed them for a while and they turned to the west. This concerned Sean some. He wondered if the riders were back behind them now. He rode back to the other men. "Them pony tracks turned to the west," said Sean. "That makes me a little edgy. They mighta headed back to a main bunch. We'll stand watches and hope nothin' happens."

They went ahead and had a fire when they set up camp for the night. Sean figured that the Comanche knew they were there anyway so why not have some hot food and stay warm. Jesse took the first watch. His turn was almost done and he was about to wake Jug. Sonny had been laying beside him. For some reason, Sonny got up and walked away from the camp. Jesse just figured he was going to do his necessaries. Jesse woke up Jug and told him that Sonny had gone off. He'd probably be back shortly. Sonny never did come back. Jug's turn was up so he woke Sean. He told Sean that Sonny was gone and had been gone his whole watch. Jeb was there and quiet so Sean wasn't concerned.

At daylight, Sean woke the others. They had some coffee and breakfast. Sonny was still not back. Sean decided he would make a sweep around their camp and see if he could see anything. He left Jeb with Jesse and Jug. About five hundred yards west of the camp, Sean spotted some tracks. He dismounted to make sure if they were dog or wolf tracks. They were dog tracks. He remounted and followed the tracks for a while. After another couple of hundred yards, he spotted some dried blood. Then the dog tracks ended. Where they ended, there were some moccasin tracks and some pony tracks. There was a big boulder out in the middle of nowhere. The tracks led behind it. Sean dismounted and eased his way around it. Now he knew what happened to Sonny. The Comanche had eaten him. Sean could tell that the fire was from last night and dog bones were all over the place. The tracks from the site headed to the northwest. Sean took a careful look around before he headed back to the others. As he neared the camp, he was wondering if Jesse was getting attached to that dog. Sean eased into the camp and dismounted. There was still some coffee in the pot so he poured himself another cup. "Jesse, I hope you weren't gettin' ta like that dog," said Sean. "Them Comanche ate'm last night."

"Son of a bitch, damn dog eaters," said Jesse. "I guess I was startin' ta like ole Sonny some. I wonder why he run off like that."

"He probly just had to do his necessaries and when he was out there, somethin' caught his scent so he went lookin'," said Sean. "Then Comanche musta stuck an arrow in'm and we never heard nothin'. They had their fire behind a big boulder so we couldn't see it. Their tracks're headed to the northwest now. We'll be headed northeast. Maybe we'll push a little harder and git outta their territory."

"They think their territory is wherever they are at the time," said Jug.

"That's true," said Sean. "We'll just hafta stay alert."

~~~~

Over at the CC, the two Comanche scouts got their hands on one of the cowboys. He was out chasing strays when they grabbed him. The cowboy was scared shitless. The two Comanche never said a word when they grabbed him. They took his weapons and tied him to his own horse. They rode a couple of miles away from the ranch's border and then dismounted. The cowboy was surprised when the two Comanche finally spoke. One of them spoke perfect American. As the Cowboy lay tied on the ground, the brave who spoke American started asking him questions. Was O'Rourke at the ranch? If he wasn't there, when did he leave? Where did he go? The cowboy was scared. He told them that O'Rourke had been at the ranch and he had gone to San Antonio and was traveling with a big colored man and a big white man.

They also had a dog. After the information was given, the brave took a hatchet and split the cowboy's skull open. They left him there and took his horse and weapons and went to tell Mad Buffalo the news.

When the cowboy didn't return from the day's work. A search was made but there wasn't much daylight left. They found nothing that evening. Late the next day, one of the men saw some buzzards circling. He checked it out and found the man's body. He saw the unshod pony tracks and knew that it had been Comanche. He slung the body over his horse and headed back to the ranch.

The man had no kin that any of them knew of, so Clancy had a small service and the man was buried. Clancy kept his crew close for a couple of days. When the men did go out three days later, they worked in two's or three's. For the next week, no unshod pony tracks were seen and no men were injured on the CC.

~~~~

The scouts who had grabbed the cowboy at the CC ranch took their news back to Mad Buffalo. Mad Buffalo figured that if O'Rourke had been at the CC and gone to San Antonio, chances are, he would head back the same way. He was right. The scouts who had headed toward San Antonio were the Comanche who had eaten Sonny. They quickly got their news back to Mad Buffalo.

Mad Buffalo and ten warriors took off at a fast pace to intercept O'Rourke. They were well supplied and had extra horses. Mad Buffalo figured he would catch O'Rourke two or three days ride northeast of the CC ranch. Mad Buffalo knew a good place where he could ambush O'Rourke. It was a place where his people had camped many times before the Army began regular patrols in the area. There was a grove of trees at the base of a small rise and there was a stream that ran through the grove. If O'Rourke headed that way, he would surely camp there for the night. He and his men got on the northeast side of the rise and waited.

They didn't have a long wait. That same day, they could see three riders approaching from the southwest. There was a big white man, a big colored man, a dog, and one other white man. Mad Buffalo knew that this was O'Rourke. He and his men would stay back and let them camp for the night. They would kill them all in the morning at first light.

Sean and the boys set up camp in the grove just like Mad Buffalo had expected. Sean had Jug and Jesse set up camp while he did a little scouting. Sean knew that this was a good spot because of the trees and stream, but someone could be right on the other side of the rise. Sean swung way out to the west looking for sign. He found fresh unshod pony tracks heading northeast. Sean figured there were ten or eleven riders and ten more horses. He headed back to camp the same way he had left. Jug and Jesse were anxiously waiting on Sean. "Well, is there anything out there?" asked Jug as Sean dismounted.

"We got company just on the other side of that rise," said Sean. "There's ten'r eleven of'em and they got extra horses. We wouldn't stand a chance if we tried to outrun'em."

"Comanche, huh," said Jesse.

"Yep, Comanche," said Sean. "Probly be in our laps at daylight."

"Any chance we could slip up on that rise and pick off a few of'em first?" asked Jug.

"Too much open ground," said Sean. "We're better off in these trees. Let's git a fire goin' and cook some coffee and supper. They know we're here anyway."

As they were eating their meal, Sean tried to think of a plan that wouldn't get all of them killed in the morning. He was sure that the Comanche had not spotted him when he was out scouting so they were probably figuring that O'Rourke didn't know they were there. Their attack in the morning would be a complete surprise, or so they would think.

After their meal, they took the horses to the stream for a drink. Then they made a rope corral for the horses. The horses were also hobbled and tied in the corral. Sean sat the men down and told them his plan. "Boys, we'll stand two hour watches. I want that fire blazing all night long," started Sean. "We'll set up our bedrolls by the fire but we won't be in them at daylight. We'll be back some, mebbe fifty, sixty feet. The man on watch'll make sure that the fire keeps goin' and that he can be seen by the Comanche who's watchin' us. They will have someone watchin' us. About an hour before daylight, I'll wake everyone up. I got a jacket and an old hat. We'll get some branches and some brush and stuff 'em in the jacket and make it look like whoever's on watch at daylight fell asleep by the fire. Don't know if they'll come chargin' in on horseback or slip in on foot, but they'll be here. Let 'm git close and kill as many of 'em as quick as you can. We're outnumbered more 'n three to one. Anybody got a better idea or anything ta say?" Jug and Jesse shook their heads no. "Well I'll take first watch. Jesse, you're next and then you Jug. That way I'll be back on watch before daylight."

Sean wasn't worried that the Comanche would try and steal their horses that night. Ten or eleven braves wouldn't be out there stealing horses. This was a war party. They figured they could kill everyone and take everything. Sean's first watch was uneventful. Jeb got some sleep on Sean's watch. Nothing happened on Jesse or Jug's watch. Sean's second watch was uneventful too. An hour before daylight, he woke the men. They stuffed the jacket and propped it up by the fire. They put the hat on it. From a distance, it could look like a man sitting by the fire. Sean placed the men on line all facing the same direction so they wouldn't accidentally shoot each other. They were about twenty five yards apart. Jeb was at Sean's side. They hunkered down and waited.

Right at daylight, some birds started singing. Sean knew they weren't birds. Two birds kept singing and they were getting closer to each other. The Comanche were coming in on foot from two sides. Jeb knew something was up and started a low growl. Sean whispered in his ear to stay quiet. They could see the Comanche now. They were quietly darting from tree to tree as they closed in on the camp. Three or four of the Comanche were armed with bows and arrows, but all of the others were armed with Henrys or single shot carbines.

The Comanche were concentrating on the camp so hard that they hadn't spotted Sean and his men. Sean and the boys weren't fifty feet from the Comanche. One of the Comanche loosed an arrow. It hit the stuffed jacket and as soon as it did, the Comanche knew they had been fooled. It was too late for them. Sean and the boys opened up. Sean fired his Winchester as fast as he could. Jug worked his Henry hard too. Jesse had his Spencer emptied in no time and pulled a pistol and began firing it. Six of the Comanche went down having been hit multiple times. There was so much smoke from their firing that they couldn't see where the other warriors had gone. It didn't take long to find out. Arrows were coming at them now and some bullets were zipping by them. The Comanche couldn't see any better in the smoke than Sean and his men. Sean told Jeb to stay put. Then he crawled over to Jug and told him to sit tight and wait for the smoke to clear and not to fire unless he had a clear target. Then he crawled to Jesse and told him the same. As he was crawling back to his position, he saw some movement in the brush. He couldn't make out what it was, but he knew by the sound that it was Jeb. A brave had gotten close and Jeb had ahold of him. There's no mistaking the sound of a man getting his throat ripped out. Jeb left the dead brave and went back over to Sean. The blood was dripping from his mouth. Sean gave Jeb a hug and told him thanks for helping.

There was no wind so the smoke was slow to disperse. Jug thought he saw some movement not far to his front. He had emptied the Henry and had been firing his pistol. He couldn't remember how many times he had fired the pistol so he decided to check it out. It was empty. He had fired so fast that he had lost count. He was loading the pistol, when a warrior stood up and charged him. Jug grabbed up his Henry to use as a club and stayed down. The warrior knew exactly where Jug was and loosed an arrow. It missed. Jug stood up now and started running straight at the warrior. The warrior almost had another arrow ready and was about to draw his bowstring when he was knocked flat to his left side. Sean had his pistol out and had put a bullet into the right side of the warrior's head. Before Sean could yell for Jug to get down, another arrow from somewhere came flying. It struck Jug in his right side. Sean could see the arrow sticking out the back. Jug went down. A warrior on Sean's left was now taking shots at him. Sean tried to spot him but couldn't because of the smoke. He waited and hoped to see a muzzle flash. Another warrior got up and was charging Jug. Jesse saw him and fired his pistol. The warrior went down but got right back up. Jesse cocked his pistol again and squeezed the trigger. Click, his pistol was empty. Jesse didn't even try to reload. He got up and ran straight for the warrior who was running toward Jug. The warrior had a knife out now. He slashed Jesse with it as Jesse tackled him. When he tackled the warrior, it knocked the wind out of him. Before he could get his wind back, Jesse punched him in the throat crushing his windpipe. Then Jesse took his powerful hands and arms and broke the warrior's neck. Sean heard the bones in the brave's neck snap and turned to see what had happened. When he turned to look, an arrow skinned along his back. He could feel the arrowhead against his shoulder blades as it went by. Then it was quiet. Five minutes went by, and then ten. The smoke had finally cleared. Then a voice could be heard.

"You are the one who kills with the long gun and the big pistol." said Mad Buffalo. "You are O'Rourke. I am Mad Buffalo. Let us fight face to face and honorably like men should."

"Why should we fight at all," said Sean. "You go your way and I'll go mine."

"Several years ago you killed my brothers with your long gun," said Mad Buffalo. "There was no honor in the way you killed them."

"If your brothers were with that war party that was coming to attack my village, then your brothers were on their way to slaughter my family," said Sean. "What honor was there in that? I killed them before they killed my family."

"The Comanche and Cheyenne have been raiding each other for years," said Mad Buffalo. "The men who died, died honorably in battle attacking or defending their people. They have never used the long gun to kill. There is no honor in it."

"There is no honor in killing at all," said Sean. "There is only death. If I kill you, there is no honor. You are just dead."

"If I kill you O'Rourke, there will be great honor in it," said Mad Buffalo. "My brothers will be avenged. My people will be avenged."

"Your brothers are dead and you will be too if you don't move on," said Sean. "Now git. You got enough trouble with the Army and Rangers. Does your woman wanna sing the death song?" Mad Buffalo didn't speak. Sean stayed silent.

"You just better kill that son of a bitch," said Jesse. "If you'd fight'm straight up and he got lucky and killed you, he'd go on a rampage killin' all over thinkin' he was invincible or something. I think you best kill'm now."

"I think so too," said Sean. After a few minutes, Mad Buffalo spoke.

"I'm coming out in the open for you to see," said Mad Buffalo. "I have only my bow and quiver. I do not use white man's weapons. If you are an honorable man, you will come out and fight me."

"I told you once. There is no honor in killing, only death," said Sean. Sean took aim with a pistol and put a hole in Mad Buffalo's forehead. Mad Buffalo hit the ground dead. The one warrior who was left, came out of hiding and went over to Mad Buffalo's body. He yelled out something in Spanish. He kept yelling it. Jug heard him and knew what he was saying. He had learned a lot of Spanish from Lolita.

"He's sayin' they'll hunt you down and kill you and your family and their families," said Jug. Sean didn't tell Jug to say anything to the brave. He took aim with a pistol and put a bullet in the brave's brain. No one said a word.

Sean went to work and got the arrow out of Jug. Sean knew just what to do. Jug's wound was just like the one he had gotten from a Comanche arrow years ago. Katie and Blue Swan had fixed him up. Jesse had been slashed across his chest. He needed some stitches. Jesse had a needle and some thread. Sean poured some whiskey over the needle and thread and went to work. Jesse didn't yell once.

Then it was Sean's turn. His back looked like someone had taken a wide bladed knife and cut him across the back at the shoulder blades. He needed some stitches too. Jesse did a fine job. After they had their medical care, they shared some whiskey. No one spoke for a while. Jesse kept looking at some of the dead Comanche. "Are we gonna bury them Injuns?" asked Jesse.

"Them boys came out here ta kill us," said Sean. "They came ta kill us fer somethin' that had nothin' ta do with any of'em. Hell no we're not buryin'em. We'll move camp to another place and then take it easy for a day so Jug can start healin'. Then we'll take Jug home. We're not that far from his ranch. We'll make a travois for Jug. He shouldn't be ridin'."

They broke camp and set off to find another spot. They took all of the firearms from the dead Comanche and just turned their ponies loose. About an hour before dark, they found a spot that Sean thought would be a good place to stay for a day. Jug had a little fever but it was gone the next morning. The boys just laid around and relaxed. Jesse was in charge of the cooking and fed them well. The next morning they got up and headed for Jug's ranch.

When they got on Jug's property, they came upon one of the hands. He was out chasing strays. He galloped over to them. He was startled some when he saw Jug on the travois. "Don't fret about me," said Jug. "I'll be up in a day'r two. Now you ride on in and tell my woman I'm back. Don't you dare tell her I'm laid up some. If ya do, I'll fire yer ass."

"Yes'm," the hand said. Then he took off for the ranch house.

~~~~

When they got to the ranch house, Josh and Wayne were there with Lolita. Lolita came running off the porch as soon as she saw them. She had a good cry going. "You haven't gotten yourself killed, have you?" said Lolita.

"No darlin', I'll be up in no time," said Jug. "These boys been treating me like I was a new baby and couldn't walk yet. This thing I'm on is embarrassin'. I should be on a horse." Lolita opened Jug's shirt and inspected his wounds. Then she looked up at Sean.

"Thank you for taking good care of my man," said Lolita. "Now let's get him inside. I'll give him a bath and then get him to bed. You men could use a bath too. Why don't you go over to the bunkhouse. Josh, tell Cook to heat up some water for them." There was a water trough behind the bunkhouse that the hands used for a tub when they took their monthly bath. Cook had some water ready in no time. Sean let Jessie go first. Sean had another set of clothes with him. They hadn't been washed for a while, but they were cleaner than what he had been wearing. Jesse had another set too.

After they got cleaned up, they went up to the house and talked with Lolita. Jug had taken his bath, but he would not go to bed while there was still daylight. The men did a little drinking while Lolita made them dinner. Lolita made them a fine meal and after it was over, she made an announcement. "You cannot have my man anymore to chase outlaws or whoever," she began. "I am with child now and his place is with me." Jug didn't say a word. He just got up from his chair and went to Lolita. He looked into her eyes and then kissed her.

"That's good news," said Sean. "Jesse's got one on the way and now you. Wouldn't surprise me if Maggie tells me she's pregnant when I get back."

"If she is, are you still going to be a lawman and chase outlaws?" asked Lolita.

"That's somethin' ta think about," said Sean. "Maggie deserves a good quiet life. I been shot way too many times already. So has Michael. I'll be thinkin' hard on this." The boys had a couple of drinks and then bedded down.

Jug surprised Lolita that night. He hadn't slept with his woman for a good while and he was very frisky. She felt the same.

After breakfast the next morning, Sean and Jesse headed for Dallas.

~~~~

When they finally rode into Dallas, Sean had no hopes of getting any good information on the whereabouts of Kid Evans. They rode straight to the Town Marshal's office. A very young looking man was sitting at a desk with his feet propped up on the desk. When he saw Sean's badge, he took his feet off the desk and stood. "I'm actin' Marshal Todd," the young man said. "I bet you're O'Rourke. What can I do for you?"

"I am Federal Marshal O'Rourke and this man is my deputy. His name is Jesse Strong," said Sean. "You can begin by tellin' me everything you know about what happened that day your Marshal got his throat cut."

"I was the one that found'm," Todd started. "So you say this here nigger is your deputy. I never heard a no nigger lawman before."

"You best show some respect'r you won't see much of anything for a long time," said Sean.

"What'r you sayin'?" asked Todd.

"He's sayin' you best watch that mouth a yours or I'll hurt you bad boy," said Jesse.

"You callin' me boy?" said Todd. "That's a big change, huh boy."

"Go ahead Jesse, teach this fool some manners," said Sean. Jesse reached across the desk and grabbed the young man by the front of his shirt. He pulled him over the desk toward him. Todd tried to reach for his pistol. Jesse let go of him with his left hand and knocked the pistol away. With his right hand, he threw Todd into the steel bars of the jail cell that was behind the desk to the right. Todd fell to the floor after his body slammed into the steel bars. He got back up and before he could say a word, Jesse hit him with a tremendous left. Todd went to the floor again. He couldn't get back up this time. Sean found a bucket of water by a stove. He threw the water on Todd. Todd came to spitting water and shaking his head.

"What the hell happened?" asked Todd as if he never knew what had happened to him.

"You just got yer assed kicked fer bein' disrespectful," said Sean. "I reckon now you'll be more respectful when yer addressin' my deputy." Todd never said a word. He just shook his head yes. "Now tell me what went on here that day." Todd really don't know much. He had found the Marshal at his desk with this throat cut. He had apparently been looking at wanted posters. No one in town knew anything. There was some story about a young fella who was in town looking for bounty hunters, but nobody went out and talked to them. "What do you know about them bounty hunters?" asked Sean.

"Well their names is Potts," started Todd. "They're brothers. Names is Chili and Stew. Some names, huh. Anyway, them boys is good at what they do. I hear their Pa was raised by Apaches and he taught them boys how to track and such. Them boys only go after men that got big money on'em and the poster's gotta say dead'r alive. They don't bring in nobody alive. They go out and get a wanted man and live off that money till it's gone. Then they go get another."

"So basically, the Town Marshal was murdered in his own office and nobody's done a damn thing about it," said Sean. "Where's them Potts boys live?"

"They got a place to the north a couple hours," said Todd. "It's not much. Just a shack and some shelters and such. I'd go in easy like. Them boys don't like nobody visitin'em. Might take a shot at ya since they never saw ya before."

"Well, you stay here and make sure that desk don't run off," said Sean. "We'll get us some food and then go see the Potts. Before we go, have you got any telegrams'r word bout any rustlin'r anything goin' on?"

"I got a telegram the other day bout some banks bein' robbed over in western Missouri," said Todd. "Most thinks it's that James Younger gang, but some say it couldn't be them cause they was farther to the east robbin' some bank when one of'em was robbed. Mebbe it's another gang."

"Well you stay here and hold that chair down," said Sean.

~~~~

While they were having their meal, Sean decided that they should head over into Missouri and visit the two banks in western Missouri that were robbed. Sean hoped that maybe someone would remember something about the outlaws, like how tall were they. What type of weapons did they carry? How were they dressed? What color or type horses were they riding? But first, they would go talk to the Potts brothers and see if they knew anything.

The Potts place was deserted when Sean and Jesse arrived. There were no horses or saddles around. Sean looked inside the shack and there was absolutely no food of any kind inside. The bucket by the well was bone dry so it hadn't been used for a while. "I'd say they'd tied up with Kid," said Sean. "Course I could be wrong but somehow I doubt it. I bet he promised'em more money than they'd ever make bounty huntin'. Well let's git back to town and catch the stage over to Missouri. May as well rest our backsides. Give the horses a break too."

They had to spend the night in Dallas because the stage wasn't leaving till the next morning. They got a hotel room for the night. The clerk at the hotel didn't want to give Jesse a room. Jesse was about to reconfigure the clerk's face when acting Marshal Todd walked in. "Go ahead and give this man a room," said Todd.

"But he's a ni-----," Todd cut him off.

"I said give him a room and I meant it," said Todd.

"All right, but I'll hafta burn the sheets off'n the bed after he moves out," said the clerk. "Nobody'll wanna sleep on them sheets after some nigger slept on'em."

"You best shut your face before this fella gets a good mean on and gets ahold a you," said Todd. "He'll hurt ya bad. Now shut up like I said." The clerk never said another word. He handed Sean and Jesse the keys to their rooms. There was no trouble that evening or night. They had breakfast at a café and were on the stage east the next morning.

~~~~

There were two other passengers on the stage with Sean and Jesse. A woman and her young son were headed back to Missouri. They had been farming in Texas for a while and had not had much luck. The woman's husband had taken to drinking and gambling and had gotten himself killed. He accused another man of cheating and the man shot him dead. Witnesses had said that it was a fair fight, but the woman knew better. Her husband never carried a gun in his life. He had been an ambulance driver during the war and was never issued a weapon. She was going back to Missouri to be with her kin.

The young boy seemed amazed by Jesse. He kept staring at him. Finally Jesse spoke. "What's up with you son?" asked Jesse. "Haven't you ever seen a colored man before?"

"Not up close," the boy answered. "Are you that color all over?"

"Well I'm not gonna drop my drawers and show you, but yes I am," said Jesse. "I'm Jesse Strong. Who might you be?" Jesse extended his hand to the boy. The boy shook Jesse's hand.

"I'm Al Snider and this is my Ma," said Al. "Her name is Alice."

"Pleased ta meet the both of you," said Jesse. "This quiet fella here is Federal Marshal Sean O'Rourke. I'm his deputy." Sean shook the boy's hand and tipped his hat to Alice. "Them's our horses tied on the back and that big dog runnin' along with us is ole Jeb." The boy hadn't noticed Jeb. He looked outside and saw him now.

"That's about the biggest dog I ever did see," said Al. "What kinda dog is he?"

"I got no idea," said Sean. "But he's a good cow dog and he loves protectin' my wife'n me'n my men. He's killed several men. Ripped their throats out."

"You didn't need to tell us that Marshal," said Alice.

"Sorry ma'am, didn't mean ta be impolite," said Sean. "It's just that sometimes this can be a tough country and a man's gotta be tough ta survive in it."

"I heard about you and that dog," said Al. "I hear you've killed a lot of men."

"Had to son, they was tryin' ta kill me or my wife or my men," said Sean. "Now I think I'll try and get a little sleep." Sean was asleep in a few minutes. Jesse woke him up at the next stop when they changed horses. An older man and woman worked at the station. He changed the horses while the woman gave them all a meal. She even had something for Jeb. Sean and Jesse ate quickly so they could make sure their horses got watered before they took off again.

They had a couple more horse changes before they got into Missouri. They had only crossed the state line by a mile or so when the stage driver pulled back on the reins and halted the stage. "What's goin' on out there driver?" asked Sean.

"I seen four men on horseback up ahead a ways," started the driver. "Two of'em still on the road and the other two split up. One's on our right and one's on our left. They're just waitin' ta see what we do. They're not wearin' masks."

"Is there anything important on this stage today?" asked Sean.

"There's a strong box," said the driver. "Got no idea what's in it though."

Sean yelled up to the shotgun rider now. "You got anything besides that shotgun?" asked Sean.

"I got my Colt revolver," said the shotgun rider. "What do ya reckon we should do now Marshal?"

"Let's just sit right here and let them come ta us," said Sean. "They'll come on in a little bit when they see we're not runnin'. When they git closer, you point that shotgun right at'em. Looks like they got pistols in their hands and maybe some Winchesters on their saddles. Is that shotgun a yers sawed off any?"

"No it's not," said the shotgun rider. "It'll reach out there purty good."

"Well when they git bout fifty yards from us, you cut loose with that thing," said Sean. "Don't worry bout talkin'r nothin'. Them boys is out there ta rob us. Me'n Jesse'll take care a them two on our sides. Make sure you don't accidently shoot my dog. He's out there somewhere. He knows somethins' up. He's probly makin's sure them fellas don't see'm. Alice, you'n Al best git as low as you can now. There's gonna be some shootin'."

After about five minutes, the four men started moving closer to the stage. All four of them had pistols in their hands. When they were about seventy yards from the stage, one of them spoke. "Throw down that strong box and your wallets and purses and we'll let you move on," he said. They kept easing closer to the stage. When they were about fifty yards from the stage, the shotgun rider cut loose. He fired one barrel and then the other. Both men were thrown out of the saddle. As soon as the rider fired his second barrel, Sean fired at the man on the right while Jesse fired on the man on the left. Both men hit the ground dead. The two men who were hit by the shotgun blasts were not dead, but in a few seconds they would wish that they were. The man who had done the talking was sitting there on the ground trying to get his wits back. He was looking around on the ground trying to find his pistol. His right hand was almost touching the pistol when he saw Jeb coming at him. He got out half of a scream before Jeb tore out his throat. The other man spotted his pistol and took off running for it. He was screaming as he ran. He was almost to his pistol when Jeb jumped on him and knocked him down. The man fell forward screaming. He turned over and tried to fight off Jeb, but it was no use. He got out one more scream before he was killed.

"Jesus, Joseph, and Mary," shouted the driver. "I never in my born days ever seen or even heard about anything like this. If someone else told me, I wouldn't believe'm. Just what kinda dog is that? Them poor outlaws never had no chance. No sir, no chance at all."

"They made their choice," said Sean. "We never asked'em to try'n rob this stage. Now they won't rob no more."

Al had kept low most of the time, but after the shooting had stopped, he stuck his head out the window to see what had happened. He had his head out just as Jeb had gone to work. He watched Jeb kill one outlaw and then the other. He was in total disbelief. "Holy shit Mom," said Al. "That dog's gotta be part wolf'r somethin'. He killed them men like it was nothin'. Holy shit!!!"

"Watch your language Al," said Alice.

"Holy shit is right ma'am," said the shotgun rider. "I can't thinka nothin' better ta say bout this. Holy shit bout covers it."

"What we gonna do with them bodies?" asked the driver.

"We'll round up their horses and tie'em to'em and take'em to the next town," said Sean. "Hope it's not too far. Don't want'em gettin' ripe on us."

"We got one more change a horses and then we'll be in the next town after that," said the driver. Sean and the men rounded up the horses and got the bodies tied to them. Neither the driver or the shotgun rider recognized any of the outlaws. "Well we know fer sure that these fellas is not part a the James Younger gang," said the driver. "Them boy's is over to the east a bit. I hope these boy's is no kin to'em. They might not take kindly ta us killin' their kin."

When the stage took off again, Sean let Jeb ride inside with them. It was apparent that Alice was totally afraid of Jeb, but Al and Jeb made friends right off. "Jeb makes friends easy," said Sean. "Dogs and a lotta other animals can sense when someone is afraid of'em or means ta do'em harm. Alice, you don't need ta be afraid a ole Jeb here. He won't hurt ya. Go ahead and pet'm."

"I don't know," said Alice. "I always been kinda scared of dogs. I seen my brother get bit once when we were kids."

"I bet your brother was doing somethin' the dog didn't like," said Sean. "Well anyway, we got a ways ta go. If we have any more robbers show up, ole Jeb'll protect you cause he knows you and me and Al are all friends now." Jeb had been laying on the floor of the stage. He sat up now and laid his head on Alice's lap. He looked into her eyes and Alice couldn't resist. She petted him and petted him some more. Then she thanked him for helping with the outlaws.

The next town was Huntsville. This was one of the towns where the bank had been robbed. When they arrived, Sean and Jesse said their goodbyes to Alice and Al and then went straight to the local lawman's office. He was a middle aged man and looked like he was well fed. He had been sitting outside of his office whittling on a piece of wood when Sean and Jesse showed up with the four dead men. "I see your badge Mr. Who are you?" asked the lawman.

"I'm O'Rourke and this is my deputy," said Sean. "Who and what're you?"

"I'm the County Sheriff. Name's Warden, Jess Warden," said Jess. "Who're these fellas?"

"These boys tried to rob the stage a ways back," said Sean. "They weren't very good at it."

"What the hell happened ta them two?" asked Jess. "Somethin' tore their throats out." Then Jess saw Jeb. Jeb gave him a low growl. "I reckon I can figure what happened ta them two now. Would ya tell that dog ta stop that growl."

"He don't like you," said Sean. "Be a little nicer soundin' and Jeb'll leave ya alone."

"Hey Jeb, good boy Jeb. Come here boy," said Jess. Jess knelt down and Jeb went over to him. He let Jess pet him once and then he backed away.

"He's just made his mind up that he don't like ya, but he won't hurt ya now unless I tell'm," said Sean. "Now do you recognize any a these fellas?" Jess went over and lifted up the heads of the dead men.

"Never seen these boys before," said Jess. "I spose you want'em buried."

"You do with 'em what you want," said Sean. "Now I wanna know everything about that bank robbery that happened here a while back."

"I'll take ya over to the bank," said Jess. "The teller and the bank manager was both there durin' the robbery."

"I heard you never formed a posse and went after'em," said Sean.

"Hell no I didn't," said Jess. "It was probly that James Younger gang and I weren't gonna git my head shot off. I couldn't get anyone ta go with me."

"Yer a brave man Sheriff. I spect you'll make it ta old age if ya don't die of over eatin' or somethin' first," said Sean. "Now take me to the bank."

"Ya got no call ta talk ta me that way. I don't give a damn who you are," said Jess.

"Jess, just shut up and give me directions to the bank," said Sean. "You just stay here and finish yer whittlin'." Jess pointed the direction of the bank and sat back down. He was mumbling to himself as Sean and Jesse went to the bank.

When they entered the bank, there was a teller on duty and they could see a man in a back office. "I'm Federal Marshal O'Rourke and this is my deputy," announced Sean. "We want to talk with whoever was here during the robbery."

"That'd be me Marshal," said the teller. "Name's Steve Long. I was here."

"And so was I," said the man from the back office. He made his way to the front of the bank.

"Well what can you fellas tell us about it?" asked Sean.

"They came in and pointed guns at us and demanded the money," said the teller. "We gave it to'em and they left."

"Well how many of'em was there?" asked Sean. "Could you identify any of them if you saw them again. What kind a horses was they ridin'? How was they dressed?"

"Well there was four of'em that came into the bank," said the teller. "They had masks on. I think there was four more outside with the horses but I couldn't see their faces. I would say that one of them was a real young fella. He was the one doin' most of the talkin'." Sean pulled out his picture of Kid.

"Could this have been him?" asked Sean. "I know you say he had on a mask, but try to imagine what he might look like without it." The teller looked hard at the picture.

"That sure could've been him," said the teller. "He was wearin' them big spurs like a lotta Texas boys do. This fella in this picture is wearin' some spurs. I noticed his saddle too when he was ridin' away. It had a high cantle on it like the cowboys like for ropin' and such. He was ridin' a big gray geldin'. Another one of'em was ridin' a big buckskin. He had a long gun in a scabbard tied to his saddle. Probly a Sharps. One of'em was wearin' an old reb cavalry hat. It had holes in it. Coulda been bullet holes. Now the four what came inside had Colt pistols. Couldn't tell ya bout them others outside. Oh, two of'em was ridin' bays and another one was a paint but the paint wasn't real colorful like some of'em are. From what I could see, they all had dark hair but one. He had yellow hair."

"You got anything to ad?" Sean asked the bank manager.

"Not really," he answered. "Was it the James Younger gang?"

"No it wasn't," said Sean.

"Well who was that fella in the picture?" asked the manager.

"That fella is Bart Evans, commonly known as Kid," said Sean. "This is probly his gang. He was wanted for several murders before he got into the banking business. If I was you, I'd get myself a different Sheriff next election. The one you got's just puttin' in time and gettin' paid fer doin' nothing."

"You're talking about my brother-in-law," said the manager.

"I don't care who he is," said Sean. "He's worthless as a lawman. Keep him around and you're just askin' fer your bank ta git robbed again." Sean didn't wait for a reply from the manager. He and Jesse just walked out. They went to a general store and got some more supplies and headed north to the next town that had the bank robbery. The town was Hillton and it was an easy two days ride. When they got to the bank, none of the employees could tell them about the robbery. They were new employees. There were only two of them. The original two were the ones killed during the robbery. Sean and Jesse went to the Sheriff's office. No one was inside the office, so they found a saloon close by and went in for a drink. They sat at a table and waited for the bartender to ask what they wanted. Jeb sat beside Sean. He started a low growl.

"Calm down Jeb," said Sean. "I don't see nobody in here who'll give us any trouble. Bartender, you best bring us some whiskey before it gets ugly in here."

"I won't be servin' the likes a him," said the bartender.

"Why are all you asshole bartenders like that?" said Sean. Sean got up from his chair and walked over to the bar. He stood right in front of the bartender. "Now you will give us some whiskey right now or we'll be gittin' it ourselves cause you won't be able to. Now I'm Federal Marshal O'Rourke and this is my deputy."

"I don't give a good God damn who the hell you are," yelled the bartender. "I won't serve the likes a him."

Sean didn't say a word. He just reached up and grabbed the bartender by his hair and slammed his face into the bar. Blood went flying. "Now we'll have that whiskey now," said Sean. The bartender wiped the blood from his face with the apron he was wearing. He kept looking down at something. "Don't even think bout goin' for that shotgun you got back there," said Sean. "I will shoot you dead." The bartender made a move. Before he even got close to the shotgun, Sean had a pistol out. The hammer was cocked and the muzzle was against the side of the bartenders head. "I never miss at this range," said Sean. "A little whiskey's not worth dyin' over, is it?"

"I reckon not," said the bartender. He pulled his hands back and started to stand up straight. Just then, the County Sheriff walked in.

"What the hell's goin' on in here?" the Sheriff yelled. "And who the hell're you and why is this nigger in here?"

"Wrong thing ta say Sheriff," said Sean. "He's all yours Jesse. Don't kill'm. We gotta ask him some questions."

Jesse got up from his chair and ran straight at the Sheriff. The Sheriff was a big man, but he was no match for Jesse. He was fumbling with his holster trying to draw his pistol when Jesse ran into him like a grizzly bear. "Time you learned bout respect," yelled Jesse as he started beating on the Sheriff. Jesse toyed with the Sheriff some. Jesse'd give a good shot to his jaw and knock him down. Then he'd let him get back up and take a swing at him. He'd either miss or Jesse would block it. This went on for about five minutes. Sean had been watching the fight but he hadn't forgotten the bartender. Jeb was watching him. Finally, Sean reminded Jesse that they needed to ask the Sheriff some questions and not to beat him to death. Jesse put a good right to the Sheriff's chin and then quit. The Sheriff went down hard and was out cold. They let him lay there for a bit. The bartender gave them their whiskey and they drank while the Sheriff was out. They had one more drink and then Sean found some water and threw it on the Sheriff.

The Sheriff wasn't very happy when he came to. "Just who in the hell are you Mister?" asked the Sheriff.

"Name's O'Rourke, Federal Marshal Sean O'Rourke, and this man is Jesse Strong, my deputy," said Sean.

"He is strong. I'll give'm that," said the Sheriff. "But we don't want none a these people in this town. They bring trouble with 'em."

"Seems ta me that you fellas're the ones causing the trouble," said Sean. "Now enough a that stuff. I wanna know all about your bank robbery and see if anybody remembers anything or might recognize one a the outlaws."

"All I can tell ya is this. I was in my office when I heard the shots," said the Sheriff. I ran out into the street and I heard someone shout that the bank's been robbed. I pulled my pistol and started over toward the bank. I seen seven'r eight men ridin' hard outta town away from me. Some of'em was wearin' masks and some weren't. I fired a few shots at'em, but I don't guess I hit any of'em. A deputy a mine was down the street some. He seen me firin' at them fellas so he fired a couple shots too. I couldn't see no faces cause they was ridin' away."

"What kind a horses was they ridin'?" asked Sean.

"One was on a big gray and there was a big buckskin," said the Sheriff. "One was on a paint but it wasn't all colored up like some of'em are. One of'em had on a reb cavalry hat. That's about all I can remember."

"Did you get up a posse and go after'em?" asked Sean.

"I did," answered the Sheriff. "We tracked'em to the county line and then headed back to town."

"So why did you quit at the county line?" asked Sean.

"Cause that's where my jurisdiction ends," answered the Sheriff. "When we got back here, I sent telegrams out to all the closest towns and told them ta be on the lookout fer that bunch. Never heard nothin' back. I spect they slipped inta "The Nations.""

"They probably did," said Sean. "But they won't stay there long. That fella that's runnin' that outfit likes killin' too much to stay there too long. Them boys a his'll be itching ta spend all that money they got. No whores'r bars in "The Nations." Them boys'll be headed where the big money is."

"And where might that be?" asked the Sheriff.

"Abilene," answered Sean. "With the railhead there and all the Texas herds comin' up, there'll be lotsa money ta be had in Abilene. Jesse, you'n me best get up there as fast as we can. I gotta get to the telegraph office and send a telegram ta Maggie." Sean went to the telegraph office and sent the following to Maggie:

Maggie O'Rourke
Abilene Kansas

Maggie<<stop>>am in Hillton Missouri<<stop>>will be back as soon as possible<<stop>>believe Kid

Evans gang headed for Abilene<<stop>>Michael can
identify Kid<<stop>>eight in gang<<stop>>one rides
big gray gelding<<stop>>one rides big buckskin
<<stop>>one rides paint<<stop>>one wears reb
cavalry hat with bullet holes in it<<stop>>be careful

Much love
Sean

CHAPTER NINE

Things had been noisy and there had been plenty of fights in Abilene, but no one had been shot for a while. Thomas Lonnigan got his herd to Abilene and got it sold. He waited for two more weeks after his herd was sold hoping his stolen cows would show up with another herd. He couldn't wait any longer. He needed to get back to his ranch and get started on another herd. Two days later his cows did show up with another herd. The buyers were told that cows with the T/M brand had been stolen and not to buy them. The buyers didn't care what brand was on the cattle. They needed cattle so they bought them. Besides, O'Rourke was off chasing outlaws and would be back who knew when. Bill Thompson was making a huge fortune in Abilene. Besides buying cattle, he owned several hotels and saloons now. He knew those T/M cows had been stolen, but what could he do. There was no law in Abilene. If he hadn't bought the cows, another buyer would have. A couple of days went by and Bill was feeling guilty. He found the ramrod from the Texas herd who had brought in the stolen cows and asked how much he had paid for them and where he had gotten them. The ramrod told him exactly what he paid for the cows. Bill sent a telegram to the nearest town where the Lonnigans lived and told him that he would send him a bank draft for the stolen cows. The draft wouldn't be for the buyer's price, but it would be $15 a head which is what was paid to the rustlers for the stolen cows. The draft would be for $7500. Bill felt guilty, but not guilty enough to pay Lonnigan full price.

~~~~

Maggie's morning sickness had eased up some, but she was still having it at least every other day. She was in her room taking it easy when the telegram from Sean arrived. She read it and then she had a good cry. She was so glad to hear from Sean, but the thought of another outlaw gang coming really upset her. She herself had already killed several men. She didn't want to kill any more. She hoped that Sean would be back soon.

Maggie regained her composure and went downstairs. It was still early in the day so the place wasn't busy at all. Michael was at his piano trying out some new songs. Maggie went to him.

"Michael, Sean believes that the young man who shot you and Betty has a gang now and he's headed for Abilene," started Maggie. "He said you'd be able to recognize him. Sean and I were in St. Louis. I have no idea what he might look like."

"I'll recognize that little son of a bitch," said Michael. "He'll be dead when I do. What else did Sean say?"

"Well he said there were eight men in the gang," said Maggie. "One rides a big gray gelding. Another one rides a big buckskin and another rides a paint. One of them wears a reb cavalry hat with bullet holes in it."

"Well we'll put out the word for everyone to be on the lookout for them horses and such," said Michael. "I doubt they'd all come in town together, but you never know. Maybe they know Sean's not here. There's a lotta money in this town now."

After Maggie talked with Michael, she went to Doug and had him round up all the employees. She sat them down and told them what Sean had told her. Then Maggie went around to all of the stores and the bank and told them what Sean had said and what to watch for. Everyone said they would be on the lookout. Paint horses were fairly common among some of the cowboys, but not too many big grays or buckskins were seen regularly. Old reb cavalry hats were seen regularly, but not usually with bullet holes in them. And who knows, maybe some cowboy or maybe a bounty hunter might be out there and recognize Kid.

~~~~

Kid knew it would be foolish to go to Abilene, but that's where the big money was and he wanted it. His men were getting restless in "The Nations" and they wanted to spend some of the money they had stolen and then steal some more. Kid knew that O'Rourke wasn't there. He was out chasing after him and was most likely still down in Texas. There was also something else in Abilene that Kid wanted and he wanted it above everything else. He had to kill the big man who almost broke his jaw. He'd also heard about the redheaded beauty who was O'Rourke's wife. He never saw her when he was in Abilene with the herd, but he did see her painting. He was going to go to Abilene and take her. He was going to rape her and then give her to his men. When they were done with her, he was going to cut her into little pieces and feed her to the coyotes. When O'Rourke came after her, he'd kill him too.

In the first town in Kansas that Kid's gang came to, he made all of his men get different horses. Some of them whined a bit, but after Kid explained to them that they had already used the same horses on a couple of bank jobs, they understood his reasoning. He had the men get some new clothes and hats too. Slim was the one who always wore the reb cavalry hat with the holes in it. He got a new hat, but he kept his reb hat. He'd wear it when Kid wasn't around.

~~~~

When they got to Abilene, Kid sent his men in two at a time. Kid went in last. He had his men get rooms in the same hotel. He was going to let them drink and whore for a couple of days and then they'd go to work. He also told them to stay out of trouble. Sol was given an extra warning. Kid told him that if he caused any kind of trouble at all, he would kill him. Sol gave Kid a nasty look, but didn't say a word. Kid would spend most of his time just mingling with people and finding out things. It only took him a couple of hours to find out who all the cattle buyers were. He also found out that Bill Thompson was the biggest cattle buyer, plus he owned several hotels and saloons in town. They wouldn't have to rob the bank. Thompson probably had as much or more money than the bank. Kid learned what he looked like and followed him around for a day and learned some of his habits. He also found out that Thompson lived in a suite in his biggest hotel. Kid started figuring out his plan.

The morning of the third day in Abilene, Kid rounded up his boys and gave them their assignments. Lukey, Slim, and Sol would rush into Maggie's Place at ten o'clock and grab the red-head. Things were always slow that time of day at the saloon. Most of the girls were always sitting around drinking coffee. The big man would probably be playing his piano. Barney and Clyde would be outside waiting and when the big man would get up and go after the redhead, they would shoot him. The Potts brothers would be with Kid. They would be in Thompson's hotel room. Bill Thompson always had his big breakfast delivered to his room every day at ten o'clock. Every-thing would happen right at ten o'clock. They would all meet a couple miles east of town at a small tree grove they had passed on the way to town.

About nine thirty, Kid had everyone ready to go. Kid and the Potts boys were sitting in the hotel lobby acting like they were reading newspapers. At just before ten, Kid saw a man carrying a tray of food up the stairs. He and the Potts followed him. Thompson's room was on the third floor. Kid and the boys stopped on the stairs just below the third floor. They heard the knock on the door and then Bill Thompson greet the server. The food was delivered and the server went back downstairs. He said hello to Kid and the Potts as he passed them. Kid and the boys went onto the third floor and looked down the hall. There was a big man standing outside the door of Thompson's suite. He was armed. The big man saw Kid and the others now. "This is a private area boys," he said. "Go back down where you came from." Kid thought for moment.

"Bill Thompson told me to meet him in his room at ten," said Kid. "He's buying our herd."

"That's a damn lie. Bill don't do no business up here, now move on," said the big man. The big man started reaching for a pistol. Kid pulled his faster and put a slug into the big man's chest. He hit the floor dead. Bill came running out of his room to see what had happened.

"Who the hell'r you. You just killed my bodyguard. I'll see you hang," said Bill.

"Shut the hell up and get back in your room," said Kid. "Chili, don't let nobody come up them stairs. Stew, drag that body into the room so it can't be seen. " Bill went into his room with Kid following him. "Now Mr. Thompson, where's all that cash a yours? Believe I'll take a quick look around." There was a medium sized safe in a closet. It was half open. Kid looked inside it. "Holy smokes, there must be over $50,000 in there," said Kid. "Find somethin' ta put it in Stew." Stew grabbed a pillow off the bed and took off the pillow case. He stuffed the money into the pillow case. "Now is there any more a this stuff around?" asked Kid. Just then someone came up the stairs, but stopped before getting to the third floor.

"What was that shot about?" yelled the person.

"Accidental discharge," said Chili. "Just dropped my pistol and it went off, sorry."

"All right, so nobody's hurt," said the person.

"Nope, nobody's hurt," said Chili. The person went back downstairs unconcerned.

"There's no more money," said Bill. "You got it all."

"We'll see about that," said Kid. Kid reached down with his left hand and pulled out the knife he always wore. He walked over to Bill and shoved the long blade into his gut and then upward. He twisted the blade a few times and then pulled it out. Blood went flying all over, but Kid was careful and didn't get much of it on himself. Bill fell to the floor dead. Kid went through his pockets and found another $500.

"Jesus Keyrist, was that necessary?" said Chili.

"Course it was," said Kid. "Dead men can't talk." The three of them left the room and walked out of the hotel as if nothing had happened. Nobody even noticed the big bag that Chili was carrying. The three of them mounted their horses and headed for the meeting place.

Back over at Maggie's Place, things weren't going exactly as planned either. At ten, Lukey, Slim, and Sol walked into the saloon. Kathleen was sitting at a table not far from the door. Before anyone in the saloon even noticed their presence, Lukey took his pistol and cracked Kathleen on the head. Then Slim threw her over his shoulder and they headed for the door. Simon was with Sara at a table not far away. As soon as he saw the man hit the redhead, he pulled a pistol and started shooting. Lukey was hit and went down. Sol pulled a pistol and fired at Simon. Simon was hit in the left shoulder and went down. The bullet passed through and shattered a beer glass that was sitting on the bar. Michael had a pistol out now and took careful aim. He fired and Slim went down. When Slim went down, Sol grabbed up the redhead and ran out the door. Michael went to the door as fast as he could. Doug was there now with his pistol in hand. As they got to the door, they were met by a hail of bullets from Barney and Clyde. They ducked down. Doug went to a window and looked out. Three men were riding away. One of them had Kathleen across his lap as he rode away. Maggie had been up in her room and came running down the stairs. More shots were fired from upstairs in the saloon. Jim had been upstairs with Sally and saw the men riding away after the shots were fired.

He fired two shots and then quit when he saw that Kathleen was laying across the lap of one of the riders.

"Someone go get the Doc," yelled Sara. "Simon's been shot." Tom was behind the bar and took off running for the Doc. Michael went over to the two other men who had been shot and checked them out.

"This one's dead and this other one will be in a few days," said Michael. "He's gut shot."

Doc had heard the shooting and was already on his way to the saloon. As he entered the saloon, he took a quick look at the men lying on the floor and then went to Simon. "You're lucky young fella," said Doc. "Went clean through. I'll have you cleaned and bandaged in no time. One a you put somethin' on that hole in that gut shot fella and try ta slow down the bleedin'." Doug pulled off his apron and held it on the man's wound.

Doc finished with Simon and started on the gut shot man. The man was conscious as Doc worked on him. "I don't know who you are mister, but I got some bad news for you," said Doc. "There's not much I can do for you. That bullet tore up some a your liver and some other vitals. All I can do is try to make you comfortable as you're dyin'."

"How long I got Doc?" asked the man.

"You could die in a few minutes or you might make it two'r three days," said Doc. "If you're a religious man, which I doubt, you should go ahead and make peace with whatever God you worship."

"That's funny Doc. Me makin' peace with God," said the man. "How bout some whiskey. Might as well die happy."

"Go ahead and give him some whiskey," said Michael. "I believe I'll join him for a drink." Maggie went to the bar and returned with a bottle and a couple of glasses. Michael filled the two glasses. They moved the man over to the wall so he could sit up and drink. As they dragged him over to the wall, a reb hat fell out of his pocket. It had bullet holes in it. Michael remembered Sean's telegram. "You must work for Kid Evans," said Michael. "You got a name?"

"They call me Slim and I'm in Kid's gang," said Slim. Then Slim took a drink of whiskey. "Holy shit that burns," cried Slim. "But it's still good."

"I told you that some a your vitals been shot up," said Doc. "Course that stuff's gonna burn."

"So why did you fellas take the woman?" asked Michael.

"Kid wanted us ta grab O'Rourke's woman and we was sposed ta shoot a big fella," said Slim. "I bet the big fella was you."

"I reckon I was the man Kid wanted you ta kill," said Michael. "So why did them fellas take Kathleen?"

"Who the hell is Kathleen?" said Slim. "We was told O'Rourke's woman was a good lookin' redhead so we grabbed the good lookin' redhead. Didn't know her name."

"Slim, I'd like for you to meet Mrs. Sean O'Rourke," said Michael. Maggie walked over so Slim could get a good look at her.

"Oh shit, they got the wrong woman," said Slim. "I wonder if Kid knows it now."

"I doubt it," said Maggie. "I wasn't anywhere near Kid when he was in town. He never knew there were two redheads here. He probably just saw that painting. Kathleen and I look enough alike that we could pass for sisters. What were his plans after I was taken?"

"I don't spose I oughta be tellin' you all this stuff, but hell, I'm dying anyway," said Slim. "We was all gonna meet a couple a miles east a town at a small grove a trees. Oh, you might wanna check around town. Kid was lookin' ta rob that cattle buyer Bill Thompson. That Thompson fella's probly kilt. That Kid sure likes killin'."

"Someone get over to Bill's hotel suite and check it out," said Michael. Tom went.

"So what else have you boys been up to since you fell in with Kid?" asked Michael.

"Oh, we rustled some cows and then robbed us some banks in Missouri," said Slim. "I reckon them fools over there thought it was that James Younger gang what done the robbin' and killin'."

"So there was some killin' too?" asked Michael.

"Yep, Kid shot a couple people at that second bank we robbed," said Slim. "Shot'em dead. I guess they was too slow at doin' what Kid told'em ta do. Fill my glass again would you please?" Michael refilled Slim's glass.

"So you know how ta say please," said Michael. "I'll bet you haven't used that word too much lately."

"No I haven't," said Slim. "When I was a little shit, my Momma always made us say please and thank you and such. If we didn't my Pa'd beat the hell out of us. He beat me once too often and one day when he come home drunk I kilt'm. I stuck him with a pitchfork. Thought fer sure they'd hang me even though I was a kid, but Momma told the law that he was drunk and fell on the pitchfork. They believed her. I found out my Pa wasn't very well liked. My Momma was glad he was gone. I left home a year later when I was only 14. My Momma married the County Sheriff a year later."

"So what did you do to survive when you left home?" asked Michael.

"I learned how to steal," answered Slim. "Got purty good at it too." Slim emptied his glass and asked for a refill. Michael obliged him. Slim took one more sip. As the glass was on his lips, he took a look up at Maggie and smiled. He nodded his head a little. His hand holding the glass slipped down to his side. The remaining whiskey spilled onto his chest as the glass came out of his hand and rolled onto the floor. His eyes were open and he was still looking up at Maggie, but he was dead. Doc reached down and closed his eyelids.

"Well, I guess I'm done here," said Doc. "Simon, I'll see you again in a few days."

Before Doc got to the door, Tom was back. "Bill Thompson's dead," said Tom. "So's that fella that was his bodyguard. Bill was stabbed and the other fella was shot. They don't need you Doc."

"I'll be on my way then," said Doc.

"I always heard that Bill had a safe in his suite," said Maggie. "Did you see the safe while you were there?"

"I did," answered Tom. "It was open and it was empty."

"I'd say Kid's got a lot of money on him now," said Michael. "Hard to guess what he'll do next or where he'll go. I wish Sean was here."

"So do I," said Maggie. "I hate to think about what they're doing to Kathleen now."

"Kathleen's a smart woman," said Michael. "She'll figure out a way to stay alive. I'll bet she'll even kill some a them boys herself."

"If they don't kill her first," replied Maggie.

"I don't think they'll kill her right off," said Michael. "They think she's you. I'm guessing that they'll keep her alive so Sean will come after them hard and fast and get careless. When he does, they'll try ta kill him and then they'll kill her."

"In the meantime they'll use her bad," said Maggie.

"Have some faith Maggie darlin'," said Michael. "Kathleen'll be all right. I just know she will."

It wasn't long and the undertaker's men had the bodies removed from the saloon. Michael had gone through their pockets and removed their valuables. Slim had $50 on him and a watch and Lukey had $100. After the outlaw's horses, saddles, and guns were sold, Michael made a deposit into the "Burying Fund."

Maggie decided to close the saloon for the rest of the day. She, Michael, and Jim sat around drinking coffee trying to think of something they could do. "I think I should round up some men and go after them fellas," said Jim. "I'm not afraid of them."

"We know you're not afraid," said Michael. "But you're not a tracker and neither is anyone here. We don't know for sure how many of them there are. Sean'll be back shortly. He'll get them fellas and he'll get Kathleen back too. Sean can move like a cat and he can sneak up on a Comanche war party. Them fellas won't know what hit'em when Sean catches up to'em. Kathleen's a smart woman. She'll keep herself alive."

"I'm hoping Sean will be back late this afternoon," said Maggie. "His telegram was from some little town in Missouri. I'll go over to the train station and check the train schedules. Let's hope he's on his way." Maggie left the saloon and went to the train station. She read the schedule that was on the side of the building and then went to the telegrapher. "Is the train that originated from Hillton on schedule?" asked Maggie. "Sean is on that train and I must know if it's on time."

"Mrs. O'Rourke, the train left on schedule," said the telegrapher. "They will have to stop and take on water one time, but they should be here around 4:30pm. If I hear of any problems, I will get word to you immediately. I heard about what happened at your place. Damn shame. What's wrong with people these days?"

"Some people just enjoy hurting or killing people," said Maggie. "I don't understand it. I never will. Well, I must get back now. Thank you for your kindness. I'll be here around 4:30 waiting on the train." The telegrapher nodded his head and Maggie left.

~~~~

"Sean's train should be here around 4:30," announced Maggie when she entered the saloon. "The rest of you can go home and relax for the day. I'll see you all tomorrow."

"Betty and me will be waiting at the train station too," said Michael. "In the meantime, I believe I'll stick around. We don't want some rowdy cowboys doing something foolish because our place is closed for the day."

"I supposed that might be possible," said Maggie. "I guess we do have the best looking girls in town. Maybe I shouldn't have closed for the day."

"It'll be all right Maggie darlin'," said Michael. "I think all of us could stand the time off. Now why don't you go up to your room and rest. I'll set out front and make sure people know we're closed for the day."

Maggie took Michael's advice and went to her room. She thought she was too upset to go to sleep, but she was asleep in no time. The next thing she knew, Betty was knocking on her door waking her up. "Maggie, it's getting close to 4:30," said Betty. "We'll be downstairs waiting on you. Are you awake?"

"I'm awake. I'll be down in a few minutes," said Maggie. Maggie got up from the bed and looked in the mirror. She dressed and then combed her hair. She looked hard at her belly. "Sean'll know I'm pregnant," she said to herself. "I know he will." Then she went downstairs. Michael, Betty, and Jim were waiting on her.

"Jim here will watch the place while we're gone," said Michael. "Are we ready?"

"Let's go," said Maggie. "I do hope it's on time."

~~~~

They weren't at the station for more than five minutes when the train pulled in. Sean had been sitting next to the window and he saw Maggie and the rest of them waiting for him. He got up from his seat and ran to the door. He was off the train before it came to a complete stop. He ran to Maggie and they locked themselves together. They hugged and kissed till they were almost out of breath. "I have missed you terribly Maggie darlin'," said Sean. "And before you say a word, I can tell that you are with child. You look so beautiful." They grabbed each other and stayed locked together for a good while longer. Finally, they pulled apart. Jeb was there now and sat patiently waiting on a hug from Maggie. Maggie bent down and hugged Jeb and gave him a kiss on the head. He let out a small howl. Maggie stood back up but kept her hand on Jeb.

"We have some terrible news for you Sean," said Maggie. "Let's get home and we'll tell you all about it." Jesse was off the train now. He gave Maggie and Betty a hug and shook Michael's hand.

"You go on now," said Jesse. "I'll take care a the horses and everything. I'll see you at the saloon after I get the horses settled. All of them headed to the saloon while Jesse took care of the horses.

Not a word was spoken by any of them until they got to the saloon. Jim was sitting our front. He stood and shook Sean's hand. "Glad you're back," said Jim. "We had some bad trouble." Jim stayed outside. The rest of them went inside and sat at their regular table. Betty got them a bottle and some glasses. She filled all of the glasses.

Maggie was the first to speak. "I will take one sip of this glass and then I shall not drink until after our son is born," said Maggie.

"So you're sure it's a boy," said Sean. "How can you be sure."

"Because you're the father," said Maggie. "What else could it be but a boy?" Sean smiled but didn't say a word. Maggie took a sip from the glass. The she let a few tears come. "Kathleen has been taken," started Maggie. "There were five of them. Three of them came inside in the morning and two were waiting outside. Before we even noticed that they were here, one of them took a pistol and cracked Kathleen on the head. He picked her up and threw her over his shoulder and started to leave. Simon saw what had happened and shot one of them. One of them shot Simon. Then Michael shot the one carrying Kathleen. The other one picked up Kathleen and ran out the door. When Michael and Doug ran to the door after them, the ones outside opened up on them. Jim was upstairs and when he saw what was happening, he fired a couple of shots at them as they were riding away. He quit firing when he saw Kathleen lying across one of them's lap."

"Why was Kathleen here?" asked Sean. "We just saw her in St. Louis."

"Oh, I guess I never told you," said Maggie. "We were so busy. I sent a telegram to Susie and Dan and asked if they could spare any extra help. They sent me Kathleen, Sara, and Doug."

"Well why would they take Kathleen and who is Simon?" asked Sean.

"They thought Kathleen was me," answered Maggie. "One of the outlaws was not dead yet and he told us he worked for Kid and they were supposed to grab the beautiful redhead and kill the big man. The redhead was supposed to be me and the big man was Michael. I guess they didn't know there were two redheads here and they looked alike. The outlaw died shortly after he talked. The other one that was shot was already dead."

"Well who's Simon and is he dead?" asked Sean.

"Simon was some nice cowboy that I hired to work for us," answered Maggie. "He's a good man and he does a great job here. He was hit in the shoulder. I believe Sara is taking care of him today. Now that's not all that happened. Bill Thompson and his body guard were murdered. There was a safe in Bill's room and it was empty when Bill was found. No one saw anything but we know it was Kid and his men. The one that talked said that they were all to meet up a couple of miles east of town at a small grove of trees."

"So them boys don't know they grabbed the wrong woman," said Sean.

"No, they don't," said Maggie. "I wasn't around when Kid was in the saloon. I guess he just saw the painting and figured there could only be one redhead here. Get her back Sean. You've got to get her back."

"I will darlin'," said Sean. "Jesse and me'll head out at first light. I'll get her back and Kid and his bunch'll be dead."

Jesse came into the saloon now. He walked over to the table and sat down. Betty got him a drink. "So when are we headin' out again?" asked Jesse.

"It'll be first light," said Sean. "We'll get some provisions today and be ready. Two a them fellas is dead so there should be six of'em left. They took Kathleen. They thought she was Maggie. It shouldn't be hard ta pick up their trail. I know Jeb can't wait to hurt them boys. I can tell by lookin' at him that he knows who we're after. Let's eat us a big supper and then rest up."

"I'll get somethin' goin' in the kitchen since Cookie and Barbara aren't here now," said Betty.

"If you all will excuse us, me and this gorgeous woman haven't seen each other for a spell," said Sean. "We'll be occupied for an hour or so. We'll be back for supper." Sean and Maggie went to their room and Betty headed to the kitchen. Michael, Jim, and Jesse stayed at the table and enjoyed some more whiskey.

Maggie and Sean weren't back in an hour, but it wasn't much over an hour and a half. Betty was bringing food out to the table as they were coming down the stairs. They talked a lot as they ate. Maggie wanted to know all about Sean and Jesse's long journey.

"I guess we had us some tough times, didn't we Jesse," started Sean. "Help me out if I miss somethin'."

"I will. There's a lot to remember," said Jesse.

"Well I guess I'll start out by tellin' you that Dawn, Lolita, and Orry's wife are all with child," said Sean. "Countin' Maggie, there's four a you women that're all gonna have babies bout the same time."

"So Jesse, was Dawn upset about you going off with Sean?" asked Maggie.

"She worries bout me, but she knows if it weren't fer you and Sean, we'd probly be dead now," said Jesse. "She's doin' fine. She'll be a fine momma."

"How is Lolita doing?" Maggie asked Sean. "I bet she doesn't want Jug running off with you anymore chasing outlaws."

"No she doesn't," said Sean. "Jug'll be stayin' home from now on. He needs ta heal up some. He took an arrow in the side when we had some trouble with some Comanche. He'll be all right. No vitals was hit. It was bout like that time I took that arrow in my side. Was sticking out both sides and was easy to pull out."

"Just why did you have Comanche trouble?" asked Maggie.

"Years ago when I was with the Cheyenne, me and Braddock killed a bunch a Comanche who were coming ta raid our village," started Sean. "We killed a lot of them with our Sharps before they even got close. That brave that was leadin' them Comanche we had the trouble with when Jug took an arrow, had some brothers in that war party. He was out for vengeance. He's dead now."

"Maybe that Comanche has kin who'll be after you now," said Maggie.

"Could be," said Sean. "But there was eleven of'em that came at us and they're all dead. Maybe if there is kin, they'll know better than ta mess with us. Anyway, I left out about Jeb bitin' that brave from "The Nations" on the ass."

"Well tell us Sean," said Michael.

"Well this one brave thought we should pay a toll for passin' through his land," Sean began. "Course we didn't pay no toll. When we got close to the Red River, we made camp for the night.

That night, that brave tried ta steal a horse and Jeb bit'm on the ass. It was funny at the time."

"It's funny right now," said Michael. "I can just see that brave runnin' off with blood on his ass and Jeb carryin' on."

"Ole Jeb done in a couple a other fellas in too," said Sean. "We was on a stagecoach in Missouri and four men thought they were gonna rob it. Jesse killed one of'em and I killed another one. The shotgun rider hit two of'em but they wasn't dead. Jeb took care a that."

"Sounds like you had yer hands full the whole trip," said Jim. "Anything else happen?"

"Kid hired four buffalo hunters ta kill us," said Sean. "They're dead. Jesse had ta teach a few fellas about respect. We found out that Kid shot his Pa and raped his stepmother. Seems like I'm for-gettin' somethin'. Jesse, did I leave anything out?"

"I'm not sure. Sounds like enough ta me," said Jesse. "Oh, Kid slit that Marshal's throat in Dallas."

"I think that's enough," said Maggie. "I think you men need to finish eating and get your supplies. First light isn't that far off."

They finished their meal and Sean and Jesse got everything ready for the morning. Jesse spent the night in one of the rooms upstairs. Maggie and Sean soaked in the tub for a good while be-fore they went to bed. Sean didn't get much sleep but he didn't care. He'd been too long away from Maggie.

CHAPTER TEN

Jason Hunter was still "Justice of the Peace" in town. Since there was no other type of law in town, he took it upon himself to find out if Bill Thompson had any kin who could be contacted. Jason went to Bill's hotel suite and went through all of the personal belongings. There was nothing there that indicated that Bill had a wife or other kin. Jason decided he would go to the bank. Maybe the banker would know something. Everyone knew that Bill did business at the bank so maybe Bill had some type of legal paper or something that listed a beneficiary.

The bank President was hesitant to show anything to Jason, but Jason convinced him that something had to be done. The President went into his office and went through a cabinet. He pulled out two folders. "Bill had two accounts here," said the banker. "One was for his businesses in town and the other was a personal account." He handed the folders to Jason. The business folder had only Bill's name on it. The personal account had Bill's name and a woman's name. The woman's name was Elizabeth Jane Thompson. Jason opened the folder. There was a legal paper inside that listed the woman as his wife and beneficiary. She had a

Cincinnati address. Jason looked through both folders. Bill had a lot of money in both accounts.

"I will be sending a telegram to Mrs. Thompson telling her of her husband's demise," said Jason. "I'm sure she'll be wanting to take care of his affairs."

"I wonder why she wasn't out here with him?" said the banker.

"That's none of our business," said Jason. He thanked the banker and then headed to the telegraph office. He sent the following telegram to Mrs. Thompson

Elizabeth Jane Thompson
Cincinnati, Ohio

Mrs. Thompson<<stop>>it is with regret that I must inform you of your husband's murder<<stop>>he was killed this morning by an outlaw named Kid Evans<<stop>>Federal Marshals are in pursuit<<stop>>
Your humble servant

Jason Hunter Justice of the Peace
Abilene, Kansas

"Now you mark that very urgent," Jason told the operator. "I don't want some grieving widow after me because no one told her about her husband. If you get a response back, you get it to me quick."

"I will Jason," said the operator. "Don't worry."

~~~~

Elizabeth Jane Thompson was born Elizabeth Jane Turner in Cincinnati Ohio. Her father was a very successful business man and Elizabeth was sent to the best schools available for women. She was a very attractive girl and had plenty of suitors. None of them could convince Elizabeth that she was the woman they would spend their lives with. She and Bill met by chance at a restaurant one day. Elizabeth was having dinner with another gentleman and Bill was at the restaurant with another woman. Bill saw Elizabeth and couldn't keep his eyes off her. The woman he was with noticed this and asked Bill to quit looking at the other woman. Bill ignored her and she got upset and left. When the woman left, Bill went over to Elizabeth's table and introduced himself. Right there in the restaurant for all to hear, he asked if could court her. Elizabeth was embarrassed at first, but she agreed. The gentleman with Elizabeth was at a loss and had no idea what to say. He regained his composure and asked Bill if he would step outside for a moment. "I'll have none of that," said Elizabeth. "This gentleman will be calling on me and that's that. Acting like some tough brute will not change that."

"Bill, that's your name, right?" said the gentleman.

"Yes, my name is Bill," said Bill.

"Well Bill, you may see her home this evening. I am leaving," said the gentleman.

~~~~

Six months later, Elizabeth and Bill were married. They had a nice house in Cincinnati. Bill did not have what could be called a regular job. He was a dreamer and had a good business head on his shoulders. Anytime something came up where Bill thought he could make money, he invested in it. He was very successful. They tried to have children but were not successful. They had been married for ten years when Bill decided to try his hand at cattle buying. He knew the railroad was going to Abilene and there was money to be made. The Texas herds would be driven north to Abilene and other businesses like hotels and saloons would flourish. Bill tried and tried to get Elizabeth to go west with him, but she would have no part of it. "I love you more than life itself," she would say. "But I am as far west as I am going. You go make our fortune. I'll be right here waiting for you." So Bill went west. He was doing exceptionally well until Kid Evans came along.

~~~~

Elizabeth was sweeping off the front porch of their house when the telegram arrived. She saw that it was marked urgent and asked the delivery person if he would wait. There could be a reply. Then she read it. Tears starting falling and she fell down. The delivery person helped her back up. She sat down now to keep herself from falling again. "Do you have pencil and paper?" asked Elizabeth.

"Yes ma'am, I do," answered the delivery person.

"Well take this down," started Elizabeth.

Jason Hunter Justice of the Peace
Abilene Kansas

Thank you for your kindness<<stop>>I will come to Abilene as soon as possible<<stop>>don't know much about such things but am posting a $5000 bounty on Bill's killer<<stop>>can you do this for me

Elizabeth Thompson

It was almost dark when Jason received the telegram in Abilene. He knew Sean and Maggie needed to be alone so he would wait till first light and let Sean know about Elizabeth Thompson. Jason got up well before daylight to make sure he didn't miss Sean.

Sean and Jesse had a big breakfast and were headed for their horses when Jason found them. "I got something you'll need to know Sean," said Jason.

"What is it?" asked Sean.

"Bill Thompson had a wife," started Jason. "She lives in Cincinnati. I sent her a telegram telling her about Bill. She answered it. She'll be coming here and she's posted a $5000 reward for Kid."

"Holy shit, $5000," exclaimed Sean. "Bounty hunters'll be coming outta the woodwork for that. They'll be tryin' ta kill us if they think we're gonna get to Kid before they do. Holy shit!!! I guess me'n Jesse better get that son of a bitch before word gets spread bout that reward. So ole Bill had a wife. I wonder why she wasn't with him."

"I suppose we'll find out when she gets here," said Jason.

"Thanks Jason. We'll be headin' out now," said Sean. Sean gave Maggie a long kiss and then mounted his horse. He, Jesse, and Jeb headed east to find the small grove where the gang was to have met. Jeb seemed anxious to go.

Kid and the Potts brothers waited anxiously in the grove of trees for the others to show. After about fifteen minutes, they could see three riders approaching. As the riders got closer, they could see the red head draped over Sol's lap. The three riders rode over to the others. Sol shoved Kathleen off of his lap. She fell limply to the ground. She was still out cold. "Where's Lukey and Slim?" asked Kid.

"Dead most likely," answered Sol. "I'm purty sure Lukey hit the floor dead and it looked like Slim was gut shot."

"Well that's more money fer the rest of us," said Clyde. "You suppose if Slim weren't dead yet he'd talk and tell'em who we are?"

"It don't matter," said Kid. "I want'em ta know it's us. Now one a you throw that woman on yer horse and let's git movin'.'"

"Can't we count that money'r get a poke first?" said Barney.

"Don't worry bout that money," said Kid. "There's plenty ta go round. And we'll get all the pokes we want after we get some distance betwixt us and Abilene. And why would you want a poke now? The woman's out cold. What fun would that be? Now let's get movin'." Sol threw Kathleen back on his horse. They all saddled up and headed east.

They rode fairly hard for around an hour and then slowed to a walk to take it easier on the horses. Not long after they slowed down, Kathleen came to. She waited a few minutes and thought about her situation. Then she spoke. "I don't know who the hell you men are or what you want, but I'd be more comfortable if I could ride sitting up," said Kathleen. They all stopped.

"Git'r down offa yer horse Sol," said Kid. "She can ride with me." Sol gave Kathleen a hard shove. She fell to the ground but immediately stood and gave Sol a defiant look.

"You sure how to treat a woman, don't you. You piece of trash," said Kathleen. "I'll enjoy watching you die."

"Sassy bitch, huh Kid," said Sol. "Believe I'll have me a poke right now."

"No, there won't be any pokin' right now," said Kid. "Now git up here woman and don't even think bout tryin' fer my pistol'r knife. I'll stove yer head in." Kathleen didn't speak. Kid pulled his foot out of the stirrup and let her mount his horse. "Now you behave yerself and we won't kill ya right off," said Kid. "How long you think it'll be afore yer man comes after us?"

"Which man is that?" asked Kathleen. "Sean will be the one who kills you."

"So that's O'Rourke's first name," said Kid. "I always heard bout O'Rourke, but I never heard his first name mentioned. Maybe him and me'll be on a first name basis now since I got his woman."

Kathleen knew now why she had been taken. This man thought she was Maggie. Kathleen decided then and there that she could not tell them that she wasn't Maggie. Maybe if she played along, it would keep her alive longer. She knew that she would be abused, but maybe if she made them all believe that they were great lovers, she would live longer. There was another thing that might help her live longer. She was due to start her cycle. Maybe the men wouldn't like the blood and would wait until her flow slowed down. If she lived a few days, maybe she could make some of the men jealous of each other and they would kill each other. "I'm a smart woman," Kathleen said to herself. "I'll keep myself alive and I'll see these men dead."

"Who painted that picture a you that's hangin' back at the saloon?" asked Kid.

Kathleen had no idea who did the painting. She thought for a moment before speaking. "It was my first husband," answered Kathleen. "He was an artist. He died from influenza not long after we were married."

"I'll be lookin' forward ta seein' if he did a good job on all a yer parts," said Kid. "I'll be havin' my way with ya tonight."

"So whom will I have the honor of being with?" asked Kathleen.

"What's this whom stuff mean?" asked Kid.

"I mean what is your name?" said Kathleen.

"Ma'am, I am Bart Evans," said Kid. "Most folks call me Kid on account a my youth."

"So Kid, how old are you?" asked Kathleen.

"I'm seventeen, but I'll be eighteen next month," said Kid.

"So young to have killed so many," said Kathleen. "Do you really think you'll make it to eighteen."

"Look bitch, we was havin' a nice talk and now yer gettin' sassy," said Kid. "Don't make me git mean. Things git ugly when I git mean. We're gonna kill you, but we might keep you around longer if you behave."

"I'm like most folks. I'm not ready to die just yet," said Kathleen. "I'll do my best to behave. You may even decide you want me around. I know how to please a man."

"Damn, never thought I'd hear O'Rourke's woman talkin' like that," said Kid. Kathleen didn't speak for a while. She felt something on her forehead and tried to wipe it off with her hand. She could feel that it was dried blood.

"How about handing me a canteen?" said Kathleen. "I'd like to get this blood off of my forehead. I'll tear off a piece of my dress and wet it down. Kid handed her a canteen. She wetted down a piece of her dress and wiped off her forehead. She could feel a fair sized bump on her head just above her hairline. "It wasn't necessary for your man to hit me over the head," said Kathleen. "If they would have just pulled a gun and said they were taking me, I would have gone. I'm not stupid. I don't want to get shot or hurt."

"How bout them others in the saloon? Would they have just let my boys take you?" asked Kid.

"I think they would have," answered Kathleen. "They would have been afraid that your man might just shoot me if there was any trouble."

"Well no matter. Two a my boys is dead so there's more money fer the rest of us," said Kid. "Now be quiet for a spell. I got some thinkin' ta do."

They rode for a couple of hours and then dismounted and walked the horses for a while. They came to a small stream and watered the horses and refilled the canteens. Clyde was getting hungry. "We gonna stop fer a minute and get somethin' ta eat?" asked Clyde.

"Chew on a piece a jerky," said Kid. "We're gonna keep movin' till almost dark. Then this woman is gonna cook us up some supper."

"I never said I could cook," said Kathleen. "We have a cook at the saloon. I never cook."

"We're just gonna have some bacon and beans woman," said Kid. "Coffee too. Any dern fool can make that stuff without messin' it up too bad. I like my coffee strong too." Kathleen didn't speak.

They rode on till about an hour before dark. Kid picked a campsite near a small hill that had a few trees at the bottom. As soon as they dismounted, Kathleen started gathering firewood and got a fire going. As she was cooking supper, the men hobbled the horses and put out their bedrolls. Kid had a bottle of whiskey so they passed it around while Kathleen was fixing supper. After the bottle had gone around the first time, Kid took another drink and started it around again. "Just wait a minute," said Kathleen. "Don't I get a drink too. I think I deserve it. It's not like I was invited on this trip." Kid took the bottle from Barney and handed it to Kathleen. Kathleen took her hand and wiped off the bottle and put it to her lips. She took a very long drink.

"Whoa, take it easy," said Kid. "Only got one more bottle till we get resupplied." He took the bottle from Kathleen. He corked it and put it in his saddle bags. "Now you get back ta makin' supper. I wanna eat and then I'm gonna have my way with you."

"How bout we count the money while supper's cookin'? said Sol.

"I guess we can," said Kid. "Gimme that pillar case." Sol got the pillow case and handed it to Kid. Kid untied it and turned it upside down. The men's eyes glistened when they watched the money fall out."

"I never knowed there was that much money in the world," said Sol. "Must be thousands and thousands."

The money was banded together. Kid counted and there was a thousand dollars in each band. There were sixty bands. "Boys, we got $60,000 here," said Kid. "That's $10,000 fer each a us." Kid gave the boys their share.

"Holy shit," said Sol. "I could have me some fun times with this money. I need me a woman tonight."

"We got us a woman and she won't cost you a thing," said Kid. "But I'm first and I'll take as many pokes as I want. You all can have her when I'm done fer the night. Now let's eat so I can git busy."

When they were done eating, Kid told the other men they could clean up the plates and such. He took Kathleen by the arm and took her a little ways from the camp. He had grabbed a blanket on the way and threw it on the ground. Kid looked into her eyes for a moment and smiled. Then he reached up and started ripping her dress off of her. "Whoa, whoa, whoa," cried Kathleen. "You don't need to do that. I'll unbutton everything or maybe you'd like to do it. It might be more fun that way." Kid smiled at her again.

"You go ahead and undo everything," said Kid. "I like to watch."

Kathleen was glad that he was letting her undress herself. She had a derringer on the inside of her left thigh that was strapped on by a garter. No one had bothered to check her for weapons or anything. She knew she could shoot Kid and maybe one other man before they would shoot her. She would bide her time and strike at the right moment. If she undressed carefully, Kid wouldn't even notice the derringer. She took her time. She could tell Kid was getting more excited all the time. Finally, she was standing in front of him totally naked. Kid had not seen the derringer. It was now in her pile of clothes. "Get down on that blanket now," said Kid as he began tearing off his own clothes.

"Slow down, let me undress you too," said Kathleen. "You'll enjoy it. I know you will." Kid undid his gunbelt and tossed it several yards away.

"Don't be gittin' no ideas bout goin' fer my gun," said Kid. "Now get me undressed." Kathleen did as instructed. She took her time and acted like she was enjoying herself. When Kid was completely naked, he stood there for a moment and looked at Kathleen all over. "That fella that done that paintin' did a good job, but not quit good enough," said Kid. "Now git down on that blanket."

Kathleen got down on the blanket and Kid got on top of her. He entered her and began pumping away. Kathleen tried to kiss him and act like she was having a good time, but Kid didn't want to kiss. He chewed on her breasts and had his hands all over her backside. He was being too rough with her breasts, but she didn't tell him that. She did her best to act like she was having a great time. After about a minute or two, Kid stopped pumping. He stayed inside Kathleen, but pulled his chest up from her so he could take a look at something. He looked down toward her crotch. There was some blood down there. "Just what the hell's goin' on," yelled Kid. "Why's there blood down there?"

"I must have started my cycle," said Kathleen. "It was due to start any day."

"So how long does this cycle or whatever you said go on?" asked Kid.

"Five or six days," answered Kathleen. "Didn't you know this about women?"

"I guess I did but I never poked a woman when she was doin' this," said Kid.

"You can still do it. It's just going to be messy till it's over," said Kathleen.

"It seems purty messy now," said Kid. "Is it gonna git any messier?"

"Well, usually the first day isn't too bad," said Kathleen. "The next few days are very messy. The end of it isn't bad."

"Well I'm gonna finish up and git me a drink," said Kid. "Then I'll see if I wanna do that again." It didn't take Kid long to finish up. When he was done, he got up and stood for a minute looking down at himself, Kathleen, and the blanket. "Holy shit, that looks like a lotta blood," said Kid. "If we keep doin' it will ya bleed ta death?"

"No, I'd still bleed the same amount of blood if I wasn't getting poked," answered Kathleen.

"And you say it's gonna git worse?" asked Kid.

"That's right. Like I said, I'll have some heavy days and then it'll lighten up and quit," said Kathleen.

"Well I'm gonna git that drink and I'll be right back," said Kid. "Don't even think bout tryin' ta run off."

"I'll be right here when you get back," said Kathleen. Kid didn't bother to put any clothes on. He grabbed his gunbelt and walked back to the campfire. He got the whiskey out of his saddle bags and took a big gulp. The other boys sat there and stared at him.

"What the hell happened ta you Kid," said Clyde. "Ya got blood all over down there. Did she cut ya'r somethin'?"

"No she didn't cut me," answered Kid. "Damn woman just started her time."

"What do you mean started her time?" asked Barney.

"Don't you fools know nothin' bout women?" said Kid. "They do this every damn month. We just happened ta grab her when she started hers."

"So how is it Kid?" asked Sol. "Is it still good?"

"It's still good but it's sloppy," answered Kid. "She says it gets worse for a few days. Then it'll lighten up and quit."

"Sloppy'r not, I'm gittin' some a that," said Sol. "I need me a woman tonight."

"Well you all can have'r when I'm done," said Kid. "You best figure out who's next and such."

Stew and Chili had been quiet but now they spoke. "Me'n Chili'r gonna be first and second," announced Stew. "Anybody says any different's gonna hafta whoop our asses."

"Hell, that won't be no problem," said Sol. "Let's git'em boys. No guns now." Sol, Clyde, and Barney, tore into Chili and Stew. Kid ignored them and went back to Kathleen.

"What the hell is going on over there?" asked Kathleen. "It sounds like they're beating the hell out of each other."

"They're decidin' who's next," said Kid. "Maybe they will beat each other senseless and won't be able to take you tonight. Hell, maybe they'll kill each other."

"Shouldn't you stop them," said Kathleen. "It is your gang. You shouldn't have them hurting each other."

"They're grown men," said Kid. "If one'r more gits kilt, that'll be more money fer the rest a us. Now you get ready cause here I come again."

Kathleen did her best to act like she was enjoying herself. It wasn't long and Kid was done. When he was finished he got off of her and sat beside her on the blanket. "I believe that'll be enough fer me tonight," said Kid. "I'll go see how the boys'r doin. Don't run away now."

"I'll be right here," said Kathleen. "How about getting me some water and some rags or something so I can clean up a bit?"

"I'll see what I can come up with," said Kid. "What do you women do about this anyway. I know you don't just let it run down yer leg'r git all over furniture and such."

"We wear pads or something that soaks up the blood," said Kathleen. "When one is full, we put on another one and wash out the other one and let it dry. If we get some supplies somewhere, maybe you could get me something."

"What would I ask for?" asked Kid.

"Just tell them you need some things for a woman's time," said Kathleen. "They'll know what you mean."

"You got some cajones woman," said Kid. "You figure I'll do this fer you when we're gonna kill you anyway."

"You might change your mind about killing me," said Kathleen.

"I doubt it, but you can think that all ya want," said Kid. "I'll be back shortly." Kid got dressed and went back to the camp. Two of the men were lying there unconscious. Two others were sitting, but were pretty beat up. Stew was the only one standing. "Looks like you're next Stew," said Kid. "Take this canteen with you. That woman wants ta clean herself up a bit. Tell her I got no rags. She'll hafta tear off a piece a her dress."

Stew found Kathleen with no problem. He handed her the canteen and told her if she wanted a rag, she'd have to tear off a piece of her dress. While Kathleen was cleaning herself up a bit, Stew tore off his clothes. Kathleen noticed right off that Stew hadn't brought his pistol with him.

It only took Stew about a minute to climax. He still thought he was in heaven. He stayed right on her and it wasn't long and he was pumping again. This time it was maybe two minutes. When he finished this time, he got up off of her. He looked down and saw the blood all over himself and her. "You sure yer not dyin' woman?" asked Stew. "That looks like a lotta blood."

"No, I'm not dying," answered Kathleen. "Now go send whoever is next." Stew said nothing. He got dressed and went back to the camp. When Stew got back to the camp, Kid was the only one who was awake.

"I reckon them others'll take a turn tomorrow," said Stew. "Mind if I get me a drink Kid?"

"No, help yerself," said Kid. "How was it?"

"Well I never poked no gal when she was doin' that," said Stew. "It weren't bad, but It'd be better without all that blood. Damn, that sure looked like a lotta blood. So are we gonna stand watch tonight? Just you'n me if we do. Them others has had it looks like."

"We won't do no watches tonight," said Kid. "Don't think anyone's on our trail just yet. We'll keep watches startin' tomorrow. Get yer drink and git some sleep." Kid walked back over to Kathleen.

"So are you back for more or am I done for the evening?" asked Kathleen.

"You can git yer clothes back on woman," said Kid. "Them others aren't in no shape fer that tonight. They'll be wantin' you tomorrow." Kathleen slowly dressed herself. She was careful to make sure Kid didn't see the derringer as she positioned it on the inside of her left thigh. She was able to do this when he turned his head for just a moment to look around.

"Where am I sleeping and what am I sleeping on?" asked Kathleen.

"You already got a blanket," said Kid. "You be right next ta me. I'll have you tied so if you move at all, it'll wake me. I don't want ta be woke. Do you understand?"

"Yes I understand," answered Kathleen. "Now can I have some more water so I can get some of this blood out of the blanket. I can hold it by the fire and let it dry some."

"That blood won't hurt ya none," said Kid. "It'll dry faster'n water anyway. Now come on. I'm ready ta sleep now." They laid down by the fire. Kid tied Kathleen as he said he would.

Kathleen thought she would never get to sleep but she was asleep in no time. The next thing she knew, Kid was waking her up. "Get up woman. Yer fixin' breakfast," said Kid.

"How about I go relieve myself first," said Kathleen.

"Sure, ya gotta go, ya gotta go," said Kid. "Go over there and squat down in the brush so I can still see the top a yer head. Kathleen never complained. She did as instructed.

While they were eating breakfast, Sol started complaining. He was mad about not having the woman last night and wanted her this morning. "You coulda had all ya wanted last night," said Kid. "But you fools had ta beat the hell outta each other. We're not wastin' time this mornin' fer that. You can have her tonight. Now finish eatin'. We probly got a posse on our trail now." They finished breakfast, mounted up, and headed east.

~~~~

Sean found the grove where the gang had met with no trouble. "There's no blood anywhere," said Sean. "Looks like they were here for just a little while and then headed east. One a the horses is carryin' two people. They didn't bring an extra horse for Kathleen. Get a good whiff Jeb. We don't wanna lose'em. They're only a day ahead of us. Jeb sniffed around and then started on the trail east. It wasn't long and they came to the place where Kathleen had regained consciousness. "They stopped here for a minute," said Sean. "There's a different horse now with two riders." They moved on. When they came to the small stream where Kid and his men had crossed and watered their horses, Sean did the same. "They probly rode till about dark and made camp," said Sean. "Let's push hard for a spell. I wanna see that camp well before dark and see what kinda sign they left."

They pushed the horses for a good bit and let them walk for a while. Then they rode hard again. Jeb was ahead of them and found the camp. He left out some howls when he found it. Sean and Jesse rode to the campsite and dismounted. "They left here early this mornin'," said Sean. "After we look around a bit, we'll ride some and get ourselves closer. They won't expect us to track at night."

"I found a piece a somethin'," said Jesse. "Looks like mebbe it's off a dress. It's got blood on it. They looked around some. Another piece of bloody material was found. Then Jeb let out a howl. Sean and Jesse went to Jeb. He was about twenty five yards from the camp. "There's a lotta blood there on the ground," said Jesse. "You reckon they done killed Kathleen?"

"Stand back and let me have a good look," said Sean. He studied the ground close to the blood and around it. "There's some barefoot tracks here. More'n one pair," said Sean. "These other ones here are a woman's track. See what direction the prints are. The woman was layin' down on a blanket or somethin' with her knees up and her feet on the dirt. The man's prints are like he was standin' here lookin' down at her. Then he got down on her. See how them toe prints are. He was down on her pumpin' away and his feet and toes was diggin' inta the dirt some."

"How can you tell that?" asked Jesse.

"Just stand back and look Jesse," said Sean. "Look and try to imagine what that would look like."

"All right, I guess I can see that," said Jesse. "So with that blood, do ya think they killed her?"

"They could have, but I don't think so," said Sean. "There's six of 'em and they'll want to use Kathleen all they can before they kill her."

"So you're thinkin' that blood might be from somethin' else like mebbe she started her time," said Jesse.

"That's just what I'm hopin'," said Sean. "If she is on her time, mebbe they won't want to use her so much. That'll keep her alive longer and give us more time ta catch 'em."

CHAPTER ELEVEN

Sam Waters grew up in Louisiana. His parents were poor farmers and the family would have never survived if Sam's father hadn't been such a good hunter. He also made a little money at times when he helped catch runaway slaves. He was very good at this and he passed on his skills to Sam. By the time Sam was fifteen, he had the reputation of being the best slave catcher in his parish. The largest plantations were always seeking his help. There were times when he went as far as two states away chasing runaways, but he was always successful. Sam never injured any of the slaves he caught if it could be helped. Some slaves owners paid a bonus if their property came back in good shape and Sam was in this business to make money. He had no feelings one way or the other about colored folks. They were slaves and that's the way it was. It must have been meant to be this way.

When the war came, Sam rode with Nathan Bedford Forrest. He started out as a private, but after his second engagement, he was given a commission. By the end of the war, he was a Colonel. He was at Fort Pillow when colored soldiers were executed. He didn't participate, but he did nothing to stop it. He felt no remorse. This was war and they were the enemy. To win the war, you kill the enemy. That's what you do.

Like a lot of ex-Confederate soldiers after the war, Sam went to Texas. He couldn't find steady work and wandered around the state. He was camped one evening almost to the New Mexico line. The next morning he was attacked by a small party of Apaches. There were three of them. Sam took an arrow in his side but miraculously, he killed the Apaches. He had just awakened and was sitting up rubbing his eyes when he heard the twang of a bowstring. Before he could react, the arrow tore into his left side. An Apache warrior came charging at him. The warrior had a cavalry saber in his right hand and was almost on Sam when he retrieved his pistol from under his blanket. The warrior was so close that when Sam fired, he landed on top of Sam. Sam was partially dazed but shoved the Apache's dead body off of him. Another warrior was close and fired a shot at Sam, but missed. The bullet struck between his legs and just missed his privates. This warrior charged Sam now and was reloading an army carbine. He was only fiteen feet away when Sam's bullet caught him between the eyes. Out of the corner of his left eye, Sam saw something coming his way. He moved just in time time to be missed by a war lance. He looked to his left now. Another Apache warrior was running towards him and firing a Spencer rifle as he ran. He was less than fifty feet away. Sam took aim and fired his pistol. The warrior was struck in the chest. He was knocked backwards, but didn't go down. He started for Sam again. Sam fired again striking him again in the chest. The warrior still kept coming. His Spencer rifle must have been empty because he never fired it again as he ran toward Sam. He was only ten feet from Sam when Sam put a bullet in his forehead. The back of his head came off as he was falling backwards. Sam got himself behind some cover and reloaded his pistol. He waited for more Apaches to come. None did.

The arrow went through and was sticking out his back. Sam broke off the end with the arrowhead and looked at the arrowhead. It was a metal arrowhead and it looked like none of it had broken off inside him. He took a couple of deep breaths and yanked out the arrow. He heard himself screaming as he did it. He had a little whiskey in his saddle bag. He poured some over the wounds. Then he got a fire going. He started a pot of coffee and then placed a knife in the flames. When the blade of the knife was glowing red, Sam took it and cauterized his wounds. Then he fashioned himself a bandage and wrapped it around his mid section.

He was on his second cup of coffee and about to start cooking some bacon when he heard a bunch of horses coming his way. He sat there drinking his coffee and waited. He figured it was a troop of cavalry. They finally came into sight. Sam didn't much care for the blue uniforms but he reminded himself that the war was over. Someone in the patrol yelled "Troop Halt." The soldiers stopped and an officer and a Sergeant rode over to Sam. "I see you had some trouble," said the officer. "You were very lucky. I am Lieutenant Sanders and this is Sergeant Collins. Were there any more hostiles?"

"Not that I know of," answered Sam.

"Well we're headed back to the fort," said the Lt., "Looks like you could use some medical attention. You are welcome to ride with us. In fact, I would recommend it. You might not be so lucky next time Mr.---. What is your name anyway sir?"

"Name's Sam Waters and I'll be goin' with ya," said Sam. "I'll get my gear rounded up." Sam got his meager belongings together and mounted up. They were about to leave when someone from the column yelled out.

"Them scalps is worth $20 a piece. Yer not leavin'em is ya?"

"Who said that?" yelled the Lt. No one spoke.

"Mr. Waters, being in the Army, I can't condone the bounty on scalps, but it is done in this part of the country," said the Lt. "If you want those scalps, I will not stop you. I have no authority over a civilan."

"Well Lt., there's $60 right there and I haven't had no money of any kind since forever," said Sam. "I'll be gettin' them scalps and them rifles. Never scalped no one afore. I guess you just cut with a knife and yank." The Lt. didn't say a word for a moment.

"We'll be moving out Mr. Waters," said the Lt. "You can catch up when you're done."

Scalping was easier than Sam thought it would be. He was done in no time. He tied the scalps and the Apache's rifles to his saddle. He was about to mount his horse when he remembered that the one Apache had a cavalry saber. Sam retrieved the saber and tied it to his saddle. He had no use for it, but he figured he could sell it and the rifles for a few bucks. When they got to the fort, the Sergeant took Sam to the doctor. "You did yourself good," said the doctor. "Couldn't a done better myself. I'll clean it up a little and put on some fresh bandages and you can be on your way. Just take it easy for a while and keep the wound clean." As Sam was leaving the dispensary, a young Lieutenant approached him.

"I heard about your ordeal and I saw the saber on your saddle," said the Lt. "I'd like to purchase the saber from you. I'll give you ten dollars for it."

"Sold," said Sam. They went to Sam's horse and he gave the saber to the Lt. "Now be careful with that thing and don't cut yerself. I bet yer having dreams a glory and such. I bet you can see yerself charging into battle and slashing the enemy."

"No Mr. Waters," said the Lt. "That's not why I want the saber. I want it because it was my father's. He was killed a few years ago by the Apache. When I first saw it, I thought it might be his. Then I took a closer look. His initials are scratched into the back of the handle." The Lt. showed the initials to Sam.

"Hell young fella, just take the saber," said Sam. "It belongs to you anyway. I can't take your money."

"Myself and my family thank you Mr. Waters," said the Lt. "I hope your wounds heal well." The Lt. gave Sam a salute and left. Sam almost saluted him back. He felt his arm going up when he stopped it.

"I never did like that salutin' stuff," Sam said to himself. "I knew I was an officer and so did everone else. No need fer all that arm stuff.

~~~~

After Sam collected his bounty money for the scalps and sold the rifles, he went to the sutler store and bought himself another shirt. He threw away the one that had the blood all over it. Then he headed for the nearest town and saloon. It was twenty miles away. He wanted a woman, some whiskey, and some food. He wanted it in that order. He hurt some but not enough to keep him from having a woman. The town was small and only had one saloon. When he walked into the saloon, a very attractive senorita went to him and grabbed his arm. Before she could speak, they were headed up the stairs to a room. Once in the room, Sam still never spoke. He gave the woman a look and she knew what he wanted. She undressed herself and laid on the bed. "Do you like what you see Gringo?" asked the woman.

Sam finally spoke. "Yes Senorita, I like what I see," said Sam. "Now don't be callin' me Gringo. I don't know for sure, but I spect it's not a nice name. I will treat you nice. My name is Sam."

"All right Sam, I will not call you Gringo," said the woman. "Now take off your clothes and join me. I am anxious to please you." Sam smiled, took off his gunbelt and clothes, and then joined her in bed. Nothing was said about money.

"I see you have been wounded senor," said the woman. "I will make sure I do not hurt you. How did you receive your wounds?"

"Apaches," answered Sam. Nothing else was said. Two hours later, they were lying in bed holding each other and covered with sweat. "You are a very good lover," said the woman. "I would like it if you would visit me again. I would not charge you. No one has been so nice with me before."

"What is your name?" asked Sam.

"It's Juanita Alverez," answered the woman.

"Well Juanita Alverez, I would like to see you again too," said Sam. "Don't know when it might be. I gotta find me a way to make some money or a livin'. This bounty money I got for them Apache scalps and them rifles won't last long."

"So you took some Apache scalps, did you?" said Juanita. "A lot of these scalp hunters go out and kill everything but Apaches and claim the scalps are from Apaches. If you really took Apache scalps, you are very lucky to be alive. Apaches are very good at killing and tracking. My family was killed by the Apache when we lived over the border in Mexico. I hid in a corn crib or they would have taken me."

"Well I'm sorry about your folks," said Sam. "Let's go down-stairs and have a drink. Then we'll get something to eat."

"I will tell the cook to make a fine meal for us," said Juanita. They got dressed and went back downstairs.

Sam sat down at a table and Juanita went to the kitchen and then to the bar. She returned to the table with a bottle and two glasses. Right after the glasses were filled, a big man came over to the table. He had a pistol stuck in his belt. He stood by the table and looked down at Juanita. "Yer spending too much time with this'un," he said to her. "There's other customers awaitin'."

"Go away Mr." said Sam.

"What'd you say boy?" said the man.

"You heard me Mr. Now go away before you get hurt," said Sam.

"Is that right?" asked the man. The man waved his arm and two other men came over to the table now. They had been on the other side of the saloon watching everything. They both were wearing tied down Colts. One was a Mexican and the other one was a Swede or something. Sam hadn't been around too many Swede's, but he met a few during the war and they talked funny like this fella did. Sam heard him answer a question from the Mexican by saying yah instead of of yeh or yes. He was a big man. He had long blonde hair and his skin was so white that Sam thought he might be albino.

"You got pink eyes there Swede?" asked Sam. "You sure look albino ta me. I bet yer name's Bjorn'r somethin' like that. The Swede didn't say another word. He just stood there and smiled at Sam. His hand was touching the butt of his Colt.

Sam Waters wasn't a big man. He was about five foot nine and weighed around 160 pounds. He was tough as nails and was a dead shot with a pistol. It was said that he could shoot a man in the head at fifty yards in a full gallop. He was fast on the draw too. Many times during the war when his unit was ambushed, being fast saved his life and the lives of some of his men. He carried three pistols and a carbine with him. One pistol he wore on his left side and was there for a cross draw with his right hand. The two other pistols were in holsters and tied to his saddle where they could be easily reached. The carbine was in a scabbard tied to the saddle. One of the first things he did when he received his pistols from the Army was to cut the flaps from the holsters. When he left the Army of the Confederacy and went west, he got himself three new pistols that had been converted to metallic cartridges and a Henry rifle. He still wore one pistol on his left side and the other two were in holsters fastened to his saddle horn. The Henry was in a scabbard on the saddle.

"What the hell's yer name Mr.?" asked the big man. "I like ta know a man's name before I kill'm."

Sam stood up now. "Juanita, you best move away now," said Sam. "There's some fellas gonna git theirself kilt." Juanita got up from her chair and moved over behind the bar. "That'll be fine right there," said Sam. "My name is Sam Waters. Now just who the hell'r you and why you think you got the right ta tell this woman what ta do?"

"Ya don't need my name dead man," said the big man. "I own this place and I'll do what I want and say what I want in here." The Mexican fella leaned over and whispered something into the big man's ear. "This Mex said he heard that some fella named Waters kilt three Apaches. I say that's bullshit. No white man can take three Apaches. He might take one'r two, but then he'd be tied to a wagon wheel with a fire goin' betwixt his legs. Whoevers spreadin' that word bout you is a damn liar. I say yer a damn liar too."

"You must be itchin' ta die Mr.," said Sam. "Now apologize to Jaunita and leave me alone. You do that and you'll live ta see tomorrow." No one spoke. Sam kept his eyes trained on the Mexican. He figured he'd be the first to draw. Sam had heard a lot of stories about Mexican pistoleeros. Now he would find out if they were true or not.

Sam was right. The Mexican went for his pistol first. Before it was out of the holster, Sam's pistol was smoking and there was a hole in the Mexican's forehead. His head came apart and blood, brain, and bone flew all over the Swede and the other man. Before the Mexican hit the floor, the Swede had his pistol out of it's holster but not up enough to fire. Sam put a hole in the Swede's chest. The Swede was knocked backwards. He landed on a table and he and the table went down to the floor. The top of the table broke off under the Swede's dead weight. The big man had his pistol out now and fired at Sam, but he missed. Before he could cock his hammer again, there was a hole in his forehead. The back of his head came off and blood flew everywhere. One end of the bar was covered with blood and brain. No one in the saloon spoke for what seemed like several minutes. Then Sam spoke. "Anybody else in here gonna call me a liar?" yelled Sam. No one spoke. "Well one a you fellas git up off yer ass'n go fetch the law."

"Are you sure you want the law Mr. Waters?" asked one of the men in the saloon. "That big fella you just shot is his cousin."

"I don't care who the hell he is. These sons a bitches tried ta kill me and now they're dead," said Sam. "Now go git the law."

"All right, Mr. Waters, I'll go get him," said the man. "But you can bet he won't come alone after I tell'm what happened."

"Just go get'm," said Sam. "You let me worry bout what might happen." The man left to get the law. Sam reloaded his pistol.

"The Marshal is not a good man," said Juanita. "He will want to kill you. You must go. Take me with you. He will want to kill me too now."

"You won't get harmed woman and nobody's leavin'," said Sam. "Now you just stay over there behind the bar. Could be some more shootin'."

It wasn't long and the Marshal showed up. He was a tall slender man, maybe thirty, and had a full mustache. He was carrying a sawed off shotgun and had a tied down Colt on his right side. He had a deputy with him. The deputy was wearing a tied down Colt and had a Henry rifle in his hands. The Marshal and his deputy stood just inside the door of the saloon and faced Sam. The Marshal was holding the shotgun across his chest. Sam could see that the hammers were not cocked. The deputy held his Winchester down to his left side with his left hand and had his right hand on the butt of his pistol. "They tell me yer name is Sam Waters and you kilt three Apaches," said the Marshal. "Well maybe you did and maybe you didn't but you sure as hell kilt these three. You some kinda gunman'r somethin'?"

"No, I'm no gunman. I'm just some fella who wanted a woman, a drink, and a meal," said Sam. "Them three started the trouble. They tried ta kill me. They're dead. I'm not."

"That's right," said Juanita. "Sam didn't do anything wrong."

"Shut up whore," said the Marshal. "If I want any lip outta you, I'll beat it out of ya."

"Marshal, you got no call ta talk to Juanita that way," said Sam. "Now be a gentleman and apologize to the lady."

"Lady hell, she's a damn whore," said the Marshal. The deputy let out a laugh.

"So you think it's funny do ya boy?" said Sam. "You apologize to the lady too."

"The hell I will," said the deputy. He was pulling his pistol as he spoke. Before his pistol left the holster, the deputy was being thrown backwards with a hole in his chest. The Marshal looked down at his dead deputy for a moment.

"Ya done murdered my deputy," said the Marshal. "First ya kill my cousin and now ya kill my deputy. I'm gonna blow you in half." The Marshal cocked the hammers on the shotgun, but before he could line it up to fire at Sam, he had a hole in his head. He hit the floor dead.

Sam holstered his pistol. "Is there any more lawmen in this town?" yelled Sam. "If there is, someone go get'em so we can git this over with quick."

"There is no one else Sam," said Juanita. "The Marshal and his cousin, who was the mayor, and his cousin's men ran this town. This was not a good town. They took a cut from every business in town. Anyone who didn't pay was beat up or killed. You have killed all of them."

"Sounds like you folks should have yourself a special election and git a new mayor," said Sam. "Then he can appoint you a new Marshal. Isn't there a county Sheriff around here?"

"There is, but he never comes here," said Juanita. "Anyone who ever tried to get him here came up missing."

"How about the Rangers?" asked Sam.

"They're too busy chasing Apaches, Comanches, and bandits," said Juanita.

"Well like I said, you need yourself a new Mayor and Marshal," said Sam. "Now can we get back to what we were doing before we were so rudely interrupted? And can we git these dead bodies outta here? I don't like ta eat with dead men close by. Does somethin' ta my appetite."

The bodies were taken out into the street. Someone came with a buckboard and the bodies were loaded onto it. Then the bodies were taken to the barber shop. Juanita and Sam went back to their table and had some drinks. It wasn't long and some food was brought out from the kitchen. Sam wolfed his food down like he hadn't eaten for a month. Then he asked for more. Before he was finished eating, three older gentlemen came into the saloon and went to his table. They didn't speak. They just stood there.

Sam stopped eating for a moment. "You three got something on yer mind," said Sam. "What is it you want?"

"Us three run businesses in town," one of them started. "I'm Paul Harden and I own the general store. This fella to my right is Tobey Smith and he owns the livery. The is other fella to my left is Bob Alexander. He runs the freight office. We'd like a minute of your time if you don't mind."

"Let me finish my food and then you boys can talk all ya want," said Sam. "Have yerself a drink. I won't be long." The three men went to the bar and got themselves a drink. "Do you know them men?" Sam asked Juanita.

"I know them," answered Juanita. "They are not customers."

"Do they talk nice to you and treat you right?" asked Sam.

"They know what I am and they treat me that way except for when I spend money at their businesses," answered Juanita.

"Seems like folks around here need some lessons on manners," said Sam. They finished eating and Sam called for the three men to come over. "Go ahead and speak yer peace," said Sam.

"I'll start," said Paul Harden. "We're glad that you killed these men today. They were evil men and were a curse on our town. They were bleeding us dry. We have a proposal for you Mr. Waters."

"Well, spit it out," said Sam.

"We would like for you to be our Town Marshal," said Paul. "We think you are the man for the job."

"You don't know a thing about me," said Sam. "All you know is that I killed these fellas and three Apaches. Is that it? You just want a killer. That way if someone does something you don't like I can kill'em for you. Is that what you want?"

"Of course not Mr. Waters," answered Paul. "We want someone who can protect us if necessary. There can be a lot of bad people this close to the border with Mexico. A lot of bad men have come here on their way to Mexico. They were most likely friends of our former Marshal and Mayor. They drank their fill, abused the women, and then moved on. If the Rangers or any other law showed up lookin' for them, no one knew or saw anything. Anyone that ever said anything was killed or beat up."

"Sounds ta me like you folks got no backbone," said Sam. "You all shoulda run that Marshal and his men outta town back when he was first gettin' started around here."

"We're businessmen," said Paul. "I myself don't even own a gun. Most of us men in town are gettin' old. We were too old for the war."

"I didn't know anybody was too old for the war," said Sam. "I seen seventy year old men fightin' and dyin'. I seen thirteen year old boys out there too. I'll tell you one thing right now Mr., if I was ta take this job, I'd expect help from the local citizens if the need come up."

"What do you mean, Mr. Waters?" asked Paul.

"Well say for example a gang of five'r more outlaws came ta town and was hurtin' folks and shootin' up the place. I'd expect some help," said Sam. "If I didn't get it, I'd leave. I won't git myself kilt for folks who aren't willin' ta help themselves."

"I'll have a talk with the townspeople and I'm sure we would do whatever we could to help you if the need would arise," said Paul.

"So how would I be gettin' paid?" asked Sam. "I hear them others just took a cut of all the businesses."

"Yes, that's what they did," said Paul. "But I propose something different for you Mr. Waters. This fella who owned the saloon had no kin around here other than the Marshal. From now on, you are the owner of the saloon. That will be your pay. How does that sound Mr. Waters?"

"Does anybody in here object to me bein' the new owner?" asked Sam. No one objected. The cook, the bartender, and the working girls were all glad to have Sam as the new owner. "I reckon I'll give it a try for a spell. There will be a condition though."

"And what would that be?" asked Paul.

"You townspeople will treat these working girls like they are regular citizens and not trashy whores," said Sam. "I don't wanna hear no Bible thumpin' shit bout sin and whores and such. Have you folks ever wondered why women become whores? I'll tell ya right now it's not cause they like pokin'. You will be nice to them all the time, not just when they come to your place to spend money."

"We'll do our best Mr. Waters," said Paul. "It's hard to change the way you were brought up, but we'll try."

"Now does this town have a jail?" asked Sam.

"There's a place down the street a bit that the Marshal used as an office," answered Paul. "We don't have a real jail. The Marshal never locked anybody up. They just beat'em up and sent'em outta town. We don't have no telegraph here either. Closest one is at the county seat over a hunnerd miles away."

"Well I want a jail cell built in that office," said Sam. "You got a blacksmith at that livery. He should be able ta make some iron bars'r somethin'. So how does any news'r anything git ta town."

"Stage comes here once a week," said Paul. "The County Sheriff used ta come ta town every few months but we haven't seen him for good while."

"Well you boys spread word that ya got a new Marshal," said Sam. "And git that blacksmith busy on them iron bars. And git yerself a new Mayor elected. He'll need ta figure on how ta pay for the jail cell."

Paul and the others left. Sam had a talk with the bartender. "So how'd that other fella pay you?" asked Sam.

"Name's Charlie Adams," started the bartender. "I was paid $20 a month and they let me stay in the back room. It's not much more than a bad shack. I won't lie to you Mr. Waters. Ever once in a while I did a little skimmin'. Mebbe $2 a week when I could git away with it. I figured he owed me that fer not payin' me much. Hell, I'm the only bartender here. Most days I'm here sixteen hours."

"Well Charlie, I'll give you a decent wage when I figure out what kinda business we do here," said Sam. "I'll start ya out on $30 a month. Does that sound fair?"

"Yes sir, Mr. Waters," said Charlie.

"Call me Sam," said Sam. "Mr. don't sound right. Now you probly got somethin' that needs done. You go on while I talk with the women."

Charlie went to work and Jaunita and the other girls joined Sam at a table. There were two other girls beside Juanita. One was named Julie and the other one was Georgia. Both girls were a little dark skinned so Sam assumed they were part Mexican or Indian. He didn't care. "Now how much do you girls normally charge and how much of it did your former boss take from you?" asked Sam.

"We charged $2 and that bastard took half of it," said Julie.

"So did you all git a cut from drinks," asked Sam.

"Hell no," answered Georgia. "Sometimes we'd do some skimmin' if a man left his money layin' on the table. But that didn't happen too often. That bastard and his men kept a close watch all the time."

"Well things'll be different from now on," said Sam. "If you charge $2, you keep it all. When I git settled in and see what kinda business we do, I'll give you a cut on drinks. How does that sound?"

"That's wonderful Sam," said Juanita. "You will be a good boss."

"There's one other thing," said Sam. "Juanita here is no longer a working girl. She's with me." Juanita was completely surprised by this. She was so happy. She went over and got on Sam's lap and started kissing him all over. "Whoa there," said Sam. "We'll have lotsa time fer that kinda stuff. Now do you women think two a you will be enough or do we need ta git another girl?"

"I think we can handle it," said Julie. "Why don't we give it a while. If we can't, I know someone who would come here."

"I have a cousin across the border who would gladly come here," said Jaunita.

"Sounds good ladies," said Sam. "Now I'll go to the kitchen and talk to the cook."

The cook was an older Mexican man. Sometimes when they got busy, his wife would help. "So what was your pay?" Sam asked the cook.

"$15 a month," answered the cook. "Any my name is Manuel."

"Well that's not near enough," said Sam. "I'll give you $30 a month."

"Muchus gracias," said Manuel. "That will be a big help. My wife and I are raising four grandchildren. Our daughter is living with us now. Her husband was killed by the French."

"Maybe I'll see if I can help her find some work to help out," said Sam.

"She already does a little laundry and sewing for some of the women in town," said Manuel. "She's a very good seamstress if you ever need a new shirt or something."

"I'll keep that in mind," said Sam. Now I'm goin' out and have a look at this town. So what is the name of this town? No one ever told me and I never asked."

"It is called Lonesome," said Manuel. "You will probably know why after you've been here for a while." Sam kind of shook his head and left. He put on the Marshal's badge and went around the town. He introduced himself to everyone. They all seemed glad he was there. When he stopped at his new office, the blacksmith was already there taking measurements.

"Won't take long," said the blacksmith. "That jail cell'll be done in no time. Let's hope ya don't need it much."

"Yep, let's hope that," said Sam. Then Sam left and went back to the saloon. Juanita was anxious to have her way with him again, so they spent the rest of the day together.

~~~~

The first month as a lawman for Sam was fairly quiet. A bunch of soldiers from the fort came into town one Saturday night and got drunk and a little loud, but there was no trouble. While the soldiers were in town, they let Sam know that about once a month, several of them would be getting passes and would be coming to town. It would be at the end of the month. That was good to know because when they came to town, two girls wouldn't be enough to handle all of the soldier boys.

During the next few months, the town started to grow. Word must have gotten around that Lonesome was now a peaceable town and people and businesses moved in. Lonesome now had a bank too. Business picked up really well at the saloon too. Sam hired another bartender and got some regular help for the cook. Three more girls were added. One of them was Juanita's cousin Maria. Maria soon became everybody's favorite.

The new jail cell had a few customers from time to time. If someone got a little too drunk and was getting loud or rowdy or was nasty to the girls, Sam threw them in jail. The new Mayor was also "Justice of the Peace," and the trouble makers were charged $2 for disturbing the peace. So far, Sam's job was pretty easy and his saloon was making him a wealthy man.

Reality set in one morning when Sam and Juanita were having their breakfast. A couple of shots had been fired and then horses could be heard riding out of town at a fast pace. Someone let out a yell. "The banks been robbed. The banks been robbed." Sam checked his pistol to make sure it was fully loaded and then ran over to the bank. The bank manager had been shot in the shoulder but was the one outside doing the yelling. "There was three of them Marshal," started the manager. "They rushed in with guns pulled and demanded the money. When I wouldn't give it to them, they shot me and took it. I had just opened the safe. I would have closed it, but I didn't have time. They got $8000."

"What did these fellas look like?" asked Sam.

"I know'em," said the manager. "They're the Barker brothers. They wasn't wearin' no masks. There's Dick, Fred, and Waldo. They all got brown hair and blue eyes. Their hair is long and they all wear full mustaches. They're all medium build and bout six foot tall. Dick was ridin' a palomino mare. Fred and Waldo was ridin' chestnut horses."

"Seems like you know a lot bout them fellas," said Sam. "Why's that?"

"Cause they're cousins a mine," said the manager. "Ya know how some families got bad relatives and they stay away from'em. Well the Barkers is my bad relatives. They musta heard I started up this bank and come ta rob it. You goin' after them?"

"Yes I am," said Sam. "I'll get my gear and be right after'em. You best git yerself patched up."

Sam rounded up his gear, said his goodbyes to Juanita, and headed out. The outlaws were less than a half hour ahead of him. Sam could tell by their tracks that they were riding hard. It wouldn't be long and they'd have to slow down and rest the horses. After a while, Sam could tell by the tracks that they hadn't slowed down. It wasn't long and Sam discovered why. Just ahead of him were three horses by the trail. They were soaked with sweat. The Barkers had changed horses. Sam continued on the trail but took his time. He stayed on the trail till dark and then made camp for the night. He didn't have a fire. He ate some jerky and cold biscuits and washed it down with some water. He was up before daylight. He chewed on some jerky as he rode. About noon, he came across three more horses. The outlaws had changed horses again. These horses were not all sweaty so the change had been made sometime earlier. These horses were rested. Sam threw a rope on one of them and took off again. He would change horses if he had to.

Sam knew he probably wouldn't catch up to the outlaws, but he knew where they were headed. The trail they were on led to Hadleyville. He figured the Barkers would want to spend some of the money they just stole on whiskey and women. Sam figured that the outlaws wouldn't expect to be followed. A town marshal had no authority outside of his town. Sam wasn't worried about authority. They robbed a bank in his town and he was going to get them. He rode carefully at all times keeping a look out for possible ambush sites.

Hadleyville was the county seat. The County Sheriff who seldom went to Lonesome would be there. Sam wasn't quite sure what to expect from the Sheriff. He figured he wasn't much of a lawman since he seldom visited Lonesome. He most likely knew the men who ran the town or was afraid of them and steered clear of them.

The livery was on the edge of town. The first thing Sam did was get his horse boarded. The man at the livery gave Sam a strange look when he first saw him. "Where'd you git that other horse mister?" asked the man. "And who're you?"

"Name's Sam Waters. I'm Marshal of Lonesome," answered Sam. "This other horse was used by some outlaws that robbed the bank in Lonesome. They had horses along the trail and traded horses two times."

"Well that horse was stolen from here four days ago," said the man.

"Well you got it back now," said Sam. "Did three fellas come here yesterday that looked like they could be brothers? They all got long brown hair and blue eyes and have full mustaches."

"I got their horses in the corral out back," said the livery man. "They come in yesterday and said they'd be here a few days."

"Well them three had yer horse and they robbed the bank in Lonesome," said Sam. "Don't spose you know where they might be."

"There's three saloons in town and they all got whores," said the livery man. "They're probly at one a them. You gonna tell the Sheriff yer in town. He might not like you comin' here since ya got no authority here."

"I don't care what he might think," said Sam. "But I will tell'm I'm here and what I'm after."

"Well good luck to ya," said the livery man.

"If I was you, I'd stay inside for a spell," said Sam. "Might be some shootin' in a bit."

Sam grabbed his two other pistols off of his saddle horn and put them across his left shoulder. He got his Henry and carried it with his left hand. He looked around town a bit until he spotted the Sheriff's office. He opened the door and went inside. A big man, maybe around thirty, was asleep at a desk. Sam saw the badge on his chest. The man didn't wake when Sam went inside. Sam closed the door hard and woke him up. "Who the hell're you and why you wakin' me up?" asked the Sheriff.

"Name's Sam Water. I'm Marshal over at Lonesome," said Sam. "Three fellas robbed the bank there and they're in this town."

"Well you got no authority here so git yerself outta town and back to Lonesome," said the Sheriff. If there's outlaws in this town, I'll git'em. Do you know who they are?"

"They're the Barker brothers," said Sam. "They got $8000 and shot the bank manager."

"I know them Barker boys," said the Sheriff. "They're good boys. They wouldn't be robbin' no bank."

"Sheriff, I may as well go piss in the wind instead of talkin' to you," said Sam. "Now I'm gonna go look for them three. Stay outta my way. Mebbe you should just go back ta sleep. You know, I bet that bunch over at Lonesome was giving you a cut ta stay outta their business. No sir, that wouldn't surprise me a bit."

"I'll round up my deputies and we'll be runnin' you outta town," said the Sheriff. Sam had enough of the Sheriff. Before the Sheriff knew what was happening, Sam pulled a pistol, reached across the desk and cracked the Sheriff's head. The Sheriff slumped down in his chair. Sam dragged him into an empty jail cell. He found some rope and tied the Sheriff and gagged him. He locked the cell door and put the key in his pocket. Then Sam headed for the nearest saloon.

As he entered the saloon, he got a lot of stares. He looked around the saloon. No one with the Barker brother description was there at the tables or at the bar. Sam went to the bartender. "I'm lookin' fer the Barker brothers," said Sam. "There's three of'em. They all got long brown hair and blue eyes. They all got full mustaches too."

"I know them boys," said the bartender. "What they done this time?"

"They robbed a bank and shot the manager," said Sam. "Now are they in here?"

"They was here last night but I haven't seen'em today," said the bartender. "They're probly at one a the other saloons tryin' ta wear out their whores. They was spendin' a lotta money in here last night."

"Are them boys friends a yers?" asked Sam.

"I know'em but they're not friends," answered the bartender.

"That's good," said Sam. "I'd take it bad if you put out the word that I'm lookin' fer'em."

"So who are you Mister," asked the bartender. "I see that badge but yer not a Federal man."

"No, I'm just the Marshal over at Lonesome," said Sam.

"Well you got no authority over here," said the bartender. "You best go git the Sheriff."

"The Sheriff's busy and can't come," said Sam. "Now remember what I said."

"I won't ferget Marshal," said the bartender. "Hell, you got enough firepower there ta wipe out the whole damn town if ya want." Sam nodded his head and headed for the next saloon. As soon as he entered the saloon, he saw two men with women on their laps. They fit the description of the Barkers. They were sitting at a table just to the right of the bar. The two men saw Sam as he entered. They didn't recognize this man but they knew something wasn't right. This man was heavily armed and wearing a badge. The two women saw Sam and tried to get off the laps of the men, but the two men held them down. Sam walked toward their table. He also made sure no one got behind him. He glanced around to see if the third brother was around. Sam worked the lever on the Henry and pointed it at the table. "You Barker brothers are goin' with me," said Sam. "Let them women up."

"I think them women'll stay right where they are lawman," said Dick Barker. "Now you ease on outta here before someone gits hurt. You wouldn't want one a these fine girls ta git shot would ya?" Sam took the Henry and pointed it right at Dick's forehead.

"You do whatever it is you think you can do," said Sam. "But you'll have a nice hole in yer head if ya try anything." Just then, a voice came from upstairs.

"Drop that rifle right now lawman," said Waldo Barker. "Ya got five seconds." Sam put the muzzle of the Henry right on Dick's forehead and smiled.

"He's a lawman. He won't shoot," said Dick. "Go ahead and shoot'm Waldo."

As soon as the words were out of Dick's mouth, Sam squeezed the trigger on the Henry. Blood flew everywhere. The two girls screamed and ran off. They were covered with blood. A split second after that, Sam trained the rifle on Fred's heart and fired. Fred was dead when he hit the floor. His right hand was holding his pistol and the pistol fired when he hit the floor. The bullet went through a front window of the saloon. It struck a horse that was tied to the hitching post in front of the saloon. The bullet hit the horse in it's left eye. It fell to the ground but lay there screaming and kicking.

Waldo started firing at Sam but he missed several times. One of the saloon girls was hit in the leg. Waldo ducked into a room upstairs and closed the door. Sam yelled for someone in the saloon to help the woman who had been shot. No one moved. "No count sons a bitches," yelled Sam. All the other patrons in the saloon were hugging the floor. Sam went to the closest man to him and grabbed his shirt by the collar. Then he gave it a yank and ripped the back out of the shirt. He took the piece of shirt over to the woman and wrapped it around her leg. "Sorry bout this ma'am," Sam said to her. Then he handed her a couple of dollars. "This is fer yer doc bill ma'am. Now if you'll excuse me, there's some fella upstairs who wants ta die." Sam moved away from the woman. Waldo did not fire any more shots. Sam stood and took took aim on the door with the Henry and fired off eight shots. They struck the door high and low and on both sides of the door frame. When Sam quit firing, Waldo's body was heard falling to the floor. Sam ran upstairs and kicked the door open. Waldo was dead. Sam checked the room to make sure there was nobody else there. Then Sam went through Waldo's pockets. Waldo had $2000 in his pockets. Then Sam went downstairs. He threw a dollar at the man whose shirt he had torn. Then he went through Dick's and Fred's pockets. They had $5000 between them. Just as Sam stood up, two men wearing stars entered the saloon. "What the hell happened here?" yelled one of the men.

"The Barker boys robbed the bank in Lonesome and shot the manager. I'm the Marshal there," said Sam. "I'm taking what money they didn't git spent and goin' back ta Lonesome."

"We'll see bout that," said one of the deputies. "Bill, you go git the Sheriff. We'll see what he's got ta say bout this."

"You'll need the key," said Sam as he threw the cell key to the deputy. "Now I'm leavin' this town. Anybody tries ta stop me'll end up like the Barker boys, law or not." The two deputies stood there sizing Sam up. One of them almost went for his pistol, but changed his mind. Sam changed it for him. As soon as Sam saw the deputy's hand just barely move, he had his pistol out and cocked. He pointed it at the deputies. "There's no good reason fer you boys ta die right now," said Sam. "Now go tend to yer boss. And someone git a doc fer this woman here. Jesus H. Christ. You dern fools'd let her bleed ta death while you was thinkin' bout gittin' yerself kilt." The deputies left and someone went for the doc. When Sam was leaving the saloon, the woman who had been shot hobbled over to him and kissed him on the cheek. Sam tipped his hat to her and smilled. The horse that had been shot through it's eye was still alive and kicking and screaming. Sam put it out of it's misery.

~~~~

Sam went to the livery and left town without incident. He took the Barker brothers' horses with him. Maybe these horses were stolen and maybe they weren't. Sam didn't care. He didn't get all the money back so the horses were worth something. He'd give them to the bank too.

The two deputies went to the jail and found the Sheriff. They unlocked the cell and untied him. He was awake now. "That Marshal from Lonesome kilt them Barker boys," said one of the deputies. "Are we goin' after'm?"

"No, that man'll git himself kilt soon enough," said the Sheriff. "A man like that gits a reputation real quick. He won't last long."

CHAPTER TWELVE

As soon as Sam left Hadleyville, he realized that he wanted to get back home. Lonesome was his home now. He liked it there. He hadn't had a real home since before the war. And now he had Juanita. He'd only been with her for five or six months, but he knew he loved her. They would be married when he got back. He knew she would have him for her husband. Maybe they would even have children one day. When he finally had Lonesome in sight, he rode the rest of the way to town at a full gallop. The first person he saw in town was the bank manager. Sam dismounted and handed a flour sack to the man. "There's only $7000 there," said Sam. "They spent the rest. They're dead now. These is their horses. They're yers now. Sam handed the lead rope to the banker. I'll be seein' Juanita now." Sam saw a look come over the banker's face, but he never said a word. Sam tied his horse in front of the saloon and went inside. Maria saw him and went running to him. She was crying hysterically. "They took her Sam. They took her," cried Maria.

"Who took who?" asked Sam.

"They took Juanita," said Maria. "There was three of them. They came in here and there was a big argument between them and Juanita. They started dragging her out the door. Charlie tried to stop them and they shot him. He died the next day."

Sam was at a loss for words. He knew he wanted to kill someone but who were those three men. He sat down for a minute and cried. "Did anyone hear any names fer them men?" asked Sam.

"One of them called another one Clyde and another one was called Sol," said Maria. "I never heard a name for the other one."

"Can you give me a description of them?" asked Sam.

"The one called Sol was a short stocky fellow," started Maria. "He had yellow hair and there was a big scar on his chin. The one called Clyde was a tall skinny man. He had black hair and was missing a front tooth. The other fella was a very ugly man. His face looked like it had powder burns all over it. He wore tall moccasins instead of boots. They were all riding bay horses."

"Which way were they headed when they left?" asked Sam.

"They went south," answered Maria.

"When did all this happen?" asked Sam.

"The day after you left," answered Maria. "We wanted to get ahold of you but didn't know how. No one here is a tracker and we have no telegraph yet."

"I'll be leavin' in the mornin'," said Sam. "You'll be in charge while I'm gone. Hire yerself another bartender if you find a good person. I'll be tellin' the Mayor what I'm doin'." Sam found the Mayor and told him his intentions. "I'll be gone as long as it takes," said Sam. "Somethin' happens ta me, the saloon goes to Maria. She's in charge while I'm gone. Don't know how long this'll take. If it takes a while, ya might think bout hirin' someone till I git back."

"We have faith that you'll be back and Maria will be safe," said the Mayor. "God speed."

~~~~

Sam didn't get much sleep that night. All he could think of was what the three men could do to Juanita. He got up a little before daylight and rounded up some supplies. He would take a pack horse with him. The cook was up and fixed him some breakfast. As he was about to mount his horse, Maria came out to wish him luck. "Viya con dios," said Maria.

"God may not want to spend much time with me after I get done with them three," said Sam. "Now Maria, do you remember what Juanita was wearing when they took her?"

"Yes Sam, I do. It was a calico dress," answered Maria. "It was the one you bought her a couple of months ago."

"That'll be a big help," said Sam. "Now you take care of the place while I'm gone. Be back as soon as I can."

~~~~

Sam left town heading south. He had no idea where the outlaws were headed or anything. One thing he did know for sure. They had Juanita with them and they would want to use her as soon as they could. He passed a few travelers on the way to the border. He questioned all of them, but no one had seen or heard anything about three gringos and a senorita. He made camp for the night and crossed into Mexico the next morning. Right after he crossed the river, he found a campsite that was a few days old. It looked like there had been three or four horses. There were some footprints but they were hard to make out. It looked like there could have been some strong winds because the prints were mostly covered. He was about to mount his horse when he saw something in some brush. He went over and looked at it. It was a piece of calico. He was on the right trail. He had ridden only a couple of hours when he ran into a French patrol. The officer in charge spoke English. He wasn't very friendly. He kept asking Sam if he was down there to fight with the Juaristas. "Look Lieutenant, or whatever your rank is, three men took my woman and I'm down here to get her back," said Sam. "I don't know nothin' bout no Juaristas and I don't know nothin' bout you. Have you seen three gringos with a senorita? She had on a calico dress."

"No we have not seen them," answered the Lt. "There are lots of places to hide here. If I were you, I'd keep heading south. There is a small village about two hours from here. They have a cantina. Your gringos might have needed a drink. Now I must continue the patrol. If I were you, I would not stay long in this country. It is not a safe place to be."

Sam continued south. The tracks he was following were several days old. Not long after he left the French patrol, Sam found a horseshoe. One of the horses had thrown a shoe. Maybe there would be a blacksmith at the village. Maybe he would know something about the three men.

There were only a few buildings in the village. They were adobe. There was a church, the cantina, a store, and another building that Sam wasn't sure about. Not far from the buildings were several shacks made of sticks and whatever else could be found. Sam went to the cantina first. Inside was an old man and an attractive, but middle aged woman. The woman went to Sam and asked if he wanted a woman or a drink or both. "I just want some information," said Sam. "Did three gringos come in here a few days ago?"

"Information can be expensive down here," said the woman.

"Not giving information can be costly too," said Sam. "It could cost you your life if you know something I want and don't tell me."

"I am not afraid of you gringo," said the woman. "I get threatened by the French and the Jauristas."

"Well senorita or senora or whatever you are, I will pay well if you have the information I want," said Sam. Sam reached into a pocket and pulled out a $20 gold piece. He tossed it to the woman. "You'll get another one if I get good answers to my questions."

The woman put the gold piece in her mouth and bit down. She looked at the piece and then put it in a pocket. "All right gringo, what do you want to know?" asked the woman.

"Did three gringos stop here a few days ago and if they did, was there a senorita with them?" asked Sam.

"Three gringos did stop here a few days ago. There was no woman with them," answered the woman. "They ate, drank, and then left."

"What did they look like?" asked Sam.

"One was tall with black hair and had a front tooth missing," started the woman. "Another one was very ugly. He wore tall moccasins instead of boots. The other man scared me. He was kind of short but wide and had yellow hair. There was a scar on his chin. What scared me was that he had deep scratches on both sides of his face and neck. A woman had to have done that to him."

Sam tossed another gold piece to the woman. "Do you reckon anyone around here might have seen the woman?" asked Sam.

"You might ask the farmers around here," said the woman. "There are a lot of small farms all over this area. They might not talk to you. They are afraid of everyone and everything. There is fighting around here all the time between the Juaristas and the French."

"Which way did the three men head when they left town?" asked Sam.

"They were headed east," answered the woman.

Sam thanked the woman and started looking for farms in the area. No one had seen anything but they would tell Sam where the next farm was. It was about an hour before dark. Sam decided he would stop at one more farm and then camp for the night. As he approached the farm, he noticed some fresh diggings about a hundred yards from the stick building that was the farmhouse. Sam looked hard at the recently turned dirt. "That sure looks like a grave," Sam said to himself. Then he rode over to the house. "Hello in the house," said Sam. A middle aged man and a woman came to the door. Sam could see some children trying to hide behind them. "Buenos dias," said Sam. "My name is Sam Waters. I'm looking for a senorita who was taken by three gringos. She was wearing a calico dress. Have you seen her?"

"We have seen her Senor Waters," said the man. "I am Roberto Gonzales. The woman is buried in that grave you passed." The man's wife started crying and grabbed the children and left the doorway.

"How did she die?" asked Sam.

"She was beaten very badly," answered Roberto. "I have never seen anyone beaten that badly before. It is hard to talk about."

"Please tell me if you can," said Sam.

"There were bruises on most of her body," started Roberto. "Most of her ribs were probably broken. Her jaw and nose were broken. Her left eye was hanging out. She had been raped. Her right arm was broken too. Please don't make me go on." Sam broke down and cried. He cried for a good ten minutes.

"How did she get here?" asked Sam after he got control of his tears.

"My daughter found her in one of our fields," said Roberto. "She saw the woman laying there and screamed for me to come. I don't know how, but the woman was still alive. We got her into the house and did what we could for her. I sent my oldest son into town for the priest. He only comes here once a month and he was here on that day. He made it out here just before she died. He heard her confession and gave the last rights. We buried her right after that."

"Was she able to say anything else?" asked Sam.

"She was asking for Sam," said Roberto. "Where's Sam. I want my Sam. That was the last thing she said before she died."

"So you never saw the gringos?" asked Sam.

"No one ever comes here," said Roberto. "Even the French haven't bothered me for a while."

"Can you show me where you found her in the field?" asked Sam.

"Yes, I can show you, but if you are looking for sign, you will not find much," said Roberto. The field was plowed yesterday."

"Well I'll just ride around the edge of the field and see if I can pick up any sign," said Sam. On the first pass around the field, Sam didn't see anything. On the second pass, he spotted some hoof prints. They looked to be a few days old. There were three horses and one of the horses was missing a shoe. Sam's anger could not be contained. He got off his horse and pulled his pistol. He fired six shots into the ground. "Sons a bitches," Sam shouted. "Use my Juanita, beat her to death, and then just toss her out into some field. I will get you sons a bitches and you will die slow."

Sam rode back over to the house. "Thank you for helping Juanita," said Sam. "I'll be on my way now."

"It is late Senor," said Roberto. "You are welcome to eat with us. Come, join us. You can continue your search for those men in the morning." Sam was too tired and upset to say no.

Roberto had four children, two boys and two girls. They looked to be aged from nine or ten to maybe fifteen. The girls were older and starting to become women. As he ate, Sam wondered what it would have been like if he and Juanita had gotten married and had a family. They didn't talk much as they ate. Roberto's wife made a place on the floor for Sam to sleep. He slept good that night. He had good dreams of Juanita. Reality set in the next morning when he woke up. Roberto offered Sam some breakfast and he accepted. Roberto's oldest son had Sam's horse saddled and the pack horse ready when Sam finished breakfast. Sam thanked everyone for their kindness and tried to give Roberto some money. Roberto would not accept any money. Sam went to the pack horse. He got some salt pork, beans, salt, flour, and gave them to Roberto. These things he accepted.

~~~~

Sam headed east. The trail was old, but could still be followed. He came to another small town. The outlaws had been seen. They had eaten and then moved on. Sam lost their trail about an hour from the town. Apparently, a troop of French cavalry had gotten on this trail and were headed the same direction as the outlaws. Sam camped for the night and then headed out at daylight. He rode east most of the day. He was hoping that he could pick up some sign, but had no luck. The cavalry troop had destroyed the tracks he needed to follow. Sam just continued eastward. Maybe the outlaws would be visiting the border towns. There was always plenty of liquor and women in border towns.

Sam was right. In every little border town he found, the three outlaws had been seen. Sam was getting closer now, but he was still maybe three days behind them. All of the little border towns looked alike. There was always a cantina, a church, a store, and a few houses. When Sam came to the next town, there were three bay horses tied in front of the cantina. Sam tied his horses to the hitching post. He took the holsters that held his two other pistols from his saddle horn, and threw them over his left shoulder. He approached the door of the cantina slowly. He could see over the top of the door. There were three Mexican men and a woman inside. They were all sitting at one table. The woman was on the lap of one of them. They had been talking and laughing, but when Sam entered the cantina, it got very quiet. Sam looked around the place to make sure no one else was in there. The three Mexicans and the woman stared at Sam for a few moments. Then one of the Mexicans stood. It was the one who had the woman on his lap. The woman went over behind the bar. "Hey gringo," said the Mexican. "You must be expecting some trouble since you are wearing three pistolas. You must be after someone. I know everyone around here. I can tell you what you want for a price."

"I believe I'll just have somethin' ta eat," said Sam. "I doubt you have anything I want."

"I have tried to be kind to you gringo and you have insulted me," said the Mexican. "You will give me $20 in gold and I will forget the whole thing. You can even have this woman."

"I don't want the woman and you're not gettin' $20," said Sam. The three Mexicans all had tied down Colts. Sam also figured that there was a shotgun behind the bar and the woman would use it.

"Well, I'm tired of your insults. I think we will just kill you and take your money, guns, and horses," said the Mexican. The two other Mexicans were still sitting. Sam figured they would draw as they started to stand. He was right. As soon as they started to stand, he saw their hands going for the Colts. The Mexican who was standing had his pistol halfway out of the holster when Sam's bullet hit him dead center in the chest. Sam turned his pistol and fired two shots so close together they sounded like one. The other two men hit the floor dead. Sam looked over at the woman. She had grabbed a shotgun from behind the bar and was cocking the hammers.

"Don't do it senorita. I will kill you," said Sam. The senorita got the hammers cocked and was lowering the barrel to fire at Sam. Sam's bullet caught her right between the eyes. There was a painting of a white horse on the wall behind the bar. The white horse was now a red horse. Sam could hear someone running toward the cantina. He kept his pistol in his hand and faced the door. An older man and a woman entered the cantina. They stared at the dead bodies for a moment. Then they looked at Sam.

"I am Manuel Moralez and this is my wife Consuela," said Manuel. "We run the store in town. I see you have killed the banditos. Are you a bounty hunter?"

"No Manuel, I'm just a man trying to find three gringos who took my woman, used her, and killed her," said Sam. "Have you seen three gringos in the last few days."

"Three gringos were here three days ago," answered Manuel. "They ate and then moved on heading east."

"I am glad that woman is dead," said Consuela. "Puta!" Then she spit toward the dead woman's body.

"I guess these folks weren't well liked around here," said Sam.

"No, these banditos have been stealing from us for years," said Manuel. "The whore was the woman of their leader. He was not one of the ones you killed. When he finds out, he will be after you. He is a very bad man Senor. The Juaristas and the French are both after him."

"Well, if he comes around here after I leave, tell him my name is Sam Waters," said Sam. "He will join his friends in hell if he comes after me. Now can a man get somethin' ta eat around here?"

"You can come over to our house," said Manuel. "Consuela is a good cook and we will be glad to feed you after what you have done here."

Sam had a good meal and moved on. Manuel invited him to stay the night, but Sam wanted to gain ground on the outlaws. There was a full moon that night so Sam rode well into the night. It was two more days before Sam got to the next town. There were ten horses in front of the cantina. They appeared to be French cavalry horses. After Sam tied his horses, he grabbed his extra pistols and went inside. There were ten French soldiers inside. They were sitting at three different tables. There were four of them at two tables, and two at the other. The two soldiers at the one table appeared to be Officers or an Officer and a Sergeant. Sam went to a table at the other side of the cantina so he could keep an eye on everyone and everything. A woman came to his table and asked what he wanted. Sam told her he wanted some food and coffee. After the woman left, one of the French soldiers came over to Sam's table. "I am Lieutenant Dupon'," he began. "I have heard a story about a Yankee who carries many guns and killed three banditos. Are you that Yankee?"

"Damn, word sure traveled fast," Sam said. "I heard that story myself."

"So if you are that man, I thank you," said the Lt. "If you are not, It looks like you are ready for trouble with all those guns. You will need all those guns when you run into the friends of the banditos who were killed. They will see all those guns and assume that you are that man. Now please excuse me. I must talk some with my Sergeant." The Lt. went back to his table. He and the Sergeant were looking at a map. The Lt. was just rolling up the map when a bunch of armed Mexicans burst into the cantina. They came in through the front door, the back door, and the windows. Several of them yelled "Viva Jaurez" and "Viva Mexico." Then they started shooting. The French soldiers were ripped to pieces.

Sam thought about trying to slip out. It was hard to see in there with all the gunsmoke. Sam decided to stay at his table. He pulled a pistol with each hand and held his hands under the table. When the smoke finally cleared, there were fifteen or more armed Mexicans standing over the dead French soldiers. They were dressed like peasants. One of them came over to Sam's table. "I am Migel Rojas. I know you are the gringo who killed the banditos," he said. We are glad you killed them. They were a disgrace to our country. You may put your pistols away. We will not harm you. We know why you are here."

"So since you know why I'm here, have you or any of your men seen the three gringos I am after?" asked Sam.

"We have," said Migel. "We did not know what these men had done when we saw them. If we had known, we would have killed them. They were here three days ago. They tried to steal some horses as they were leaving. My men chased them all the way to the border. They are now in Texas."

"Well I thank you for your kindness," said Sam. "I'll be on my way. And good luck with the French."

Sam didn't wait on the food that he had ordered. He mounted up and headed for the border. After he crossed into Texas, he rode till dark and then made camp. Sam had no idea which way to go. The outlaws could have gone anywhere. Once they got to a town, they could have taken a stage and gone anywhere. Sam didn't sleep much that night. Texas was full of outlaws, bandits, and Indians. When daylight came, Sam made up his mind he would head to San Antonio. He figured that if he was the outlaws, that's where he would go.

It was a long ride to San Antonio. He had to avoid Comanche country too. It took him a week to get there. The first thing he did was find the Town Marshal. He gave him a description of the three men. The Marshal had not seen anyone fitting the descriptions, but he would notify Sam if they showed up later. He'd have to write Sam in Lonesome because Lonesome didn't have a telegraph yet.

"You should get them fellas on some wanted posters," said the Marshal. "Maybe some bounty hunter might get'em if there's a price on'em."

"I don't know all their names," said Sam. "One goes by Sol and another goes by Clyde, but I don't know the other one's name and I don't know no last names."

"Well if you got descriptions and first names, that can be used on a poster," said the Marshal. "As long as someone can positively identify them when they're brought in, that's good enough. There's lotsa men outta work cause a the war. Lotta men bounty huntin' hopin' ta make a dollar. Them posters'll be sent all over ta Town Marshals and Sheriffs. Sooner'r later, someone'll see'em. It might take a while, but they'll get caught. Most outlaws do."

Sam made up his mind. He'd go ahead and get some wanted posters made for the three men. He'd also post a $200 reward for each man, but it wouldn't be dead or alive. Sam wanted the three men alive. After all of this was done, Sam went around town and looked around. He asked everyone he saw if they had seen the three men. No one had. He had a meal at a café and spent the night at a hotel. The next day, he was on a stage to El Paso. It would take several days to get to El Paso. After he got there, he might get lucky and catch the weekly stage to Lonesome. If not, he'd ride.

Sam lucked out. When he got to El Paso, the weekly stage to Lonesome would be leaving the next morning. He spent the night at a hotel and was on the stage in the morning. Sam noticed something on the road to Lonesome. Telegraph poles were being set. It wouldn't be long and Lonesome would have the telegraph.

~~~~

Sam was glad to be home, but it wouldn't be the same without Juanita. After his horses were taken care of, Sam went straight to the saloon. Maria saw him and ran to him. She hugged him and then wanted to know if he had found Juanita. Sam went to a table and sat down. He almost cried, but he kept his tears back. "They killed her," said Sam. "They raped her and beat her bad. Then they threw her out in some field to die." Maria was crying now.

"Did you catch them?" asked Maria after her tears stopped.

"I was on their trail," said Sam. "They crossed back into Texas and I lost'em. I'll get'em though. I don't care how long it takes. I'll get'em and when I do, they'll find out what hell's like." They both cried together for a while.

~~~~

Two weeks later, the telegraph was in Lonesome. Sam was in contact with lawmen all over Texas, New Mexico, and Kansas. No one had seen the men in question, but they would contact Sam if they did. It had been quiet in town during Sam's absence. Maria had hired another bartender and he was doing a good job. The girls were all making plenty of money and everyone was happy. A month rolled by and Sam could tell that Maria was starting to have some feelings for him. He had a long talk with her and explained that he was just not ready for her. He had to get Juanita's killers before his mind would set him free. Maria said that she understood and could wait.

Maria did wait a year for Sam, but after that year, she found someone else. He was a young business man and he was starting a newspaper. It didn't bother him that Maria had been a whore. The wedding was held in the saloon and Sam gave the bride away.

CHAPTER THIRTEEN

Things stayed quiet in Lonesome the during the next year. The jail cell had not gotten much use. Sam locked up a couple of drunks because he was afraid that they might accidentally hurt themselves. One time he ran a couple of men out of town because they were acting nasty to the girls in the saloon. They left without incident.

One Saturday afternoon, Sam was sitting on the porch in front of the saloon reading a newspaper. There was a story in it about this Federal Marshal named O'Rourke up in Kansas. He had been having a lot of shoot outs and had killed a lot of outlaws. "Maybe one day I'll meet O'Rourke,"

Sam said to himself. "Sounds like my kind a lawman." Sam finished the article and turned the page. He leaned back in his chair and yawned. As he was yawning, he caught sight of three Mexicans on horseback in the street. They were riding toward him. Sam carefully looked them over. All three of them wore two pistols. They also had rifles on their saddles. Sam put the newspaper down and stood. He knew his pistol was not fully loaded but had five rounds in it. The Mexicans stopped in the street about twenty feet from Sam and dismounted. They let their horses stand with their reins down and all three of them stood facing Sam. The one in the middle spoke.

"Gringo, I have looked for you for a long time," he began. "I am El Tigre. You killed my woman and now I shall kill you."

"Oh yeh, so yer that bandit from down Mexico," started Sam. "That woman a yers was gonna blow me away with a shotgun. I told her not ta try it, but she wouldn't listen. I reckon you think yer better with a gun than them three men a yers I already kilt."

"I am better gringo," said El Tigre.

"So are them other two fellas gonna help ya?" asked Sam.

"Pedro and Chico are grown men and do what they want," said El Tigre. "I have not asked them for help, but I think they want to kill you too. Those three men you killed were their friends."

"Those three men were loudmouth idiots," said Sam. "Now are you gonna talk me ta death or can we git this over with?" El Tigre never said a word. He went for a pistol with his right hand. Before his hand even touched the pistol, he was falling backwards with a hole in his forehead. The man on the left of El Tigre had his pistol out now and about to fire when Sam's bullet caught him dead center in the chest. The other Mexican had his pistol out and fired at Sam. Sam fired again at almost the same time as the last Mexican. The Mexican's bullet caught Sam's upper left arm and turned him sideways. As Sam was turning, he saw the Mexican falling backwards with blood on his chest. Sam cocked his hammer again and walked over to the last Mexican. He was dead. The bullet had gone through his heart. Sam checked the other two to make sure they were dead. Several people ran out into the street to find out what had happened. The Mayor was the first person in the street.

"What the hell was this all about?" asked the Mayor.

"Oh, Just a little leftover trouble from down in Mexico," said Sam.

"Well we don't need that kind of gunplay in this town," said the Mayor.

"Well don't you worry yerself sick Mayor," said Sam. "These three won't be havin' any more shootouts anywhere."

"That was not my meaning," said the Mayor.

"I know what yer meaning was," said Sam. "This town is gettin' civilized and civilized folks don't go shootin' each other. Well Mayor, I wasn't gonna stand there and let that son of a bitch kill me. Now maybe you and some a these other fine citizens'll git these dead bodies off the street. The Mayor shook his head and walked away. Sam knew what the Mayor was thinking. He wanted law and order but he didn't want anyone to die while the law was being enforced.

Lonesome was still slowly growing. They didn't have an undertaker in town yet but they had a new young doctor who was just starting his practice. The dead bodies were taken to the barber shop and Sam went to the new doctor. Sam knew that the new doctor had come to town but he had not met him yet. The doctor was excited when Sam went to his office. "My first bullet wound," said the doctor. "Oh, I'm sorry. I'm Jonas Wilson. Dr. Jonas Wilson.

"Sam Waters," said Sam. "Patch me up Doc."

"Have a seat on that table there and we'll get your shirt off," said Doc. Sam sat down and tried to take his shirt off. Doc could see that he was hurting and helped him. Doc cleaned off his arm so he could tell what was going on. "The bullet went through," said Doc. "But it clipped the bone some. I see some bone chips that'll have to be removed. I can put you out if you'd like. This is going to hurt."

"Just git it done Doc," said Sam. "I been shot before."

"Yes, I can see that you have," said Doc. Doc looked at the scars on Sam where he had been shot before. He had been shot in both shoulders and his left side. "Were you in the late war?"

"I was," answered Sam.

"What side was you on," asked Doc.

"What does that matter?" asked Sam. "Are you gonna refuse to help me if I say I was on the wrong side."

"No Sam," said Doc. "I didn't mean to be nosey. I was just looking at your old scars and admiring the work that the doctors did on you. They did a very good job."

"Well, not much to bullet holes sometimes," said Sam. "Ya clean'em up and plug'em up and then hope ya don't die from infection. I was one a the lucky ones. Seen too many men gittin' their arms and legs cut off. So you think you could cut off a man's leg Doc?"

"I would do whatever was needed to save a life," said Doc. "Now hold still. Like I said. This is gonna hurt."

It did hurt. It hurt a lot, but Sam didn't yell or scream. When Doc was done with the bone chips, he bandaged up Sam and put a sling on him. "How long I gotta wear this sling?" asked Sam.

"I'm treating your arm just like it was broken," said Doc. "And it could very well be broken. The bullet might have cracked it and a wrong move could break it the rest of the way. I want you to wear the sling for six weeks. And I want you to see me again in a week. Change that bandage every day until it scabs over well. Do you have any questions?"

"What do I owe ya Doc?" asked Sam.

"$2.00," said Doc. Sam paid Doc and headed back to the Saloon.

Before Sam got to the saloon, he was met by the Mayor. Sam gave him a look of disgust. "Just what is it you want now?" asked Sam.

"I was thinking, that is, some of the other citizens and I were thinking that maybe you should get yourself a deputy," said the Mayor. "Your left arm is laid up plus the town has been growing and will continue to grow."

"And how will this deputy git paid?" asked Sam.

"Why you'll pay him of course with money from the saloon," said the Mayor. "We gave you that saloon, remember."

"Yep, I remember," said Sam. "I spose I could pay a deputy $40 a month. Just where am I gittin' this deputy? Haven't seen one man in town I'd want standin' by me when I needed'm."

"I have just the man for you," said the Mayor. "My son has just finished law school and will be home later this week. Being a deputy would give him some good experience. He will see what a real lawman does before he sets up his law practice."

"Just how long do you think your son will stay alive if he's my deputy?" asked Sam. "What if the bank'd git robbed again? Could yer son break up a bar fight? Has yer son ever shot a gun?"

"I took him bird hunting when he was younger," said the Mayor. "He's a fine shot."

"I'll bet them birds weren't shootin' back," said Sam.

"Look Sam, I can't make you hire my son, but I can fire you," said the Mayor. "Don't make me fire you."

"You know Mayor, you do whatever the hell you want," said Sam. "I'll think I'll hire yer son as a deputy just ta see how soon he'll git hisself kilt. Now if you'll excuse me, I've got to rest some,

Dr.'s orders." Sam went into the saloon and sat down at the near-est table. The Mayor took off muttering to himself.

~~~~

The Mayor's son arrived in town the next week. After a day with the family, the Mayor took him over to meet Sam. Sam was sit-ting in a chair in front of the saloon when the mayor found him. "Sam, this is my son Daniel," said the Mayor. "Daniel, this is our Marshal, Sam Waters." They shook hands. As they shook hands, Sam was sizing up Daniel. He wasn't a bad lookin' kid.

"There's no way the Mayor coulda been Daniel's Pa," thought Sam. "The wife musta snuck out one night." Daniel had a good firm handshake. He was maybe six feet tall, medium build, and had a full mustache. He had blonde hair and blue eyes. The Mayor's eyes were brown and his hair was dark brown. Daniel was wearing a suit and had on a boler hat. "All right mayor, you go on about yer business," said Sam. "Daniel and me got things ta do." The Mayor nodded his head and left. Sam and Daniel headed to the jail. Once inside, Sam told Daniel to have a seat. "Let's git started off on the right foot young fella," said Sam. "Yer here cause a yer old man. I'll do what I can ta keep you alive. You'll do what I say and when I say. Do you understand?"

"First off, my name is Daniel, not young fella. You can call me Dan if you want," started Daniel. "And I'll tell you right now that this was my idea, not my father's."

"All right Dan, I'll try ta teach you ta stay alive," said Dan. "Now the first thing yer gonna do is git rid a that stupid hat and git outta that suit. This is west Texas, not Boston'r New York City."

"What's wrong with this hat?" asked Daniel.

"A hat is fer keepin' yer head warm and the sun off a you," said Sam. "That ugly lookin' thing don't do neither, now git rid of it before I shoot it full a holes. And git some boots too. Now go back home and change them clothes. If ya don't have somethin' ta wear, git over to the general store and buy some. I'll see you back here in a couple hours." Daniel didn't say a word. He headed back home.

Sam went over to the saloon. He had some whiskey and talked with some of the girls. Then he headed back to the jail.

Daniel showed up right after Sam. Everything he was wearing was brand new. Sam looked him over. "Best git them boots broke in," said Sam. "Never know when yer horse might git shot and you'll hafta walk some. Now Dan, can you ride?"

"Of course I can ride," answered Daniel. "I've been riding since I could walk."

"That's good," said Sam. "But I bet you never rode very many horses. Ya need to be able ta handle different horses. We're goin' down to the livery and git you a horse."

The livery had several horses for sale. Sam told Daniel to pick one out. Dan went into the corral and came back with a chestnut gelding. I like the looks of this one," said Daniel. "He's nice and gentle."

"That's cause he's damn near twenty years old," said Sam. "Look at them teeth." Sam took the horse by it's muzzle and opened it's mouth exposing the front teeth. "See how them teeth are all worn down. This horse is old. Go pick out a different one." Daniel picked out a bay mare. He looked at its teeth.

"I don't know how old this one is, but she's younger than that chestnut," said Daniel.

"She's maybe ten," said Sam. "And she might be a good horse, but I think you should get a gelding. You don't want some stud horse climbing up yer back when yer mare's in heat."

"That makes sense," said Daniel. He picked out another horse. It was a bay gelding. Sam said it was maybe six years old. They saddled up the gelding and Daniel rode it around the corral.

"I'll git my horse saddled and we'll take a ride," said Sam. Sam had the man at the livery saddle up his horse.

"The fella that owned that horse said it was a little gun shy," said the livery man. "I wouldn't do no shootin' first time out." Sam nodded his head and he and Daniel headed out of town. They didn't talk as they rode. Sam was just seeing how Daniel handled himself and the horse. He was doing fine.

"All right now, you take off in a full gallop now," said Sam. "You go bout a mile'r so and turn around and come back. Daniel gave the horse a kick and took off. Sam watched as they rode out of sight. "Looks like he's handlin' it all right," Sam said to himself. It wasn't long and he was back. The horse was covered with sweat. "Well, git off and we'll walk a while and cool off yer horse," said Sam. As they were walking, they talked. "Do ya reckon you could shoot a pistol and hit something while you was in a full gallop?" asked Sam.

"I seriously doubt it," answered Daniel. "I'm not planning on shooting at anyone ever."

"Most people don't plan that, but it happens," said Sam. "You wear a badge and some men'll wanna kill you just cause you are a lawman. Talkin' don't work fer some men. Guns're all they understand. You live long enough, you'll find out."

"I became a lawyer so I could see things done properly, in courts of law and such," said Daniel.

"That's admirable Dan, but outlaws don't care about such things," said Sam. "Now when we git back ta town, we'll git you a pistol and I'll teach you how ta shoot proper."

"I wasn't going to wear a gun," said Dan.

"You'll wear a gun or I'll go ahead and shoot ya myself," said Sam.

"I'll wear it but I won't like it," said Daniel.

"I don't like wearin' my gun neither, but it keeps me alive," said Sam.

After they took the horses to the livery, they went to the general store. Sam picked out a pistol that had been converted to metallic cartridges. It was used but it was a good pistol. The holster was worn some but was still good. Sam also got a couple boxes of shells. They went to the edge of town for some target practice. Sam gave Daniel a good safety lesson on handling the pistol before he would even let Daniel touch it. After the lecture, he handed the pistol to Daniel and told him to repeat everything he had just told him. Daniel did, and Sam handed him six cartridges and told him to load up. Daniel loaded the pistol and then stood there with the pistol in his right hand and down to his side. "Get yer finger outta that trigger guard," said Sam. "Don't put it in there till yer ready ta shoot." Daniel did as instructed. "Now see that piece a old wood out there bout sixty feet," said Sam. "Take yer time and try ta hit it." Daniel raised the pistol, took aim, and fired. He hit the wood. "That's good," said Sam. "Now do it again and again till yer empty." Daniel fired five more times and hit the wood every time. "Not bad," said Sam. "Just remember. That wood wasn't shootin' back at ya. Now that'll be all fer today. You head on home and meet me at the jail right after daylight. Oh, and clean that pistol tonight." Daniel nodded and headed home.

~~~~

Everyday, Sam gave Daniel some lessons. They were not always about shooting. They were about whatever Sam thought that Daniel would need to stay alive. Daniel seemed to absorbing the things Sam was teaching him. Sam was beginning to be glad that he had a deputy. The town was still growing. Another saloon had come to town. Sam didn't mind the competition. What he did mind was that the owner of the new saloon let his customers get too rowdy from time to time.

Sam still had another week to wear his sling when a huge fight broke out in the new saloon. Sam and Dan went there to put a stop to it. They entered the saloon and looked around. "Tell me what you see Dan." said Sam.

"I see a bunch of drunks beating the hell out of each other," answered Dan.

"Are any of them wearin' guns?" asked Sam.

"Yes, some of them are," said Dan.

"So someone could end up gettin' shot," said Sam.

"Yes they could," said Dan.

"Now what do you spose we should do bout that?" said Sam.

"We gotta get their attention," said Dan.

"That's right," said Sam. "Now pull yer pistol and have it ready. Don't use it less'n I tell ya." Dan pulled out his pistol. Sam pulled his pistol and fired two shots into the floor. The saloon got very quiet. Everyone looked around to see who had done the shooting. "All right, now that I have yer attention," started Sam. "You fellas fightin' and wearin' guns, take them guns off and I mean right now."

"What if'n we don't," asked one of the fighters.

"I'll shoot yer eyes out," said Sam.

"Bullshit," said the fighter. "You won't shoot nobody."

"Try me pigface," said Sam. The fighter stood there for a moment and then went for his pistol. A split second later he was holding his hand screaming in pain. Sam had shot him in the hand. "Sorry, I guess I missed yer eyes," said Sam. "Now the rest a you fellas, if yer gonna fight, git them guns off right now. If yer not gonna fight, then drink up and have a good time. I bet most a ya don't even know what you was fightin' bout." Most of the fighters started laughing and went back to drinking. "Dan, take pigface here over ta Doc's," said Sam. "He probly needs looked after."

"You shouldn't be callin' me pigface," said the wounded man.

"I'm sorry," said Sam. "I won't call you that no more. And you shoulda known better than ta try and draw on me."

"I know Marshal," said the man. "Guess I was just drunk and stupid. Won't happen again."

~~~~

Over the next few months, Dan got better at his job. He was even involved in a shootout one day. A couple of men had tried to rob the general store. The store owner had chased the two men out with a shotgun. They were exchanging gunfire when Dan went running over to see what was happening. The store owner was standing in the doorway with a double barreled shotgun. The two would be robbers were down behind a water trough. The store owner saw Dan approaching and quit shooting. Dan pulled his pistol and walked to within forty yards of the two men. They had no idea he was there till he yelled at them. "You two, drop your weapons and stand up with your hands in the air."

The two men were startled when they heard Dan's voice. Then they turned to see Dan standing there with his pistol in his hand. He did not have his pistol pointed at the two men. The two men looked at Dan. Then they looked at each other. Then they opened fire on Dan. Dan just stood there taking aim as the bullets whizzed by him. His first shot hit one of the men, but he didn't quit shooting. Dan fired again. This time the other man was hit. The bullet struck him in the head. When the wounded man saw that his partner was dead, he dropped his pistol.

"I can't stand up lawman. Ya done gut shot me," said the man. Dan kept his pistol aimed at the man and approached him. When he got close, he kicked the man's pistol away.

"You just sit quiet like," said Dan. "Your partner is dead. I'll get the Doc for you." As Dan turned from the man to go after the Doc, he almost ran into Sam who was standing there.

"You sure were lucky Dan," said Sam. "Just standin' there like that. You should be dead. Them boys was bad shots."

"I guess that wasn't a very smart thing to do," said Dan. "Could you get the Doc? I'm not feeling too well." As soon as the words were out of Dan's mouth, he ran over behind the general store and threw up. Sam watched him for a few minutes. Sam didn't need to fetch the doctor. He had heard the shooting and was on his way. When he got there, the gut shot man was already dead. Doc never said a word. He just walked back to his office.

Sam grabbed a couple of men and had them take the bodies to the barber shop. Then he went to the office and waited for Dan. Dan arrived about fifteen minutes later. "It doesn't feel good killin' a man, does it?" said Sam.

"No it sure doesn't," said Dan.

"Well you go ahead and feel bad for a spell," said Sam. "Then you try to remember that them boys was shootin' at you. Coulda been you dead in the street out there."

"You've killed a lot of men haven't you?" asked Dan. "Does it always feel bad?"

"Depends on how hard they're tryin' ta kill me," said Sam. "I got three men I'm gonna kill one a these days and I'm really gonna enjoy it."

"I heard your woman was taken," said Dan. "Are them the ones that done it?"

"That's them," said Sam. "It's been two years now. They're gonna find out what hell is all about." Just as Sam finished his words, the telegraph operator came in with a telegram for Sam. It went as follows:

Marshal Sam Waters
Lonesome Texas

Three men you are after are believed to be in Kansas headed for Abilene<<stop>>Potts brothers are in Kid Evans gang<<stop>>brothers have kin in gang<<stop>>believe Potts kin are men you are after<<stop>>gang believed to have robbed two banks in Missouri<<stop>>figure Abilene is next because money is there

Travis McCord
Marshal Dallas Texas

"That was the telegram I been waitin' for," said Sam. "I'll be goin' ta Abilene. You'll be the law while I'm gone."

"So what was the telegram?" asked Dan.

"Them three that took Juanita are up in Kansas now," said Sam. "They think they're in that Kid Evans gang. They figure they'll go ta Abilene cause that's where the money is now that the rail head is there. Lotta Texas cows goin' ta Abilene."

"I've seen the posters on Kid Evans," said Dan. "He's a killer. There's $5000 or more on his head. He must be a real bad man."

"He must be, but he's not the one I'm after," said Sam. "Course I'll kill'm if I hafta. Now I'll be leavin' in the mornin'. Don't be gittin' yerself kilt while I'm gone. I'll be takin' stages to the nearest railroad station. Then I'll take the train into Abilene. If somethin' comes up, send a telegram ta Abilene."

"That O'Rourke fella is up around Abilene isn't he?" asked Dan.

"Yep, he is and they say he's a hell of a good man," said Sam. "Maybe I can tie up with him. I'm sure he wouldn't mind catchin' that bunch."

~~~~

When Sam finally arrived in Abilene, it was the day after Sean had left to go after Kid and get Kathleen back. Sam went all around town looking for O'Rourke. Everyone told him to ask over at "Maggie's Place." Sam had on his regular pistol and the two from his saddle were thrown over his left shoulder. He wasn't wearing his badge as he entered the saloon. Michael saw Sam first and went over to him. "Check your guns at the bar," said Michael.

"I'm lookin' fer Federal Marshal O'Rourke," said Sam.

"And why would you be lookin' for my friend?" asked Michael.

"That's between me and him," said Sam.

"Well I'm a deputy of his and you can tell me," said Michael.

"I never seen a deputy with a wooden leg before," said Sam.

"Me neither," said Michael. "At least I never did till I got my leg shot off. Now who are you sir?"

"I haven't been called sir since the war," said Sam. "Please don't call me that. Name's Sam Waters. I'm a Marshal in a little town called Lonesome. It's in west Texas."

"Well Sam Waters, I'm Michael O'Connor. Pleased to meet you," said Michael. They shook hands. "Now why are you here? Hey, we had a cook on a cattle drive a while back named Sam Waters. Any relation?"

"No, no relation. I'm after three men," started Sam. "They are believed to be in the Kid Evans gang. One's called Sol and another one is called Clyde. Got no name fer the other one."

"What would these three look like?" asked Michael.

"One's tall and has black hair and a muctache. He's missin' a front tooth," Sam began. "Another one is real ugly and wears tall moccasins. The other one is short and stocky. He has yellow hair and has a scar on his chin."

"That yellow haired fella is in that gang," said Michael. "They were here two days ago. They took a woman thinking she was Sean's wife and they killed a cattle buyer named Thompson. Sean's tracking them right now. He left yesterday." Maggie had been upstairs and was coming down the stairs. She saw Michael talking with a stranger and went over to them. Sam hadn't really paid attention to the painting on the wall. There were always pictures of women with their clothes off in saloons. When he saw

Maggie coming down the stairs, he looked at her in disbelief. He looked back and forth from the painting to Maggie.

"Yes, that' me," said Maggie. "I'm Maggie O'Rourke. And you are?"

"Sam Waters ma'am," said Sam. "I come here hopin' ta tie in with yer husband. There's three fellas in that Kid Evans gang I'm after. I'm a Marshal in Lonesome Texas."

"You've come a long way," said Maggie. "Sit down and have a drink. I'll have the cook make you something to eat. And call me Maggie."

"Don't wanna stay long Maggie," said Sam. "I wanna git on the trail."

"You gotta eat," said Michael. "We got the best cooks in town. So you don't want to be called sir anymore. I take it you were an officer in the late war."

"I didn't start out that way, but that's how I ended up," said Sam.

"I would guess that you wore gray," said Michael.

"Does that matter? The war's over," said Sam.

Yes, the war is over and whether you wore gray or blue doesn't matter," said Michael. "But Sean and myself wore the blue and we wouldn't want any problems because of that. Our good friend, Jon O'Brien, was killed not long ago. He was Sean's deputy and was a Confederate Major in the late war. We were all close friends."

"Well maybe one day I can be your friend too," said Sam. "I was a full Colonel and rode with Nathan Bedford Forrest. As far as I'm concerned, the past is the past."

"You said you started out as enlisted man and became a full Colonel," said Michael. "You must have been good at what you did."

"I was good, but I got promoted a lot because we were gettin' killed so fast," said Sam. "You Yanks saw to that. So, I've heard stories about Sean O'Rourke. Is he as good as they say he is?"

"No Sam, he's better," said Michael. "You can't blink when he draws or you'll miss it. He can do it with either hand. He can kill a man at 1000 yards with his Sharps. He is a master with his fists. He's the best tracker in this part of the country. He lived several years with the Cheyenne and he can sneak up on a wolf."

"Sounds like a good man to side with," said Sam.

"None better," said Michael. "Now there's something I should let you know so you won't be surprised. Sean has a deputy out there with him."

"We could probably use some good help," said Sam.

"Well his deputy is a colored man," said Michael. "His name is Jesse Strong. He was born a free man and was blacksmith before the war. He's the strongest man I've ever seen. He's been a deputy for a while and he's a very good man."

"Well I never heard a no colored deputy," said Sam. "But if Sean and you say he's a good man, then he must be."

"He is," said Michael. "Now will you be needin' a good horse?"

"I will," said Sam. "I didn't want to haul my horse all the way from west Texas. I'll need a pack horse too."

"You can use my horse," said Michael. "He needs rode some anyway. I haven't ridden a lot since I lost my leg. We'll get you a good pack horse too." Jim entered the saloon and went over to see who was with Michael. Michael introduced them and asked

Jim to go over to the livery and get his horse saddled up. He was to get the paint horse for the pack horse also.

Sam's food arrived and he ate his fill. He thanked everyone and then got himself provisioned. Michael told him where he could pick up sign and Sam was on his way. He wanted to push as hard as he could. He rode well into the night. The next morning, he was up well before daylight and on the move. The trail was not fresh, but Sam could follow it. He continued to push hard. As a cavalryman, Sam knew how much his horse could do. Michael's horse was strong and Sam got everything out of him that he could. After the second day, Sam figured he was less than a half day behind Sean.

~~~~

Sean and Jesse were gaining on Kid's gang. "I figure he wants us to catch up," said Sean as they rode along. "I figure he'll try to set up some type of ambush. That's what I'd do if I was him."

"That's what I figure too," said Jesse. "I also got me a feelin' that we're bein' follered. It's just a gut feelin' more'n anything."

"I kinda got that too," said Sean. "I think ole Jeb's got it too. He keeps lookin' back. Tell ya what. Bout two hours before dark, I'll stay back. You keep ridin' till bout dark. I'll see if we got company'r not. I'll join ya soon as I can. Jeb'll go with you."

Sean stayed back as planned. It wasn't long and a lone rider with a pack horse was in sight. Sean stood right on the trail so the rider would see him. When the rider got within 200 yards, Sean got his Winchester, got down on one knee and took aim at the rider. The rider kept coming and never made a move to pull a weapon. When the rider was 100 yards away, Sean yelled. "State yer business and leave them hands where I can see'em."

"Name's Sam Waters. I'm lookin' fer Marshal O'Rourke," said Sam. "I'd say yer him. I seen that badge flash in the sunlight."

"I wanted you ta see it," said Sean. "Now Sam Waters, state yer business."

"I'm a Marshal in west Texas. It's a small town called Lonesome," said Sam. "I'm after three men. Them men are part a the Kid Evans gang."

Sean lowered his Winchester and stood. Sam rode the rest of the way to Sean. "I don't know all their names," said Sean. "I know the Potts brothers are with Kid."

"The others are kin to the Potts brothers," said Sam.

"You come a long way Sam," said Sean. "What'd them fellas do over yer way?"

"They took my woman," started Sam. "They raped her and beat her almost to death. Then they just threw her out into some farmer's field to die. Been two years ago'r better. Michael O'Connor told me that this gang took another woman and kilt a cattle buyer. They were thinkin' the woman they took was yer wife."

"That's what they did," said Sean. "And I'm gonna kill'em and get her back."

"Mind if I join you?" asked Sam. "I'm pretty good with my guns and I can track some. Mebbe not as good as you, but I get it done."

"Sure, can always use a good man," said Sean. They shook hands. "We'll move out now and meet up with my deputy."

"That'd be Jesse Strong, right?" said Sam. "Michael told me bout him."

"He told ya Jesse was a colored man, didn't he?" asked Sean.

"He did," answered Sam. "Don't bother me none."

"That's good cause he's the strongest man I know," said Sean. "You'll meet ole Jeb too. Don't be afraid a him. Don't know what kinda dog he is, but he loves me and my friends. He's the biggest dog I ever did see and he can rip a man's throat out faster'n any wolf can."

"I'll try ta stay on his good side," said Sam.

"Sam Waters huh. We had a cook on a cattle drive a while back named Sam Waters," said Sean. "Any relation?"

"Michael asked me that," said Sam. "No, no relation. My Pa's name was Ben. He had one brother named Zeb and he had two girls and no boys. Now my Pa's Pa was named Sam, but he's long dead."

~~~~

When they got to Jesse, Jeb went over to check out Sam. "Just talk to him nice and pet'm some," said Sean. "He'll like ya fine." Sam dismounted and made friends with Jeb. Then he went to Jesse, introduced himself, and shook hands.

They didn't have a fire that night. Sean figured that they were close enough to Kid's gang that a fire out there could be seen from several miles away. When they took off again a little before daylight, Sean swung out to the right and then the left. He wanted to see if anyone had been watching for them. He found fresh tracks on the south side of the trail. One of Kid's gang had stayed back to see if they were being followed.

CHAPTER FOURTEEN

After a half day's ride, Kid's gang stopped for a while to rest the horses. When Kathleen dismounted from the back of Kid's horse, Kid saw that she had blood all over her. There was blood on his horse and blood on the saddle. "Damn woman, you sure yer not dyin'?" said Kid.

"No, I'm not dying," said Kathleen. "I told you it would be like this for a few days."

"Well you shoulda spoke up," said Kid. "That's a thirty dollar saddle. That damn blood better come off."

"What if it doesn't?" asked Kathleen. "Are you going to kill me? You said you were going to do that anyway."

"I am gonna kill you woman, but I'll do it when I'm good and ready," said Kid. "I really wanna do it when O'Rourke's watchin'."

"If you see Sean, then he's seen you a long time before you've seen him," said Kathleen. "He'll kill you so quickly, you won't know it happened."

"We'll see bout that woman," said Kid. "Boys, mount up. Stew, you stay back. Swing out to one side a bit and see if we been followed. I got me a feelin'. Catch up when ya find out." Stew stayed back when the others moved out. He moved south of the trail and found a spot where he wouldn't be spotted.

Two hours before dark, Kid's gang came to a small stream. On the opposite side were three hills. Kid decided to camp on the other side of the stream. One hill was to the right about two hundred yards from the campsite. Another hill was to the left about two hundred yards away. The third hill was centered between the two hills and was about a hundred yards from the campsite. There was nothing on the hills except tall grass. The whole area was open plain except some small trees near the stream. Kid stood for a moment and looked over the area. "This is it," said Kid. "This is where we'll kill O'Rourke. We'll wait right here on'm. I figure he'll be along directly. We'll find out when Stew gits back."

"Are we gonna get us a poke tonight?" asked Sol.

"Yep, ya can have all the pokes ya want after this woman fixes us some supper," said Kid. "You can even go before me." Kathleen never said a word. She just went ahead and gathered some wood for a cook fire.

The others had just started eating when Stew got back. "We're being follered," said Stew. "There's three of'em. I seen a badge on one of'em. That's gotta be O'Rourke."

"That's good," said Kid. "We'll kill all of'em tomorrow. Now get yerself fed. I reckon you'll be wantin' ta git a poke."

"I aim ta git me some," said Stew. "So who's first?"

"I reckon I'll let Sol go first," said Kid. "We'll see if he likes that blood'r not."

Kathleen knew that all of them would be taking turns that night. She knew if she fought them too hard, they would probably beat her half to death. She decided she would just lay there and take it. As soon as she was done eating, she grabbed her blanket and went about twenty five yards from the campfire. She undressed carefully so if the boys were watching, they wouldn't spot her hidden derringer. She put the derringer under her clothes and laid naked on the blanket.

After Sol finished eating, he got a bottle of whiskey from some saddle bags and took several long swigs. Then he went for Kathleen. He stared at her for a few moments. "Damn bitch, you sure are a looker," said Sol. "You'll be even purtier after I blacken yer eyes and bruise ya up some." Kathleen didn't respond. Sol didn't undress. He just pulled down his pants and got down to mount Kathleen. He entered her and started pumping away. After several pumps, he looked down and saw the blood. Then he finished. He pulled out and got to his knees. "Shit woman. If yer bleedin' down there, ya might as well be bleedin' up here," said Sol. Then he started hitting her. He punched her in the face several times. She was bleeding around both eyes. Sol kept hitting her. Kid heard the punches and ran over to see what was going on. He pulled Sol away.

"You son of a bitch," said Kid. "I'm gonna be the one that kills her. You git the hell away you crazy son of a bitch. Can't you see she's out cold."

"I'm not done yet," said Sol.

"Yes you are," said Kid as he pulled a pistol and stuck the muzzle against Sol's head. "Now git before I kill ya." Sol pulled up his pants and left cursing. Kid looked down at Kahtleen. He got closer to make sure she was still breathing. Then he went back over to the campfire. "You other boys can have'r, but she's out cold. Hard ta tell when she'll come to."

"I don't care if she's awake'r not," said Barney. "I'm gittin' some a that."

"Me too," said Clyde.

"How bout you Potts boys?" said Kid. "You best git some to-night. I'll most likely be killin' her tamarra."

Kathleen was out cold while the rest of the boys took a turn. She didn't come to till well into the night. She was on her back when she came to. She looked up at the stars for a moment. They were hard to see because her eyes were almost swollen shut. She thought of being with her husband one night long ago before he was killed in the war. Then she remembered where she was and what was happening. She curled up in a little ball and cried for a while. Then she put her clothes on. Kid and the others had not spotted her derringer, so she placed it back on her thigh with the garter. Then she rolled up in the blanket and fell asleep.

Kid wasn't worried about Kathleen trying to run away that night. He knew she probably couldn't see where she was going anyway. At daylight, Kid woke up Kathleen and had her come over by the campfire. He had already started a fire and some coffee was cooking. Stew was getting ready to fry some bacon. When breakfast was ready, they all sat down and ate. Kathleen didn't eat. Her jaw hurt some so she just drank some coffee. When they were finished, Kid told them his plan. "All right boys, here's what's gonna happen taday," started Kid. "Stew, yer gonna be on that hill on the right. Chili, you'll be on that hill on the left. You other three'll be spread out on that hill in the center. You can see fer a long ways from them hills. You'll see O'Rourke before he ever spots us. I'll be right here with his woman. When ya spot him a comin', don't shoot till ya see me kill his woman. I want him ta git close enough ta see it."

The men saddled up their horses and went to their positions. Kid stayed at the campsite with Kathleen. When the men were in position, they signaled Kid. Kid sat down and had some more coffee. "Bitch, git yer blanket out and git yer clothes off," said Kid. "I'm gonna git me one more poke before I kill ya."

Kathleen did as she was told, but she was just about to boil over. She was going to kill this son of a bitch even if it cost her own life. She would grab her derringer when he was on her pumping away and gut shoot him. She slowly undressed and laid on the blanket. Kid did not watch as she undressed. He finishd his coffee and got undressed. He went over to Kathleen and mounted her.

~~~~

Sean and the men only slept a few hours that night. They were up and moving several hours before daylight. There was a half moon and Sean could see well enough to track. Just before the sun rose, Sean saw a small stream and three hills on the other side of it. "That's where I'd be if I was gonna bushwack somebody," said Sean. "Kid's probly got'em on them hills waitin' for us." Sean got out his spyglass. "I can make out a horse just on the other side a that stream, but I can't make anybody out yet. Too far away yet. Sam, I want you to swing out to the left and then try and slip up on that hill and kill whoever's up there. Use a knife if ya can. Hopefully they'll be looking this way and not spot ya comin' up behind'em. I'll swing out and work my way up the hill on the right."

"What about that hill in the middle?" asked Jesse.

"We'll worry bout it after we take care of the other ones," said Sean. "I'll have ole Jeb stay with you Jesse. You give us bout an hour. Then you ride over there nice and easy like. Keep yer hat down low so they can't make out yer face." Sean and Sam took off.

There was no cover for Sean or Sam as they moved. As Sam got closer to the hill, there were a few small tress and some brush. He tied his horse to a small tree and started working his way up the hill as best he could. About halfway up the hill, he came across a horse. It was tied to a small tree. Sam was careful not to spook the horse. As he got closer to the top of the hill, he could see a man laying in the tall grass. He had a Sharps rifle in his shoulder but it was not being aimed. Sam moved as quietly as he could. He was about ten feet from Chili when Chili turned and saw him. By then it was too late. Sam sprang at him before he could turn the Sharps to fire. The big knife in Sam's hand went deep into Chili's throat. Sam covered Chili's mouth so he couldn't yell or scream. Then he started cutting with the knife. He worked the blade until he felt bone. Then he turned the blade and cut the other way. Chili's head came off in his hands. Sam was covered with blood.

Sean was able to sneak up his hill totally undetected. Stew never knew Sean was there until he felt the knife blade cut into his throat. Sean was working his way over to the other hill when he saw three riders riding away. "There were six of'em," Sean said to himself. "Three of'em's run off. Must be only one on Sam's hill. Kid must be down below with Kathleen." Sean turned and headed up the hill. When he neared the top, he crawled the rest of the way. Down below he could see Kid pumping away on Kathleen. Sean had his Winchester with him. He was an excellent shot, but he couldn't risk shooting Kid and hitting Kathleen. A bullet could go through Kid and kill her. Even if he shot Kid in the leg, a bullet could still hit Kathleen.

Kid had no idea that the Potts brothers were dead and the other three had run off. He was going to shoot his wad and then take a dip in the stream. Then he would wait for O'Rourke. He didn't figure O'Rourke would show for several more hours. Kathleen was about to reach for her derringer when Kid climaxed. As he climaxed, he grabbed her arms. She would have to wait for another chance to gut shoot him. As he was pulling out of her, he punched her in the jaw with a right hand. Kathleen didn't move. Kid assumed she was out cold. He got up and headed for the stream. Kathleen was not out cold. She reached over and got her derringer. She pointed it at Kid and fired. The bullet hit Kid in the back of his right knee. Kid screamed in pain and went down. Sean was taking aim on Kid now. Kid stood back up and started after Kathleen as best he could. Sean was squeezing the trigger on his Winchester when he heard the pop of the derringer again. This time Kid was hit in the left knee. He went down hard. Sean had kept the rifle in his shoulder and was taking aim again when he saw some movement. It was Jeb. He was headed for Kid at a dead run.

Kathleen had never met Jeb, but she had heard stories about the big dog. She saw the big dog coming toward them but she didn't know if it was Jeb or some other dog that might hurt her. She curled herself into a ball and covered her neck with her arms. She watched as the huge dog got closer and closer. When the dog tore into Kid, she knew that it was Jeb. She uncurled herself and sat up so she could watch. She had heard the stories about Jeb ripping out men's throats. She wanted to watch as it happened.

Kid never knew Jeb was coming for him until it was too late. Kid saw that Kathleen was looking at something. When he turned to see what she was watching, Jeb was on him. He tried to fight off Jeb, but his attempt was futile. Jeb ignored his throat and went straight for his privates. Jeb tore off his pecker and then backed up a step or two. He sat down and stared at Kid.

Then he spit out the pecker. Kid was screaming at Jeb and cursing him. Kathleen watched Jeb as he sat there. She thought it looked like he was grinning. Then Jeb let out a low growl and went at Kid again. This time he bit off his cajones. He backed up all the way over to Kathleen. He sat down beside her and then spit out the cajones. Kathleen put her arms around Jeb and hugged him. "You are such a wonderful dog Jeb," said Kathleen. "I never had a dog, but when I do get one, I want one just like you. I love you Jeb. Let's sit here and watch this son of a bitch bleed to death."

"I'm not dead yet bitch," said Kid. He started crawling to where he had left his gunbelt. He was bleeding badly. Jeb let him get almost to his gunblet and then attacked again. This time Jeb grabbed ahold of his right wrist and shook ferociously. Kid's hand came off. Blood gushed out from Kid's arm. Jeb spit out the hand and picked up the gunbelt and took it over to Kathleen. He sat down beside her and the two of them watched Kid bleed.

Sean got to his horse and rode to Kathleen as quickly as he could. Kid was just barely alive when Sean got to Kathleen. "It's a pleasure watching you die you piece a trash," said Sean as he dismounted. "I'd hang ya too if there were any good trees around here."

"You couldn't kill me, you son of a bitch," said Kid. "It took a woman and a dog ta do it."

"I'd put a bullet in yer brain right now, but I promised a friend you'd die slow," said Sean. Kid tried to get out some more words, but couldn't. He was dead. Kathleen stood up now and grabbed Sean. She held him so tight he thought he might not be able to breath. She cried some and then stepped back. Sean wrapped the blanket around her.

"I knew you would come for me," said Kathleen. "I knew you would."

"I wish we could have been sooner," said Sean. "Let's get you cleaned up as best we can. Jesse's coming now and I'll have him and Jeb stay with you. Me'n Sam's goin' after them other three."

"I want the one with the yellow hair to die slow," said Kathleen. "He hurt me bad."

"He will," said Sean. "See that rider comin' down that hill now." Sean pointed Sam out to her. "That's Sam Waters. He's been lookin' fer him fer two years. I guarantee that son of a bitch will die slow." Sam rode over to them and dismounted. Kathleen turned to him.

"Sean tells me you are Sam Waters. I am Kathleen Jameson," said Kathleen. "Sean tells me you have been after those men for two years."

"That's right ma'am," said Sam. "Them three took my woman. They raped her and almost beat her to death. Then they threw her out in some farmer's field ta die. The farmer found her and she died shortly after that. I will kill them slow Kathleen. I have some special plans for the one with the yellow hair. I figure he's the one that beat my woman the most. He had scratches on his face and neck and I know she put'em there."

"What are you plans Sam?" asked Kathleen.

"You sure you wanna hear this Kathleen?" asked Sam.

"That son of a bitch raped and beat me," said Kahtleen. "I want to know how he's going to die."

"All right, here's what I aim ta do," started Sam. "I'm gonna shoot or break his knees so he can't walk or run. Then I'm gonna shoot him in both shoulders and elbows. Then I'm gonna take one a his eyes. Then I'm gonna back off a ways and watch him watch what the buzzards or coyotes eat on'm." Kathleen got closer to Sam and gave him a kiss on the cheek.

"Sean, I have a request," said Kathleen. "I don't want any of these other sons a bitches buried. They don't deserve it. I want them to rot in the sun and the buzzards to pick their bones."

"Don't worry Kathleen," said Sean. "They won't git buried."

"All right Jesse, you'll be stayin' with Kathleen," said Sean. "Help her as much as you can. When she's good enough to travel, head on back ta Abilene. Sam'n me'll be back after we kill them three fellas."

Jesse helped Kathleen clean up as best they could. He took his blanket from his bedroll and wrapped Kathleen. Then he took her clothes to the stream and washed them out as best he could. He did the same with the blanket that had the blood all over it. Then Jesse built a big fire and drove some sticks in the ground near it so he could hang Kathleen's clothes on them to dry. "Are you hungry Kathleen?" asked Jesse. "I can fix ya sonethin' ta eat if you want."

"I don't think I can chew very well," said Kathleen. "But I am hungry."

"I'll make ya a nice broth," said Jesse. "Be ready in no time." After Jesse made the broth for Kathleen, he rounded up Kid's horse and went through the saddle bags. He figured there would be some money in them, but he was surprised when he saw how much. "Damn, there's over $30,000 in them saddle bags," said Jesse. "Ole Bill Thompson musta had a lotta money in that safe a his." Jeb kept a vigil watch while Jesse talked with Kathleen and tried to comfort her.

~~~~

Sean and Sam rounded up the Potts brothers horses before they took off after the other three men. Sean wasn't really surprised when he found that there was over $10,000 in both of the saddle bags. "They musta all got even splits after they killed Bill," said Sean. "That'd be $60,000 all told unless Kid took a bigger cut. I spose some a this might be from them bank jobs over in Missouri. Tell ya one thing right now Sam. There was a $500 reward on Kid from the start. Bill's wife added $5000 to it. Kid's Pa mighta added another $1500 to it. I'll be givin' all that money to Kathleen."

"Sounds good ta me," said Sam. "She was the one taken and she was the one that shot him. Ole Jeb helped her finish him off. That money won't git rid a the scars she'll carry in her mind, but it'll sure make her life easier. Are you sure Maggie'n her aren't related. They sure do resemble each other."

"Nope, they're no relation," said Sean. "My Ma always said that somewhere in the world there' s another person that looks about like you do. Mebbe she was right. Let's move."

Sol had made up his mind that sooner or later, he was going to leave Kid's gang. He had thought about it before, but when Kid stuck his pistol against his head as he was beating Kathleen, that made up his mind. They knew O'Rourke was coming and Sol knew of O'Rourke's reputation. He was a killer, plain and simple. No matter what kind of plan Kid had, O'Rourke would kill them. Sol and the other two had all that money on them and hadn't spent a dime of it yet. Right after they signaled Kid that they were in position on the hill, the three of them slipped away. They could put some distance between them and Kid. Besides, it would take

O'Rourke a little while to kill Kid and the Potts boys. They could be a full day or more away from O'Rourke.

Sean and Sam got on the trail easily. After a short distance, Sean could tell something by the tracks. "They're not moving fast," said Sean. "They musta been too far away to hear Kathleen's derringer. Let's push a little harder. If we're not on'em by dark, we'll take'em sometime in the mornin'."

Sean and Sam did a lot of talking as they rode. "So Sean, they say you lived with the Cheyenne for some years before the war," said Sam. "How did you end up with them?"

"My family was in Tennesse. My folks knew a war was comin' so they decided ta go ta Oregon," started Sean. "Our small wagon train got massacred by white outlaws. I was out huntin' at the time. I killed some a them outlaws. I was only twelve then. Some Cheyenne came by. They happened on one a the outlaws. They heard all the shootin' and come over ta see what was goin' on. They brought that outlaw with 'em. I put a bullet in his brain. They Cheyenne took me in. I was with 'em till right before the war started."

"How was it with 'em?" asked Sam.

"It was a good life," Sean began. "I lived with a Cheyenne woman and her mountain man husband. He taught me how ta hunt and track and everything ta stay alive. They had a daughter. She became my wife later. We had a daughter. She was with child again when the cholera came. It took them and a lotta people in the village. I left them not long after that."

"How come the cholera didn't take you?" asked Sam.

"Me'n Braddock, that was my father-in-law, was in a town shoppin' fer nice things fer our women," answered Sean. "They got took while we was gone."

"So how did you end up wearin' the blue?" asked Sam.

"I ran into a cavalry patrol while I out was out wanderin'," answered Sean. "I made friends with a Sergeant. You met him. He's Michael O'Connor. I was hired to scout for the Army and git them through Indian territory and back east when the war started. I joined on the way east. We made it through the war. We always had this toast and we still use it sometimes. It goes, "Here's to not getting killed.""

"That's a damn fine toast," said Sam. "I sure coulda used that one. So how'd you become a lawman?"

"I met this Colonel who was a Federal Judge before the war," answered Sean. "He heard all about me and asked me to be one a his Marshal's after the war. I did, and here I am."

"So what did yer family do back in Tennessee?" asked Sam.

"We had a small farm," said Sean. "My Pa was a also a horse trainer and a blacksmith. My folks come over from Ireland. We never had no slaves and my Pa got inta a scrape'r two because we had a colored family workin' fer us. Folks there didn't like that. That's enough bout me. Where're you from and such?"

"We had a small farm in Louisiana," answered Sam. "It weren't very good. We'd a starved ta death if my Pa hadn't been such a good hunter. He also did somethin' that you might not wanna hear."

"What's that?" asked Sean.

"You sure you wanna know?" asked Sam.

"Sure, I didn't know yer Pa," said Sean.

Yeh, but ya know me now and I did what he did," said Sam.

"Can't be that bad," said Sean. "Tell me. I won't hold it against ya. Past is the past."

"All right, here goes. My Pa made extra money catchin' runaway slaves," said Sam. "He taught me and that's what I did when I got older. I was very good at it."

"Did you like doin' that?" asked Sean.

"Not really, but that's what I knew and I was good at it," answered Sam. "I never hurt no slaves. I needed the money and sometimes I got bonus money from some a the plantations cause I brought'em back in good shape."

"I bet others didn't care how they brought'em back," said Sean.

"No, they didn't," said Sam. "I'm sure since you was from Tennessee, there was slave owners that whipped and beat their slaves. And there was probably some that treated'em nicer."

"Yep, there was good ones and bad ones, but ownin' a person is still wrong even if ya treat'em nice," said Sean.

"Well I was raised thinkin' that slaves was property," said Sam. "I never knowed nothin' else. Don't really know why I rode with Bedford Forrest. I reckon I just went along with my state like a lotta other boys. Hell, most a the men in the Confederate Army never had no slaves. There's no good reason we fought so them rich folks could keep theirs."

"Was you at Fort Pillow?" asked Sean.

"I was," answered Sam. "I never murdered no colored soldiers, but I didn't stop it either. At the time, I just figured it was war and in war you kill the enemy. I can still see some a their faces."

"So would you live next to some colored folks if they had a spread next to you?" asked Sean.

"Sure, don't bother me none," said Sam. "War's over. I try ta treat folks nice unless they wrong me first. Don't make no difference what color they are. My woman was a Mexican. She was so beautiful. Folks in Lonesome weren't very nice to her unless she was spendin' money at their place. She was a whore before she took up with me. I told'em if I was gonna be their Marshal, they was gonna treat all the women proper. They did after a while."

"So how'd you get ta be the Town Marshal?" asked Sean.

"I'd been wanderin' round and ended up there," Sam began. "I went into this saloon ta have a woman, a drink, and some food. I found out the owner of the saloon and the Town Marshal were a bunch a crooks. They owned the town and extorted money from all the businesses. Anyway, I was with Juanita, that was my woman's name, and the owner of the saloon started givin' her some shit. We had some words. Two of his men come over too. They tried ta kill me and now they'r dead. Then the Marshal and his deputy showed up. We had more words and now they're dead. The town folks were so glad them fellas was dead that they asked me ta stay on and be Town Marshal. They didn't pay me. They told me since the previous owner of the saloon was now dead and he had no kin, I was now the owner. That's how I would get paid."

"So does yer saloon do a good business?" asked Sean.

"It did all right and then the town started ta grow," said Sam. "It does real good now."

"So when did yer woman get took?" asked Sean.

"I was out takin' care of some bank robbers when it happened," answered Sam. "Charlie, my bartender tried to stop'em and they killed'm. That was over two years ago. I been lookin' for'em ever since."

"Well we'll get'em now," said Sean. "No way in hell they'll get away from us."

"Remember now, the one with the yellow hair's gotta die real slow," said Sam.

"He's all yours," said Sean. "We'll kill'em all slow if we can."

~~~~

They rode till almost dark and made camp. "We'll take'em some-time in the mornin'," said Sean. "We'll show them fellas what hell is like." They never had a fire that night. They took turns standing watch. Sean figured the outlaws knew they were being followed. It was doubltful they would try to circle back on them, but Sean wasn't taking any chances.

Sean and Sam moved out about an hour before daylight. Three hours later, Sean thought he saw some movement ahead of them. He got out his spyglass and took a look. Three riders were ahead of them. Sean could see that one of them had black hair and another had yellow hair. They weren't pushing their horses hard at all. They were riding next to each other. The one with the black hair was in the middle and yellow hair was on the right. "Yer man's on the right," said Sean. "Let's get closer and I can use my Sharps. If we can git about a thousand yards from'em, I'll hit the one in the middle. Mebbe when he gits hit, it'll spook them horses. Mebbe they'll go ta buckin' and them boys'll get throwed. If they don't, we'll keep after'em."

"Are you really that good with that Sharps?" asked Sam.

"I've killed men at around eight and nine hundred yards," an-swered Sean. "A little bit farther shouldn't be no problem."

"They might spot us," said Sam. "There's no cover. It's bout all open plain."

"Well, we can hope them fellas don't look back before I take my shot," said Sean. "Now let's pick it up some and close in." They gave the horses a kick and picked up the pace. When Sean thought they were close enough, they stopped and dismounted. Sean pulled his Sharps from its scabbard. Sam held the horses and kept watch with the spyglass. The three outlaws had not looked behind them yet. Sean laid down on the ground and put the Sharps in his shoulder. He picked up some dirt and checked the wind. He adjusted his sights and took aim. Finally, the Sharps roared. Sam thought he had missed because he didn't see anyone fall right away. Two to three second later, the bullet struck the black haired man at the base of his skull right where it connects to the spine. The man's face was blown off as the bullet tore through. The other two men had not heard the shot yet. The two outlaws and all of the horses were sprayed with flesh, blood, and bone from the man's face. All of their horses went crazy and started prancing and bucking. Barney was the first to get thrown. He laid on the ground and didn't move. Clyde must have somehow yanked back on his reins because his horse reared straight up and fell to the left. Clyde and the horse landed right on top of Barney. Sol was finally thrown. His horse took off at a dead run after he was thrown. Barney's horse followed Sol's horse. Sol got up and ran after his horse for a while, but stopped when he realized he could not catch the horse. Then he realized he was in trouble. He looked back and saw two riders coming at him. They were in a full gallop. Sol tried to find some cover. There was nothing but a few scrub bushes. He laid down behind one and pulled his pistol.

Sean and Sam stopped just out of pistol range. Sol fired a couple of useless shots at them. "Let's see if we can keep'm shootin'," said Sean. "We'll stay just outta range and take a shot at him now and again. Maybe he'll use up all his ammunition." Sam grabbed his Henry and Sean got his Winchester and they spread out maybe fifty yards. They took turns shooting at Sol. They tried to see how close they could get to him without actually hitting him. The tactic worked. Sol wasted all of his ammunition. After his last bullet was fired, he pulled out a knife and ran right at Sam. He was cursing as he ran. Sam waited till he was only fifteen feet away and shot him in the right knee. Sol went down hard. Sam walked over to Sol. He didn't say a word. He chambered another round in his rifle and shot Sol in the other knee. Sol did not scream. He just gave Sam a look of pure hatred.

"What'd I ever do ta you?" Sol asked Sam. "I never seen you in my life."

"You remember that Mexican woman you took a couple years ago?" asked Sam. "She was my woman."

"Oh yeh, I remember her," said Sol. "She fought me hard. I liked it."

"Well yer gonna git what you give her," said Sam. Sam didn't say another word. He chambered another round and shot Sol in the left shoulder. Then he shot him in the right shoulder. Sol still didn't scream in pain. Then Sam shot him through both elbows. "Now I'm takin' an eye," said Sam. Sam took his big knife and jammed it into Sol's left eyeball. Then he twisted the blade some before he pulled it out. Sol still didn't scream. "Now, I'm gonna git back some and watch the buzzards and coyotes eat their fill," said Sam. "Don't you be bleedin' ta death just yet."

Sean had gone over to make sure the other two men were dead. They were. Barney had been crushed. Sean looked down at the faceless man. He knelt down so he could see where the bullet had struck him. Sean found the hole at the base of his skull. "Hmm, reckon I shot a little high," Sean said to himself. "Meant ta hit'm right between the shoulder blades. Oh well, got the job done." The horse that had fallen on the man had a broken leg.

Sean put it out of it's misery. The other two horses were nowhere in sight. Sean checked the saddle bags on the dead horse and found another $10,000. "I'll be after them other two horses," said Sean. "Gotta git that money back. Be back shortly."

Sam put his rifle back in the scabbard and mounted his horse. He rode away but stopped around four to five hundred yards from Sol and dismounted. He dropped his horse's reins and sat on the ground. About a half hour later, Sean returned with the horses. "Let's git goin' now," said Sean. "Them critters'll be all over that horse and them fellas shortly."

"I'll be stayin' fer a spell," said Sam. "I'm gonna watch them buzzards pick that fella's other eye out. And I'm gonna watch as them and the coyotes fill their bellies. You go on now. Make sure Kathleen gits back and sees a doctor. She sure is one fine woman."

"All right, I'll take care a things," said Sean. "You come inta Abilene when yer ready." Sean left with the other two horses.

It wasn't a full hour later and the buzzards started circling. Sam watched as they came in lower. "Won't be long now you son of a bitch," Sam said to himself. Then Sam saw some movement on the ground. "Damn, coyotes already. That was quick," said Sam. Then he took a closer look. They weren't coyotes. They were wolves. "Haven't seen a wolf since forever," said Sam. "Wonder what them wolves'll start on first?" Sam's horse was getting a little jittery. It didn't want to be anywhere near those wolves. Sam picked up the reins and talked to the horse. "Easy now boy," he said. "Them wolves over there got plenty ta eat. They won't be botherin' us." The horse calmed down some. Sam started making bets with himself on what the wolves would eat first. Would it be the horse.? If not the horse, which man would they start on? Sam decided they would do the horse first. There were six wolves in the pack. Sam guessed right. They started on the horse first, but it wasn't long and they got to fighting with each other. Only one wolf stayed on the horse. He must have been the pack leader. The other five wolves started on the dead men. Two of them started on Sol and two started on the black haired man. The last wolf started on the other man. Sam couldn't get Sol to scream at all as he shot him and took his eye, but when the wolves started on him. He let out a couple of screams. After the second scream, his throat was ripped out.

Sam watched the wolves feast for about an hour. He was about to leave when several coyotes showed up. They stayed back and waited for the wolves to get their fill. Sam decided to watch until the coyotes had their chance. It wasn't long and the coyotes were able to slip in and grab a bite. The wolves didn't bother them much. They had already gorged themselves. Sam mounted up and headed back.

~~~~

Jesse and Kathleen had not started for Abiline. They were still in the same place when Sean got to them. "Let's git ready and head back ta Abilene," said Sean. "We gotta git you to the doc."

"Where's Sam?" asked Kathleen. "I'm not leaving without Sam."

"Sam'll be along directly," said Sean. "He's doin' what he said he was gonna do. Now let's get movin'."

"I won't go without Sam," said Kathleen. "I mean it. I'm not going without him."

"I already tried ta git her to go," said Jesse. "I wasn't gonna force her. She been forced enough lately."

"All right, we'll wait on Sam. "He should be back before dark."

"Are those three dead?" asked Kathleen.

"They been sent ta hell where they belong Kathleen," said Sean. "Sam did as he said he would on the yellow haired one."

They didn't talk anymore for a good while. It started getting late so Jesse got a fire going and started on supper. Kathleen said she felt a little better and would try to eat. They were about to start when Sam arrived. He rode into the camp and dismounted. "The critters ate good today," said Sam. Then Sam looked after his horse. As he was rubbing his horse down, Kathleen went to him. She never said one word. She just grabbed him and hugged him. She hugged him hard. Sam found himself hugging her back. They stood and hugged for a good while. Finally they separated. "You go on now and get some food Kathleen," said Sam. "I'll finish my horse and be over." Kathleen smiled at him and then went over by the fire. She wouldn't take any food until Sam came over and sat beside her. That night, she wouldn't lay down unless Sam was next to her. They spent the night rolled up in their blankets and facing each other. The next morning after breakfast, they headed back to Abilene.

CHAPTER FIFTEEN

Elizabeth Jane Thompson was on a train headed for St. Louis. While she was in St. Louis, she had plans to meet with Judge Sharpton. It was her intent to find out everything should could about the Federal Marshals who were pursuing her husband's killer. She had also gotten ahold of the Pinkerton Detective Agency. She knew nothing about the wild west. All she had ever heard about was wild Indians and outlaws. People were getting shot and killed on a regular basis in the west. Her husband was proof of that. She had hired a Pinkerton man to be her bodyguard and he would meet her in St. Louis. When the train pulled into the station in St. Louis, Elizabeth noticed a well dressed, big and handsome man. He appeared to expecting someone on the train. When Elizabeth stepped down from the train, the big man went straight to her. "Mrs. Thompson, I'm Detective Alan Cooper," he said. "I am at your service."

"How did you know who I was?" asked Elizabeth.

"I'm a detective Mrs. Thompson," Alan answered. "It's what I do. I have a carriage here for you. I'll have your luggage loaded and then we can go see Judge Sharpton if you'd like."

"That's what I'd like Mr. Cooper," said Elizabeth. Alan took Elizabeth over to the carriage and helped her onto it. Then he had her luggage loaded. They didn't speak as the carriage started moving.

After a while, Elizabeth spoke. "Are you armed Mr. Cooper?" asked Elizabeth.

"Yes I am," answered Alan.

"Are you a good shot Mr. Cooper?" asked Elizabeth.

"I am a very good shot Mrs. Thompson," answered Alan. "I'm also very good with my fists and I can use a knife."

"Sorry, I'm new at this," said Elizabeth. "I'm just wanting to know what I'm paying for."

"I will take care of you Mrs. Thompson," said Alan. "If anything happens to you it will be over my dead body."

"Let's hope that doesn't happen," said Elizabeth.

It wasn't long and the carriage arrived at the Federal Court House. Alan helped Elizabeth down from the carriage and escorted her inside. They went into an office that had "Clerk" above the door. A middle aged man was sitting at a desk. He seemed to be ignoring them. "I'm here to see Judge Sharpton," said Elizabeth. The man looked at Elizabeth for a second and then went back to whatever he was doing at his desk. Elizabeth was about to verbally abuse the man when he spoke.

"What is your name and do you have an appointment?" asked the clerk.

"My name is Mrs. Bill Thompson. My husband was murdered in Abilene by an outlaw named Kid Evans a while back," said Elizabeth.

"Oh yes, I heard about that," said the clerk. "O'Rourke's after him. He's as good as dead."

"So you know this O'Rourke?" asked Elizabeth.

"I don't know him personally. I just know what all he's done since he's been Marshal," said the clerk.

"Well am I going to see the Judge or not?" asked Elizabeth.

"Follow me. I'll take you to his chambers," said the clerk. "He just got out of court." The clerk took them to the Judge's chambers. "You wait here and I'll tell him who's here," said the clerk. The clerk went into the Judge's chambers. "Excuse me Judge Sharpton. There's a Mrs. Bill Thompson here and she wants to speak with you," said the clerk. "That was her husband Kid Evans killed in Abilene."

"Send her in," said the Judge. The clerk went out and brought Elizabeth and Alan to the Judge.

"Good day, I'm Judge Sharpton and you are Mrs. Bill Thompson," said the Judge. "And who might this gentleman be?"

"This gentleman is Detective Cooper from the Pinkerton Detective Agency," said Elizabeth. "I have hired him as my bodyguard."

"Do you think you need a bodyguard Mrs. Thompson?" asked the Judge.

"Yes I do," answered Elizabeth. "My husband was murdered and I have no intention of letting that happen to me."

"Well from what I hear about the Pinkerton's, you are in good hands," said the Judge. "Now what can I do for you?"

"I want to know all about the Federal Marshals who are pursuing my husband's killer," said Elizabeth.

"Sean O'Rourke is the Federal Marshal and he has several deputies," said the Judge. "He is the best qualified man for the job. He has all the skills and knowledge required for the job. He has proven his kills numerous times. Justice will be done. I assure you."

"What will happen when the killer is caught?" asked Elizabeth.

"If he is captured alive, he will be hung by the neck till he is dead," answered the Judge. "But chances are that he will be killed and not taken alive. Very few outlaws are brought in alive."

"Good, I just want to make sure that man is dead," said Elizabeth. "Now I thank you for your time. I will go to Abilene and await the return of Mr. O'Rourke."

~~~~

The train from St. Louis to Kansas City did not leave until the next morning so Elizabeth got them a hotel room for the night. The room was a big suite and it had two bedrooms. Elizabeth wanted to make sure Mr. Cooper was not far from her. That evening, they had dinner at the hotel. Elizabeth was very curious about her bodyguard and asked him question after question. Alan answered very few of her questions. "Why won't you answer my questions?" asked Elizabeth.

"The questions you have been asking me are personal in nature," answered Alan. "A person in this line of work does not get personal."

"So what's wrong with asking you if you are married or not?" asked Elizabeth. "A question like that can't hurt anything."

"What if that man sitting at the table close to us was listening in on our conversation," started Alan. "What if he knows I'm a Pinkerton and he's after me for some previous job I've been on. If I said I had a wife, it wouldn't be too hard for that man to track her down and put her in harm's way while I'm on this job. He could use her to get to me. There's a lot of bad people out there

Mrs. Thompson and us Pinkerton's have helped get rid of some of them. Bad people do not like us."

"So are you married or not?" asked Elizabeth.

Alan gave her very stern look. "No, Mrs. Thompson, I am not married," answered Alan. "Now no more personal questions."

"All right, no more personal questions," said Elizabeth. "So do you like what you do Mr. Cooper?" And are you good at it?"

"I like what I do and I am very good at it," answered Alan.

"So were you in the late war?" asked Elizabeth.

"I was but I can't reveal what I did," answered Alan.

"I bet you were one of them spies that went down south and gathered information on all kinds of things," said Elizabeth.

"No more questions Mrs. Thompson," said Alan.

"So, Mr. Cooper, do you know anything about this Federal Marshal O'Rourke?" asked Elizabeth.

"I have heard a lot of stories about the man," said Alan. "If they are only half true, then O'Rourke is still one hell of a lawman. I would say that your husband's killer's days are numbered."

"Do you believe in an eye for an eye?" asked Elizabeth.

"I do, but I also believe in the law," said Alan. "There must be certainty in someone's guilt."

"So Mr. Cooper, if you were married and someone killed your wife and you saw the person do it, would you kill that person?" asked Elizabeth.

"Without hesitation Mrs. Thompson," answered Alan.

"What about the law? Would you want that person to have a fair trial?" asked Elizabeth.

"You push pretty hard Mrs. Thompson," said Alan. "If I witnessed my wife's death and definitely saw the person who did it, there would be no trial. That person would end up dead. Now let's get to our room and get some sleep."

"Very well Mr. Cooper, we can retire for the night," said Elizabeth.

~~~~

The train ride to Kansas City was uneventful. The passenger car they were in was only about half full. When they got to Kansas City, they had to spend the night. The train to Abilene did not leave till 10am the next morning. The hotel in Kansas City didn't have a suite with two bedrooms, but it did have a big suite that had a big bedroom and another room with a sofa and chairs. Alan spent the night on the sofa.

When they boarded the train the next morning, Elizabeth started noticing that most of the men wore pistol belts. Other men who didn't wear pistol belts were carrying some type of rifle or shotgun.

"I guess I'm in the wild west now," said Elizabeth to Alan.

"Not quite, but we're getting there," said Sam. The passenger car they were on was not even half full. The seats in the car were arranged so that some of the seats faced forward and some faced backwards. Alan had them sit where he could have his back to the end of the car and Elizabeth sat facing him. This way he could see everything that was happening in the car. The train was about to depart when a man boarded at the last minute. He walked through the car looking around. He looked toward Elizabeth and Alan and went that way. He stopped right beside Eliabeth. Alan sized him up. He was probably just some cowboy. His clothes needed some patching and his hat was well worn. But the thing

Alan noticed the most was the Colt revolver the man was wearing. It was tied down.

The cowboy stared at Elzabeth for a while. The train started moving. "Mind if I sit next to you lovely lady?" asked the cowboy.

"She does mind," said Alan. "There's plenty of other seats."

"No one was talkn' ta you fella," said the cowboy. "I was talkin' to the lady."

"There are plenty of other seats," said Elizabeth. "So please take one of them."

"Are you sure ma'am?" said the cowboy. "I'm an awful nice fella once ya git ta know me."

"I'm sure you are," said Elizabeth. "Now please go."

"You heard the lady," said Alan. "Now move."

The cowboy stood facing Alan now. "Take a look Mr.," said the cowboy. "You can see that my Colt's not lashed down."

"I can see that," said Alan. "That just means you're careless. Now move on." Just then, the conductor came through the car.

"What's going on here?" the conductor said. "Is this man bothering you Miss?"

"He wants to sit beside me and I don't want him to," said Elizabeth.

"Take a seat somewhere else," said the conductor. "You cause trouble on my train and you'll be off at the next water stop." The cowboy turned to face the conductor now. As he was turning, he was drawing his Colt. Alan saw him drawing and reached out and grabbed the man's arm. He forced the pistol out of the man's hand and cracked him over the head with it. The cowboy slumped to the floor. "We'll toss him off at the water stop," said the conductor. "And thank you sir. I spose that fella mighta shot me'r you or both of us." The conductor left for a moment and returned with some rope. He tied the cowboy's hands behind his back and he and Alan dragged him to the caboose. The conductor put the cowboy's pistol in a cupboard on the caboose. When Alan got back to his seat, Elizabeth was stiil in disbelief.

"What just happened?" asked Elizabeth. "Was that man really going to shoot someone because he couldn't sit next to me?"

"I believe he would have," said Alan. "Some men who wear guns think they can do whatever they want."

"Well maybe people shouldn't be allowed to wear guns," said Elizabeth.

"There's no law against it," said Alan. "That's just the way it is."

"Well people back east don't wear guns," said Elizabeth. "That is unless they're in law enforcement."

"It'll be that way out west some day when civilization catches up," said Alan. "We might see it in our lifetime and we might not. Now let's relax and enjoy the scenery."

At the next water stop, the cowboy was put off. The conductor untied him while the brakeman stood there with a big wrench in case the cowboy tried something. When they started to pull away from the stop, the conductor threw the cowboy's pistol to him. The conductor had removed the bullets from the pistol.

~~~~

When they got closer to Abilene, Elizabeth started wondering what she was smelling. "What is that I'm smelling?" asked Elizabeth. "Smells kind of like manure and something."

"There's no kind of like manure to it Mrs. Thompson," said Alan. "You're smelling thousands of cows and their business.

There are thousands of cows being driven here from Texas to ship to the slaughter houses."

"So that's what Bill was doing," said Elizabeth. "He bought those cows and then sold them to the slaughter houses. Does that smell like a lot of money to you Mr. Cooper?"

"No Mrs. Thompson, smells like you know what to me," said Alan.

"Well when we get to Abilene, the first person I need to see is Jason Hunter," said Elizabeth. "He's the Justice of the Peace there. He's the man who informed me of Bill's death."

"We'll find him Mrs. Thompson," said Alan.

Elizabeth had no idea what Abilene would look like. She was totally amazed when they pulled into the station. A herd had just come in and the pens were bulging with cattle. They left the luggage at the station and went looking for Jason. Elizabeth seemed shocked when she looked around. "Seems like there's several saloons in town," said Elizabeth. "I bet they all have ladies of the evening."

"From what I understand, your husband owned some of these saloons and hotels," said Alan.

"He did Mr. Cooper, and now I own them," said Elizabeth. "I just don't know which ones they are. Mr. Hunter probably knows." As they walked the street, there were several drunk cowboys. One of them was leaning over a hitching post and vomiting. "Disgusting," said Elizabeth. "I wonder what his mother would say."

"She'd probably say, you made the mess, you clean it up," said Alan. And then he let out a laugh.

"So you do have a little humor in you Mr. Cooper," said Elizabeth.

"Well what you said struck me as funny," said Alan. "Some a these cowboys aren't much more than boys, but they've been out doing a man's work. They feel they have the right to get blind stinking drunk and spend time with a soiled dove."

"Soiled dove huh, I haven't heard that term for a while," said Elizabeth. "Let's go into that General Store and ask someone where we can find Jason Hunter." When they went inside, there was a man talking to another man who was behind the counter. When the two men saw Elizabeth and Alan enter the store, they turned to look at them. "Excuse me gentlemen, I am trying to locate Jason Hunter," said Elizabeth.

"Well you've found him. I am Jason Hunter," said Jason. Jason had been in the store buying some dry goods.

"I am Mrs. Bill Thompson," said Elizabeth. "I need your help. I do not know which businesses in town were my husbands. And where did he do his banking?"

"There is still only one bank in town Mrs. Thompson," said Jason. "Now if you will follow me, I can show you the hotels and saloons that your husband owned."

"Pardon me for my rudeness," said Elizabeth. "This gentleman with me is my bodyguard. He is with the Pinkerton's and his name is Alan Cooper."

"Pleased to meet you Alan," said Jason. They shook hands. Bill owned three hotels in town and Jason took her to them. Each hotel had a manager. Elizabeth informed them that nothing had changed for the time being. They had worked for her husband and now they worked for her. She would be back in a few days to go over the books. The last hotel Jason took them to was the one where Bill lived when he was in town. Elizabeth wanted to see Bill's suite. Jason took them to it.

"Is this where my husband was killed?" asked Elizabeth. "I can make out some blood stains on the floor."

"Yes, this is where Bill was killed," answered Jason.

"How was he killed?" asked Elizabeth.

"Are you sure you want to know?" asked Jason.

"Yes, I am sure," said Elizabeth.

"He was stabbed, Mrs. Thompson," said Jason. "And his bodyguard was shot."

"I never knew about the bodyguard," said Elizabeth.

"I never thought to put that in the telegram Mrs. Thompson," said Jason.

"Well, no matter now, and call me Elizabeth," said Elizabeth. "I'll be staying in this suite. After you show me around, could you get someone to bring my luggage from the train station?"

"I'll see to it Elizabeth. Now if you're ready, I can take you to his saloons," said Jason. Elizabeth nodded and they headed for the saloons.

They arrived at the first saloon just as a fight broke out. "I'll not go in there just now," said Elizabeth. "Jason, would you go in there and tell whoever runs the place to come out here." Jason nodded his head yes and went inside. He returned in about five minutes.

A middle aged, bald headed man came out of the saloon with Jason. The bald headed man went to Elizabeth and extended his hand. "I'm Oscar Landon, Mrs. Thompson," he said. "I ran this place for your husband."

Elizabeth shook his hand. "Mr. Landon, if you want to keep your job, you will do your best to keep these brawls from happening," said Elizabeth. "Do I make myself clear?"

"Yes ma'am. I'll do my best," said Oscar.

"See that you do," said Elizabeth. "We'll talk again in a couple of days and we'll go over the books. Come on Jason. Let's see the other ones."

There were no fights happening in the other saloons. Elizabeth was quick to lay down the law to the managers. She also seemed a little snooty when she saw the working girls, but she didn't say anything about them. Then they went to the bank. Jason went on back to his store. Elizabeth introduced herself and the Bank President took her to his office and showed Elizabeth the two accounts that Bill kept. "Oh my, Bill was doing very well out here," said Elizabeth when she saw how much money there was in the accounts. "For the time being, I will keep the accounts until I decide what I will do."

"Do you have an idea of what you might do Mrs. Thompson?" asked the banker. "I don't mean to pry, but if you decided to sell all of the businesses, I'm sure that you would do very well. Abilene is just getting started as a cow town. Business will be very good so all of your properties will bring very good prices if you were to sell."

"So are you interested in buying any of the properties?" Elizabeth asked the banker.

"No Mrs. Thompson, I would rather make money by lending money to someone who wanted to buy your property," answered the banker.

"You sound like a banker sir," said Elizabeth.

"That's what I am Mrs. Thompson," said the banker. "Now is there anything else I can do for you?"

"No, and thank you for your kindness, good day to you," said Elizabeth. Elizabeth and Alan headed back to the hotel where Bill stayed when he was in town. When they got to the hotel,

Elizabeth went to the manager and told him some things she wanted done.

"I want another bed put into the bedroom in my suite," started Elizabeth. "Mr. Cooper will be sleeping in the same room. You will hang a big curtain or something so I can have my privacy. Is any of this a problem?"

"No Mrs. Thompson, I'll have it done as soon as we're done talking," said the manager.

"Then about 6 o'clock this evening, I'd like some dinner for Mr. Cooper and myself brought to the suite," said Elizabeth.

"It will be done Mrs. Thompson," said the manager.

"Mr. Cooper and I will be walking around the town for a while," said Elizabeth. "We should be back in an hour or two." As they walked down the sidewalk, Elizabeth saw a sign that said "Maggie's Place." "Do you suppose that place is a saloon?" said Elizabeth.

"I know for a fact that it is," said Alan. "Maggie is Sean O'Rourke's wife. They own the saloon with their partner Michael O'Connor."

"How do you know all that?" asked Elizabeth.

"I'm a detective, Mrs. Thompson," said Alan.

"Well let's go over there," said Elizabeth. "I'd like to meet Mrs. O'Rourke." Alan escorted her to the saloon. When they walked in the front door, Elizabeth was impressed right away. "How about that," said Elizabeth. "They don't allow guns or knives in here. I like this place already."

Michael had been at his piano and noticed when Elizabeth and Alan entered the place. He went over to them. He figured that Elizabeth was a woman of quality or something because not too many other women came to "Maggie's Place." "Good afternoon,

I'm Michael O'Connor and welcome to "Maggie's Place," said Michael. "Is there something I can help you with?"

"I am Mrs. Bill Thompson and this is Mr. Cooper," said Elizabeth. "I would like to meet Mrs. O'Rourke if it is possible."

"Yes, that is possible," said Michael. "Now Mr. Cooper, are you armed?"

Before Alan could speak, Elizabeth spoke. "Mr. Cooper is a Pinkerton Detective and he is my bodyguard," stated Elizabeth. "Of course he is armed."

"So yer one of them Pinkerton's," said Michael. "I've heard of'em, but I never met one before. I've heard about some of the things you fellas have done. Anyway, you two take a seat at any table you'd like and I'll get Maggie. She's upstairs resting. She's with child and she needs her rest. Can we get you anything to drink while you're waiting?"

"Mr. Cooper, have yourself a drink if you'd like," said Elizabeth. "I doubt if they have any wine here."

"Oh, but we do have some wine here," said Michael. "We have white and red. We don't sell much of it, but we do have some."

"In that case, I'd like a glass of some red wine, and how about you Mr. Cooper," said Elizabeth.

"I'd like a glass of some Irish whiskey if you have it here," said Alan.

"Oh, a man after me own heart," said Michael. "We always have Irish whiskey. I'll have Tom bring over your drinks while I get Maggie." Tom got the drinks while Michael went upstairs and got Maggie. "Maggie darlin'," said Michael as he tapped on the door. "You have a visitor downstairs. Bill Thompson's widow would like to meet you."

"I'll be down in a few minutes," said Maggie. Talk with them till I come down. Michael went back downstairs and sat down with Elizabeth and Alan.

"Maggie will be down in a minute," said Michael. "She asked me to sit with you till she arrives. Is that all right?"

"Of course it is Mr. O'Connor," said Elizabeth. "Now tell us all about this town."

"First off, please call me Michael. Mr. sounds too formal," said Michael. "I'll tell you what I know about this town. Sean came out here not long after the war. He had just become a lawman. There was a lot of outlaws along the Kansas Missouri border and down in the "Indian Nations." Sean ended up here because of some outlaws. He met Maggie and they've been together ever since. I joined him as his deputy after I got discharged. We have had our hands full with outlaws and gangs. Even Maggie has had to kill some bad people. It was bad around here for a good while, but things finally quieted down some. When they decided to put the railhead here, the town started growing. It's still growing. Now we have drunk cowboys all over the place. Sometimes they can get pretty rowdy, but they behave themselves in here. We see to it. The town makes a lot of money off of the cowboys."

"So I understand that O'Rouke is a Federal Marshal," said Elizabeth. "What does that mean."

"It means he can go anywhere in this country or the territories in pursuit of lawbreakers," said Michael. "But he is not the local law here. Abilene doesn't have a Town Marshal."

"What if something happens in town?" asked Elizabeth. "Do you ignore it?"

"Of course not Elizabeth," answered Michael. "Sean is out after your husband's killer as we speak. Now a Town Marshal has no authority outside of a town and a Sheriff has no authority outside of his county. Sean can go anywhere."

"I saw that your leg was injured," said Elizabeth.

"It surely was Elizabeth," said Michael. "It got shot off." Maggie was coming down the stairs now and headed to Elizabeth's table. Elizabeth had seen the painting when they had entered the saloon, but hadn't said anything. Now that she saw Maggie, her head went back and forth from Maggie to the painting.

"Yes, Mrs. Thompson, that's me," said Maggie. "It's nice to finally meet you." Maggie went to Elizabeth. Elizabeth stood and they gave each other a little hug. "Now is there anything I can help you with or do for you?"

"I just really wanted to meet the wife of the man who is after my husband's killer," said Elizabeth. "Oh, and pardon my rudeness. This gentleman with me is Alan Cooper. He is a Pinkerton Detective and my bodyguard." Alan went to Maggie and extended his hand. Maggie took it and when she did, Alan bent down and kissed Maggie's hand.

"It's an honor to meet you Mrs. O'Rourke," said Alan. "You husband's exploits are well known all over this country."

"It's nice of you to say that Mr. Cooper," said Maggie. "Sean will catch Kid Evans and he will be dead. I promise you."

"That's good to hear," said Elizabeth. "Now could you answer this? Why does it seem to me that your saloon is so much nicer than the places my husband owned?"

"I'd say it's because we have very nice people working here," said Maggie. "Most people go to a saloon to relax and have a good time. We try to make sure that they do. My girls are beautiful and the men love them. We have had trouble at times, but we try to end it as quickly as we can. Not allowing guns or knives in here has helped some."

"I can see how that might help," said Elizabeth. "Maybe we should try it at my places. Of course I'm not sure what I will do. Should I sell everything, or should I just keep them and make money off of them as long as I can?"

"I can't tell you what to do, but I will tell you this," said Maggie. "If you do start a policy of no guns or knives in the saloons, you'll have to have good people so it can be enforced. Most cowboys or men don't want to give up their weapons. That's where the girls can help. You can catch more with honey than you can vinegar, if you get my meaning."

"I don't know if I could get used to having prostitutes working for me," said Elizabeth.

"Well, they say it's the oldest profession," said Maggie. "There are way more men than women around here. We simply supply a service. My girls are here because they want to be here. They were not forced and I never allow them to be mistreated. They can leave any time they want. I'll tell you this right now Elizabeth. If you didn't have working girls in your saloons, you may as well just board them up."

"You're probably right Maggie," said Elizabeth. "I'm tired now. Too much time on trains. I'll finish my wine and we'll go back to the hotel. I need to lay down for a while. I'm sure we'll talk some more."

"It was nice meeting you," said Maggie. "I have a strong feeling that Sean will come riding into town tomorrow and he'll have good news for us."

"Let's hope so," said Elizabeth. She finished her wine and Alan finished his whiskey. They went back to the hotel.

When they got back to Elizabeth's suite. Everything had been done that she had requested. Their luggage was there too. Alan locked the door and both of them took a nap. They were awakened at 6 o'clock when their dinner arrived. The didn't talk much as they ate. There was a nice bathtub in the suite and Elizabeth had some hot water brought up so she could bathe. After she was done, she had more water delivered for Alan.

Before they retired for the evening, Alan did some checking. He found out who was staying in what room and he went around the outside of the hotel to see how access to the suite could be gained by someone if they wanted. When he was satisfied, he went to the suite. He locked the door and checked the windows. Elizabeth was already fast asleep. Alan watched out a window for a couple of hours and then laid down. About 2am, both of them were awakened by some gunfire. Elizabeth ran over to Alan in fear. "What was that?" she cried.

"You go on back to bed Mrs. Thompson," said Alan. "I'll check it out." Elizabeth got back into bed and Alan slipped over to a window. He stood to the side so he would not be a good target if some drunk cowboy needed a target. He saw a couple of drunk cowboys in the street. They were so drunk they could hardly stand. They fired their pistols in the air a couple more times and then passed out in the street. "Just drunk cowboys," said Alan. "They passed out in the street. Maybe a stage or something'll run over them in the morning."

"I hope this doesn't go on every night," said Elizabeth. "And I think you should start calling me Elizabeth. That's my name. And I shall call you Alan"

"I will call you Elizabeth if that's what you want," said Alan. "It's not necessary for you to call me Alan."

"I hired you and I will call you Alan," said Elizabeth. "Now I will try to get back to sleep."

CHAPTER SIXTEEN

Ned Conrad was the cowboy who Alan Cooper had cracked over the head on the train to Abilene. Ned was basically a drifter. He didn't take orders very well so he couldn't hold any job for very long. He had worked for a lot of ranches down in Texas and some in Kansas. He was usually let go after a few months. Ned was always busy trying to keep from doing work. He tried gambling for a while and he actually won once in a while, but the games were always with cowboys and there wasn't much money involved. Cowboys only made $30 a month on the average. Ned got himself into a card game in a small town in Texas with some real gamblers. He won a few hands and one of the gamblers accused him of cheating. Ned told his accuser to meet him out in the street. They went out into the street. Both men pulled their pistols at about the same time and opened fire. After four shots had been fired by both of them, neither one of them had been hit. They were both down to their last shot when Ned's accuser was finally hit. The bullet struck the man in his left foot and he went down. Just as the last shot was fired, the Town Marshal came running to see what all the shooting was about. He saw Ned standing there and the other man laying in the street. He didn't ask what happened or anything. He just ran Ned out of town and told him to stay out. Ned moved on to another town. The same thing happened. He won a few hands at poker and was accused of cheating. This time the gunfight was in a saloon. Ned's accuser pulled his pistol first and started shooting , but he missed. Ned drew his pistol and fired, but he missed too. Ned's accuser took another shot and the bullet grazed Ned's left arm. Ned fired again and this time the bullet struck the man dead center in his chest. When Ned saw that the man was dead, he high tailed it out of town as fast as he could. Even though the other man drew first, Ned wasn't taking any chances on what might happen. As he rode away, he started thinking of himself as a gunman. Maybe this was his calling. He felt no remorse about the dead man. Yes, he would be a gunman. Somehow, he ended up in Kansas City. He would get himself to Abilene. Abilene was a cowtown now. There was lots of money in Abilene. It would be a good place to prove himself.

When Ned was removed from the train to Abilene, he made up his mind that he would find the big man who had taken his pistol and cracked him over the head. He would get even with this man and maybe even the woman who wouldn't let him sit next to her. He took his empty pistol and loaded it with bullets that were on his gunbelt. Then he took off walking. He had walked for a couple of hours when he came to a farm. There were a couple of horses out in a corral. Saddles and bridles were on the fence. No one was there to be seen. Ned saddled up one of the horses and took off for Abilene.

~~~~

Kathleen rode next to Sam on the way back to Abilene. When they stopped for a night, Kathleen slept next to Sam. When they ate, she was right next to Sam. Sam realized that he had only just met Kathleen, but he knew that he already felt something for her. He hoped her feelings for him were not just because he had killed the yellow haired outlaw. The two of them talked all the way back to Abilene.

There was no more shooting that night in the streets of Abilene. When Elizabeth woke up the next morning, Alan was sitting in a chair by the door. "Good morning," said Elizabeth. "I slept really well after that shooting stopped. How did you sleep?"

"I slept well," answered Alan. "Can I have them bring us some breakfast?"

"Yes you may," said Elizabeth. "It doesn't matter what it is. I feel very hungry. See if we can get some coffee while we wait for breakfast."

"I will. Now I'll lock the door behind me and be back in a minute," said Alan. Alan returned shortly with a pot of coffee and two cups. Elizabeth wasn't dressed but had on a robe. She poured them some coffee.

"What do you think I should do today Alan?" asked Elizabeth.

"That's up to you Elizabeth," said Alan. "If I was you, I'd just nose around town today and take it easy. I wouldn't see any of the managers today. They're probably busy trying to make the books look good."

"So what are you saying?" asked Elizabeth. "Are you saying that my managers might not be honest?"

"No, but I am saying that it could be possible," said Alan. "Please don't let me influence you in any way. Your husband must have trusted them and from what I have heard, your husband was a good business man."

"Yes he was Alan," said Elizabeth. "The accounts at the bank prove that." They didn't talk for a while. They drank coffee and looked out the windows. Breakfast arrived and they ate. After the meal, Elizabeth decided they would just walk around town and maybe get to know some of the other business people. They had come out of one of the general stores and were in the street when Alan thought he saw someone coming into town that he recognized. He thought as they walked. It was the cowboy that was thrown off the train. The cowboy spotted Elzabeth and Alan a split second after Alan figured out who he was. Without saying a word, Ned rode right at Elizabeth and Alan and was firing his pistol. It was too late to run so Alan shoved Elizabeth to the ground and laid on her to protect her. Ned had fired two shots and missed. Alan had his pistol out now and was about to fire when he heard two shots that came from somewhere besides Ned.

Maggie was in her room and looking out the window when she saw some man on horseback shooting at Elizabeth and Alan. There was a Henry rifle in her room by the window. She picked it up, chambered a round, took aim, and fired. As her bullet struck the man in the front, another bullet struck him from the back. Sean had just arrived in town when he saw a man riding toward a man and a woman and the rider's pistol was out. When the man started shooting, Sean pulled a pistol and fired. His bullet caught the man dead center in the back. As the man was struck in the front and a split second later in the back, he wasn't knocked out of the saddle. Alan fired now. His bullet hit Ned in the forehead and he was knocked out of the saddle.

"You stay down now Elizabeth," said Alan as he got up off of her. "I need to make sure he's dead." Elizabeth didn't say a word. She was crying hysterically. As Alan made his way over to Ned, Sean rode over also. Both Sean and Alan had their pistols ready. Ned was face down on the ground. Alan and Sean could see that the back of Ned's head was missing.

"I spect we got'em," said Sean. "I'm Sean O'Rourke, and who might you be." Sean dismounted and extended his hand to Alan.

"I'm Alan Cooper," said Alan as they shook hands. "I'm Mrs. Bill Thompson's bodyguard. That's her over there on the ground. I told her to stay there till I made sure this fella was dead."

"Smart thing ta do," said Sean. "Who was this fella anyway?"

"He was just someone we had a run in with on the train here from Kansas City," said Alan. "He wanted to sit next to Elizabeth and she didn't want him next to her. There was plenty of other seats on the train. Anyway, the conductor happened by and had words with that fella. The fool tried pullin' on the conductor. I saw what was happening and I grabbed his pistol and cracked him over the head with it. The conductor put him off the train at the next water stop."

"So you never saw this fella before that, and you don't know his name or nothin'?" asked Sean.

"That's right. I have no idea who he is," said Alan.

"Well, it looked like he wanted you and Mrs. Thompson dead," said Sean. "I guess you earned yer pay. So you said you were her bodyguard. Are you one a them Pinkertons'r somethin' like that."

"Yes, I am a Pinkerton," said Alan.

"Well Pinkerton man, I never met one a you guys, but I heard some stories," said Sean. "Let's go over and tell Mrs. Thompson she can get up now." Maggie came running out now and glued herself to Sean. They hugged and kissed for a good while.

"I have missed you darlin'," said Maggie.

"I have missed you too Maggie," said Sean. Jesse, Sam, Kathleen, and Jeb came into town now. As soon as Maggie saw them, she ran over to see how Kathleen was.

"Oh Kathleen, I am so sorry this happened," cried Maggie. "Let's get you over to Doc Rawlins and have you checked out."

"Don't be sorry Maggie," said Kathleen. "It was those bastards who did me harm, not you. I will be all right. I'm just beat up and bruised some."

"You'll be goin' to the doc's," said Sam. "We need to make sure nothin's broken or anything like that."

"All right Sam, I'll go if you go with me," said Kathleen. Michael and Betty came out in the street now.

"Jeb looks happy," said Michael. "I guess he got even with Kid."

"He got even and then some," said Sean. "Now while Sam takes Kathleen over to docs, the rest of us can go get some coffee or have a drink."

"I'm gonna get somethin' ta eat and then I'm headin' home," said Jesse. "Haven't seen my woman fer a good while. I miss her."

"Jesse, I'll tell ya right now so I don't ferget," started Sean. "I thank you fer helpin' me out again. Yer a good man, none better. Go home to yer wife. We won't be out chasin' any outlaws fer a good while. Stay home and be there when yer baby's born." They shook hands.

~~~~

They went into the saloon and Tom brought them all some coffee. Michael was the first to speak. "I want to know how Kid died," said Michael.

"Well he did die slow," started Sean. "Kathleen shot him in both knees with a derringer. He was naked cause he was about to take a dip in a stream. After she shot him, ole Jeb attacked. Jeb bit off his pecker and then bit off his cajones. When he tried to crawl over to where his pistol belt was, Jeb bit off one a his hands. Me'n Kathleen and Jeb watched him bleed ta death."

"He got what he deserved," said Betty. "Did Sam do what he said he was gonna do to that one fella?"

"He did," answered Sean. "He surely did."

"So Kathleen was abducted by the man who killed Bill," said Elizabeth.

"That's right," said Sean. "And she's the one that shot him too. I intend ta give her all the reward money."

"That's only proper," said Elizabeth. "I do hope she's all right."

"I'd say she'll be all right," said Sean. "She's a strong woman. And she's got Sam now."

"So how did she keep herself alive?" asked Elizabeth. "I'm sure them ruffians abused her."

"They did," said Sean. "It's lucky fer her that she was on her cycle when they took her."

"What do you mean?" asked Elizabeth.

"I'm saying that since she was on her cycle, them outlaws didn't like all that blood and didn't want her all that much," said Sean. "I figure that helped keep her alive."

"That might be true," said Elizabeth. "But why didn't they just kill her?"

"I reckon Kid wanted to kill her while I watched," said Sean. "He thought she was Maggie. That's why she was took in the first place."

"I guess she does look like Maggie some," said Elizabeth. "It's kind of hard to tell with her face all bruised and swollen. I do hope she'll be all right."

"Well folks, I don't want to sound rude, but my woman and I will be occupied for a while," said Sean. Maggie and Sean went up to their room.

~~~~

Doc Rawlins gave Kathleen a thorough examination. Sam stayed with her the whole time. "It'll take time Kathleen, but you'll be fine," said Doc. "You could have used a stitch or two in a couple of places, but it's too late now and they're healing fine. The swelling in your face should go down soon and after those black eyes go away, you'll be as good as new. Your nose wasn't broken and none of your teeth seem loose. The rest of you looks good. You go on home now and rest up. I'll check on you in a few days."

"What do we owe you Doc?" asked Sam.

"Not one red cent," said Doc. "I'm just glad she'll be all right. She's been through some ordeal. Just who are you Mr.?"

"Name's Sam Waters," said Sam. "I'm a Town Marshal from Lonesome Texas. I was after some men who were in Kid Evan's gang."

"Well it looks like Kathleen here has latched onto you," said Doc. "She's a fine woman. I hope you two can make a go of it." Sam nodded his head and he and Kathleen headed for her hotel room.

Jeb had been sitting beside Maggie and when Maggie and Sean went upstairs, he went over and sat beside Elizabeth. Elizabeth was mesmerized by Jeb. "Just what kind of dog is this?" Elizabeth asked. "He's so big and he seems so gentle." Elizabeth was petting Jeb and making friends with him.

"We have no idea what breed he is," said Michael. "We got him and some other dogs from some outlaws. The outlaws'r dead now. Anyway, they were usin' them dogs as cow dogs. Ole Jeb here just loves Maggie and Sean and all of us. Looks like he likes you too. Anyone who don't like us, best look out. Jeb's very good at rippin' a man's throat out."

"And other body parts too," said Elizabeth. "Well, I'd like to go back to my hotel right now. I'm sure we'll all get together again shortly. If you'll excuse us." Alan nodded and he and Elizabeth left. They talked as they walked. "Alan, thank you for saving my life," said Elizabeth. "I had no idea what was happening at the time. I was afraid for you and me."

"I was just doing my job," said Alan.

"Well I'm glad I hired you Alan," said Elizabeth.

"I'm glad you hired me too," said Alan.

Alan unlocked their hotel room and checked it out before he let Elizabeth enter. Elizabeth entered the room and locked the door behind her. "Alan, do you think I'm pretty?" asked Elizabeth.

"I can't answer questions like that as you are my employer," said Alan.

"Is that right?" asked Elizabeth.

"Yes that is right," answered Alan.

"I want you to kiss me Alan," said Elizabeth. "I want you to kiss me now."

"I can't do that Elizabeth," said Alan. "You are my employer. It wouldn't be right."

"Well, Alan Cooper, you are fired. Now kiss me and tell me I'm pretty," said Elizabeth.

"I will kiss you, but you are not pretty Elizabeth. You are beautiful," said Alan as they locked themselves together. Two hours later, they were in bed holding each other.

"I should feel guilty, but I don't," said Elizabeth. "Bill hasn't been gone very long. Why don't I feel guilty?"

"I can't answer that for you Elizabeth," said Alan. "My wife's been gone for a long time and I do feel guilty. I haven't been with a woman since she died."

"May I ask how your wife died?" asked Elizabeth.

"I lost her and the baby during childbirth," said Alan. "She was the love of my life."

"Bill was the love of my life too," said Elizabeth. "I should have come out here with him when he decided to get into cattle buying, but I wanted no part of anything west of Cincinnati. Maybe I was selfish. There were times I missed him and times I didn't. We tried to have children but were not successful. Anyway, I don't believe I can live out here. I need more civilization. I need to feel safe too. I do not feel safe out here."

"I understand that, but there are more murders and crimes committed in the big cities back east than there is out here," said Alan. "There are so many gangs in New York that it would boggle your mind. You probably lived in a nice section of town and bad things didn't happen close to you."

"Well it bothers me that almost all the men out here wear guns," said Elizabeth.

"That's because you can see the guns," said Alan. "Now if you didn't know me and saw me on the street, would you think I was armed?"

"No, I wouldn't," said Elizabeth. "I would probably think that you were just some nice businessman."

"See, there you go," said Alan. "I always have two pistols, a knife, and some brass knuckles on me."

"What are brass knuckles?" asked Elizabeth.

"I'll show you sometime," said Alan. "Now no more talking. I want you again."

~~~~

Maggie and Sean made love for the rest of the morning and then decided to soak in their tub for a while. Sean could tell that something was on Maggie's mind and he had a good idea what it was. As they gently washed each other in the tub, Maggie told Sean what was on her mind. "I don't want our son to be born in a place like this," said Maggie. "I don't want to worry that some stray bullet from a drunk cowboy's gun will come through a wall or a window and kill him. I had to shoot another man today too. I don't want to shoot anyone else. I am tired of worrying when you're out chasing outlaws. I'm tired of watching Doc patch you up. I am tired of cleaning blood off the floor in this place. I want us to have a life without blood and killing. I don't want any more blood."

"I love you darlin'," said Sean. "We'll have us that life."

Here ends Book 5 in the Sean O'Rourke Series, *Quiet Times?* For a preview of Book 6 in the Sean O'Rourke Series, *Blood Flows in the East*, continue reading.

The Sean O'Rourke Series
Book 6

Blood Flows in the East

by

Michael E. Cook

TELEMACHUS PRESS

CHAPTER ONE

The first thing Sean did the next morning was send a telegram to Judge Sharpton. It went as follows.

Federal Judge Sharpton
Federal Court House
St. Louis

Kid Evans and gang dead<<stop>>Abducted woman rescued<<stop>>over $80,000 recovered<<stop>>will put money in bank minus reward money<<stop>>reward money goes to Kathleen Jameson<<stop>>$30,000 stolen from Clancy Evans<<stop>>$5000 from bank in Missouri <<stop>>$10,000 from another bank in Missouri <<stop>>unknown amount stolen from Bill Thompson <<stop>>unknown amount from cattle rustling <<stop>>will distribute recovered money when hear from you

O'Rourke

Sean had the money stashed in his room. He took the money to the bank and explained to the banker about the money. Then he went to Kathleen's room at the hotel. Sam answered the door when Sean knocked. "Mornin', how's Kathleen doin'?" said Sean. "I got somethin' for her."

"Come on in," said Sam. "We was just havin' some coffee and then was gonna go have some breakfast." Kathleen was sitting on the edge of the bed sipping her coffee. She smiled at Sean and then went over and gave him a hug.

"Hope yer feelin' better," said Sean. "I got some reward money for you."

"Reward money! Why would I get that?" asked Kathleen.

"Cause you purty much caught that son of a bitch by yerself," said Sean. "Jeb just put on the finishin' touches. Jeb don't need no money anyhow. It's all yours." Sean handed the money to Kathleen. He counted it out as he gave it to her. "There ya be, $7000."

"Oh my, what am I going to do with all that?" said Kathleen. "Maybe I will have my own place soon."

"Maybe Sam can help ya with that," said Sean. "Looks like you two'r made fer each other. Well, I'll leave you alone now. Me'n Maggie got some serious things ta talk about." Sean gave Kathleen another hug, shook Sam's hand, and then left.

As soon as Sean was out of the room, Kathleen wrapped her arms around Sam. "Will you help me figure out what to do with this money?" asked Kathleen. "I was figuring on having my own place someday."

"I was hopin' that you'd go with me back ta Texas," said Sam. "I already got a place and I sure would like it if you were my partner. I want you for my woman Kathleen. I know we just met, but I got strong feelins' fer you. I think you got them fer me too."

"I do have strong feelings for you Sam," said Kathleen. "I was hoping that we could become more than just partners."

"You just say when and we'll git ourselves married," said Sam. "I understand there's a Justice of the Peace in this town. Are you sure you wouldn't mind bein' married to a lawman?"

"I like the idea of being married to a lawman," said Kathleen. "I know you're a good man and will protect me and our children if we have children. I'd like to get married next week. I want to be pretty for you. Maybe some of the bruising will be gone by then."

"Kathleen, you'll always be beautiful to me," said Sam. "Nothin'll change that."

"I do love you Sam," said Kathleen. "Now let's get this money to the bank and then have some breakfast."

~~~~

Maggie, Sean, Betty, and Michael sat down at their regular table and sipped coffee while they waited on their breakfast. Betty was the first to speak. "Michael and I have decided that we're going back east," said Betty. "We love you two and all the people here, but things have gotten worse lately. We would like to own a nice neighborhood pub maybe in Boston or a big city like that. We need a more peaceful place. Abilene will only get worse before it gets better."

"I fully understand," said Maggie. "I don't want our baby to be born here. I need some quiet too."

"You'll have that quiet," said Sean. "How bout we stick it out till the end of this season and then sell the place. We can go back to St. Louis for a while. We can stay there till the baby is grown some and then go wherever you want."

"What about that Federal Marshal's badge?" asked Maggie. "Would you be willing to give that up?"

"I think I could give it up for you and the baby," said Sean. "I've done my duty and then some. But you gotta remember darlin', I've made a lot of enemies. Lawman'r not, there could always be some trouble."

"I know that," said Maggie. "But I'm willing to take those chances. So Michael, is there a place back east that's for sale that you've been thinking about?"

"I haven't been looking yet," said Michael. "I'll be sendin' out some telegrams and maybe I'll put some ads in some papers back east sayin' I'm lookin' for a place to buy. If we haven't heard anything after a couple of months, then we'll head east anyway. Maybe we'll build a brand new place."

"What would you call your place?" asked Sean.

"I haven't thought about that yet," answered Michael. "I guess I better."

~~~~

Elizabeth Thompson decided she would sell all of her properties and then go back to Cincinnati. She would stay in Abilene till all of her places sold. Ads were placed in papers all over saying that there would be an auction. The places could be separately or together. Elizabeth would have the right to reject bids that she thought were too low. The auction would be held in a month. That would give any interested party plenty of time to check out the places.

When Alan Cooper's assignment with Elizabeth was terminated, he reported to his office that his assignment was finished. He stayed with Elizabeth while he waited for his next assignment. At times he wondered if Elizabeth was just using him. Other times he was sure that she felt something for him. He knew that he was having strong feelings for her.

A week later, Alan received his next assignment. There was some politician in Chicago who wanted Alan as a bodyguard. This job would start in eight days. Alan figured it would take him three days to get to Chicago by train so he and Elizabeth made the most of those five days. On the first of those five days, they never left the hotel room except to eat. That evening as they lay holding each other, Elizabeth looked into Alan's eyes. "I want you to be with me," Elizabeth said. "You don't have to marry me. Whenever you have time between assignments, I want you to be with me."

"What if I don't want that?" said Alan.

"What do you mean? I know you have feelings for me," said Elizabeth.

"I do have strong feelings for you Elizabeth," said Alan. "I just don't want to be your man. I want to be your husband too."

"Oh Alan, I want that too," said Elizabeth. "I have hoped that we could be married some day. You know that you'll be marrying a rich woman, don't you?"

"I don't need your money Elizabeth," said Alan. "I just need you. Besides, I'm not a poor man myself. I inherited a lot of money and some properties in Washington D.C."

"So why are you a Pinkerton?" asked Elizabeth. "You don't need to work."

"I guess it's kind of like why Sean O'Rourke is a lawman," said Alan. "He doesn't need to work, but someone has to do what he does and he's good at it. I'm good at what I do and I like it. So when can we get married?"

"Jason Hunter is the Justice of the Peace in this town," said Elizabeth. "We can talk with him tomorrow if you'd like."

"I'd like that," said Alan. "I'd like that a lot. Maybe if I tell my boss I'm getting married, he'll let me have some time off."

"What about that Chicago politician?" asked Elizabeth.

"The Pinkerton's have plenty of good men," said Alan. "That politician'll be taken care of."

~~~~

The next morning, Alan sent a telegram to his boss and asked for some time off to get married. He received a reply later that morning. The Chicago politician had changed his plans. Alan could have a month off. Instead of talking to Jason Hunter about the wedding, they stayed in their room and celebrated. The next day after breakfast, they talked with Jason about performing their wedding.

"You know what you folks might think about," said Jason. "I'm doing another wedding next week. Sam Waters and Kathleen Jameson are getting married. They'll be asking Sean if the wedding can be at Maggie's Place. We could have a double wedding."

"That would be nice," said Elizabeth. "We'll go over and talk with Maggie now. Thank you."

"It'll be my pleasure to get you two hitched," said Jason. Kathleen and Alan thanked Jason again and headed for Maggie's Place. When they got there, Sam and Kathleen were there talking with Maggie and Sean. They could see Maggie and Sean were happy to have Kathleen and Sam's wedding in the saloon. Hugs and kisses and handshakes were being exchanged. Elizabeth and Alan waited for a break in the action and then joined them.

"I could tell by all the hugs and kisses that you are having Kathleen and Sam's wedding here next week," said Elizabeth. "Would you consider having a double wedding that day? Alan and I are getting married."

"Of course we can do it," said Maggie. "Everyone knew that you two would be getting married. We'll be glad to have a double wedding here. Kathleen, you and Sam don't mind do you?"

"Of course not," answered Kathleen. "It'll be a wonderful time."

"Let's all sit down and have a toast to your upcoming nuptials," said Sean.

"Nuptials, I've never heard you say that word," said Maggie. "It sounds strange coming from you."

"Well sorry, let's have a toast to their upcoming weddings," said Sean. They all laughed a little and sat down. Tom brought over a bottle and some glasses and they had their toast.

~~~~

The next few days in Abilene were very quiet. There were plenty of drunk cowboys and cattle herds, but it had been unusually quiet. Sean and Michael were worried that something was about to happen. Sam was beginning to think the same thing. He was a lawman and knew that with that many cowboys and that much liquor, trouble always comes. Even Alan thought it was too quiet. He and Elizabeth were on their way to the general store one day when Alan noticed four riders coming into town. They had two pack horses with them and all four of them were heavily armed. Each man wore a pistol belt and had another holster and pistol tied to his saddle horn. Each man had a repeating rifle and a long gun in scabbards on their saddles. Some shotguns were tied to the packs on the pack horses. They looked like they had been in the saddle for a good while. They stopped at one of the other saloons in town. They tied their horses and went inside. "I need to tell Sean about those men," said Alan. "They didn't come here for a church social."

"Why should Sean know about those men?" asked Elizabeth. "Everybody carries guns around here."

"Most of them do, but for most men, one is enough," said Alan. "I'll be telling Sean."

When they got to Maggie's Place, Sean and Michael were standing there looking out a front window. Maggie was over by the bar so Elizabeth went over to talk with her while Alan talked to Sean.

"I came to tell you about some men I saw coming into town," said Alan. "There was f____."

Sean interrupted him. "Michael and I saw them too," said Sean. "They look like bounty hunters ta me. Probly come here hopin' ta find the whereabouts a Kid and his bunch. They're gonna be disappointed. I'll wait a bit and then go over there."

"You want me to go with you?" asked Alan.

"No need, but thanks fer the offer," said Sean. "If there'd be any trouble, I can handle four of'em." Sean and Michael went over to their regular table and drank some coffee. Alan joined them. Elizabeth was still talking with Maggie. No words were spoken. Sean finished his cup of coffee and then checked his two pistols and made sure they were fully loaded. "I'm goin' over there now," said Sean. "I doubt there'll be any shootin', but if ya hear shootin' and ya see them four runnin' out the door, you kill'em. Michael, git yer Winchester and give Alan my Winchester. You two wait here just inside the door." Michael got the rifles and Sean headed to the other saloon. Jeb went with him. Sean stopped and looked over the swinging door. Jeb stayed to the side so he couldn't be seen. The four men were at the bar drinking whiskey. There was a big mirror behind the bar. Sean was sure that the four men saw him. Sean entered the saloon and moved to the right away from the doors. Jeb came in and sat down on Sean's right. Jeb had a very low growl going. Sean was about forty feet from the bar. He could see that the four men were watching him in the mirror.

"Well lookey here boys," said one of the men. "We got us the famous sharpshooter and lawman a watchin' us. He must figure we're bad men. What do ya want O'Rourke? And that's bout the ugliest dog I ever did see."

"I wanna know what you boys'r doin' here and don't insult my dog. He don't take insults too good." said Sean. "You got names?"

"Name's none a yer," said the man who was doing the talking.

"None a yer what?" asked Sean.

"None a yer damn business," said the man.

"Oh that's funny," said Sean. "That's so funny I might laugh so hard that I'll shit myself. Don't you think that's funny Jeb?" Jeb increased his growl a bit. "I figure you boys'r bounty hunters and yer here hopin' ta find out somethin' bout Kid Evans and his gang. Well boys, yer too late. Kid and his bunch'r in hell where they belong."

"Did you kill'em?" asked the man.

"I had some help," answered Sean.

"What about all that money they stole. Was any of it recovered?" asked the man.

"That's none a yer," said Sean. "None a yer damn business."

"Haw haw haw," said the man. "You know O'Rourke, these boys'n me fought fer the stars and bars. We was all sharpshooters. We never wasted no time like you shootin' Corporals and Sergeants. We went after big game. I'd a got ole Grant one time, but some stupid Lieutenant got in the way after I squeezed the trigger. I got me several Colonels and a lotta Captains. Ronnie down here on the left almost got Sherman onest. We all got us a passel a officers. We was after that bounty they had on you too. No one saw you after Atlanta. We figured you was hidin'."

"Look, I don't give a shit how many men you killed durin' the war," started Sean. "The war's over and while yer in this town, it better stay over. You look at me the wrong way or even make me think yer goin' fer iron, I'll shoot you dead. I'll kill you so fast you won't know yer dead till you don't wake up the next mornin'."

"Don't go gettin' so all high toney," said the man. "We all know how fast you are. You probly could kill us if we tried to pull on ya. We never come here ta git shot by you. We come here hopin' ta hear somethin' bout Kid Evans. I reckon we're too late. Ya got any new posters on anyone?"

"Nothin' that'd be worth yer time," said Sean. "Nobody's worth more than $50 right at the moment."

"Well I reckon we'll have us some more drinks and some food and then we'll move on," said the man. "Don't you worry O'Rourke, we're not gonna bushwack ya."

"Does yer momma know what you grew up ta be?" asked Sean.

"Does yers?" asked Ronnie.

"Nope, she doesn't," answered Sean. "My Ma and Pa was murdered by some white scum. I helped kill them scum. Now you boys make sure you stay away from me." Sean turned and left. He watched in the mirror in case one of the men would try and back shoot him. Jeb watched the four men until Sean cleared the door and then he followed Sean. As soon as Jeb cleared the door, the four men turned and continued their drinking.

"They was bounty hunters," said Sean as he entered Maggie's Place. "Just like I figured. They was after Kid Evans. They said they'd be movin' on after eatin' and gettin' some drinks. I don't trust'em. I figure they'll go after the bank. Looks like they put in a lotta time chasin' Kid and they don't wanna leave empty handed. I'll be keepin' an eye on'em."

"I'm here if you need me Sean," said Alan.

"Thanks, I might need me another good man," said Sean. "With me and Michael and you, we oughta be able ta handle things. Think I'll talk ta Sam too." The three men sat down at the regular table and had some drinks. Maggie and Elizabeth joined them. It wasn't long and Sam and Kathleen joined them. It wasn't another fifteen minutes and the four bounty hunters rode out of town heading west. Sean didn't want to upset the women but he figured they had a right to know what he thought could happen. He got right to the point. "Ladies, there was some bounty hunters in town a little while ago," started Sean. "They was after Kid Evans and his bunch. Now that they know Kid and his bunch is dead, I figure they'll be after the bank. Them boys was all sharp-shooters for the south durin' the war. That means they're good shots and they'd like ta see me dead too. I'm gonna wait a bit and then go track'em. I figure they'll set up camp a few hours from town. Hard ta tell when they'll come if they're comin'. Could be tonight or in a few days."

"I'll give a hand," said Sam.

"Why do you think those men would want to rob the bank?" asked Elizabeth.

"Cause they put in a lotta time chasin' after Kid," answered Sean. "That was a big reward fer him. Them fellas don't wanna come up empty handed. They know there's plenty a money in that bank."

"I know that," said Elizabeth. "I have a bunch in there."

"We all do darlin'," said Michael. "Sean and us'll make sure it stays there."

"I'm gonna get somethin' ta eat and then I'll be trackin' them fellas," said Sean. "I'll get back soon as I can."

~~~~

The four bounty hunters rode for about three hours and set up camp. The land was mostly all open plain with a few rolling hills. When they had their campfire going, the smoke could be seen from more than a mile away. The four men's names were Ronnie, Amos, Tully, and Saltie. Saltie thought he was the leader of the group. He was the one who had done most of the talking with O'Rourke. They had a bottle with them and they passed it around as they sat by the fire. "We're takin' that bank in Abilene," said Saltie. "O'Rourke or no O'Rourke, we're takin' that bank. We come too far to come up empty handed. I bet that money that Kid and his boys took is in that bank. Plus Abilene's a cow town now. Gotta be lotsa money in that bank."

"So you think we can take O'Rourke?" asked Tully.

"We better if'n we want that money," said Saltie.

Other Books By Michael E. Cook

<u>The Sean O'Rourke Series</u>

Book 1: A Killer for the Common Good

Book 2: A Killer For The Common Good – Lawman

Book 3 :O'Rourke's Revenge

Book 4: O'Rourke's Law or No Law at All

Pitcher

Available in paperback and eBook formats
at Internet retailers everywhere.

ABOUT THE AUTHOR

Michael E. Cook (Mike), was born in Chillicothe, Ohio and grew up loving and playing baseball. After high school graduation in 1969, Mike served 4 years in the U.S. Marine Corps. In Vietnam, Mike was a Field Radio Operator in a Forward Observation Team, and was attached to the companies of the 3rd Battalion 5th Marines. During the "Easter Offensive" of 1972, Mike was with 2nd ANGLICO (Air and Naval Gunfire Liaison Company) and was attached to South Vietnamese Marines as a Naval Gunfire Spotter. After military service, Mike attended and graduated from Ohio University, Athens, Ohio and received a BA with a major in Psychology. "I did not pursue my major," Mike says. "The more classes I took, the more I disliked Psychology." At Ohio University, Mike met Eleanor, his wife of 40 years.

After college, Mike worked as a maintenance man, and then a brakeman and locomotive engineer on the B&O Railroad. When the division was shut down, Mike took a job at a snack food manufacturer, and retired after 31 years of service and was Plant Manager for almost 30 years. "Pitcher," is Mike's first attempt at writing outside the Western genre. He currently has 5 books of "The Sean O'Rourke Series" published, and is working on a 6th.

Mike's hobbies are fishing, turkey hunting, and shooting. He has two grown children and two grandchildren. He resides with his wife on their 31 acre mini-farm in southwest central Ohio.

www.ingramcontent.com/pod-product-compliance
Lightning Source LLC
Chambersburg PA
CBHW021942170626
46808CB00001B/6